SLATED SCARS

A TRIED & TRUE NOVEL
BOOK FOUR

CHARLI RAHE

TRIED AND TRUE PUBLISHING

First ebook edition June 2023

First paperback edition June 2023

First hardcover edition June 2023

Cover Art by Miblart
Chapter Art by Etheric Designs

ISBN (ebook) 978-1-958055-10-6

ISBN (paperback) 978-1-958055-11-3

ISBN (hardcover) 978-1-958055-12-0

✺ Created with Vellum

Note from the Author

Scarlett's fantastical story follows a woman's journey through her magical heritage in which she encounters several dark scenarios. It is not intended for readers under 18 years of age and includes adult content.

While I'd prefer you to experience it as you go, your mental health matters. Please refer to www.charlirahe.com for a detailed list of possible triggers.

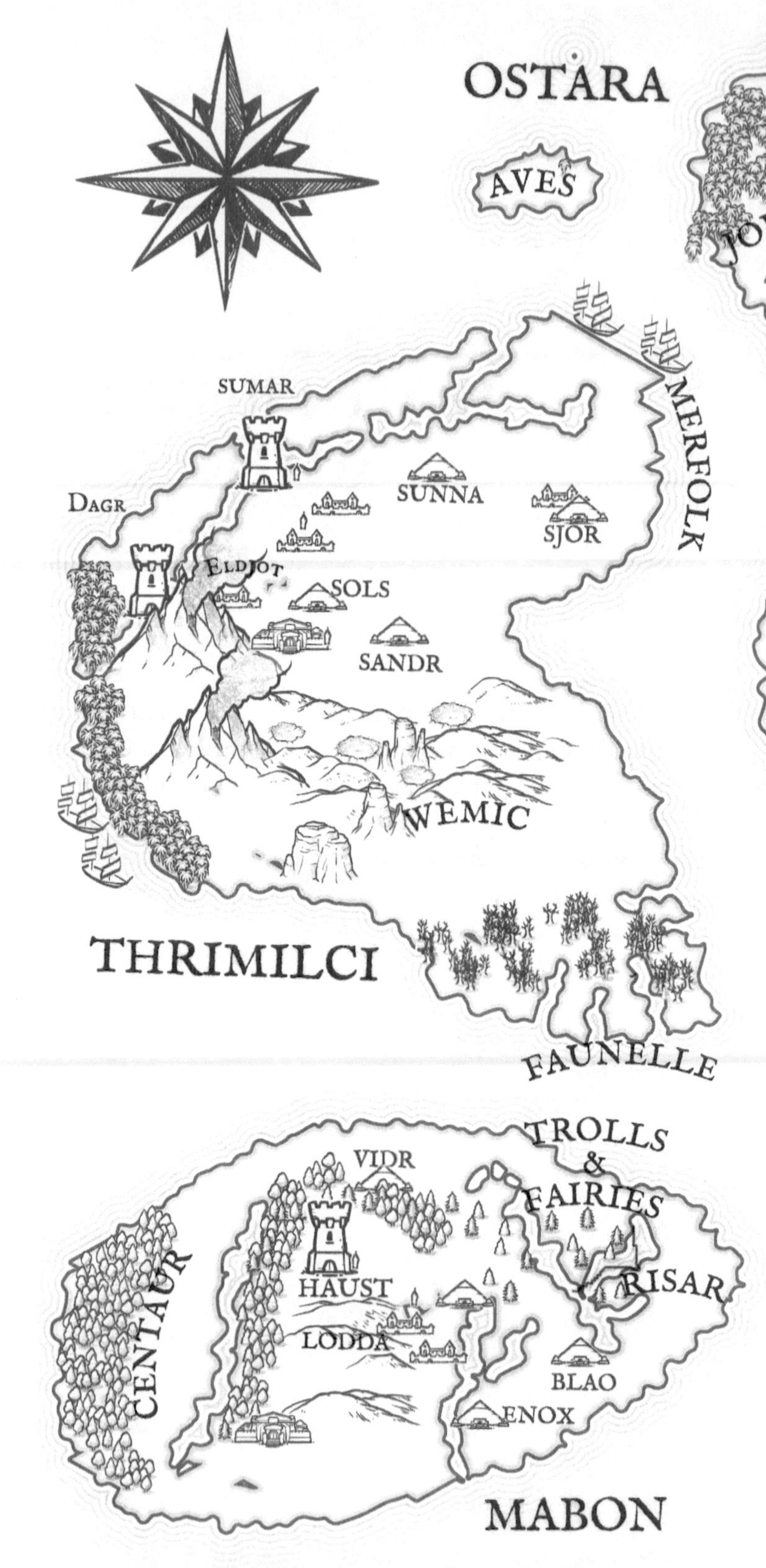

OSTARA
AVES
JOR
SUMAR
MERFOLK
DAGR
SUNNA
SJOR
ELDJOT
SOLS
SANDR
WEMIC
THRIMILCI
FAUNELLE
TROLLS
&
FAIRIES
VIDR
RISAR
CENTAUR
HAUST
LODDA
BLAO
ENOX
MABON

TIDINGS
ELIVAGAR
ANGUILLAN
LITR
REGN
ROT
VAR
GORGONS
LYCANS
NATT
BIORN
CRATHODE
VETR
SVELL
GLITRA
MINOTAUR
KALLA
SNJAR
KALDR
JOTNAR
STRAUMR
MOSSUR
TOWN CENTER
STOKER
TIO
HVALL
JARN
VALKYRIES
ALLA

PROLOGUE

Wren scowled at Lark's knowing smirk as she set Sumy down on the blanket she had spread on the floor. Lark's nameless son toddled past. She had taken to calling him Stoic. Sumy seemed determined to catch up with the older boys wandering, who attempted to toddle along with Steel.

"Quite the party here," Lark said. "How far along are you this time?" He claimed to scent it on her.

Wren glared. "Two months. Right after I finished the Wild Hunt, Alder came to visit Sumy for the first time." Wren folded her arms and watched the boys. "Delta is pregnant. Alder says it is his."

"I know."

Wren had purposely been away or busy during Lark's last five weekly visits, knowing he would find out about her twins the moment he hugged her. He patted the couch beside him and she sat.

She'd given up on attending Valla U and retreated to the Tio palace again and away from prying eyes. Lark wrapped his arm around her shoulders and pulled her close so she could lean on him.

"Will you help me plan a birthday gathering for my son?" Lark asked, his voice muffled by her hair.

"I have already started. It is next week," Wren replied, and Lark sighed.

"Wren?"

"Hmm?" she pondered, watching Stoic plop down beside Sumy who immediately beat his shin with a rattle.

Steel took the rattle from Sumy and scolded him, making Wren smile at the funny little trio.

"Daughters?"

"Yes. Two girls," she replied. "How is Hawk? He has refused to come see me. He thinks, *knows* I do not think clearly with Alder. I cannot stop myself. I feel like such a fool. He is bedding her. His Guardian wife. While I sit within these walls with his children, counting the days since his last visit, praying for the next. I am the most pathetic version of myself."

"The same. Love makes fools of us all. Hawk is certainly not the exception. It has been over a year since he has been with Sparrow, and he is even further away from finding a suitable wife. Though he has lost himself a few times in the wiles of lesser family daughters," Lark said ruefully.

"And you? Have you been enjoying anyone's wiles? It has been a year, Lark. No one would fault you. You certainly have enough prospects," Wren said, clasping his hand on his lap.

"I love Sea. It does not seem fair to bind a woman to me who would only be second to her. I have only enjoyed your wiles, Wren."

Wren could certainly understand that sentiment. "Been enjoying them as I sleep? I think I would have remembered," she teased.

"Not everyone's wiles are of the carnal kind. You are a truly wonderful mother, your sons, my son — we are all lucky to have you."

He puckered his lips where his face buried against her hair. "Jasmine and roses. You smell the same way you did when I stole your first kiss."

Wren laughed, and it surprised her. It was a long time since she'd heard her own laugh.

"You tried to steal a lot more than that if memory serves."

"That I did," Lark murmured and she could hear the smile in his voice. "I am sorry about that day. I enjoyed your momentary lapse in judgement far more than I had expected."

She sniffed. "I will try not to take offense."

Lark chuckled. "Before I met Sea, I always assumed we would wed —"

Wren pulled away from him and knit her brows, looking at him. "Truly?"

"Yes, you never thought of it?" Lark asked in all sincerity.

She shook her head. "I was scrawny and you treated me like a sister. You only showed interest in me like a girl once, and then you shouted at me and told me to leave you alone."

Lark made a pained face. "I forgot about that. No wonder you did not speak to me for months. Not until you met Alder, and he soothed whatever I had ruined by my coarse words."

"You are forgiven," she said, settling back against him, but he stopped her and took her hands in his.

"Wren. Something just came to me. You are miserable here raising my son and yours alone, yes?" Lark asked excitedly.

"Not miserable. Lonesome for companionship, but you come and keep us company," she said, offering him a smile.

"Right. You and me. We make a very good pair. We have always been companions and, under the right circumstances, find one another appealing as a man and woman." She arched her brow in question and he angled his body towards her. "Be my Guardian wife, Wren."

"Do not be ridiculous, Lark. That was a lousy proposal. What *are* the right circumstances?"

"You have me there. Hear me out, though. I cannot get through a single day without thinking about Sea. May I assume you feel the same way about Alder?" She nodded, and he continued smiling as if he was onto something he thought monumental. "We both love someone we cannot be with. The solution to both our problems is to be together, publicly anyway. The daughters would stop coming to my castle and you can show your face again and be tried and true."

Wren scanned his face. He was being earnest, and she was speechless. It would solve their problems, and they were always together — had been since they were little.

"I would have to tell Alder first," she breathed.

Lark's smile grew and a lock of his midnight waves fell from behind his ear. "You can reassure him; I have an heir. I need no more children and I would not prevent you from seeing each other."

Wren's mouth sat ajar. "*Need* more children, but what about wanting them?" she asked, blushing.

Lark had the grace to avert his eyes as his deeply tanned skin reddened. When he looked back to her, his soft grey eyes were mirrored orbs reflecting her own flushed face back to her.

"That would be entirely up to you, Wren. My wife has passed, and she has my love. I have not been with another woman in any capacity since the morning of her death."

Wren swallowed. "You are twenty years old; do you plan on being chaste the rest of your life? Never mind," she said, shaking her head. "We can address that later if it comes up. Yes. My answer is yes. Bring your father to ask my father because... Goodness, I have never had a true suitor before." She giggled and slapped her hand over her mouth and gave him a sidelong glance, daring him to laugh at her.

Lark was smiling at her. "I have missed your giggling."

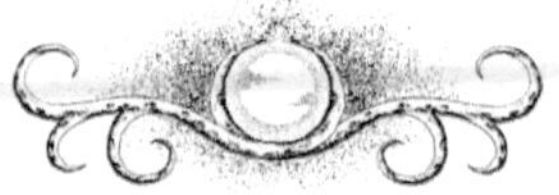

Wren crumpled Alder's message, then decided it wasn't nearly destructive enough and lit it on fire. He could have been less understanding. She was distraught when he married Delta, but Alder seemed almost... relieved.

"If we cannot be together, I am glad you find happiness with Lark," Wren mocked.

She was back at the Sumar palace in a wing of their own since she would officially adopt Lark's son as soon as they were married. For the time being, no one outside of Hawk, Flint, and Pearl knew about the boy. They couldn't stay at the Haust castle because Peak had married Willow and there was no way she would bring her children around a Natt.

The door opened in the front room and Wren left the bedroom where Stoic and Sumy napped in the large four post bed big enough for a half-dozen people.

Steel barreled into the room as fast as his little legs could carry him, and Wren caught him and set him on her hip. "Lark says I can stay with you if I want, and Stoic and Sumy can be my brothers! That I can have sisters too!" he said gleefully, his turquoise eyes wide.

Lark walked into the room, carting in boxes and bags. The staff set it down inside the door and left. The wry smile she gave him when he entered fell as she looked about his things.

"What is all this?" Wren asked.

"I am moving in. I had it packed after I received a messenger from Alder. He said he gave his approval, and that he was glad you were not alone anymore. My father and I just spoke with Hawk and Flint. I expect your mother will burst into the room at any moment. That is why you moved into a wing, is it not?" Lark asked, moving past her and into the bedroom.

Steel giggled. "Does Wen love Lark?"

Wren's dark eyes went as wide as saucers. "You little rapscallion. Trying to get me into all sorts of trouble. If it is a secret between us two, I suppose I love Lark. Of course, you are welcome to stay with us, my little love bug." Wren nuzzled his neck, and he twisted in her arms so he could beat her into the bedroom.

Lark was hanging up his clothing in the closet and turned to give her a smirk. "How does early autumn sound to you?"

She shrugged as she sat down on her trunk to watch him organize his things and rubbed her small belly. "Not too chilly. All you would need is a light cloak. The girls are due in late fall. I did not tell Alder I was pregnant. I did not want it to fall into the wrong hands." She sighed. "He does not know about Steel, either."

"No matter. When all is settled, we can have him over for dinner and set things right. I was asking about early fall to marry, Wren." Lark poked his head out of the closet.

"Oh!" she said, startled. "Autumn is lovely. That is not much time to plan."

"We can do it in Mabon, just our immediate families. It is not peculiar because it is my second marriage and you will be noticeably pregnant."

"You are going to break my mother's heart, having planned it all out already," Wren said, giving him a wry grin.

Lark came to kneel in front of her. "Am I overwhelming you? The idea of having a family with you, so neither of us has to be afraid any longer, has given me joy I have not felt in a very long year."

Wren balanced her weight on her palm as she pushed one of his loose waves behind his ear. "A little, but I will come around. I am... happy too."

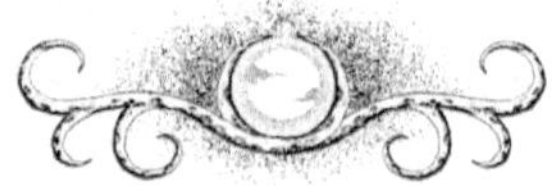

She had gotten used to sleeping next to Lark in their overly enormous bed with Stoic, Sumy, and Steel between them. Wren had even stopped blushing when nursed Sumy in front of him, but their wedding day was different.

Sparrow set a crown of harvest wildflowers on her head, and Wren reached for her hand to give it a squeeze. Sparrow gave her a tight smile.

"Better you than someone else I would hate. I knew they were sending him daughters by the score and he was spending all his time with you." She sighed.

"You knew that?" Wren asked, running her hands self-consciously over the cream pleated fabric of her empire waist dress.

"All of Tidings knows when Lark is not in classes at Valla U, he is with you. You have been living together for the last four months."

Wren looked away. "How is your daughter? She looks like Ridge."

Sparrow's lips curled reluctantly. "Fiery little whiner. She never sleeps. Someone must hold her at all times, but Ridge adores her. He is an excellent father... and husband."

"That is good, Sparrow. I am happy for you," Wren said, sounding preoccupied.

"Are you? I never see you anymore. I know I hurt Hawk. I hurt Hawk badly, but Ridge showed out of nowhere with his proposal. We signed it on the spot. I hardly had a choice. Hawk never asked."

Wren turned to her incredulously. "Do not play coy with me. Hawk only ever loved you. The only reason he did not propose sooner was because you are a free spirit, you always have been. He wanted you to be impressed with his proposal, so he waited for the perfect moment. All of Tidings knew you were together. You never made it a secret. Hawk and Sparrow. You could never say only one of your names without the other. I am sore. You broke his heart. He has not been the same. Never did he think you would choose another over him."

Sparrow's olive cheeks were splotchy with either anger or shame. "So there it is. After all this time — the truth. Good. I am glad we got it out of the way so we can go back to normal. Sorry. I am sorry to you, to Hawk, to your family. It was stupid and childish and part of me thought I could get out of it and it would push Hawk to act. Never did I think I would ever marry anyone other than Hawk. I owe Ridge for keeping me together when I wanted to fall apart. I love him in my own way. It is not the same as Hawk. No one could be, but he is the father of my daughter."

Wren ran her fingers through the big curls they had styled her dark hair into and picked up her harvest flower bouquet. "I suppose I should let it go. Neither of us saw our lives taking us here."

"You do not have to let it go. I would be mad if we were reversed but stop shutting me out. I only have Ridge and his evil sisters, whom I hate, and Robin, who is going to wind up with another child from how she gropes that Regn."

Wren chuckled. "I saw that too. Her sons are too handsome. We will have to keep them away from our daughters."

Sparrow smiled, and it felt like old times.

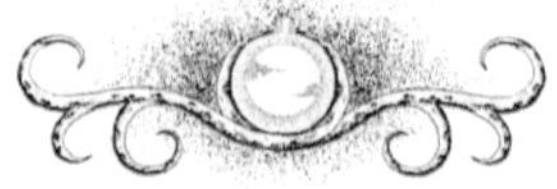

Wren's flowers shook as she walked down the aisle of crunching fall leaves lined by only their closest family and their spouses. Wren had two women walking down the aisle before her: Sparrow and Robin. While Lark had Peak and Hawk. They had to mismatch the partners because Hawk was enduring enough torture with Ridge there holding their daughter born at the end of last spring.

"Nerves are good. It means you have thought it through," Flint said.

Wren tried to focus on Lark ahead. The boy she knew was now a man. He would never hurt her, he would always protect her, and it was all for show so they could live as normally as possible.

Still...

Wren's stomach was in knots at having to say the Guardian vows complete with hand-fasting ceremony. Her father's calloused palm scratched her sheer butterfly sleeves where they met her bare arm as he handed her off to Lark.

Lark took her hand, and they faced the Valkyrie they'd selected to perform the speaking portions.

"You are shivering," Lark whispered from the side of his mouth.

"Naturally, you are calm. You have done this before. Everyone thinks my children are yours. As if you cheated on Sea. I despise it," Wren hissed.

Lark gave her hand a squeeze. "We know the truth. Sea knows the truth. Their opinions do not matter."

It was time for them to address one another. Wren thought her face must have been beet red the entire time. Lark looked dapper in the silver they had selected to contrast with the bronze the girls wore. Wren could see Steel and Brass playing a dozen feet away from where their guests sat. They did the ceremony in the leaf laden woods on the side of the Haust castle. No one but Sparrow, Hawk, Lark, and Wren knew it was where her first kiss was stolen.

They didn't exchange rings, so when the Valkyrie stared expectantly at them after they had said the vows, Wren only stared back. Flint cleared his throat and a round of chuckles began. Lark gave her bound hands a squeeze, and she started.

"Oh!" Her face heated again.

Lark held up his finger for them all to wait a moment and turned around, using the air to float something into his palm. He turned around, and the chuckles continued. Wren joined in, though no one else could understand why he held a golden maple leaf before his lips, below his twinkling eyes.

She hadn't kissed Lark. Not once. On the cheek, sure, but at night in the privacy of their bed once they had tucked their kids in. Not in the bright afternoon, with scores of people watching them intensely. Wren had never kissed any man in front of other people other when she and Alder had married in front of Hawk.

"I am giving you time to plan," Lark teased.

Wren's nerves faded. Lark would always be the boy she knew. There was nothing to be nervous about.

She closed her eyes and canted her chin up. Wren felt as he neared. She could smell his spicy scent just before his lips slanted over hers. She breathed deep. It was a big kiss for them both. Lark hadn't kissed another since Sea's death, and Alder had been the only man Wren had kissed since her first one six years past. She supposed it had been that long for Lark, too.

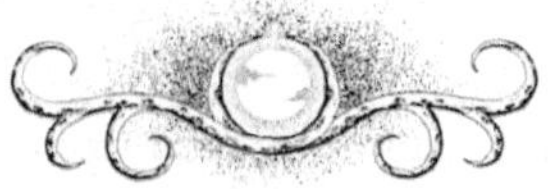

"How was it?" Lark asked as they walked back to their wing.

Wren buried her nose in Stoic's hair. "It impressed me. Almost as good as the second one. Much better than the first." Wren teased.

Steel slept on Lark's shoulder and he cradled Sumy in his other arm. The feast in the Haust great hall had been beautiful, and Wren had had to fake her happiness less and less. Lark stole two more kisses through the night. Once when they danced and again when he thanked everyone for coming.

"How are you doing, really?" she asked.

She watched his broad chest rise and fall with a heavy sigh. "I miss her. Today, more than I have in a long time." When he turned to look at her, she gave him a sympathetic smile.

"The hard part is over. Now we go back to normal. *Our* normal," Wren promised.

"Our normal," he agreed.

They both stopped at the end of the hall, looking towards the door of their wing.

"What are you all plotting?" Wren asked, narrowing her eyes at Pearl, Flint, and Hawk.

"Come, darling. Give us the children," Pearl said, taking Stoic from her arms.

"What? Why?" Wren protested as Lark passed Steel to Flint and Sumy to Hawk.

"Because it is our wedding night," Lark said, smirking.

Wren's mouth fell open. "But who will feed Sumy? He just started sleeping through the night... Stoic has night terrors. He wakes up —"

"It will be alright, darling," Flint said, giving her a kiss on her forehead.

She gaped after him and Pearl, who walked down the hall with her children.

Hawk chuckled. "See you both in the morning. Congratulations — again."

"That is tremendously inappropriate, Hawk," Wren grumbled as he walked away.

"I do not think it was," Lark said and opened the door to their wing but put his hand on her shoulder. "Allow me."

Wren yelped as he lifted her off her feet and carried her into the wing. He carried her all the way into the bedroom despite her protests and set her on her feet before the bed.

"I am going to get ready for bed. I do not know what to do without the babies to take care of," she said awkwardly.

Lark simply nodded and went into the closet.

Wren went into the bathroom to stare at herself in the mirror. She didn't look any different. She didn't feel married. She hadn't felt married when she had been with Alder, either.

"Lark?" Wren called once she was finished getting ready for bed, but still in her gown.

Lark was already in bed. She searched the drawstring pants he discarded each night before climbing under the blankets and didn't find any of his undergarments with them.

"We are not taking that step tonight, Wren. It has been a long day for both of us," Lark said from the bed.

Wren was embarrassed to feel a sting of rejection at his words, but then relief overwhelmed her and she unzipped her dress and crawled into bed wearing just her slip.

"Thank you. I do not know if I will ever be ready for something more, Lark. If you... sought comfort. I will not begrudge you," Wren said softly.

Lark turned her around, so she slept facing away from him and he wrapped his arm around her waist. His lips pressed to her ear as he sighed.

"I will never stray. I may be your Guardian husband, but you are my wife."

"Good night, Lark," she squeaked. "This... is nice."

"Mm-hmm. We may need to look into building a room for the boys, so we have the bed to ourselves from now on. This *is* nice."

More time passed and Wren had received word that Alder's son had been born. She knew that meant he wouldn't be visiting her soon. It had been a terrible day.

Wren laid back on the chaise waiting for Lark to get home from Valla U. He'd be proven tried and true at Yuletide and she tried desperately not to be jealous. She would take the test once the girls were born, as she did with the Wild Hunt.

She had researched in the technology room before coming back to the wing and had grabbed everything she thought she needed.

The door opened, and she bolted upright. Lark looked dubiously at the food she had a staffer bring up as he shut the door.

"Please, come in. Come in. Welcome to Wren's official eviction notice. I thought you might like to help." She batted her eyelashes at him, and he chuckled.

"Whatever I could do to help my ailing wife. I will have to let Hawk know we will not be joining him and the flavor of the week for dinner."

Wren waved a hand. "He will forgive you."

"Where are the boys?" Lark asked, sitting down next to her.

"My parents are watching them. We went for a walk in Ostara, then took a bumpy carriage ride back *after* I used the evening primrose." She spread out the papers she'd printed on the table for him to see.

"You have done your research." Lark suppressed a smile.

"This is no laughing matter. I can hardly breathe with them in me, one of them is always in my ribs, and-"

Lark held up a hand. "You have persuaded me." He looked at one sheet. "I will provide the hands for the foot rub and you eat the spicy foods."

Wren smiled as she leaned back in the chaise and swung her freshly polished feet into Lark's lap. "There is enough food for you, too. I did not want to be the only one feeling awful after eating all of this."

Lark smiled as Wren balanced the plate on her belly and had fed him while he rubbed her feet.

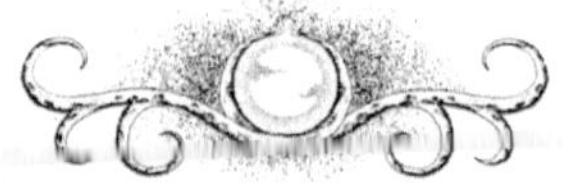

"How long is it supposed to take?" Lark asked three hours later.

"I do not know." Wren groaned. "All I have is heartburn and moisturized feet."

"Up. We will take another walk."

Lark helped her up and Wren waddled down to the first floor, where they went for a swim and checked on the boys.

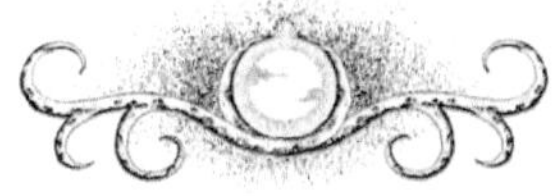

"Well, thank you anyway," Wren grumbled as they readied for bed.

She changed into her baby doll nightgown and collected the papers spread out on the table, sighing. Lark walked out after her and rubbed her lower back and took the papers from her hands.

"What else is there? Perhaps I should be very trying for the time being. Stress should induce labor," Lark teased.

"I think that happened when Sumy was born," Wren said, looking over the papers in his hands.

Her eyes widened when she realized she'd printed out *all* the pages she found. She slapped the pages out of his hand, making him chuckle.

"I did not mean to print that page," she said, blushing as she used air to pile them neatly on the table.

She rushed out of the room and cursed because she'd meant to leave the wing to get the boys. She turned around and Lark filled the doorway.

"Let your mother watch the boys tonight. You deserve a night to yourself." Lark took her hand and brought her to the bed.

"They will complete their nursery at the end of the week. I think I will miss them sleeping with us, but I suppose the girls will fill their place soon enough. Goodness, we will have to build another room for them when they come of age," Wren said, climbing into bed.

"Perhaps," Lark said, sliding in behind her. "We have time to think about it."

Wren hummed an agreement and shifted her head back to give his cheek a kiss goodnight, as they did every night. They hadn't kissed since the day of their wedding. Only Lark shifted his head at the last moment and her lips caught his.

"Oh, sorry," Wren stammered and turned away to face the windows.

"You are my wife. You may kiss me. Wren?" he whispered.

"Hmm?" she asked with her heart thundering in her ears.

"You have my permission, if you want more."

Wren twisted in his arms. "More?"

Lark's eyes had changed from their usual soft grey to silver orbs that reflected the light coming in through the stained-glass windows behind her. Instead of answering her question, Lark took her hand that rested over her belly and placed it on his hip where his undergarments should have been.

Wren's lips parted. "You are ready?"

"Whenever you are," he breathed.

She turned fully to face him. "Are we under the right circumstances?"

The corner of his mouth tugged up. "I have always been attracted to you, Wren."

"It could help to induce labor."

"Yes, I saw the sheet," Lark said dryly.

Before she lost her nerve, Wren used where her hand rested on his bare hip to leverage herself high enough to kiss his lips. He caught her and spun her onto her back and deepened the kiss.

It differed from their kiss in the woods. They were fifteen and had gotten carried away. Now they were adults and married. Wren knew she could stop him at any point and he wouldn't be upset, but she didn't want him to stop.

"Wait. Wait," she groaned under his weight and the awkwardness of her belly.

Lark was breathing harshly and seemed to throw himself back, hands balled into fists as his chest heaved.

"Yes?" he asked roughly, and Wren worked her tongue to loosen it from the roof of her mouth.

She had never seen Lark fully unclothed and obviously aroused. Lark's smile was a salacious curl of his lips. Wren blinked several times, as if she was seeing him for the first time.

She was sure he had never looked at her with such lust before.

"On your back," she said, wriggling out from under him.

Lark wasted no time rolling off her and took her hips so she strad-dled his hips. "Are *you* ready, Wren? No one waits for me. Not in this world," he asked, kneading her thighs.

Alder laid with his wife. They had a son together. Maybe he didn't like her, but part of him must've loved her enough to make her the mother of his son. It eased some of her guilt. She wanted Lark... since they were children. She never thought he saw her that way and when

Sea sauntered into his world, she felt discarded. The feeling quickly passed, but there it was.

"I want to make love to you. Not only because I want these babies out of me, but because I want to," Wren whispered.

Lark growled and where his hands had been on her thighs gripped her nightgown and tore it to her neckline. Wren stared in disbelief at his strength and how all his muscles had seemed to flex at once as he bent forward to press his open-mouthed kisses along her breasts.

His big hands cupped her backside and guided himself into her. Wren gasped and for a moment, neither of them moved.

It had been done.

Sea was no longer the only woman he had been with, the last woman he had been with and Alder was no longer her only lover.

"I watched you make love to Alder that night," Lark confessed.

"Why?"

"I do not know. It changed the way I viewed you. You became a woman."

Wren blushed, and Lark kissed her again. "Wren, I should warn you. I am already on the cusp."

"Oh." She averted her eyes despite their intimate position.

He stopped and leveled his eyes at her. "But I can go again. I want to. I want you as long as you are giving yourself to me."

"All night?" she squeaked.

Lark kissed along her collarbone. "Unless you can go into the morning as well. I am already mentally planning my excuses for why I will not be present in my classes."

Wren's skin prickled with excitement at his words and she shoved him back so his head hit the pillow. "There is nothing worth doing unless you are going to do it extremely well," she said as she moved.

CHAPTER 1
JETT
WHAT DOESN'T KILL YOU, MAKES YOU STRONGER

Slate,

Trust this is for the best. Please forgive my deceit and know that my love for you will never fade. It is for that reason that I must leave. You need an heir I can't provide, and you won't move on unless I am out of your life. Please don't waste my sacrifice.

I expect I will see you again. I hope when I do, you

*will be happily married or betrothed to a worthy woman. Do
what needs doing.
Please do not search me out.
Love, Forever and Always, Yours, Mine, The World's,
For all Time
Your Torch.*

Slate had broken every piece of furniture in their wing, save the nursery. The big man had finally passed out and Jett went to check on him. He'd found the letter crumpled on the floor of their bedroom where Slate's six-foot six form laid atop a mattress that's insides spilled from the side. He was naked as the day he was born, and Jett tossed a shredded blanket over his adopted brother's waist. Slate was one of the few men in Tidings who was as big as Jett.

Jett hadn't slept all night; he'd paced the halls of the palace and lingered close to the portal room to keep an eye out for Slate after he'd put Indigo to sleep. He'd watched Brass and Scarlett leave together and no one came back. If they only knew how close they'd come to running into Slate... it had been hardly a minute before Slate had charged through the portal door and didn't stop until he reached the wing.

Jett had followed and waited to see if Slate would search him out either to question him or kill him, perhaps both. Slate had roared after a long silence. That was when the destruction began. He stood guard outside the wing while Slate raged until he only heard silence hours later.

Jett's boots crunched over the debris that littered the room as he took in the mayhem's scope. He stood in the doorway to the nursery, its vacant crib and toys that'd never known the grubby touch of children's fingers seemed to mock him. He guessed they mocked Scarlett and Slate even worse. Jett wasn't one for crying. He'd cried when his mother died, in bed with his wives when his father died, but he'd stove off the tears at Scarlett's leaving. He slid down the sea foam green wall, plucked a stuffed toy from the rocking sofa chair.

Damn the Gods, he thought as his tears slid over his chiseled features.

Scarlett's letter was unlike her, so matter of fact, no genuine warmth to it at all. It must have eaten Slate from the inside out. No woman had ever left him. Jett doubted Slate thought it was possible until he'd met Scarlett. A trail of broken hearts in her wake, that's what Quick had said.

"Did you help her?"

Jett jerked from the wall and wiped a hand over his face, clearing the tears. He hadn't snuck up on like that in years. It was a minor concession that it was Slate who had done it. The man was a master assassin. Truth be told, Jett didn't know how six different people could have known about Scarlett's plans and Slate not found out.

She'd chosen her conspirators wisely; Brass was hopelessly devoted to her. Jett and Indigo would never betray her. Pearl thought this way the best choice and would keep her secret. Lera had seen an alliance with the Guardians, which could later result in a favor. Chafer did what Lera said. It didn't hurt that he was no fan of Slate's.

Jett cleared his throat. "Some." He croaked and cleared his throat again.

"She did not say goodbye." Slate slid down the wall next to Jett and rested his head back.

"Didn't she though?" Jett's voice was thick with emotion still and he swallowed hard. "If she had tried to tell you, you wouldn't have let her go. She did what she thought was right. If we hadn't helped her, she would have been out there on her own with no one."

Like their mother, but she had had Hawk and Sparrow. Scar had no one. Jett sucked in a sharp breath. Every time he thought about it, he felt like he'd somehow failed her. Slate blew out a deep breath.

"She will come back," Slate said, and Jett shut his eyes again.

Out of all the scenarios Slate must have gone over in his head, the ways she would try to push him away, to get him to leave her, Jett knew Slate never imagined she might give up everything and everyone so that he could live a full life. Slate had told her not to sacrifice herself for him, but it was her way. Everyone was put before her own wishes. Their mother had been the same way.

"She left Tidings. Right now, she is on a flight far away from here,"

Jett said, turning his head against the wall to view his brother's expression.

Slate pressed his lips firmly together. "Brass did not persuade her to go to Ostara?"

"No. He tried. Right until the end, he helped her get through tonight. She turned him down." Jett wasn't proud of his spying, but he'd wondered if Brass pushed if she would go.

Slate's chest rose and fell with a hefty sigh. "Did you know she took down the Stygians? Lera said she had been plotting away from the past month, that she had loose ends she needed tying up before she could leave. They caught the men who gave her to the Merfolk. All of it, she did without me."

"To protect you and herself. Self-preservation. Don't you dare degrade her love; you did not see how hard it was for her. She did it all for you, you bastard." Jett promised himself he wouldn't blame Slate, but that grew harder by the minute.

"Who else?" Slate asked, and Jett rattled off the list of conspirators. "Not Tawny?"

"No, she thought she might go to you. Tawny hates you, but she'd go to you to keep Scarlett. Breakfast will be brutal. No one else knows yet," Jett said and dry washed his face. "I told the girls. They know when something is wrong with me. It's been a tough secret to keep."

"What would you have me do? If you were in my place and one of your wives left you?" Slate turned his head to face Jett.

Pain filled grey eyes gazed back at Jett and his chest constricted. If Amethyst or Cerise left him, he'd drag them back kicking and screaming. He'd not been whole until he found love with them.

"My wives can have heirs, Slate. It is a unique situation. Don't waste my sister's love. Find a wife, have tons of children, you'll keep Scar as an adopted sister. You can love one another on the inside but do as she asks. Continue the Dagr line. It's all riding on you."

"Tell me where she went," Slate rumbled.

Jett furrowed his brow. "I don't know. She doesn't have anywhere to live." Jett cleared his throat again and shifted his head back so Slate couldn't see the anger and frustration in his eyes.

"No one, nowhere, nothing. I will be dead within the next few years.

I never wanted children, I did not want a wife, now I am forced to have both." He blew out a breath. "Will you tell me when she contacts you? Let me know she is all right?"

Jett nodded and got to his feet. He didn't much feel like eating, but he had letters to deliver.

"I swear it."

"She did not need me. As soon as she could function without me, she left," Slate said to his retreating.

"Nah. She didn't need you, but she wanted you anyway."

In no way could Jett have predicted just how badly Tawny could have taken the news. She'd flown from her seat and tried to beat Slate with her tiny fists, all the while bawling and cursing that he'd ever been born. Slate took it and then some. He'd gently wrapped his arms around her until she wore herself out and sobbed, clutching his shirt.

Gypsum sat stoically, staring at his breakfast. "I could have gone with her until I started at Valla. I don't need to be here; she doesn't have to be alone."

"Scarlett said she wanted you here," Jett said mechanically, and Cherry slid her hand into his.

Gypsum was soulful. She thought if Slate was going to open up to anyone about his hurt, that it would be with Gypsum. Indigo stroked the snowy white fur of her kitten Bee-Gold, who purred contentedly in her lap. Her face was a blotchy, reddened mess. Her powder blue eyes, unseeing.

Steel took Tawny from Slate and led her upstairs. Hawk and Sparrow would still need to be told. Jett didn't think that would go ever very well. Pearl was making the trip to the old Dagr palace after breakfast and Slate had agreed to go with.

In March, the Dagr portal door was repaired. Sparrow and Hawk were nearly finished with its rehabilitation and spent almost every dinner at the Sumar palace. It had shocked the tyros at Valla University to find Scarlett had dropped out.

Jett had nearly spluttered when Ash approached him and asked after her. In some peculiar way, the Straumr boy had fallen for Scarlett. Jett didn't think Ash would ever really love someone. He loved himself far too much for that. If he did, though, it would have been Scarlett. A lot of what Ash did made more sense with that knowledge.

Jett hadn't known what to expect with Slate when they got back to classes. He hadn't expected him to keep his head down and drift through the days like a shadow of a man. Since Scarlett was out of the picture, women flocked to Slate like never before. He'd shown that he could commit to one woman, and they all strove to replace his sister.

None could. Slate rejected them left and right.

Slate's birthday was in March, and that had been a hard day. Jett had tried to take him out and drown his sorrows, but they'd sat at the bar swamped in melancholy with Brass, Quick, Gypsum, and Steel. They were a poor party. Brass and Slate had repaired things without a foul word between them. They'd both lost her and misery loved company.

Then one morning at the end of March, Jett woke up in Valla to find a girl in Slate's bed. His heart leapt at the sight. Scarlett had been emailing him regularly, and she hadn't mentioned she'd be coming back for a visit. The girl turned under Slate's blankets, and Jett's stomach dropped. *Not* Scarlett.

A poor man's Torch — Amber.

Jett had stormed from the room and slammed the door so the wall trembled. He didn't know why he was so upset. He shook with anger. Why did it feel so much like a deep betrayal? Amber had been Slate's most ardent pursuer, and she was a lesser family, but it felt like a slap to Scarlett after their previous scuffle.

Things escalated quickly after that, despite Tawny and Jett's disdain for the strawberry blonde. Amber started coming to family dinners on the weekends and staying the night in Slate's bed. With more Amber came more Garnet and things ended between Quick and Indigo for good. In mid-April came the ring. An oval Baltic amber stone in a gold setting rested on Amber's finger when they announced their engagement. They planned to wed during the Midsummer festival.

Jett sat in front of the computer in the technology room in Valla with Tawny, trying to break the news. "Just tell it like it is, but don't say to who. I doubt she wants to know that much. Oh! Tell her about the baby shower, too. That'll soften the news a bit."

Jett licked his lips and began.

To: Scarlett Tio (ScarlettSunset@Sunsettravels.com)

Hey Baby sis,

Jett and Tawny here. Glad work is going well, and you met someone. Great news, it wasn't for nothing. Slate got engaged over the weekend. The wedding is being planned for the Midsummer break. They finished building the Dagr palace, and Slate will move out next month. In other news, Amethyst is as big as a house. She wants to have the baby shower in two weeks. Last minute, I know, but the family wants to see you. Bring your man with, let's see if he passes our tests. There's a protocol for bringing in myopics, so we'll take care of that on our end. Tawny says she misses you like a fat kid on a diet misses cake. We all do. We'll have your old room ready for you.

Jett & Tawny

Jett sat back and waited for her reply. She always did in a few minutes. He flexed his fingers and leaned back. Tawny hovered over his shoulder impatiently waiting for word back.

Scarlett had been cryptic when it had come to her main man. No names, no details. Only that they had worked together at the gym she did personal training at and that they were talking about moving in together. All great news. Jett was worried she'd cocoon herself and hide from the world.

That hadn't happened, and Jett knew she had pushed herself to be happy — to *try*, anyway.

Gods, how Jett hoped she didn't ask who the fiancée was. Tawny and Jett had talked a lot more since Amber joined their group. Cherry and Tawny got along very well and weren't particularly fond of Amber as well. They left it to Amethyst and Indigo to make Amber welcomed. Indigo was indifferent, at best. She mostly stuck to herself and Bee, wandering around the palace like a ghost. She needed to find a husband, too. Gypsum and Steel were the only ones who showed any genuine support aside from Hawk, Sparrow, and Pearl.

The wedding would take place at the Dagr palace and Sparrow was preparing a statement revealing Slate's true heritage. Amber hadn't cared that they wouldn't say oaths to one another. They'd bound one another in a way she found acceptable. Dhole had given them bonded tattoos on their ring fingers.

The love rune, Amber's choice.

An email popped up in Jett's inbox when he refreshed the screen.

To: Jett Var (JettSetter@VallaU.com)

That is great news. Send Slate my congratulations. It's been a long time, I think a visit would be fantastic! I would love to bring my boyfriend; I know he is dying to see all of you. Try to keep an open mind. I'll send you my flight itinerary once I book it. Give me dates and times and I'll do the rest.

Tell Indigo Tree is a she-beast, who knew cats got this big!

I know it's fast, but my boyfriend is moving in the first week of May. It's seriously going better than I could've dreamed. I'm happy. :)

Send my love to everyone!

Scar

P.S. Ask Tawny when she's going to get knocked up next. I think I'm going to love being an aunt.

Jett frowned at the screen and looked back at Tawny, who snorted. "I wish I could see her face. Do you really think she's as happy as she pretends? Who is this guy? He better not be like forty and divorced. That girl has serious daddy issues."

Tawny folded her arms below her curvy chest.

"I guess we'll find out when she gets here. She won't be able to hide it then," Jett said and replied.

Breakfast with Chris led to me staying the night at his house. He had the furnished basement to himself and told me to take the bed and he'd sleep on the futon. He wouldn't take no for an answer, and I grudgingly accepted. We'd sat at breakfast for two hours after our two-hour flight from Providence, Rhode Island to Chicago.

I told him that my parents died and that we'd moved to Tidings to be closer to family. That things had ended badly between Slate and me after we had gotten very serious. I told him and gave him a general idea about Tidings without talking about the perpetual weather islands, the magic, or hybrid tribes. I mentioned getting engaged and that I'd found out I couldn't have children, so my fiancée had ended it. Chris couldn't understand why we didn't just adopt, and I didn't go into depth about the greater family names and bloodlines.

He told me about the girl he had dated on and off until his hip surgery and how she left him when he couldn't play football anymore. Then he told me he'd tried to talk to me for months after prom. That whenever we were at a party together that he couldn't muster up the nerve to apologize. The last time we'd hooked up, he had already been drunk when I arrived and it hadn't been as hard, but then he screwed it up again by being pushy when he got me alone.

I remembered it vividly. It was my last night in Chicago two Decembers ago, and now I was back.

"I won't let you stay in a motel. My parent's basement is basically an apartment, and the futon is cozy. I've slept on it dozens of times. Don't argue, you get the bed." He dropped his dreamy baby blues and added, "The door has a lock, too."

I'd agreed and taken the rental car to his family's house. It was well after dawn at that point and we snuck in the back so we wouldn't have to explain anything to his parents. It brought me back. I actually enjoyed sneaking into his parent's basement.

I had brought in pajamas and a toothbrush and got ready for bed before him. We smiled nervously as we passed one another and I went into the bedroom and closed the door. I laid in his queen size bed and listened to the television murmur beyond the door. Left alone with my thoughts, I'd bawled.

My sobs grew so loud I pulled the blankets over my head so Chris wouldn't hear them. I squeaked when I heard knocking on the door of the bedroom.

"Scar? Are you okay?" Chris asked through the door.

"You can come in." My voice was barely more than a whisper, and he opened the door.

He was tall, just a couple of inches shorter than Slate, with chestnut hair that was always stylishly tousled. He wore flannel pajama pants and a white men's tank top.

"I brought you a box of tissue."

Chris crossed the room, and I sat up and smiled gratefully as I patted the bed. He stared down at me and knit his brows. I was wearing my Bears t-shirt and a pair of white boy shorts. I piled my hair atop my head as I wiped my eyes and looked up at him.

I was vulnerable and alone. There was one thing I knew, and that was that I didn't want to sleep by myself.

"Do you want to lie down?" I asked in a small voice. "I'm tired, but I'm having a hard time falling asleep."

Chris sat down on the bed but made no move to lie down. "I've screwed this up twice... badly. I had a huge crush on you in high school and blew it." His baby blue eyes shifted to mine. "Don't sleep with me because you're hurting and never speak to me again." He paused. "I haven't done *that* since before my hip. It's been too painful."

My mouth popped open, and I denied trying to sleep with him, but stopped. "I could really use a friend. I'm not over my ex. Obviously."

Chris smiled, finally looking at me.

That smile used to make my heartbeat faster and slower at the same time. He swung his legs over and tucked them under the blankets. I turned on my side to face him and he smiled nervously at me.

"It's been a long time since I've had a girl in my bed," he confided.

"Think of me as your friend and not a girl," I said, and he smiled.

Healing Chris had been harder than I thought it would be. He had pins in his hip and I had sedated him with my *calling* after he fell asleep on his own and remove them to mend the bone. I was the strongest tyro at *calling* at Valla University for Guardian Mastery, and this translated into my healing. Watching Chris hobble around with his cane made me feel like a terrible person.

When Chris had woken up, he'd reached for his cane and stood stock still. "The pain, the stiffness... it's all gone." He looked at me in disbelief, and I shrugged.

I'd fallen asleep with my head on his shoulder and hadn't moved so much as an inch. I had been in puppy love with Chris when I was sixteen, even after everything, old habits died hard.

Chris went with me to my appointments with the landlords until we found a one bedroom in the Mayfair area of Chicago only a few blocks away from where I lived with my mother. I drove the rental car in front of the house I shared with her and the one next to it that Tawny and her family had lived in and cried again. Chris had been with me and held me as I sobbed.

The following week, Chris helped me buy my car. I left the car dealership with a Dodge Challenger Blacktop and Chris shook his head.

"I was supposed to help you get something practical," he chastened when I revved the engine.

"This is practical. It's *practically* sinful. I love it. I wouldn't complain. As my unofficial best friend, you are privy to borrowing it to impress your hot dates." I teased and Chris had smiled and looked away as he sat in the passenger seat.

Chris took me to his old gym, and they referred me to one in Old Town. I took home a stack of papers on becoming a personal trainer and got to work. Chris and I started doing two-a-days, once before his classes and one at night. We went to dinner together after our nightly work out.

Chris helped me pick out my *practical* furniture. Everything but the bed, which I couldn't resist getting into a thick four-post bed with a leather padded headboard and matching dresser. It was my only extravagance. Well, the car too, but Chris drove it more than I did.

Once I had a furnished apartment, a job, and a routine, I emailed Jett. I told him everything I'd accomplished and how well I was doing. I didn't tell him how empty I felt and how nights when Chris didn't hang out until I passed out, that I cried myself to sleep.

Jett, Tawny, and Indigo emailed me daily. Indigo was the only one who gave me details. Slate had dated Amber. He hadn't slept around like I thought he would. That was a good thing. Indigo said he still wore Alder's ring; he never took it off. The same couldn't be said for me. I'd taken to wearing it on my right ring finger.

I couldn't say I was happy for Slate.

I wasn't — part of me hated him. My choice had been Crimson. I'd told Indigo so, and she had tried to push it, but Slate rejected everyone. Only Amber had stuck. Indigo thought it was Slate's way of fighting back because we pushed him into getting married. He'd do it, but it would be with someone they all hated. I told Indigo to be nice to the girl and try to get Tawny to come around.

Chris and I had been working out one night after work and a

photographer had approached us. "You two look amazing. Do you do fitness modeling?"

Chris and I smiled at one another. "No," I said.

Chris was bulking up after losing muscle from after his injury. His doctors couldn't explain what happened to his hip, but it cured him. Hips weren't supposed to mend, they'd told him. Now, after a month of hard training, there wasn't an ounce of fat on him. He'd rival Quick and Ash's bodies.

The plan was to pick up football again and finish college. He had a year and a half left. We were both personal trainers and clients flocked to us.

"Here's my card. We're doing some outdoor fitness modeling in Miami next week. Call me if you're interested." He looked us up and down and walked away.

Chris took the card and hooked his arm around my waist and lifted me off my toes as I giggled. "It's you. You're always smiling and your body is killer. Toned, but with curves. That's why your business is so good. You should blog about it. Put the college degree to work."

I patted his chest, and he set me down on my feet. "Don't be silly. I don't have any right to be telling people how to live their lives."

Chris leveled his dreamy baby blues at me and pivoted me to the wall of mirrors. "You're hot. Scorching." He laughed. "You're new nickname, Scorch. No more Sugar Lips."

My stomach twisted, and I looked away from the mirror. Scorch was too close to Torch. He was right. I'd worked harder than ever to be mommy's murder machine.

"I like sugar. Maybe not sugar *lips*," I said, going back to the machine we were working on.

"How about Shug?" Chris teased.

He flashed me a smile that sent a little thrill through me, and I blinked at him. Chris hadn't even tried to kiss me. We were friends, and he never crossed that line.

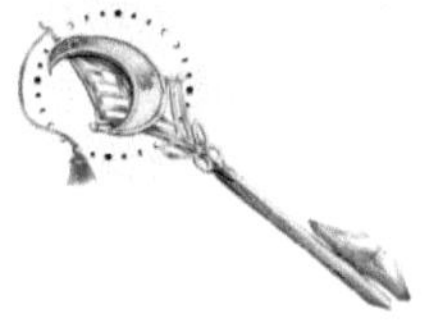

Chris and I went to Miami. It was a swimsuit shoot, and we were both oiled up and strategically dusted with sand as we played through the clear waves. It was a couple's shoot. We hadn't known that. The photographer had assumed we were together.

Chris and I frolicked along the white sand together under the tropical sun. The photographer had given us directions on how he wanted us and a lot of the shots were sexually suggestive, which made Chris and I giggle like a couple of kids. At some point, the giggling stopped.

When the shoot was over and we went back to the hotel they'd paid for, I got in the shower and tried to forget about how Chris and I had been gallivanting about all afternoon. We had another day of shooting with the other couple that would be there tomorrow morning, and we flew back the next night.

When I got out of the shower, Chris mumbled he ordered dinner from room service and that we could eat out on the balcony. He came out of the bathroom with a plush white towel wrapped around his waist and dried his chestnut hair with a towel. His body had changed so much since we started training. He had always had a six-pack, but now muscles defined across his perfect body.

Chris caught me staring and blushed. I licked my lips self-consciously and stood up from where I sat on the balcony. Open doors allowed ocean air filled the room. I walked over to where Chris stood and he watched me with glittering baby blues.

"Chris, what if I wanted a little more?" I said, chewing on my lip.

"More?" he asked and tossed down the towel he'd dried his hair with on the ottoman.

I stepped closer and placed my palms on his hard pecs. "More," I breathed.

Chris had dated no one since I'd been back. We spent all our time together. We slept in the same bed when he stayed over. I thought he wanted more and was afraid to make the first move because of our history, but it had been two months since I'd been back. While I was still heartbroken, I refused to become my mother. I wanted happiness. I wanted a life. Things were going well and with Slate out of sight, he was out of mind.

Chris licked his lips as he looked down at my too full mouth. "I care about you, Shug. A lot. Too much." He placed his hands over my palms. "I can't have more with you without having it all. I want you to be my girlfriend. I practically live at your place. We do everything together. I know it's bat shit, but I want to have a place to put my things."

"Like, move in?" I asked, knitting my brows.

Chris chuckled nervously, "A drawer first, maybe some space in the closet, but yeah, eventually. I've been in love with you since your freshman year, Shug."

My mouth popped open, and he seized upon the opportunity. Chris bent his mouth to mine and kissed me deeply. I let out an embarrassing moan and drew back. Chris's eyes flitted between mine anxiously. He was still afraid of overstepping.

"I love spending time with you and I wouldn't know what I'd do without you. I want to be your girlfriend and you can definitely have a drawer. We can talk about —"

Chris covered my mouth with his, and he swallowed my laugh. "Christ, you taste as sweet as ever, Shug," he breathed.

I pulled the white maxi dress over my head in a heartbeat. Chris sat back with wide eyes as he took me in. I reached for his towel and he held my hand.

"It's been over six months," he said nervously, and I let my lips curl.

"I promise to be gentle," I purred and his lips parted as he pulled in a deep breath.

I kept my eyes on his as I removed his towel. I'd never seen Chris naked. It was quite a sight. My eyes dropped, and I could *feel* his anxiety. Then I realized I had to worry about something I never had to do before — condoms. I *called* the care package the fitness magazine had left for us that contained a six-pack of condoms when I stopped myself.

"Come," I ordered, and led him over to the bed and sat him down.

I retrieved the allusive condoms and saw how hard Chris was. The first time would be fast. I pushed my white thong over my hips and heard Chris suck in a breath. I lifted my head and smirked before I climbed into the bed, straddling his thighs.

"I've wanted this for a long time," Chris breathed, and his fingers curled at his sides.

"Shh," I said, and put the condoms on the nightstand.

He lifted his mouth to my breast as it grazed his face, and I pushed him back to the bed. He smiled, and that thrill shot through me. I scooted down his body, and he tossed his head back as his stomach muscles flexed. I kissed down his chest, inhaling his clean fresh scent and down his tan skin, where I swirled my tongue above his manicured hair.

He was already gritting, even before I wrapped my mouth around him.

I was right. It didn't take long, and he moaned aloud.

"Oh shit, Shug."

I laughed as I sat up and his muscled chest rose and fell heavily. He licked his lips as he panted. I could read what he wanted, but he was still too nervous to push.

"You have my approval to do all kinds of wonderfully dirty things to me," I teased, and his eyes ignited.

My words were a game changer.

I learned a valuable lesson that night. Guardians were freaks of nature. Chris was not an easily exerted man. We made love five different times that didn't include when he took me with his mouth. When he passed out, I could've kept going, but he was spent. Blissfully sated and looking gorgeous in the hotel bed, I cuddled with Chris. Slate would have gone all night and into the morning if he'd gone six months without sex.

It was an unwelcome thought.

At our photo shoot the next day, it elated the photographer that our intimate poses had a newfound comfort. He said we'd probably get a cover shot. We took the flight back that night and Chris drove my Challenger home.

We moved my stuff around to make space for his things and all bets were off. Chris couldn't wait to get his hands on me.

I stared at my computer screen. Chris was at class, and I didn't need to be at work for another hour. I'd checked my emails to see if my family had sent anything. They didn't know who my boyfriend was. I didn't think they'd approve. I knew Tawny wouldn't.

To: Scarlett Tio ScarlettSunset@Sunsettravels.com

First weekend in May, we're having all the families over. Unfortunately. Pearl says we have to. Bring the b.f., we can have a rumble of the exes. We tried to line it up with Tawny's bday so you can celebrate with her. She liked POP, so I'm planning to get us a table. Tawny says she's not having any babies until after she's proven tried and true. And we know your cat must be a beast. Bee-Gold is the biggest skogkatt I've ever seen.

Jett & Tawny

To: Jett Var JettSetter@VallaU.com

Awesome. Booking flights now. We'll stay at the Sumar palace if that's cool. The b.f. and I are going on a vacay for the second week of May, so it's kind of perfect. See you then!
Baby Sis

MY HANDS SHOOK as I shut down my laptop and I wrung them as I readied for work. Pretending like my life in Tidings had been a bad dream was easy when I was in Chicago. Seeing everyone would be hard. I wanted to back out, and it'd only been a minute since I agreed. I didn't know what would happen when I saw Slate again.

Chris and I were great. It'd only been a couple of weeks since we were officially dating, but it was effortless. We'd started going to Sunday dinners with his family at their house and slowly, but surely, he'd been bringing his things over. Our life together was so normal and wonderful. After dinner at his parents, we picked up a six-pack and watched our favorite show, Game of Thrones on HBO. Normal, like two regular people in their twenties.

We made love like normal people. I wasn't being accosted in alleys or closets anymore. No one stabbed me, and Chris told me he loved me every day. What woman wouldn't want that? I never thought I would be the corrupter, but I was. Chris enjoyed every second.

My fetish... sex in bathrooms. There wasn't a bathroom stall in a building I hadn't forced Chris into.

The months sped by and soon it was May. Chris had lost his nervousness towards me, but it had resurfaced when we flew to go see my family. He looked like he was going to his execution on the plane ride to Providence, Rhode Island, and I teased him relentlessly until we joined the mile high club. Then, he relaxed.

"You are an animal," Chris said, kissing my cheek as he sat back down next to me on the plane.

"I'm not hearing you complaining," I said, wryly with a smirk.

"Christ, no. I can't believe I've missed out all these years. I love you, shug," Chris said and flashed me a killer smile.

I smiled at him and tucked my hair behind my ears. One day, he'd ask me why I never said it back, but today was not that day. In a life before Tidings, I would've married Chris and had two kids and a dog in another five years. I realized every day that I still could, but the kids would be adopted as well as the dog.

I got our rental car and told Chris I would drive. I was going to have to knock him out with my *calling* before we reached the portal. There was a strict no *calling* before marriage rule with the Guardians. Everyone would stick to it while we were back, and Chris couldn't see it. We were only staying two nights and that would be stressful enough.

When we arrived at Colt State Park in Bristol, Rhode Island, I *called* touching Chris's leg and he fell right to sleep. I squeezed my eyes shut and breathed. It'd been three months since I was back. I was living with an old boyfriend and Slate was engaged. So much had changed in such a short time.

I drove forward and saw the same patch of grass where Brass had said his goodbyes. I turned the car onto the grass and drove through the trees that made an archway for us.

CHAPTER 3
JETT

You'd think Freya herself was descending from Folkvangr the way everyone was acting since Scarlett was coming back.

Okay, so maybe Jett had been a little obnoxious about preparations as well, but she was *his* sister.

They were finally meeting her mysterious boyfriend. Jett had been the one to tell Slate, who acted as if he hadn't even spoken and walked away. Once Jett had told him she was safe and had found work and a place to live, all the news about Scarlett had fallen on deaf ears.

"She'll be here any minute." Tawny whined as she fidgeted.

They looked ridiculous, Jett thought. Hardly anyone ever left Tidings for an extended amount of time. It was a big deal. Scar had been gone for three blasted months. Even Brass and Quick had shown up for Scarlett. Ama and Shale would be at Tawny's birthday party tomorrow, so they hadn't come. Amber, looking as smug as ever, looped her arm through Slate's as they waited for Scarlett's arrival. Jett didn't even know why they bothered.

Bright light lit the portal room as a car drove through. Jett spotted

Scarlett at the wheel and a brown-haired man asleep in the passenger seat. Cherry squealed and Scarlett flashed a megawatt smile, waving like a lunatic as she put the car in park. Jett would not cry like a baby. All the girls were already tearing up, and she hadn't even gotten out of the car.

Scarlett leaned over to the man and cupped his face. Amber watched Slate carefully, but his face was smooth. Brass was another story as his arms fell to his sides and he went rigid. The man roused groggily, and she pointed out the front window with a beaming smile and the man's eyes went wide. Perhaps they had overdone the welcome wagon.

"Motherfucker," Tawny cursed.

Jett guffawed at Tawny's curse. She never cursed. Then Gypsum cursed and Jett furrowed his brows. What were they seeing that he didn't?

Scarlett gave the man a peck on the lips and unbuckled her seat belt before scrambling out of the car. She looked terrific. Her hair was light blonde though. When had she done that?

Tears streaked her beautiful tan face as Tawny collided with her, and the two girls hugged it out. The little spitfire nearly strangled her in a whirlwind of wide hazel eyes and long dark tresses. The man exited the car and nervously looked about the unfamiliar faces and something nagged at Jett's mind. There's no way the guy could look familiar unless he was famous.

He was tall, almost as tall as Jett himself, and powerfully built. Jett didn't think many men outside of Tidings were built like that outside of professional athletes. Maybe that's how they recognized him.

Scarlett disentangled herself from Tawny and wrapped her arm around the man's waist. and he relaxed visibly and flashed her a killer smile. "Family, Chris. Chris, family."

Jett's mouth dropped open, and he looked at Slate. No longer smooth faced and hands balled into fists. Jett laughed heartily, Slate may have slapped Scar in the face with Amber, but Scar did the same with Chris and *they* looked like they actually liked one another.

Jett strode forward and took Chris's hand in a firm handshake. "Nice to see you again. No wonder she was so mysterious about who her boyfriend was. We already know him." Jett patted him on the shoulder and Scarlett jumped into his arms, nearly knocking him back.

"I've missed my big brother," she said, her voice thick with emotion, and Jett almost lost it.

"Careful, shug. You're going to strangle him. She doesn't know how strong she is, does she?" Chris said with an amiable smile.

Jett gave him a thankful nod.

Scarlett went around, hugging and introducing Chris to everyone. He got hugs from Sparrow and Pearl. Sparrow and Hawk remembered him from Scarlett's prom. Tawny looked very much like she wanted to give him the cold shoulder but didn't.

"Chris. This *is* a surprise," Tawny said, glaring at Scarlett.

"For me too. I never thought she'd give me a second chance. She's wonderful, so of course she would." Chris hooked an arm around Scarlett's waist and she tiptoed to kiss him.

If they were faking, they were doing a convincing job of it. Indigo's long blonde hair fell over her shoulder as she pulled out the cat carrier from the car and pulled out Tree so she could frolic with Bee before hugging Scarlett. Indigo's slender form turned to Chris and hugged him as well.

"I've heard so many great things, Chris. It's so nice to finally meet you. Scarlett sent me the link to your magazine shoot. It's amazing. I was reading the blog yesterday. I'm glad to see you're sleeping again," Indigo said playfully, and Chris laughed and squeezed Scarlett tighter.

"It's all her. I can't take any credit," he said.

"What's all this?" Jett asked, unable to hold back his curiosity.

Chris cocked his head at Scarlett, who blushed. "She is so modest. I had a feeling she didn't tell you guys what she was up to."

He left Scar's side and went back into the car. Scarlett hugged Amethyst and rubbed her belly, then embraced Cherry. Brass hung back with Quick near Slate and they were obviously Scar's last destination.

Chris walked back with a broad smile and a magazine in hand. He held it out for Jett and he almost dropped it.

"Chris! Put that away." Scarlett's face turned bright red, and she tried to nab it.

Jett dodged her easily, and she hung on his elbow.

"Jett, no. It's too cheesy."

The others crowded around and Scarlett faded into the background, trying to hide her embarrassment. Chris pointed down at the cover.

"Your sister is a model. I wish I could take the credit, but if it wasn't for her, I'd probably be miserable in my parent's basement playing video games. Not that there's anything wrong with that, but now I play video games in my hot-as-all-fuck girlfriend's place." He chuckled. "She writes a fitness blog for us. Next week is my birthday, and she arranged for us to do a photo shoot in the Bahamas. Totally paid for by the magazine. She's a rockstar."

Jett stared at the cover. Scarlett and Chris, like a couple of models — flawless skin and she's topless. Chris's corded arm is across her chest, so you can't see anything and her face is turned away, so you can't tell it's really her and his face is buried in her new blonde hair. Shadows defined her abs, and they highlighted his arm and chest. The caption related to them is *Workout: Have Better Sex.* Jett flipped to the center and there was an entire article about the benefits about couples working out together and a mentioning about Scarlett and Chris, their blog and how they train local celebrities together. There were also another dozen photos of them on some beach in all sorts of impossible positions that display their physiques.

Their heads were touching as the group huddled around. Chris chuckled. "She's embarrassed. I thought you guys might like to have a copy, so I brought a few more."

"Chris!" Scarlett chastened and Jett looked up to see Chris blow her a kiss, which she shook her head at. "It's not that big of a deal. You guys work out all the time. I'm doing what I know. Chris just needed an extra push."

"You push me to be a better man, Shug. I love that about you." Chris shut the car door and came back with three more magazines and Scarlett groaned with frustration.

"No one wants to see that. They didn't tell us what the cover would say. We weren't even officially dating when the photographer approached us," Scarlett said in a rushed voice.

Chris laughed. "But we were when we left the shoot."

"Chris!" Scarlett cried again, and she crossed over to him and nudged him playfully.

Quick walked over and Scarlett turned with a big smile.

"Hey there, handsome," she teased. "Chris, this is Quick. I think you two are going to get along very well."

Quick cocked his brow with a smile. "Do you say so?"

She wrapped her arm around Chris's waist, and the two men shook hands. "I do. Quick here is our resident womanizer. I am ever so proud to call him my friend."

Quick and Chris chuckled. "I have never been a womanizer, but I have been known to be an enormous dick. Scar is still training me to be a good boy. I'm a work in progress."

"Good is overrated. Let me see one of those magazines," Quick said and crooked a finger.

Chris handed Quick the magazine and he let out a low whistle. "We do not have things like this here. Frigga's sweet grass, Scarlett, you let someone photograph you naked?"

Chris laughed. "She wasn't. It was only the strategic placement of my arm. I framed this shot for her. She looks hot as hell in it."

Quick lifted his head to Chris and gave him a slow smile. "She does. I like the blonde, by the way. But then, I have always had a thing for blondes."

Indigo's back was to Quick, and she snorted. Quick's head shot to her; it was the most interaction they'd had in weeks. Jett handed the magazine to a stunned Gypsum, who thumbed through the pages and watched Chris and Scarlett interact with the others.

The eighteen-year-old was taller than his father now. His raven hair fell down his back, away from his olive face. They called him chief because he looked like he would be at home in a feather headdress and hide pants. With their enigmatic heritage, there might've been some native in their ancestry.

Quick held the magazine on its side and cocked his head. "This is giving me ideas. Brass, come look and see what our sweet Scarlett has been up to."

Brass's eyes slid to his brother with a cool expression, but Scarlett and Chris were both looking at him, so he had no choice but to walk over to them. Scarlett would not let Brass sulk. She patted Chris's back and slipped away from him. Brass froze when she came at him with that drop dead gorgeous smile and she hooked her arms around his back and squeezed him tight. He held his hands up for a moment, seeming to debate whether he should touch her. Jett saw the moment he gave in and embraced her fully.

"I've missed you," she said unabashedly and peered up at him with her arms still around his waist.

"You were missed," Brass responded, trying to maintain the cool facade, but Jett could see him melting in a puddle around his boots.

She chuckled and hopped up to kiss him on the cheek, surprising him and she slid her left hand through his and led him towards Chris and Quick. "I have someone I want you to meet. Chris, this is Brass."

Chris took his right hand and shook it fervently. "Scar says so many nice things about you. It's great to meet you. She tells me if it weren't for you, she might not have come back to Chicago. That you helped her. I got to say, I am glad you did. She's changed my life."

Brass sighed, and the thaw was complete. "Good to meet you. Scarlett is dear to me."

"I strive to deserve her," Chris answered, and he raised in Brass and Jett's eyes.

"Look at this one." Quick shoved the magazine and half naked pictures of Chris and Scarlett on a beach in Brass's face.

His amber eyes widened comically, and Chris chuckled. "You'd never guess what's under those clothes." He wrapped his arm around her waist and her face was as red as her namesake.

Quick chortled, "Right."

Scarlett's eyes flitted past the group to land on Slate and Amber, who stood just past them. She nudged Chris, and he smiled down at her as she nodded towards the other couple. Chris's smile faltered for a moment, but he recovered admirably in Jett's eyes.

They held a collective breath as Scarlett was the bigger person and strode over to Slate and Amber with their arms around one another's waists. If they'd taken a moment to look around, they would have found every set of eyes fixed on them.

Scarlett acted first. She reached forward, and Amber flinched, but Scarlett pulled her in for a hug.

"Congratulations, Amber. I'm so happy for you both. I hear the wedding is next month? Children will follow soon, I hope?" Scarlett shone her sunniest smile and Amber's eyes were wide.

"Yes, next month. Thank you. We have already started trying," Amber responded.

"That's wonderful. I wish you the best of luck. Amber, Slate, this is

Chris, my boyfriend." She turned to Chris and showered him with her warmth and reassurance.

Chris held out his hand to Slate, and Jett sucked in a deep breath.

"I think we might have gotten started out on the wrong foot. When I saw you with Scarlett, I may have gone temporarily insane. Everything is as it should be now, and I'd like to start over. A clean slate, even though you kicked my ass last time," Chris said and met Slate's silver eyes.

It took a brave man to meet Slate's eyes and hold his gaze. Chris kept rising in Jett's mind. Perhaps he wasn't so bad after all. Slate relented and took Chris's hand and shook it once before releasing it. Jett thought he could hear the loud exhale from everyone involved.

Scarlett turned away from the other couple and led Chris away. Scarlett had addressed everyone except Slate. It must have been eating him up, but it wasn't visible on his stony face.

"Do we have time to catch a quick nap? We're spent," Scarlett said, moving back towards Gypsum, who she wrapped her arm around while Chris got out their luggage.

"Of course, darling. They made your old room up. I know you and Chris are living together, so I assumed you would share a bed. I can have a meal sent up if you are hungry?" Pearl answered.

Chris and Scarlett gave one another a look, and they both blushed. Jett pursed his lips. They were adorable.

"Yes, we can share a bed. Food would be good. Are you hungry, babe?" Scarlett called.

"Famished, Shug," Chris said, slamming shut the trunk and carrying their bags around.

Jett moved to help him, but Scarlett beat him to it. "I've got it. Okay, well, I know where my room is. What time should we be back down?"

Scarlett licked her lips, and Chris gave her a side glance. "Two," Jett said and Scarlett smiled and nodded.

Pearl, Sparrow, and Hawk didn't get the hint and walked with the two from the portal room as they dragged their suitcases behind them. Scarlett stopped at the doorway and looked back after the others passed her.

She bit her lip before she spoke. "I've really missed you all. *A lot.* It's good to be home."

She disappeared behind the wall, and Jett sighed. Clever Scarlett.

Cherry moaned. "Freya's burly boar, that man is a slice of beefcake! I am so jealous right now. Did you see the way they were looking at one another? *Gods*! I thought this was going to be bad, but she seems..."

"Free." Slate finally spoke.

Cherry nodded with enthusiasm. "Free, yeah. It's crazy. I feel like I'm meeting her for the first time."

Jett looked at Brass, who was still staring at where Scarlett had stood. Tawny snorted.

"That wasn't Scarlett. That was an invasion of the body snatchers. Something is wearing her face, pretending to be all happy and carefree. Baloney," she said, crossing her arms.

"She's made her own kind of happiness. What did you expect? For her to shrivel and give up? This is who she could have been if she had never met us. We ruined her life. They were better off in Chicago. I hope she never moves back. I hope she marries that man and they buy a cheap split-level house and fill it full of adopted children spending their days making love and growing old without politics and *calling* and stupid arranged marriages." Indigo snapped and stormed off.

"What did you do?" Tawny accused Quick, and he held up his hands.

"She broke it off with *me*. I do not know what triggered her. She has been odd as of late."

Gypsum was kneeling beside the green-eyed skogkatt and chuckled. Jett wished he'd stopped doing that. He looked insane.

"Tree here says Scarlett and Chris have a happy, healthy relation-ship. They don't fight, they don't worry about money, they work together, they have the same hobbies and she helps him with his classes after she finishes her blog. It's all rather boring, really. Tree says Scarlett cries a lot, but Chris knows how to handle her." Gypsum smiled and his dimples popped into his olive cheeks.

Brass closed his eyes. "He's in love with her." He shook his head with a dry smile.

"Does she love him?" Amber asked, cocking out her hip.

Brass's eyes slid to hers and up to Slate's, then down again. "She wants to. She wants to fall in love with him more than anything."

"That'd be a *no* then," Jett said, irritated.

"Trail of broken hearts, that one. She means well, but she shoves her pretty pink nails into a man's chest and caresses his heart until she's done, then she rips it out and stomps it into oblivion. I wish him luck and I am happy she turned me down or else I might have been one of her victims."

"She never would have slept with you, Quick," Tawny said, making a face at him.

Tawny was in a foul mood if she was arguing with Quick. He was her second favorite after Steel. "She's brainwashed or something. I don't get it. She hated Chris."

"There's a thin line between love and hate," Steel said and she glared at him.

"I'm just saying Scar could get any guy she wanted, and she went back to *him*."

"Cause he's hot. Smoking hot. Did you even look at these photos, Tawny? Leaves little to the imagination, though, as to what they're doing right now," Cherry giggled as she cocked her head to look at the pictures.

Quick rolled up a magazine and tucked it under an arm. "For research. I wonder if the photographer told them what to do or if one of them came up with it." Quick rubbed his chin. "I think I will have to speak to Chris."

Amethyst slid her thin hand into Jett's and he looked at one picture in the magazine again. Scarlett doing a handstand in her bikini with Chris laying on the shore beneath her and their lips pressed together.

Jett growled and threw it on the floor. It landed open to the one picture everyone kept cocking their head to at Slate and Amber's feet. Chris laid on his back with his feet on Scarlett's backside, she's backwards bent with her toes pointed and her head by his, her hand braced to either side of his face and you could see a hint of someone's tongue between their mouths.

Quick bent down and picked it up. Jett scowled at him and Quick shrugged.

"What if one gets damaged?"

Slate growled and *called,* incinerating the two magazines in Quick's hands before he stalked off.

CHAPTER

FOUR

Chris's face was flushed as he fell back against my royal blue stain blankets. "Christ, we should come back more often."

An archway hid from the rest of the room the enormous four-post canopy bed. Royal blue and gold upholstered love seat and matching chaise lounge were in the seating area on the other side. There was an octagonal table and the end table around the seats resting atop a large blue and beige fringed rug.

I swung my leg over him and walked into my bathroom to dispose of our condom. I hated those things, but it was what you did when you weren't a Guardian. Chris seemed to think it was a good idea.

The bathroom was just as elaborate as the bedrooms. A huge bathtub sat in the middle of the room, all done in pearl and iridescent tiles. The bathtub was two split sides so one person could sit facing the other in two completely separate baths. My favorite part of the palace was the shower. Water sprayed from every direction. There was even a waterfall of sorts at the entrance that fell across the low wall so no one

46

could see you if you were showering past it. The opposite side was a wall-to-wall mirror with double sinks trimmed is swirling champagne and silver mosaic.

I came back out of the bathroom and set my alarm on my cell phone before climbing into bed next to Chris. He'd been in awe of the Sumar palace. its windowless windows that held a view of the desert landscape and town's heart below from the Moroccan style palace that stood atop the cliff-side. I'd asked him to keep an open mind, and I'd answer as many questions as I could. He seemed content to just enjoy the new surroundings.

"Are you okay?" Chris asked when I rested my head on his chest.

How could I tell Chris rousen caused a sexual addiction to Slate? His own personal khoraz and being near him made me want to tear my clothes off and offer myself up to him on a silver platter?

"Yeah. It's hard being back and seeing him, but I am happy he's happy. That was really big of you. Makes me proud." I pressed a kiss to his prefect pink nipple.

"Tawny still hates me."

"She'll come around. You're doing great, babe. Really. You won over my brother and Indigo. Those two matter to me. All the adults love you too. You're a big hit, but then, I knew you would be. Steel will go along with Tawny, but I bet my brother's wives love you. I know Cherry did. She kept staring at your pants." I teased.

"It's the ridge. All the ladies love it," Chris joked, and I laughed full and throaty and fiddlestick. Did it feel good.

Seeing Slate and Amber live and in person had done a real number on me. It was like I left my body and watched someone else interact with them. Even in that state, I couldn't bring myself to touch Slate. He had always been too much for me and tightly reined emotions. He was still wearing Alder's ring, and he had the jade love rune carving I'd given him in his hair.

I saw the bond tattoo Indigo had told me about. I knew I couldn't be upset, especially because Brass and I had gotten similar bonded tattoos but seeing them with their matching bonds had hurt. No, it had all hurt. I was in an enormous ball of pain and the only thing I'd wanted to do was lose myself in a tangle of Chris's limbs. He read my body language well, and he knew what I wanted with just a look.

The nights when I couldn't stop my thoughts from running away from me, or if I had the dream with Slate dead in it, Chris was always there and he'd make love to me if I needed him to. I usually did. Other nights, he'd let me vent about nothing. He knew I was emotionally crippled and I couldn't love anyone, including myself. Every day was a battle. I had to force myself to live my life. When I did, though, it was wonderful. I had good days, and I had bad days. I lost both my parents in a year and moved across the country, so I allowed some slack.

"Do you want me to dress like them for this baby shower thing? It's kind of strange men are going."

"I want you to be yourself. If you want to wear something traditional, I can get some clothes for you. If not, then you don't have to," I said, shutting my eyes and inhaling his clean, fresh scent mingled with the scent our bodies made together.

"When in Rome, right?"

I smiled as I dozed off. Chris had come a long way.

It was a recipe for disaster. They had decorated the rarely used drawing room in pale pink blooms that hung in loping garlands. White, gold, and walnut decorated the drawing room, sheer panels of white draped in front of each mosaic column that divided the platform seated section around the circular room. They set food out around the small fountain in the center. It was softly lit by long multilayered metal lanterns that hung in a ring at the center of the room and on each column decorated in intricate filigree.

The mosaic styled palace had seated alcoves that comfortably fit six at a time. I hadn't been in the room since my mother's funeral and I clung to Chris's side. He looked dapper with a white sleeveless shirt and white waistcoat; he tucked dark brown pants into brown boots. The only thing that diminished his Tidings makeover was that he kept grabbing himself to adjust in the snugger styled pants.

I had chosen an ivory dress of flowing chiffon with off the shoulder sleeves and a tightly fitted bodice. Chris kept glancing down at my cleavage and waggling his brows, making me laugh.

I was going to need his carefree attitude to help me through the day. They invited all the Straumrs, Vars, Tios, Vetrs and Cherry's dad. I had already warned Chris about Ash, so he knew that he might have something nasty said to him. I knew Chris would laugh it off. Since we'd been together, I'd cowed his temper, but he could still be defensive, especially with me.

Chris was a brawler; he wasn't a trained fighter. He was big enough to handle more than his own, but Tidings men were dangerous. I didn't want them tainting Chris.

Viper Enox, Cherry's dad, looked lost. His peppered long hair tied away from his equally greying beard; his green eyes took in everything as he shook Jett's hand. The Straumr's brothers, Jackal and Nova, arrived next. River's wife stayed home with their children, he explained, and I greet them all, even Nova. She was equal parts beautiful and evil. Her long dark hair grew to her waist, her almost too large hazel eyes in her narrow face. Fox gave me a hug, which did nothing to improve her mood. Jackal was there, and I relaxed a bit. His witty humor would diffuse some tension.

Ruby Geol had shown up with Orion Vetr and stood near Pearl, murmuring. Her dark, luminous eyes took everything in. My father's mother was rail thin, her short dark hair pulled high from her fair-skinned face. Orion was Tawny's grandfather and had a lot of influence with the Guardians. Moon had arrived with Basil, Dahlia, and Diamond. Sterling had come shortly after and avoided Indigo, who sat next to me in one alcove with Chris.

The heir to the Haust's violet eyes caught on Indigo and slid past. She glanced away, not allowing his disregard to get to her. Sterling was boyishly handsome with stylish chocolate brown hair and was Slate and Brass's cousin.

The whole Tio brood was there with Reed and Fern. Red heads were everywhere. A frequent occurrence when congregating with the Tio side of the family. Quartz and Ash blessed us with their presence five minutes past two. I pointed him out to Chris so he knew to steer clear. Ash strode in tall and muscularly built, not an ounce of fat on him. His dark hair was close cropped, and I resisted the temptation to duck my head from those light green eyes.

His sensual mouth curled at something his petite blonde fiancée said. Quartz was a Natt/Haust, another of Slate's cousins and Sterling's sister. The curvy blonde had a rosebud mouth and green eyes that were almost too big for her heart-shaped face.

Peak Haust was the last one to arrive. His bright green eyes scanned the room until they landed on Sterling and he stood near his son and Diamond. Since I'd found out he was Slate's uncle, I saw the resemblance more and more. The same bronze skin and wavy dark hair, though Peak's, was dusted with silver. Peak didn't have Slate's straight, masculine nose, but one that rounded at the tip.

Brass and Quick sat in the alcove in front of us with Garnet, Amber, and Slate. The Regn brothers all had dark hair and powerful builds over six feet tall. The youngest Regn swaggered like a man who knew he would blow your mind if you ever let him into your bed. Girls flocked to 'Quick' Silver Regn like bees to honey. Brass was a balance between their older brother and Quick. He had a darker complexion than Quick's olive tone, with plump defined lips and soft amber eyes that saw straight through you. It didn't help that he could read minds and images.

We all seemed to hide out. I realized I didn't want to be there with all of those people that I knew were judging Chris, even though he blended in with the rest of them.

"We should go talk to Jackal," Indigo said, rubbing her temple.

She was colder somehow. When she proved tried and true, I would make her come stay with Chris and me for a while so she could experience a different life. Maybe she could meet a nice normal guy and we could be neighbors.

I nodded and sighed. "Are you ready? I'm down to bail if you hate this."

Chris's baby blues were soaking in all the people. I remembered what it felt like the first time I'd seen Guardians. As beautiful as they were, deadly, and they smelled like power and money. Chris flashed me a smile that sent a thrill through me, and I gestured to the main floor.

I felt like someone shone a spotlight on me when we emerged from the alcove. It had been Pearl's duty to make sure the Guardians knew not to *call* in front of Chris. He wasn't the first boyfriend to be brought from the States.

We made a beeline for Jackal; he'd be the easiest to talk to. My uncle was laughing at something Crag said when we caught his eye. He gulped down his drink and placed it down on the tray of a passing server.

"My, my. You know how to pick them, Ms. Scarlett," Jackal said, sliding his blue eyes up and down Chris.

Chris's hand went to his groin, and I nudged him. He laughed nervously, "I'd shake your hand, but as you can see, I'm not used to these tight pants. I'm Chris, Scar's boyfriend."

Jackal laughed and drew even more attention as he hugged me and Indi. My father's brother was as tall as he had been, as tall as Jett. All the Var men were giants. Jackal had floppy blonde hair, the same corn silk as Indigo's. He was normally a jokester; he hadn't been since Alder died.

"I would gladly shake your hand, anyway. I have touched my fair share, trust me."

Indigo giggled, and I guffawed. "Jackal, my uncle," I said, introducing them.

"Oh, Christ. Your uncle? Sorry, man, about the crotch thing." Chris winced, and I laughed.

"Jackal is not the judgmental type," I reassured him.

"Is that my favorite knife fighter? Oh, sorry."

Fox caught himself and took me up in his arms. The youngest Straumr brother's blue eyes rivaled Chris's. He had caramel skin like Ash, with tight dark curls. He was my favorite Battle Trainer at Valla U.

I gave him a rueful look and shook my head. "Fox helped train me. This is Chris, my boyfriend."

"Where do you keep finding these giants? Pleased to meet you. Any friend of Scarlett's is a friend of mine. Has anyone told you about the Stygian trial?" Fox asked and my stomach dropped.

"No, we only got here this morning. I'll get details later — don't want to spoil Amethyst's baby shower." I also didn't want to relive my last night in Tidings.

Fox nodded, and I led Chris through the throng, introducing him to everyone with Indigo. Jett was busy caring for Amethyst with Cherry and keeping Viper from wanting to jump out the window. They brought food out, and the people retreated into the alcoves with their plates.

Steel, Tawny, and Gypsum sat across from us as we ate and I waited for the questions to start. I didn't have to wait long.

"How did you two get back together?" Tawny asked straightaway.

"I got this. She doesn't like this story, but I do. So there I was, having one of the worst days of my life because I'm leaving my college to move back home after I lost my scholarship. I'm still using a cane at this point because of my hip and I reach the terminal at the airport ready to wallow in my misery when I overhear these young guys talking about this sleeping beauty who's crying in her sleep. Well, I look to where they're glancing at and there's Scar. She's got this painting in a seat next to her and she's slumped down in the seat with tears just pouring down her face. I asked the flight attendant for some tissues and hobbled on over to her." Chris sighed as he looked at me. "I didn't want to wake her, but I can't stand it when she cries. So I wake her up and she's pissed. She hates me, I can tell right away, and she is kind of bitchy until she makes up this game."

"It wasn't a game," I said, shaking my head.

"Hush now, this is my story. Anyway, I'm apologizing profusely and she's not taking it. I think she's going to get off the plane and walk out of my life. I asked her what's wrong, and she actually talks to me and tells me she's gotten out of a terrible relationship and had to leave. We take our separate seats and I'm just staring like a creep because I don't have the balls to go talk to her. Then she looked over her shoulder and caught me. So I'm thinking, well now she's never going to talk to a stalker."

Gypsum laughed at his story. I'd heard it so many times already, but it still made me smile. Chris was animated when he retold it using wide gestures like he did when he was passionate about something.

"My heart jumped into my throat when I saw her get up and she sat down next to me. She holds out her hand and says, 'Hi. I'm Scarlett Tio — twenty, single, with no job, and no place to live. I just got out of a relationship and am on my own for the first time in my life. Pleased to meet you.' I think this is my chance. It's fate that brought us together, destiny, whatever. So I say, 'Pleased to meet you Scarlett. I'm Chris Moore, twenty-two, single, no job. I live with my parents and have recently dropped out of college because a girl I screwed over's boyfriend beat me down and I lost my scholarship.'"

"Slate broke your hip?" Gypsum interrupted.

Chris pulled his tongue between his teeth and nodded. "It's done. That day at the theater." He shrugged. "He did me a favor. I think the only reason Scarlett went home with me was because she felt sorry for me." Chris nudged me with his shoulder and I rolled my eyes.

"No, I didn't want to sleep alone." I shook my head.

Chris guffawed and popped a carrot into his mouth. "Little did I know she wouldn't even kiss me for months."

"You guys were just friends?" Tawny asked, confused.

"I wasn't in the right mindset when I left here. Chris helped nurse me back to health, and I returned the favor. We helped fix one another. In the beginning, we were basically dating, but without all the benefits." I tilted my mouth up and Chris planted a kiss on my lips.

Reaching down to place my plate down on the low table, I met silver eyes past Tawny's head. They stared right through me. I'd forgotten they were sitting there, and we'd not monitored our voices. I looked over my shoulder and found Jett and the girls were sharing the alcove behind us with Diamond and Sterling.

Once everyone finished eating, Amethyst opened the plethora of gifts and we *oohed and ahhed* with gusto. She held up a painting and knit her brows at me. It was identical to the one my mother painted, but not the original. I'd done that one.

"Scar painted it. It's just like the one her mom did. Multi-talented, my Shug," Chris said, unabashedly bragging about me.

"Thank you, Scarlett," Amethyst said, and Jett held the painting and sighed.

I slightly turned my head and was caught again by the silver eyes that were so intense I had to look away. I couldn't even meet Slate's *eyes*. What would happen if he touched me? I'd probably disintegrate.

"Many know how talented Scarlett is," Ash said low, but he had taken the seat in the alcove behind us Jett vacated.

The innuendo was clear in his tone and in Quartz's chortle. Chris turned and put his arm on the back of the seat.

"I'm sorry. We haven't met yet. I'm Chris, Scarlett's boyfriend. You are?" I recognized his tone and the cant of his chin. All bad news.

Ash sneered at him. "Ash Straumr."

Chris nodded. "See Ash. Here's my problem. You can't talk about my girl like that. Where I come from, we don't talk to our women like dog shit. I'm going to have to ask you to apologize."

I open mouthed gaped at Chris and, out of the corner of my eyes, I saw Tawny doing the same. Gypsum and Steel were wide eyed, not knowing how to intervene.

Ash's eyes slid to mine coolly and back to Chris. "Careful, myopic. Straumrs do not take threats lightly."

Chris chuckled and shook his head of chestnut hair. "I'm from Chicago. I don't care who the Straumrs are and being careful has never been my strong suit. Apologize to Scar and we can go back to pretending like we all enjoy looking at baby socks."

Chris didn't know what a myopic was, but he knew when he was being insulted and his muscles flexed beneath his white shirt. Ash shifted in his seat and faced me full on.

"Control your boy, khoraz, or —"

Ash never finished his sentence. Chris jabbed him right in the mouth and his head snapped back.

"I thought I was clear about how you should speak to women. Respect. Especially when you address *mine*."

I shot to my feet to stop what could end in the revealing of a magical world to a man who knew absolutely nothing about it. Chris was pressing against my back and I tried to push back while monitoring Ash, whose legs something still slumped over the low table. The present opening had stopped and Dahlia was pitching a fit.

Just once, I'd like to have been a wallflower. Sterling was bending over Ash and he raised his violet eyes.

"It knocked him out, but he is fine." Sterling waved his hands at everyone. "He is fine. Never mind us."

I spun on Chris and his gorgeous face had gone hard, his baby blues like pools of ice when he looked down his nose at me. My skin prickled.

"Sorry about the fight, Amethyst. I'm going to take Chris to cool off," I said without looking at them.

I licked my lips, and he grabbed my wrist and turned around, leaving the drawing room. We didn't get far.

Inside a China closet, Chris cursed his tight pants and hooked a finger in my panties, pushing them aside before driving into me. My hands rested on the shelves with my legs wrapped around his waist.

Why hadn't someone said that to Ash before? Why did we always let him suck us in and bring us down to his level?

Chris's cool calculated words had made pleasure coil up in me like a sweet caress. Then he gave me that hard look. I'd lost all sense and could only think of having him. He'd seen it too; his testosterone levels were sky high, and he needed me.

"Fuck, Shug," Chris groaned. "I don't have a condom."

"Wait for me," I ground out, and he grunted ascension.

I clenched tight around him and threw back my head with a moan. Chris cursed, and I hopped from him and got down on my knees. He fisted his hand in my hair as he shuddered, and I held my mouth around him while his tremors subsided.

The door opened, and I fell down on my backside. Amethyst looked wide eyed and then spun around. I clambered to my feet as she rushed an apology.

"I didn't pick the China pattern for the dessert plates, so I thought I'd sneak a peek before the cake was served. *Oh,* my," Amethyst said and Chris blushed as he smirked.

"That's okay, Amethyst. The only difference between us and animals is that we're housebroken." I tugged Chris past her and we went back into the drawing room.

CHAPTER 5
JETT

Jett, Cherry, Slate, and Amber walked down to the conservatory; it was where they trained. Many plants and trees lined the gravel track. It was divided into several sections: an obstacle course, a weightlifting area, an area that held all different weapons with mats, and a section for archery.

Jett hadn't asked why Slate wanted to train before breakfast instead of after, as they usually did. Jett wondered if it was Amber or Slate who had come up with the idea. After Chris knocked Ash out with a single punch, Jett had decided he liked the guy. He wasn't the only one. It seemed Tawny had overcome her dislike for him. Quick wouldn't shut up about it, and Brass had given the myopic some acknowledgement. Myopic wasn't really a bad term. It all depended on how you said it.

To have the freedom not to care what anyone thought and to sock a Straumr in the face? Priceless.

Scarlett had killed it by pulling him away, as if everyone in the room didn't know what that look she'd been giving him meant. Amethyst had told him what she walked in on in the China closet. They had a bedroom. Scarlett was obviously a bad influence on Chris.

Cherry was pretending to like Amber for his sake when the two girls ground to a halt just inside the conservatory. Jett looked past Cherry's head and saw why. Apparently, they hadn't been the only ones who had thought to avoid one another. Scarlett had her legs locked around Chris's waist as he stood, and she was doing sit-ups. When she was upright, she pecked Chris on the lips and went back down again. They weren't wearing training clothes; they were wearing gym clothes from the States and Scars left little to the imagination.

She was going back down when she spotted them and smiled upside down. "We're early risers. Come on in, we'll knock this off."

"Speak for yourself, Shug." Chris grabbed her around the waist, lifted her up and she unlocked her legs, but not before he'd given her another kiss and set her on her feet.

Scarlett had on a magenta spandex outfit that exposed her sweat slicked stomach and the new blonde hair piled on top of her head. "I was just telling Chris that the combination of Fox, Slate, and Brass's training is to thank for how well work is going. We should pay them some kind of finder's fee, right, babe?"

Chris gave her a slow smile and lifted his eyes to where Slate rigidly stood.

"I would think it'd be hard to talk while doing things like that," Cherry said, putting an extra roll on her hips as she walked over to them.

Jett looked up to the heavens. Cherry thought Scarlett's boy toy was attractive. Okay, they got it. Chris ran a hand through his hair and flashed her a smile similar to Quick's lecherous one. Scarlett had been right about those two getting along.

"My Shug is tough as nails. You'd be surprised at what she could do when she puts her mind to it or maybe you wouldn't. She just needs the proper motivation."

Scarlett looked over her shoulder at him, and Jett imagined she gave him a mischievous smile.

"We don't want to bother you guys," Jett said, coming up beside Cherry.

Chris had on basketball shorts and a man's white tank top. Jett could see now how much the man had changed since he'd last seen him. Scarlett caught Jett looking and beamed with... pride?

Chris chuckled when she turned to him. Slate and Amber had walked up to where they were all standing.

"She calls it the cheese grater," he said, and Scar laughed.

"It is," she teased.

"It can't possibly be that hard," Cherry said and Chris lifted the hem of his shirt.

"You can touch, Shug doesn't mind. I secretly think she likes it." Chris beamed down at her.

Scar shrugged and folded her arms. "We've worked hard on that body. I don't mind other women appreciating it."

Cherry needed no more encouragement. Jett suppressed a groan when she ran her fingers down his abs. Scarlett giggled when Cherry snapped his waist band. Chris blushed and pushed her hands gently away.

"Don't think you want to see all that."

"Amethyst did." Cherry teased, and both Scarlett and Chris blushed.

Scar took Chris's hand and pulled him away. "Let's go for a run." He looked grateful as she dragged him over to the track.

Jett growled at Cherry. "Not fondling my sister's boyfriend would be nice. I don't know what's gotten into you and Amethyst. It's not like you haven't seen a man before."

They moved over to the machines. Amber and Slate were quieter than usual. Cherry rolled her cobalt eyes at Jett.

"They're so playful. Remember when we were like that? Now you're grouchy." Cherry pouted.

Jett walked over to the free weights and lifted as he watched Scar and Chris smiling and laughing as they ran. When they came around the bend Scar flashed Jett her drop dead gorgeous smile. You didn't want to get caught in the updraft of that thing.

"Chris wants to see more of the town. Would you mind taking him? I wanted to go see Lera if that's okay." Scar ran backwards to wait for his answer.

"Of course he will. I'm sure Steel and Gypsum would love to too," Cherry answered for him, and Jett plastered a smile and nodded.

"Thanks, man." Chris beamed.

They ran back along the track, and Amber sniffed. "They certainly seem cozy. He is so..."

"Hot?" Cherry offered.

"Mundane," Amber said coolly.

Cherry's temperature rose and Jett interrupted the tirade that was sure to come. "He's good for Scar. When she's happy, I'm happy. *He* makes her happy." Jett turned around and mumbled. "And if it wasn't for her, Slate never would've looked twice at your conniving ass. You should kiss the ground she walks on."

Not even Cherry heard Jett's mumbled words, but when Jett turned back around, Slate was staring right at him.

SIX

"I'll be back before dinner."

I pulled the clothes I'd set or dropped on the floor before my tryst with Chris on. He laid on his side, watching me pull clothes on.

"No rush. I have a feeling your ex wants to speak with you. He's been quiet."

My stomach flip-flopped and I nodded. "He has. I think it's that adage, if you have nothing nice to say, say nothing at all. I ran out on him with nothing but a note. All in all, he's been rather amiable."

Chris swung his legs over the side of the bed and pulled the golden sheet into his lap. I loved his modesty; he'd been so uncomfortable with the fact that Amethyst had seen him exposed in the closet the day before. We watched her finish opening the gifts from the doorway and slunk off to my room. Ash had walked out on his own two feet and since Sterling had proclaimed everything A-okay, there had been no repercussions.

I'd tried to keep things the same way they were back in Chicago. I didn't want to act less affectionate than I typically was with Chris and I hadn't wanted to rub it in anyone's face. It was a different version of happiness. I was uncomfortable with my family seeing our magazine shoots; they were very intimate photos. It was just as bad on our blog so I'd only sent Indigo the link, that, and because Tawny would've known Chris the instant she saw him.

Slate and Amber had walked in on us doing one of our fun workouts and I'd wanted to go hide under a rock, but for Chris's sake, I acted like it wasn't a big deal. It was. What was worse was that Amber and Slate acted miserably. I had dulled my empath abilities from the moment I left Tidings and had kept it that way. I couldn't turn down the new scent talent. Whenever anyone expressed sexual attraction to me, I could smell their lust. It had been thick in the air with Brass and Slate despite themselves.

"His fiancée looks just like you, but bitchier," Chris said as I buckled on my wrist blades.

He didn't know they were wrist blades, but I couldn't wear my knife belt. Otherwise, I was wearing my usual Shadow Breaker garb.

"I can be bitchy," I said, looking up at him from my angled position.

"Don't I know it? I know you still care about him. You won't even look at him, and I get it. I do, but if he wants to get back together or something, do me a favor and let me go home first. I don't want to be stuck here —"

I pressed my finger to his lips and ran them through his hair. He loosely wrapped his arms around my waist. "Baby, I'm not going anywhere. I promise. We're not getting back together. We have nothing to offer one another except more pain. I'm happy with you in Chicago."

Chris pulled me closer and gave me a thorough kiss. "Just checking. Now go. I think it took a lot of his pride to offer to go with you. I know Amber gave him hell when she got him alone." Chris laughed.

He was so secure with us; I hoped I had instilled that in him. "Have fun with Jett and the boys. Don't let them cajole you into sparring with them. They're ruthless."

"I've given as good as I get," Chris said, feigning a knuckle crack.

I giggled and kissed him once last time before walking from the room.

"Hey Shug," Chris called. I turned around from the open door and raised my brows at him. "Love you," he said with a killer smile.

I blew him a kiss and left.

IT WAS A TERRIBLE IDEA. I liked it better when Slate had been chillingly cordial. Alone, I walked the halls to the portal room where we'd agreed to meet. I was sexing Chris up more than usual, but I felt like if I kept my body sated, there would be less temptation. We wouldn't get back together, but that wasn't the same as being his own personal khoraz. I liked to think my moral compass was fully functioning again.

Slate leaned against the far wall of the portal next to the door. His body bathed in the blue light and I could imagine his scent from there. His silver eyes reflected the blue back at me and I tried not to falter. I had to stay strong, to present a happy front. Any cracks and he'd exploit it to whatever his end was.

Controlling my emotions meant being able to control my scent. I needed to be aware of both. I slid a calm smile onto my face as I approached and hoped I looked friendly, not too eager.

It was a bad idea.

"All set?" I asked, stopping a good ten feet away from him.

Slate pushed off the wall, and butterflies beat in my stomach. Please don't come too close, I thought. He didn't, merely straightened.

"Just us. Come along, Rabbit."

I was back to being a rabbit again. Slate turned and gestured for me to lead the way. I'd have to walk right past him. Instead of arguing, I walked up to the portal door and turned the knob, feeling the electricity from his body brush against my right side, making my insides warm. I hurriedly opened the door and walked into the bright light.

Slate didn't give me a moment to catch my breath when he came out on my heels, forcing me to hurry so he wouldn't graze me. The town heart of Valla was crowded. It was early spring, and all they set the vendors up alongside the shops, shouting their wares. I stopped for a kabob and offered to purchase one for Slate as well. He looked down at me and gave a single slice of his head in negation.

Fashion changed with the seasons in Valla. The townsfolk dressed in the Ostara style of light pastel caftan dresses and thin fabric short sleeve jerkins. I ate my chicken and peppers on the wooden stick as I took in the smell of food and flowers in the air. Spring in Valla was glorious. The promise of new beginnings and growth reinvigorated me.

We reached the dead-end alley, not having said more than a few words to one another. I'd made love for the first time in this alley with Brass. It triggered so many memories for me.

I reached up to *call,* and he caught my wrist. I sucked in an involuntary gasp as my skin thrummed. Slate spun me around so my back was against the entrance. It was midday, and the sun shone down warmly on us. I'd worn a charcoal cotton 'V' that was comfortable in the spring weather and pulled my blonde hair back into a ponytail that swished when I walked. I thought it looked perky enough for the new Scarlett.

"You're hurting me," I whispered, even though he wasn't. I just needed him to stop touching me.

His wavy mane fell forward, making the beads click softly as he lowered his face level with mine. "I am intimately familiar with hurt. Betrayal, rage, and dolor have made good bedfellows."

Darkness stirred in his silver eyes, predatory and wrathful.

"Slate." My lips uttering his name seemed to pain him. "I'm sorry. About everything. I did what I thought was best. Aren't you happy? You were with her before. It's just more of the same. Like coming home."

Slate snarled; his nostrils flared as he brought up my wrist to pin between us. "Happy? I fuck her, like you wanted me to. She asked me to marry her, and I gave her as much as I could to satisfy her. Happiness was not part of the agreement. A wife and children. I give up everything for duty."

I felt myself slump and slid my eyes closed. He wasn't happy; he didn't even look content.

"Find someone else who makes you happy. There are so many women out there in the world. No one said you had to choose Amber."

"You judge *me* for Amber? What about Chris? You reek of him and sex, rubbing him in my face," Slate growled. "How skillfully you moved on to him mere hours after you left me with nothing but a note. You put yourself in danger that night, concocted your plans, and lied about it for an entire month. You laid in our bed, whispered sweet words, and looked me in the eye, all while conspiring behind my back."

I felt my chin wobble, and I pressed my lips together firmly until the need to scream that I still loved him passed. "I didn't trick you! You wouldn't have moved on any other way and I couldn't try to push you away by hurting you. I —" I swallowed hard. "I gave *you* a second chance. Chris was young and stupid; he's paid his dues. I was alone and so sad it made me sick. He was there when I needed a familiar face. I didn't act rashly with him. I waited and made sure I was making the right choice. I don't mean to rub him in your face. This is how we are. He would do anything for me. He loves me and he's not afraid to say it." I blinked away tears that welled in my eyes. "I can tone it down. Chris is understanding; I know he won't mind."

"Because he has you now," Slate breathed. "He says your his. Are you? I see where his heart lies. What of yours?"

Slate took his hand from my wrist and slid it up my jaw. I felt weak and tingly while my stomach roiled.

"Stop," I whispered, but he didn't listen as he slid his hand into my hair at my nape and closed the small distance between us.

I could smell him, not just what my mind told me his scent was. It filled my lungs and caused my brain to play memories before my eyes like a picture show. Cloves, fallen leaves, spicy, and man. My mind floundered as I tried to get a grip.

"Who holds this now?" Slate purred as his hard planed cheek grazed mine. His other hand was at my chest over my pounding heart. I could hardly hear over it.

"Don't," I whispered softly, and I felt his lips brush my ear.

My insides jingled like a ring of a bell in anticipation of the blow horn to come. Slate puckered his lips and kissed my earlobe, tickling the fine hairs at the back of my neck. My lips parted; this wasn't going well for me.

"Who?" Slate repeated, and I felt his hand slid down between my breasts and ever south.

My eyes had slid shut, and I stood pinned against the cool wall and Slate's body. I heard the zipper of my pants fall and he kissed me on my cheek.

"No," I said feebly, not remembering what the question was, only that my red flags were all flying, and I was helpless.

"Your heart, Rabbit. Who holds it?" Slate purred, and he placed an open-mouthed kiss at the corner of my mouth.

I sucked in a sharp breath as I felt his fingers slip into my pants against my skin. My knees buckled and my eyes snapped open. I pushed him as hard as I could.

"What are you doing!" I cried as I fastened my pants with trembling fingers.

"What you want. Do not bother denying it," Slate growled.

My face wanted to crumple, but I had to set him straight. "Of course I'm attracted to you. I know every inch of your body like my own. I can't even look at you without imagining you naked. None of that matters. I've given up my entire life, my family, so you could bring your mother's family honor. Yet you take mine. I have nothing left to give you, Slate *Dagr*! You've taken everything I love away, and I'd do it again just so your family could have a future. It's the only way I can give one to you!"

"Scarlett." Slate started towards me again, face softer somehow, and I held up my hands.

"Please, just stop. I can't fight you. With you, I have no honor, no dignity. I am nothing. My strength lies in staying away from you, so we can both try to find a different happiness. You have my heart, always will. Does that make you feel any better? It sure sugarfoot doesn't make me feel better."

My body shook visibly. He took a step closer again and my back was against the wall. Slate's eyes scanned my tear-streaked face and carefully took my outstretched arms in his hands and pulled them around his waist until our bodies touched. My body shuddered as I drew a wet, ragged breath and he folded his arm around me. My fingers clutched at his shirt, at his back, and my nose burned with a cry that threatened to undo me. Permanently.

Slate's palms slid up and down my back as he made soothing noises deep in his hard chest. I felt like I'd been unfaithful to Chris even though I'd put a stop to it. It'd gone too far. We'd grown used to people trying to sleep with us after training them, or if we were out doing some kind of promotion for the magazine or the gym. Women touching Chris didn't bother me like it would have if he was Slate, and not because I didn't care about Chris, because I did. I loved him in my own way. I trusted that when it came down to it, he would turn them down because we had a good thing. Flirting was part of the business, not unlike the patrons after competitions. You wanted their money; they wanted your attention.

I allowed myself a moment of weakness there in Slate's arms, possibly the most dangerous place for me. "I've missed you, Slate. If I could change things, I would."

Slate held me tighter and rubbed his cheek along the top of my head. My ear pressed against his chest; I could hear his heart *THUMP thump* in a rapid beat.

"*Torch*. I am not a gracious man. Do not say those things to me. I would try to keep you. I have a mind to, anyway. One time is all it would take; you would be mine again," he said in his growly purr of a voice, and a traitorous thrill shot through me to my toes that left them tingling. "Vanilla and warm spice. Your scent has not changed. Are you happy with him?"

I nuzzled his chest, unable to stop myself. "I'm happy in Chicago. If I had to be with anyone there, Chris is it for me."

"He knocked Ash out for you. I thought only I had the luxury of doing that. Everyone has dreamed about doing it, and in front of all the Straumrs no less." I heard the amusement in Slate's voice and lifted my head to look at him.

Huge mistake. Slate lowered his head and brushed my nose with his. My breath caught and Slate hovered his mouth next to mine.

"Will you marry him?" he breathed, and I sighed.

"I'm already married. One husband is painful enough. I have nothing left to sacrifice for another man," I said, looking at his full lips.

"Look who's back. I thought you were engaged now, captain?"

I tried to pull away from Slate, but he loathed to let me go. Mirage smirked smugly at the entrance of the dead end and my blood boiled.

"You did not fiddlestick her again, did you?" I asked so low it was more of a thought than an uttering.

"Not on your life," Slate growled low and let me go with so much reluctance, I thought he would move next to me so we could keep touching.

He slapped his hand to the concrete wall, and it grated open. Mirage radiated smugness as she followed behind us to the rumpus room. Leather, metal, and whatever the cook was making in the room behind the bar mingled in the room. Excitement bubbled up, and I realized I'd missed this place.

"I'll see you later."

Slate grunted. "Where do you think you are going?"

Despite my anxiety, I smiled at him. "I wanted to get briefed on what happened after I left with the Stygians and to say hi, is all."

"I could brief you," Slate offered, and I ran my teeth over my bottom lip.

"We'll go sit with Lera. Come with me," I said, and Slate's eyes dropped to my mouth.

He gave a curt nod, and we crossed the room to the door that led to Lera's office. I mentally reached out for Brass so he and Quick would join us. Slate knocked on the door before me and Chafer opened it before he could finish. Chafer's wide mouth slid apart in a wicked grin, and he cocked an eyebrow at Slate.

"Together again, how sweet," he chided, and I pushed the door open further.

"Chafer. I didn't miss you at all." I teased, and he smiled again, more sincerely at me with his eyes.

Lera stood when we entered, and her red lips curled. It was like the previous months never happened. She gestured to the blood red couch, and I noticed Brass was already sitting there.

"Hey, I was just thinking about you," I joked, and Brass's lips quirked.

"Have I told you that I am a mind reader?"

I laughed and plopped down beside him as I greeted Lera. "Brass said you would come today. You are well, I trust?" His arm snaked around the couch behind me.

My lips quirked. Maybe things had changed.

"I am very good, actually, thank you. I came by for a visit and to find out what happened after I left."

Slate had taken the sofa chair beside me and looked perturbed we weren't closer. It was better that we kept our distance. Nothing good would come of us being close.

"Of course. The Guardians tried the higher ups of the guild and found enough evidence against them to send them to Karkinos. They did not, however, find the lead Knights. They believe there were four men that escaped justice. One of which presided over all the Stygians and the man who killed your parents included. I apologize for that, but it would seem that they have gone to ground. When they resurface, we shall catch them." Cordillera informed me.

Brass, Slate, and Lera took turns telling me the events which unfolded during the trials. Fenrir killed six Guardians before they sedated him and brought to Karkinos. He wasn't the true Fenrir the same way Karkinos wasn't the same from the myths; we were watered them down descendants of their ancient lines. They had high hopes of rehabilitating the animal and were going to try it before euthanizing it.

We left Lera's office and went down to the Crash Course. I joked about how rusty I was since I hadn't fought since the night I left. Brass and Slate had promised to ease me into it.

Shale and Ama were on the Crash Course with Quick and had bombarded me with questions and Ama with hugs. "Quick says your boy toy is *delish*!"

"I most certainly did not," Quick said, making a face at her.

Ama giggled, making her blonde curls bounce. "Not in so many words, but I get the visual and look at you! Of course, he would have to be gorgeous to get you. I cannot wait to meet him tonight." She clapped her hands and bounced off her heels.

"He is her boy toy, not yours. I doubt Scarlett shares. She seems the greedy type." Shale chided, and I smirked, just like old times.

"We have an uncomplicated relationship. Under the right circumstances, I could be amenable to sharing, but you're right. I'm greedy."

The sparring got too intimate, and it had been getting late. Slate had sparred with me many times before, but this time everything he did lingered. Trails of where his hands had seared into my skin and I couldn't get into the swing of things. I would spar with the girls again, but somehow Slate always inserted himself.

My body responded to his touch.

I had a hard time blocking my thoughts from Brass and keeping my scent strictly business when Slate pinned me in the combat circle on my back. Inappropriate thoughts ran rampant and I could see Ama and Shale's knowing glances.

We had a late lunch in the rumpus room and Brass told me how his team was doing. Many of them were hanging around while we ate to say hello and thank me for recruiting them. It made me miss it all the more.

I'd see all the Shadow Breakers later tonight at *POP* so my goodbyes were short. Slate and I walked back to the portal together and the tension slowly built between us. Anger, lust, sadness, frustration... it was a cornucopia of emotions.

The sun was still high since it was early evening and the vendors had switched the meals they pedaled to focus on the dinner crowd. Slate walked so close that he occasionally bumped my shoulder. I tried to ignore it, but his scent was difficult to disregard. It intoxicated me like the rousen.

"Did Amber give you a hard time about coming with me today?" I asked.

"No. She knows better."

I took a deep, fortifying breath. "Why don't you leave her if you're so miserable?"

"She is one of the few who does not care that I cannot say the blood oath words."

The truth hit me like a ton of bricks. I'd thought of that at some point, but I didn't realize what that would mean for him.

"No man is an island, Entire of itself, Every man is a piece of the continent, A part of the main. If a clod be washed away by the sea, Europe is the less. As well as if a promontory were. As well as if a manor of thy friend's Or of thine own were: Any man's death diminishes me, Because I am involved in mankind, And therefore never send to know for whom the bell tolls; It tolls for thee."

Slate sighed at my quote of John Donne.

"So she knows you said it to me then?"

"No. She does not ask questions. An attribute that counts in her favor," Slate said coolly.

"You're moving out after the wedding?" I asked, trying not to let the lump spring up in my throat.

"The Dagr door is complete. Pearl and Sparrow announced I was Lark Haust's son at the baby —"

"What! When?"

"Before the guests left last night. That was why Peak Haust was there. He did not seem shocked to hear of it. You must have been busy. I heard you mistook a closet for a bedroom." Slate's tone was arctic, but it was better than being too friendly — too friendly would get me into trouble.

I cringed at his words. "Did Peak deny it?"

"No. Astonishingly, he said he had his suspicions. I no longer carry the secrets I did. It thrilled Amber. She will be the matriarch of the Dagr house once Sparrow steps down."

We reached the portal gate at the hexagon town center. I had been silent for a time; I didn't enjoy hearing about Amber and nor did I care what she felt about anything. The mood changed right before I crossed through the door. Slate's hand found mine while the white light flared and when we crossed into the Sumar palace, he was still holding it.

"Do not go back."

Slate drew my arm towards his body and lifted my right hand. He kissed my emerald ring and gazed at me through his lashes. This had been my worst nightmare, that he'd beg me to stay. I never could deny him.

"Stay with me, Scarlett. Children be damned, the Dagr line be damned. I need *you* and nothing more."

"It's not that I don't want to. If it was all about me, I would. You have responsibilities. People are depending on you. What kind of person does that make me to let you abandon all that and steal you away?"

Two words that would accurately describe how I was when Slate was tender, foolish, and pliable. I saw the resolve in his eyes, and he led me from the portal room and into the hall.

"Where —"

He had a destination in mind. I was spending too much time in closets. He pulled me through a small utility closet off the hall and didn't give me a chance to object. He kicked the door closed with his heel and effortlessly picked me off my feet.

I opened my mouth to protest, but he slanted his mouth over mine and common sense evaded me. I was putty. My brain went to mashed potatoes, and I melted like ice cream in July. Our tongues slid into one another's mouths; my hands fisted in his mane of waves. I loved his hair.

He moaned against my mouth and I felt a pull deep inside me. His big hands slid over my body unfettered, and I panted against his mouth for air.

"I *need* you, Scarlett."

I wished he hadn't spoken, or that he'd spoken sooner. I drew back and swallowed. He shook his head, seeing my eyes.

"No," he growled.

I pushed at him and he struggled to keep me in his arms. "This isn't *right*."

"What is not right is that I have to watch *my* wife, *my* mate, *my* torch making a life with another man!" he shouted.

I could think of only a handful of times I'd heard him shout. He never needed to. His low, dangerous tone was effective. It was a testament to how helpless he felt.

My whole body shook as I pushed away from him and used my *calling* to open the door. I ran and didn't look back.

CHAPTER 7

JETT

They stepped from the portal room and into the hall to see Scarlett emerge from the closet and sprint down the hall with only her sobs to follow her. She ran as if Hel herself chased her.

The five men had frozen in place. Steel, Gypsum, Hawk, and Chris watched her go. Jett looked at Chris from the corner of his eye and realized he didn't look the least bit surprised. The men started forward again, an uncomfortable silence grew in the air when Slate entered the hall from what Jett knew was a closet. He moved slowly and thickly, as if in a fog.

Slate turned his head, and his eyes zeroed in on Chris. Hawk stepped forward, but Chris raised his hand to keep him back. Jett watched the train wreck unfold. Slate stormed over to Chris so they were eye to eye and Slate snarled.

"Break her heart and I will break something she cannot heal," he growled.

Chris looked back smugly, and Jett thought he must have lost his mind. "I'm not the one who breaks her. That's you. I'm the one who shelters her after you've shattered her. Hope you said all you needed to because she won't let you near her alone. Now excuse me, I've got to go repair the damage you've done. *Again.*"

Slate was speechless. Chris skirted him and strode down the hall before he stopped and chuckled.

"I do not know how to get back to the room from here."

Jett moved past a dumbfounded Slate and walked down to Chris. "I'll show you."

"Much obliged," Chris said with a tight smile.

It wasn't until they got to the stairs that Chris leaned against the wall and took a deep breath. Jett noticed he was shaking. Chris lifted his head and gave him another tight smile.

"I'm more than just a pretty face. I knew he'd try something. How he looks at her? I catch that expression on my face every once in a while. His fucking fiancée is her doppelgänger."

"Why'd you let her go with him, then?" Jett couldn't help but ask.

Chris's smile was extra dry. "No one 'let's' Scarlett do anything. She makes the hard choices, and she does what's right as she sees it. I had to take a gamble because if I didn't, he'd win, and he would've cornered her eventually. This way, he does a little damage, but I'm the good guy. I get to help her through it and she'll be closer to me for it. Besides, she's loyal. Maybe he snuck a kiss or two, but she's coming home with me and he won't be stealing anymore of those kisses or her time."

He pushed off the wall, and they walked up to her old bedroom. "Do you mind if I check in on her?" Jett asked, processing Chris's words.

"She's your sister. Be my guest, but I doubt it'll be pretty," Chris said, opening the bedroom door.

Jett hadn't expected how ugly it'd be. Scarlett formed a ball on her chaise, sobbing. When they opened the door, she wiped her face, shaking, and got to her feet. She curled her hands to her sides and Chris went to her side, dropping his bag on the octagon table.

She fended off his efforts, her whole-body trembling. Jett felt powerless. He thought the scene looked like it had happened much too often. Chris was relentless in his effort to pull her close.

"You won't want to touch me when you find out what I've done!" she shouted.

"Kiss an old flame? Are you coming home with me, Shug? Do you want to leave me?" Chris asked, and Scarlett blinked at him.

Chris pulled her to him then and did as he said he would. Jett could almost see Scarlett heal. "I need *you*. I'm so sorry, Chris."

"*Shh*. He was going to try something, eventually. We rather it be sooner so we could put this behind us. I love you, Shug. Please don't hurt. I don't even blame him. If I were him, I wouldn't want to let you go, either."

Chris cupped her face and kissed away her tears. Jett saw where it was going and started towards the door.

"I'll be going," he mumbled.

Scarlett turned her face.

"Sorry Jett, could you ask someone to send up dinner?"

"Sure thing, baby sis. Chris." Jett inclined his head to Chris and closed the door behind him.

"Is she...?"

Jett turned to Slate, who detached from the shadows. "He played you. I'm a little impressed. I didn't think he had it with him, but he knew exactly what you were going to do."

Slate sighed. "All is fair in love and war. He plays dirty."

Jett snorted, and they started down the hall together. "Look who's talking. You might have stood a chance if you didn't push her so hard. Not that that was what I was rooting for. She'll be fine. He knows how to handle her."

"I bet he does," Slate growled, and Jett put his hand on Slate's shoulder.

"It might be time to throw in the towel."

"Never," Slate said, shrugging off Jett's hand and stalking off.

POP had two levels decorated in ambient pink, blue, and white and all the latest American hits. It was cool in the club despite the warmth outside. Tufted pink couches revolved around round white tables on the wood floor next to the bar with more couches against the far wall opposite the bar. The ceiling over the bar was lit with the blue and pink back lit lights on the white ceiling and floor.

Scarlett, Tawny, Indigo, and Cherry stood at the sleek black bar that had white lights lighting around it and the DJ on a platform at the end, a black screen was between the bar and the DJ that showed the sound waves of the songs she was playing. They appeared to be on a mission to get good and stinking drunk.

The Shadow Breakers had only just arrived and Ama and Shale went to join the girls at the bar after fawning over Chris, who sat on Jett's other side. Amber and Amethyst were the only two girls sitting on the couches next to them. Amber glued herself to Slate's side as usual, keeping her blue eyes on him to make sure he wasn't looking at a certain someone.

Scarlett looked amazing; she'd said Chris had bought it for her. A white lace bodycon dress that displayed those long legs of hers. Chris chatted with Gypsum on his other side about high school days while he drank a beer. He acted as if he hadn't caught Scarlett in a closet with her ex-lover just a few hours earlier. If anyone was acting oddly, it was Slate who seemed well aware he had lost this battle and possibly the war.

Quick had shown up with Garnet. He had been seeing her steadily, though Jett knew she wasn't the only woman in his life. Quick made no promises.

"By the Mother, I'm going to go check on the girls. My wife is determined to make me carry her home," Steel said, getting to his feet.

"Let them play. I've never seen Scarlett drunk. She's always very careful. The drinking age must be younger here, huh? It's good to see her indulge." Chris told him, watching Scarlett throw her head back and hold her stomach as she laughed.

A smile pulled at Steel's lips, and he sat back down. Tawny turned and tossed her mane of dark hair, flashing Steel a smile she reserved only for him. Jett had never seen her smile at anyone else like that. The little spitfire had burned brightest just for Steel. Indigo slid her arm around Scarlett's waist and the two girls took their drinks onto the dance floor, quickly followed by the other girls. Ama started speaking animatedly to Scarlett, and she raised her head to Chris and gave him one of her heart bursting smiles. She blew him a kiss that he pretended to pluck from the air and put into a shirt pocket. Scarlett laughed and danced.

Jett groaned. Indigo, Scarlett, Cherry, and Tawny were already drunk. The scandalous dancing began. Indigo was in a tight little black dress which was very *un*Indigo like, but she looked phenomenal. Quick would kick himself tonight. Brass sat down on Steel's other side and they watched the show the girls were performing. It *was* a performance. Cherry would catch Jett's eye every so often before she did something particularly naughty. They danced with multiple male counterparts, and Steel laughed when Tawny yelled at her third hopeful dance partner. She wasn't interested.

Tawny leaned into Scarlett's ear, and the girls smiled. They came off the dance floor and approached them, glistening with sweat and beaming smiles.

"Shots time." Tawny told them.

"Amethyst, can I steal Jett for a while?" Cherry asked sweetly, and Amethyst gestured for him to go have fun.

"Come on, babe." Scarlett took Chris's hand, and he wrapped his arm around her waist and swung her around as she giggled.

Indigo walked up to Brass and held out her hand. "Don't make me drink alone."

Brass gave her a warm smile. "I would not dream of it."

Quick made a noise that was quickly covered up with a cough as Brass looped his arm through Indi's and they all glided to the bar. Ama and Shale were coming up to the bar with Gypsum. His cheeks dimpled as he joined them. This was how Jett had imagined times would be when his family finally came together.

Scarlett and Indigo were smiling and laughing in between their drinks. Tawny and Cherry kept getting swept away in giggle fits. Jett chuckled with Brass, Chris, Steel, and Gypsum about this thing or the other. It'd been ages since Jett had let loose. Everyone needed tonight. He tried not to feel guilty that Quick and Slate shackled themselves to the other two girls who didn't quite fit in with the others. When Jett turned back to check on them, Amber had poured herself into Slate's lap and was giving a show of her own. If it was Scar's benefit, she misunderstood how Scarlett worked. It might hurt to see them together, but what she wanted most of all was for them to be happy.

Brass and Chris had found some common ground and were joking around beside Indi and Scar. That was an excellent sign. Brass was careful around people because he knew their every intention, every thought. Brass speaking to Chris with a genuine smile comforted Jett.

Ama and Shale dragged Gypsum towards the dance floor. Indi, Scarlett, Cherry, and Tawny slammed another round of shots and dragged the men out to dance. Jett was feeling pretty tipsy, Cherry gave Amethyst a little wave and another fuck-me pop song came on. The dance floor smelled like booze, sweat, and lust.

Indigo had brought Brass out onto the dance floor and she must have been taking classes from Scarlett because her moves had gone to the risqué side. Cherry was drunk and was all over Jett. His eyes drifted to Amethyst, who gave him a small smile and Jett tapped Cherry's hip before nodding to the couches.

Chris met his eyes over the girls' heads and nodded. The two men left the girls on their own devices and walked back to the couches. Jett ordered another round for them, ignoring the way Amber rubbed along Slate's thigh suggestively, and how Quick seemed to set the dancers on fire with his eyes.

They sandwiched Brass, and he looked wasted. The girls were laughing, having a good old time. Brass was single, Indigo was single, Scarlett… not so much.

Chris clinked his bottle to Jett's glass and settled back on the pink couch. *POP*'s dance floor was black lined with tiles that graduated from blue to pink with pink and blue laser lights that shone from the vaulted white ceiling. The dancers changed color with the lights.

"Is that common here?" Chris asked, pointing to where Ama and Shale had been, even worse than Scarlett and Indi with poor Gypsum. Not that he looked to be having a terrible time. "I only ask because you have two wives," Chris said with an impish smile.

Jett flashed him a grin. Chris was quick on the uptake. They hadn't said Cherry and Amethyst were both his wives, but he knew it. They'd tried to be careful, but there had been several slip ups while Chris had visited. Slate mentioning healing, trying to explain the portal door by saying it was just *really* bright in town. That had been a major slip up. Jett hadn't thought twice about going to town through the portal door until Chris came out on the other side wide eyed and frozen in place.

"Yup," Jett answered.

"That does not bother you?" Quick asked, leaning forward to look at Chris.

Chris looked at Scarlett, who slid down Brass's front, her fingers trailing behind her, but it was Indi who Quick was angry with. She had her hands resting lightly on Brass's belt as she swayed flush to his body.

Chris chuckled and leaned forward to answer him. "Scar and her dirty dancing?" He shook his head. "I keep telling her she gives guys the wrong idea, but she thinks I'm being jealous. I don't *get* jealous. She's mine, she comes home with me, and she's devoted to whomever she's with. So no, it doesn't bother me. He might enjoy himself for now, but later, it's my bed she'll be in. She'll make it up to me." He gave Quick an impish grin.

Jett didn't miss Slate's sneer or the fact that Chris wasn't only speaking to Quick.

The girls danced and drank while Jett sat on the couches. Brass hadn't made a return from the dance floor or the bar when the girls dragged him over there. Chris seemed content to chat with Amethyst and Jett while the others had fun. Slate, Amber, Quick, and Garnet eventually got up to dance, but away from the others and not as spirited. Amber had claimed she wasn't drinking when Scarlett had told her to join the other girls. She said she wasn't sure if she had conceived. Scarlett hadn't missed a beat.

"Better not risk it then." She'd said with a sunny smile and stumbled over to Chris and fell into his lap, laughing.

"You're shit-faced," Chris teased.

"How would you know? You've never seen me drunk." She protested.

"Because you're slurring your words and you can't walk in these things." Chris held her long tan leg up and pointed to the five-inch silver heels she wore.

"I can walk. I can do a lot of things right now," she purred and gestured wildly with her arm as she spoke aloud.

"That crazed girl improvising her music. Her poetry, dancing upon the shore, Her soul in division from itself Climbing, falling She knew not where, Hiding amid the cargo of a steamship, Her knee-cap broken, that girl I declare, A beautiful lofty thing, or a thing Heroically lost, heroically found. No matter

what disaster occurred, she stood in desperate music wound, wound, wound, and she made in her triumph. Where the bales and the baskets lay No common intelligible sound But sang, 'O sea-starved, hungry sea."

CHRIS CHUCKLED as she whispered in his ear and they both got up. "Excuse me, gentlemen."

They disappeared into the bathrooms, and Jett shifted uncomfortably. He was drunk. He never got drunk. Brass, Indigo, and Cherry surfaced from the sea of swaying, grinding bodies and plopped down on the couches out of breath. Gods, they were all wasted.

Scarlett and Chris exited the bathrooms, looking disheveled and flushed, when they stumbled back onto the dance floor. Any toning down Scarlett had done for Slate's benefit had gone out the window.

Whatever they did in the bathroom together only roused them both as they ground against each other full on making out. Jett shifted on the couch and Cherry cat called out to them.

They were a good distance away from the music the DJ spun blaring, but Chris still heard her. He broke his kiss with Scarlett and gave her a light pat on her backside to knock it off. She smiled up at him and they said goodbye to the others out there drunkenly gyrating.

Scarlett nearly fell as she climbed onto the platform, and Chris caught her around her chest as she let out a yelp. "When did they put that there?" She giggled. "Indi, are you staying?"

Indigo slumped against Brass's shoulder, nearly passed out. Brass smiled down at her.

"I can help you get her home," Brass offered and stood, lifting Indigo up with him.

"Thanks man, I don't know where I'm going and Shug is looking less and less reliable." Chris teased, and Scarlett gave him a playful swat to his backside.

"Are you serious?" Quick spluttered.

Brass turned with Indigo under his arm and gave his brother a look that said, *don't be ridiculous,* but Brass was drunker than Jett had ever seen him. Indigo could do worse, but Jett didn't think that was Brass's style.

Jett watched them leave the club and sat back to drink water and sober up some before having to drag Tawny and Steel home, who may have been more inebriated than anyone else. Quick's mood soured rapidly, but that only made him drink more and become determined to have a good time forcing Garnet out onto the dance floor for the rest of the night only to break when they got more drinks.

Amber was pouting and whining until Slate snapped at her and she left him to go drink and dance with Quick and Garnet. She started putting on a show Quick was the center of, but Quick was in just the right mood to let her. Slate didn't care in the least. Jett knew the four of them had had an interlude more than once in the past, prior to Scarlett and Slate's brief relationship.

Jett got up and slumped down next to Slate, bringing him a fresh glass. "Drink up. It's going to be a fun night," Jett said, trying to boost his spirits.

Slate glanced out to the dance floor where Amber was running her hands all over Quick's back and Slate grunted. "He can keep her."

"You could always date someone you like better, or at all," Jett offered.

"No. Amber is it." Slate growled. "She does not ask questions. When she wants something, she asks point blank. No games, or if she tries to play a game, I already know the end. Sparrow will help her raise the children after I am gone, and she will not have a hard time finding a second husband. It all works out."

How bleak, Jett thought. Slate sounded like he was looking forward to his death when he used to rue it.

They stayed until the club closed and then went out for breakfast in Valla. Gypsum, Ama, and Shale had disappeared at some point, probably back to headquarters. Steel and Tawny had been so drunk, Jett had to hold up Steel while Cherry led around Tawny, who was shoeless.

When they finally stumbled into the Sumar palace, it was well after dawn. Pearl, Hawk, and Sparrow would be sitting down to breakfast.

Hawk and Sparrow wanted to say their goodbyes before Scarlett and Chris's flight back.

They were coming through the portal door when Brass froze and his face smoothed expressionless. Jett cocked his head and Cherry giggled, catching on a moment faster than he had. It had been *hours* since Brass left the club. Quick had come back with Garnet and them intending to join Slate and Amber in their rooms, but all that was forgotten.

Quick was angry. He usually let things roll off his back, but not this.

"I thought you would not fuck her!" Quick shouted at Brass.

Brass held up his hands. He couldn't hide what he'd been doing. He smelled like sex and the hastily knotted hair at his nape displayed the love bites along his throat.

"I did not sleep with Indigo," Brass tried to whisper.

Quick was an interrogator. He should have been able to glean the truth from that one utterance, but he was livid with the idea that his brother had slept with the girl he liked.

"Then who the fuck else is there!" Quick shouted, getting in Brass's face.

Jett sucked in a breath and got to Slate a second too late. Slate unleashed. The girls screamed when he sucker punched Brass, knocking him on his ass. Steel was sober enough to catch the drift and launched himself at Slate with Jett and Quick, who had finally grasped what had happened.

Brass worked his jaw and got to his feet. He clenched his jaw and sucked in a breath. "Still worth it," he said before leaving.

Slate roared.

CHAPTER

EIGHT

Brass had just left my room, and I climbed into the shower, wondering how the night had gotten so crazy. I was still drunk. I was stumbling into every wall like the world had conspired against me and shifted positions every time I took a step.

Hot water poured over me as I processed what happened.

Indigo was dead to the world when we'd placed her in bed. Brass and Chris went into my adjoining room as I removed her shoes. When I got back, they had two carafes of wine waiting and three glasses in my sitting room.

By the Mother, I didn't know if I could drink anymore.

Chris beckoned me into his lap and I happily obliged as Brass handed me a glass of wine. Both men had removed their boots. Brass's unbuttoned modern black shirt revealed his dark honey chest dusted with silky dark hair. Chris's vest was open and his white shirt unbuttoned as they both joked and laughed.

Chris knew all about Brass. How he was my first lover and how it

82

had gone on once more, but we remained the best of friends afterwards. Chris had been eager to meet him, and glad he hadn't ruined my first experience.

Chris took my chin in his hands and slanted his mouth over mine. I knew from the start it would not be a chaste kiss, but was too drunk to care. We heard Brass shuffling as he collected his boots to leave and Chris had gotten up helping me up to stand in front of him.

"Stay. Hang out for a while," Chris encouraged.

My whole body felt tingly. Brass had strong features, but not hard like Slate's. He lifted those soft amber eyes to us and Chris slid his hands down my thighs to the hem of my clingy white dress. My heart thundered as I faced Brass and Chris lifted the dress over my head so all I wore was my strapless bra and white lace thong.

Chris kissed along my neck and gave my hips a little nudge. "Brass looks lonely over there, Shug. I think he deserves a goodnight kiss for all his help." He coaxed.

My eyes locked on Brass. Permission to kiss him.

The boots fell from Brass's hands as I walked around the coffee table to where he stood. Brass's chest rose and fell heavily until I stood before him, my eyelids sliding low. He was drunk. I'd never seen him so drunk.

Brass's arms flashed out, yanking me so I raised up on my tiptoes and kissed me deeply. He still tasted like cinnamon. I felt my bra release and heard Chris's chuckle. I gently pushed on Brass's shoulders. His lips were swollen and his dreamy amber eyes were glassy when they hitched on my chest.

Chris's hands slid over my hips as I turned my mouth to his. Our tongues met, and I felt the lace slide down my legs as he helped me step out of them.

"Want to have some fun tonight, babe?" he asked.

"Uh, huh," I moaned and felt him smile against my ear.

Chris had taken off his clothes while I had been kissing Brass. He kissed along my throat as I unbuttoned Brass's shirt with trembling fingers. It was adrenaline. I knew it was now. I placed my palms on Brass's chest before I pushed his shirt off his shoulders and glanced up at his eyes.

I *felt* desire and lust with my empath abilities and took it as the go ahead.

I didn't even think twice about it. While Chris kissed behind me, I used my *calling* to expedite the removal of Brass's pants. His sculpted, dark honey body was just as I remembered it. Three months hadn't changed him at all. Chris's hands cupped my chest as Brass's defined lips molded over mine.

"I have to taste you," he whispered against them and I nodded absently as I turned around and started kissing down Chris's chest.

Before I knew it, we were in a tangle of limbs on my bed and it scattered my wits across the room from the exquisite pleasure overwhelming me; my body felt torn asunder from the orgasms that ripped through me. Chris had initiated it, but I was the one who interacted with both men. He and Brass never touched. I felt worshipped. Then Chris had fallen asleep, or rather passed out, after an intense session.

I panted, rolling off of Chris and onto Brass, where he'd fallen back.

"Should I go?" Brass had asked breathlessly.

I wasn't done yet. Chris wasn't inadequate. He usually fell asleep before I did, but Brass was here and Chris gave his approval. Then it had to be okay, right?

"The floor. I don't want to disturb him." I'd said throatily and Brass sat up, pulling me with him effortlessly, lifting me from the bed as he got to his feet.

I covered his mouth with mine, winding my arms around his neck as he carried me into the sitting room with my legs wrapped around his waist.

Then it had been just me and Brass. He was a mind reader. We wasted none of his touches. They were all designed to the greater scheme of extracting every ounce of pleasure that could be given. I didn't know how long Brass and I were together in the sitting room alone, but we hadn't stopped until I begged because I thought my muscles would turn inside out if I climaxed again.

"That differed from our first nights," he said, holding me so our stomachs touched, kissing me in between words.

I blushed.

His hands ran down my spine and squeezed my backside. "By the Mother, how I missed you." He kissed me again.

"I missed you, too," I whispered and blushed at how much I meant those words when I shouldn't. "I should go to bed."

"I believe that is my cue to leave." Brass pushed himself up on an elbow as he trailed his fingers down my leg.

"You could stay on the couch, Brass. You don't have to leave," I said, feeling guilty for making him feel like our use of him was at an end.

"I had better go. Chris felt one-way last night, but waking up to his decision may be another matter," Brass said, and I watched his dark honey muscles move as he collected his clothes.

I *called* my champagne robe from the closet and tied it around myself as I moved onto the couch, watching him dress. Every movement he made reminded me of some hedonistic act from last night.

"Did he really want to?" I asked, feeling anxious.

Brass sucked in a breath and pulled his shirt over his head. "That is what I read in his mind. Otherwise, I would not have stayed."

I licked my lips and laced my fingers in my lap. I tasted like cinnamon and salt. That was only slightly reassuring because that meant he had read that I wanted it, too. What did that say about me?

Brass sat down next to me and tied his hair back; I saw the marks I'd left on his neck and blushed. "Someone is going to have to heal you."

He ran his hand over his neck and smiled mischievously. "I will wait until my hangover kicks in." He held up his hand, and I nodded as he did what healing he could to me before the alcohol was out of my system. "Scarlett, when I leave this room, things go back to how they were. That is how these things work," Brass told me and shifted on the chaise next to him.

"Have a lot of experience with these, do you?" I was going for playful, but my voice had an edge to it.

Brass smiled and leaned forward and fitted his mouth to mine. I kissed him back, bringing my hands up to twine in his hair. Why was it so hard to let him go?

"I have done this once before, with two women. Neither of which I was dating, but I doubt Chris would like us seeing one another this way once I leave. I admit, it surprised me, but I would be lying if I said I did not enjoy it." He kissed my lips again and my insides heated when he got to his feet. I followed him as he dressed.

"Are you sure? I... I've done nothing like this. Brass, there's just been you, Slate, and Chris..." I said, feeling my face heat.

I never counted the Merfolk. While I kept the lessons and experience from them, they were a nightmare I escaped.

"I do not regret it, perhaps only that I had to share you," Brass whispered. "Besides, you let me taste you this time." He smirked. "And I finally understand why your mouth deserves worship."

My insides coiled, and I walked over to him now that he was dressed and tilted my chin to kiss him again. "I don't know how I feel about this. Guilty, mostly, if Slate finds out..."

"I will do my best to keep it from him. I know you are in love with him and you care about him, but he is not yours to caretake anymore." Brass said in his smooth, deep voice.

"He will always be mine to caretake, Brass. If not me, then who? I wouldn't trust him completely to Amber. Who do you think had Indigo invite Amber out the night they got together? I didn't like it, but she told me once that she would take whatever scraps he threw her. Indi did it for me, knowing Quick would likely end up with Garnet. We have made sacrifices so Slate could move on. Things he can never know about. Part of me wants Slate to find out about tonight because he would never forgive me for... what we did."

He kissed me again. He couldn't seem to stop himself. I couldn't stop either, as I curled my hands tighter in his hair.

"Chris knew what he was doing when he asked me to stay," he whispered. "He is hoping Slate finds out. Chris would take whatever scraps you feed him, but he is smart about it. He knows even though he shared with you last night, in the long run, it means he gets you to himself. I am jealous," Brass said ruefully and I could hear the smile in his voice.

"Do you really think so?" I asked.

"I do. I have got to go before Silver thinks I slept with your sister. That would be bad. He carries a bright torch for her." Brass took my hand as I followed him to the door.

He turned around and looked me over.

"This will make me look forward to your next visit even more. I will have to get Chris drunk again," Brass teased, and I felt a little of my tension ease.

"We'll see."

Brass smiled and reached for me. I came to him willingly as he held me close and gave me a thorough kiss that left me feeling lightheaded. "I grudgingly like Chris. It makes losing you to him somewhat tolerable. Goodnight, Scarlett. I would like to say goodbye later if that is all right?"

I nodded. "I didn't think you lost anything last night."

Brass chuckled and looked at me with a knowing gleam. "If we lost anyone last night, it was me. You have ruined me for other women."

"She has laughed as softly as if she sighed, She has counted six, and over, Of a purse well filled, and a heart well tried - Oh, each a worthy lover! They "give her time"" for her soul must slip Where the world has set the grooving; She will lie to none with her fair red lip: But love seeks truer loving."

BRASS GAVE ME A DRY SMILE. "Get out of here," I said, blushing, and Brass started down the hall.

I finished giving myself a good scrubbing so the only scent on my skin was soap and crawled in bed next to Chris. He was still naked on his back where we'd left him. When he felt me slide over him, he smiled with his eyes closed and wrapped his arms around me, letting me be the little spoon.

"How you feeling, Shug?" he asked huskily as he kissed the back of my neck.

"Okay. Exhausted. You?" I asked in a squeak.

"Fucking fantastic. Last night was wild. Cross that one off the bucket list. How much longer did he stay?"

My stomach flip-flopped. "He left before my shower."

"Did you have fun, Shug? Brass is a pretty cool. I figured for something like that you gotta have someone you trust who respects boundaries."

"Yeah, good choice," I mumbled, cozying up to Chris.

I *called*, putting Chris back to sleep and hoped my guilt would ebb so I could sleep myself. It would be a long while before that happened.

As Chris showered, I packed up our luggage. Chris's hangover was gone before he woke with a bit of healing. I'd only gotten about three hours of sleep when I got ready. I could sleep back in Chicago. My empath abilities cranked to get a read on Chris, and while he was a little wary and eager to get home, he wasn't upset at all. I thought what Brass said had a ring of truth to it. People were always underestimating Chris because he was a good-looking jock, but he could be clever when the time warranted it.

He could have enticed Brass to stay so Slate would hear about it, in which case I should be ashamed that they could easily manipulate me. We brought our luggage down to the portal room where a car was already waiting for us and packed it up and walked to the dining hall. Everyone was already there since we were late.

I turned down my empath abilities, but had caught the blind rage that Slate was in. He must have only come to lunch to make me aware that he knew. Brass was there and so was Quick. Indigo and Tawny looked miserable. One thing healing didn't fix was exhaustion. I hoped I looked better than them.

Brass was sitting in my old seat next to Indi and Quick sat next to Amber and Garnet across the table. I looked at Chris, who nodded and sat down next to Brass. Slate's whole body went as stiff as a statue.

... He knows?...

Brass gave a slight nod, and I felt bile splash in the back of my throat. Chris sat down and took my other hand. My right hand and kissed my emerald ring. Brass inhaled sharply. Never a good sign. I asked Indigo how she felt when Slate stood up and slammed down his palm on the table. I didn't need to look to know what would be there.

I slid my hand from Chris's and removed my emerald ring. I tossed it into the air and Slate's hand snapped out and caught it. I stood and palmed Alder's ring and sat back down. My stone pendant slid when I pulled it to slide the ring on. The silence was deafening.

"I cannot believe how much I drank last night." Tawny gave me a sorrowful look.

I couldn't wait to leave.

"You only turn twenty-one once," Gypsum chirped in.

"Gods, I don't think you're the only one who over indulged. Jett carried me home." Steel joked.

"How was *your* night, Scarlett?" Slate growled.

I put on my coolest expression. "Wonderful, thank you for asking."

Slate's face darkened, and I thought he was going to lunge across the table at me. It wouldn't be the first time. Amber opened Slate's palm, distracting him, and slid the ring onto her finger and I balked. I wasn't the only one.

Sparrow had a knee jerk reaction to lift her hand as if to stop her. "Lovely." Amber purred and Slate went rigid.

I filled my plate with squash stuffed with rice, chopped mint, lemon juice, pepper, minced lamb and bulgur rice, tomatoes, scallions, parsley, olive oil, red pepper paste. My stomach rumbled despite the churn of emotions. I was intent on ignoring the hurt that I felt after what I had done last night. A silly ring was hardly a logical reason to be hurt. I knew I wouldn't be giving Alder's ring to Chris, though; it signified something. Her wearing it took away from what we *were*. Slate wouldn't take the ring from Amber; he'd let her have it just to spite me.

Chris was in good spirits as he chatted with my family. He had won them all over, all except Slate, not that there was any surprise there. Chris even pulled Brass aside, and they shared a private conversation that was watched intently by us all, but the two men were smiling at the end and when they glanced my way, I blushed tomato red and ducked my head. When I lifted it, Slate was glaring at me. He might still attack me.

Jett looped his arm through mine as Chris fell back to chat with Steel and Gypsum as they walked us to the portal room. "So."

"So."

"Brass, you, and Chris."

"I don't think you of all people can judge."

"Nope, but then, I'm not married to one of their best friends."

I sighed. "I *know*. Slate would never give up if he thought there was the slightest chance. Now he can't possibly hope to get back together."

"How true. Out of curiosity. Was it Chris who asked Brass to join?"

"Jett, you are the most inappropriate brother ever," I hissed.

"Humor me."

"Yes, and that's all I'll say about it. Why is Slate even bothering to walk us out? Does he want to glower at us as we drive off?"

"I thought so. Who knows why Slate does the things he does? Probably to attack Brass again. You know we caught him leaving, that's how we found out," Jett said and I cringed.

Brass would've been smelling of sex and me with rumpled clothes. He might as well have been wearing a sign that read, **I Banged Your Wife**. I cringed again. It was a detail I loved to avoid. I may have been with Chris, but I would always be Slate's wife and I'd just slept with his friend. A lot. Like, all night and then some. A special place in hel awaited me.

We said our goodbyes, and the waterworks began. I couldn't help myself as I hugged Pearl and Sparrow. They held me so tightly, as if by strength alone, they could keep me there. Tawny was bawling. It was our first-time saying goodbye, and I remembered why I had chosen not to tell her I was leaving the first time. I was a coward.

Amethyst cried, and I rubbed her baby bump and bent down to speak to my niece or nephew. "Be nice to mommy. Auntie Scar will come back the second she goes into labor to meet you." I stood and wiped my tears. "You'll email me. The second you go into labor. I don't care what time it is. Chris and I will hop on a plane and be back within hours. I swear it."

Amethyst smiled through her tears. "We will. You may be back in a few weeks then; I am ready to pop."

"Then in a few weeks it is, right?" I turned to Chris, where he spoke with Jett.

Chris flashed me a smile that made my heart leap. "Whatever you wish, Shug."

I made my way through the others, saying my goodbyes as Indigo put Tree in her carrier and into the car. Chris nodded as I approached Brass and he winked at me, letting me know it was okay. I didn't know what the rules were at that point. It was beyond anything I was comfortable with.

Brass wrapped his arms around me and lifted me onto my tiptoes. "I cannot tell if this time is harder or easier."

"It still sucks," I said, sounding strangled.

He chuckled, making me smile, and I kissed his cheek before he set me down. He wiped at my tears with his thumb and I ducked my head. People were watching.

"I will miss you," Brass whispered as I took a step back.

"Me too," I whispered harshly and turned to Quick.

Quick seemed conflicted, but I hugged him anyway before moving to Amber. She didn't move away from this time; I hugged her for all I was worth and hoped she understood what lengths I'd gone through that attributed to her happiness.

"Next time we see you. We will probably be expecting," Amber said, hugging close to Slate and rubbing her stomach.

Tears burst forth and I covered my mouth with a hand, appalled by my outburst. "Sorry. I'm just so happy for you both. What a blessing."

Brass held out his hand as I walked past and I shrugged past him to Chris with my hand still covering my mouth.

"I'm ready," I choked out, and he swept me around to the car.

Chris gave them a lopsided smile and held the door open on the driver's side for me. I climbed in shaking and snapped my seatbelt on and turned around to scratch Tree through the carrier. She'd been off with Bee the entire visit. I didn't think she missed me.

Chris walked back to Hawk and shook his hand and placed it on his elbow. I couldn't hear what they said from inside the car, but Brass, Jett, and Slate all turned to me in unison. I knit my brow and Chris walked to the car, giving them all one last wave. Neither of us had said goodbye to Slate. I didn't know what had happened between Chris and Slate, but something had changed again.

I gave a little wave, pasting a smile on my face as I turned to reverse out. Chris closed his eyes when I *called*, making him fall asleep. I turned back to my family one last time and waved again. Indigo ran forward with tears falling. She hadn't cried yet, and I felt my eyes burn. I put the car back in park and jumped out of the car, nearly strangling myself on the seatbelt as I met her hug.

"I miss you so much, Scarlett," Indigo cried.

"Maybe when you're tried and true, you can come live with me and

Chris for a while or until you get sick of us." I was a sniveling mess, and we held each other, not caring who saw.

"Whose woods these are I think I know.. His house is in the village, though; He will not see me stopping here. To watch his woods fill up with snow. My little horse must think it queer. To stop without a farmhouse near. Between the woods and frozen lake. The darkest evening of the year. He gives his harness bells a shake. To ask if there is some mistake. The only other sound's the sweep. Of easy wind and downy flake. The woods are lovely, dark, and deep, But I have promises to keep, and miles to go before I sleep, and miles to go before I sleep."

SUGARFOOT, I missed Indigo — all of them. I needed them to understand I wasn't choosing to be away from them. Chicago made me happy, but I wasn't completely myself outside of Tidings. I couldn't call, I couldn't fight. I enjoyed the *shing* of metal and the smell of leather. My heart felt like it was being squeezed. I reached into my hair and unbraided the turquoise tree of life carving Solder had given me. I braided Indigo's hair with trembling fingers and threaded through the carving.

"Now you have a piece of me with you at all times," I said.

She ran her fingers over it and gave me a teary smile. "Take care of Tree. You can think of the crazy cat lady whenever you pet her."

I laughed with a hysterical edge and hugged her once more and raised my teary eyes. Silver gleaming eyes met mine, and I looked away. I turned without raising my head again and reversed the car without looking forward or putting on my seatbelt.

I had to get out of there.

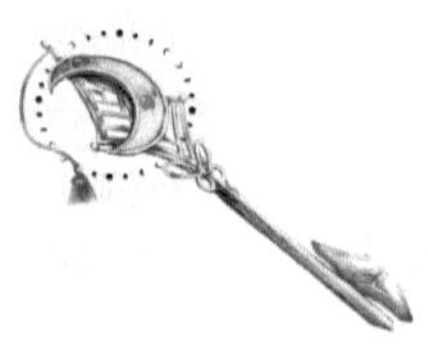

Chris and I went on our trip to the Bahamas and we got on the cover of a different fitness magazine. They were doing an exposé on us and the blog. Northwestern recruited Chris, and life had gone back to normal. I'd sent the links to both the blog and the magazine to Jett and Indigo.

It was like our trip to Thrimilci had never happened. Except. I'd slept with Brass again. My father's ring hanging around my neck was a constant reminder of the irreparable damage that had done. So was my bare finger. My thoughts were traitorous when I was alone. I'd tasted Brass, felt him inside me, and I should have known better. I wasn't the girl who could have casual sex. Whatever I had thought before about how I felt about Brass was reaffirmed. I'd left Brass that morning with a piece of me.

CHAPTER 9
JETT

When Scarlett and Indigo had cried in one another's arms, Jett had felt a bit of himself die. The backlash at Slate and Sparrow was swift. They needed someone to blame. Plain and simple. They had only known their own pain at Scarlett's departure when she first left, so covertly. Now she bared it for everyone.

The low wail she'd choked off when Amber had rubbed in her face that she could carry Slate's child had made Jett want to puke. Humans shouldn't be capable of making that noise. She'd recovered with dignity, Jett had thought, and masked it as happiness. He'd seen her eyes, though; how crestfallen she was. It had been all her plans and she could barely live with her decisions. That bastard had taken away his mother's ring and let that dingbat brandish it around in front of Scarlett. He'd given back their father's ring. Jett thought he would kill him. For real, this time. Scarlett had put on a brave face again and plowed through it.

As if Slate hadn't slept with everything and everyone, as if he had some right to cast judgement on Scar for one man. Granted, it was Brass not just *any* man, but didn't that make it better than some casual fling?

Chris had orchestrated the entire event, and they had been like puppets. Jett would have done the same thing if he had been in Chris's position. Chris set up the dominoes and had Slate completely alienate himself from Scarlett in forty-eight hours, all on his own.

Brass and Slate weren't on speaking terms. It had somehow flipped, so it wasn't Slate who wasn't speaking to Brass, but Brass who was angry with Slate. Jett knew it had to do with that brutal afternoon. Scarlett had her heart broken in front of everyone. All the things she'd given up for him. Slate would forgive her; Jett was certain of it. Slate had needed to let her know how angry he was, so he had tried to humiliate her and punish her, but what he didn't realize was that Scarlett was holding on by a thread. No need to push Humpty Dumpty off the wall. He was already broken.

"Indigo!" Quick moved to comfort her, unable to stand how alone and miserable she was.

She swiped at tears down her beautiful face and turned hard blue eyes on Quick. Her look would've frozen other men in their tracks, but Quick didn't falter as he reached her.

"Get over yourself, Regn." She spat without the vehemence of the words implied.

She shrugged free of him with a deep sorrow that she could no longer hide. She was slipping from them. Quick's jaw clenched at her rejection, but he let her go with a heavy sigh.

Brass stepped forward and set his hand on his shoulder. Only a few of them were close enough to hear.

"She does not trust you. Earn it and earn her."

CHAPTER
TEN

To: Scarlett Tio ScarlettSunset@Sunsettravels.com

Get your ass here now! Baby on the way!
Love You Lots,
Tawny

I squealed in delight, clapping my hands, and Chris poked his head from the bathroom with a toothbrush dangling from his mouth. I pulled it out and kissed his minty lips.

"The baby!" I shouted, and he laughed.

"Okay, crazy. Take it easy." Chris teased and walked into the bedroom to get the bags we'd packed just this past weekend, knowing the due date was around the corner.

"I'm going to get the plane tickets right now. Should we get open ended? I don't want to have a timeline. What if I fall in love with the little bundle of joy and never want to return? Will you leave everything behind and be my kept man?" I teased as I sat back down at my laptop and strummed away on the keys.

Chris laughed from the bedroom and shouted, "Your family has money! One more mouth to feed won't kill them, even if it is a mouth as big as mine."

I smiled with a lunatic grin as I booked our flights. We'd be cutting it close, but I was desperate to be there when the baby was born.

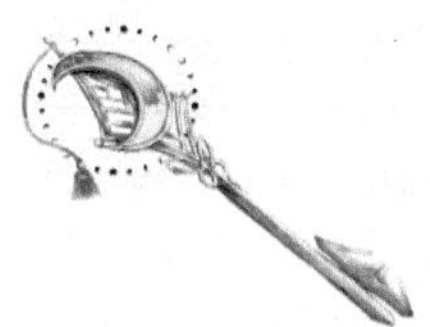

We pulled into the portal room. No one was expecting us, so I woke Chris up and set Tree free in the portal room before we brought our bags up to my old room that was already turned down for us. I was practically bouncing on my toes to go find everyone.

The palace was seemingly abandoned. Considering it was the middle of the night, it was understandable.

Gypsum ran into us as we descended the stairs and sighed in relief, hugging me. "Frigga's sweet grass, you're here. Chris." He inclined his head.

Gypsum led us through the halls to the room the palace had reserved for medical attention that would require a longer stay than a typical healer call to the bedroom would. My stomach knotted when he told me where we were going, but he said it was typical for births.

Gypsum led through an arched entranceway where several plush couches were with pitchers of water and wassail. Loud groaning came from behind the closed door to the right. Jett sat with his face in his hands, helpless, with Steel sitting to his right, trying to distract him. Hawk sat on his other side with one of his hands on Jett's back. Slate, Amber, Brass, Quick, and Tawny sat scattered on random couches, not paying much attention to anything. The Straumr brothers and Moon sat opposite one another on chairs towards the back, their faces tight, staring holes in the floor.

"Look who I found," Gypsum said as we crossed the room.

Jett's head popped up, eyes red rimmed and wide, jaw clenched, and I ran into his arms. He desperately needed a hug and his usual providers helping to give birth to his first child.

"I'm so glad you're here," he whispered into my ear, his arms crushing me to him. I knew he must be distraught to not have said something witty.

"I'm always here for you." I told him, squeezing him back, my face pressed against his chest so I could hear the rapid pace of his heart.

"She won't let me in." His voice is thick, and he swallows audibly. "She is asking for you. Indigo is already in there."

I took a deep breath, and he released me. I cupped his powerful jaw and gave him a reassuring smile. Chris had crossed the room to where Steel sat and greeted everyone. The Straumrs had given their greetings and were now back in their seats, looking despondent. Let's hope nothing ever happened to Amethyst;

We heard the doors open and Sparrow poked her head out, dark hair tied back, making her high cheekbones and deep-set eyes more prominent.

"You're here, thank the Mother. She won't push without you. Come on," she said, gesturing us in.

Licking my lips, Chris flashed me a smile as I tied my hair up on top of my head.

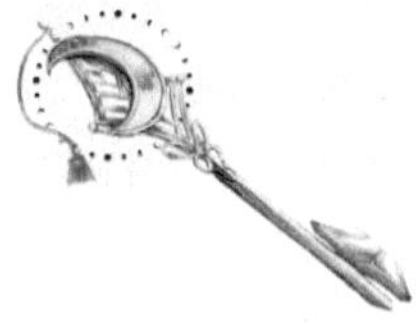

The room was more like a bedroom than I thought it'd be, but considering we didn't use any machines, I guessed that made sense.

They did the room in pristine white and mahogany. There were no rugs on the mahogany wood floors. A white triangular jacuzzi was paneled into the wall to the left next to a door I assumed led to the rest of the bathroom, but other than that the only other item in the room was the four-poster mahogany bed with all white bedding, heavy white paneling hung from the canopy on rings to shut and a flick of your wrist.

It was open. Amethyst laid back in the center of the bed, sweat glistening on her brow, arguing with Wisteria Rot and Cherry. "Amethyst, look who's here. It's time to push," Cherry said after she saw Sparrow return.

Amethyst's head snapped up, and she gave a pained smile. I hurried to her side. They pulled her black hair on top of her head, lines creased her mocha forehead as she strained, her long fingers curled into the white sheets at her sides. Leave it to Amethyst to look stunning while giving birth in her black cotton camisole nightgown. They pushed it under her heavy breasts as Wisteria sat on the bed between her legs.

I climbed onto the bed beside her on my knees, ignoring the pink stain under her. Her cheeks were flushed and her full wide mouth down-turned even as she tried for a smile. I was wearing a white ribbed tank top and skinny jeans, not very Tidings friendly, but I gripped her hand and let her squeeze to her heart's content. Indigo brought in a bowl of water and towels, placing them on the nightstand.

"It is time, darling," Pearl said patiently. She had probably said it a few times already.

Amethyst nodded and Cherry mouthed *thank the Gods*. "I didn't want you to miss it," she said, wincing as she slid off the bed.

Cherry sat behind her and hooked her arms around Amethyst's

shoulder from behind. Wisteria kneeled in front of Amethyst, her hands between her legs. I gripped Amethyst's hand from where I sat on the bed. Her legs were bent as she leaned her back against the side of the bed, most of her weight supported by Cherry's arms. Sparrow was preparing a bassinet in the background, and Indigo kneeled next to Wisteria, looking awed by Wisteria's healing abilities.

Now and then, I watched Wisteria place her hand on Amethyst's stomach, finding out where the baby was at the moment. Women in Tidings gave birth au naturel. It was one of the few things they did unassisted by *calling*. I took a dampened rag from Indigo and dabbed Amethyst's forehead.

"I wouldn't miss the birth of your child." I told her softly, and Indigo nodded in agreement so hard I thought her head might fall off.

"Time to push," Wisteria said, shimmying closer on her knees. Wisteria tightly pulled back red hair at her nape and she wore a white apron over her dress.

"Just breathe, baby," Cherry said softly to her.

Amethyst nodded, and I saw her face contort with the effort. Perspiration sprung forth and she let out a loud grunt that progressively got higher. She panted when extended grunt left her throat.

Her hair stuck to her neck and face, so I dabbed with the towel as she squeezed my hand, which was white where her finders grip it. I was too afraid to ask her to ease her squeeze.

She pushed again, over and over. She got louder and louder with each push, visible in pain. Cherry speaking soothingly to her, holding her up with all her might, and it struck me how much they were a couple as Jett was with either of them.

"The head is out. One more big push, Amethyst. You can do it," Wisteria said to the women, nearly touching her.

Amethyst nodded, her mouth open, her air coming in bursts. Her face contorted, and she loosed a loud, strained scream. Wisteria caught the baby in a fluffy white towel, and Indigo hurried to take the baby to the bassinet and clean it up with Sparrow. Pearl kneeled before Amethyst next to me while Cherry was cooing and crying. My head felt like it was going to explode with all the sensory stimulation and emotions around me.

"Amethyst, do you want to lie down? Your baby is born. You can relax now." I aimed for the most reassuring tone possible and loosened my hold on my empathetic abilities just enough to soothe her.

Pearl grabbed a nearby bowl knowing she still had more to birth and thanked my sex ed classes in high school when I heard a wet *plop* in the bowl. She shoved it away and out of sight.

Amethyst regarded me while weeping prettily, and she nodded, letting Cherry lift her on to the bed. We moved her back with a little push of air and I handed Cherry a freshly dampened towel as she cleaned the blood off of Amethyst's legs.

"How is she?" she asked breathlessly, turning her head towards the bassinet.

Indigo carried the bundle over. And she's crying, but they're happy tears. "You have a beautiful baby girl."

She leaned down to hand Amethyst the baby, but she gestured to Cherry. Cherry threw the towel she was using on the floor beside the bed and leaned forward to accept the bundle from Indigo. Indigo hugged herself as Cherry took her. Cherry's face transformed and her fair skin flushed and bright while she cried, leaning back against the headboard, low enough so Amethyst saw into the blanket.

"She's perfect," Cherry gushed.

Amethyst let out a half laugh, half sob and nodded. Cherry kissed her lips.

Amethyst took the baby girl from Cherry, and I got my first look at my niece. A head full of jet-black hair covered her tiny head, her creamy skin promised a mocha color like Amethyst's and two big blue eyes peered out from its squished face. She was beautiful. Amethyst laughed again and held the baby girl to her breast.

Wisteria came by and healed Amethyst before leaving. "Your girl is healthy, and we healed you as much as we are able. Thank you for letting me be a part of this," she said before saying her goodbyes to all of us.

"Did anyone tell Jett?" Amethyst looked at us and we realize we hadn't. The baby had us enraptured.

She had fallen asleep and Amethyst swaddled her in a new pink blanket patterned with little red flowers. "Will you take her out to meet her father?" Amethyst asked, offering me the baby.

I swallowed hard. It hurt to even look at a baby. To know I would never experience what Amethyst had. To never know what it felt like to nurse my newborn at my breast.

"I want to stay with Amethyst. You haven't held her yet." Cherry smiled reassuringly at me and I took the baby in my arms.

I couldn't believe how light she was, her little face, and tiny fingers. I wanted to unroll the blanket and count them along with her toes so I could have scientific proof that she was as perfect as I thought she was. The mattress lifted as I carefully slid. I felt like I was walking on air. The whole thing was surreal. My brother was a father, I had a niece.

Indigo crowded around me. "What do we call her?" I asked, and my voice sounded far away.

"We call girls by their mother's last name until their Ausa Vatni," Amethyst said, and she looked euphoric. Her and Cherry's fingers intertwined as Cherry stroked her hair.

"But instead of Geol, Gigi," Cherry amended.

I turned back towards the door and headed for it again. Indigo and Pearl came with me. I was so afraid of tripping or dropping her I walked at a snail's pace. Cherry and Amethyst chuckled behind me, but it didn't make me walk any faster. The closer I got to the door, the sooner I had to give her up and I wanted as much aunt time with her as I could get.

Indigo unlocked the door and opened it for me. I took two steps into the room and looked up. Jett's arms folded across his broad chest and his face pointed down at his boots. When I came out of the room, his head slowly rose and his eyes were wide. His full lips parted as he saw the bundle in my arms, and I realized I was crying and smiling at the same time.

"Congratulations, Jett. You're a father," I whispered, and his face split with a smile.

Most men were nervous about holding their newborn babies, but not my brother. He rushed to me and took her out of my arms as gracefully as he would draw his long seax.

"A Geol! I have a daughter!" he cried as he held her about carefully.

The Straumrs swarmed him and I watched as Steel wrapped his arms around Tawny. Amber slid her hand into Slate's and Hawk patted Gypsum on the back. Brass and Quick were beaming smiles at Jett. He was doing great until Hawk came to congratulate him and the two men's faces twitched with struggling emotions. They embraced and when they come apart, tears streaked their cheeks.

Chris made his way to me and I realized I was trembling; my teeth were chattering. "Shug, what's wrong?"

Too much. It was too much. I swallowed convulsively and my breaths are shallow.

"I can't," I gasped, and Chris's tan brow furrowed with concern.

"Sit down, Shug. I'll get you some water." He led me over to the couch and I fell into it.

CHAPTER II
JETT

She was perfect.

Jett had never seen such a perfect human being before. He couldn't help but show her off to every single person in the room. Passing her around before he would go check on Amethyst. Brass rose to his feet in his periphery and his expression made Jett frown.

Jett heard Scarlett's soft wail of helplessness and spun around to see her shatter a glass on the floor. She slumped on the couch and sobs raked through her body as she stared blankly ahead.

Jett gave Geol to Moon, who was itching to hold her, and started towards Scarlett. She was coming undone. He should have seen it coming. How could they have expected her to sit here and watch them rejoice in this new life she would never experience? What a dumb bastard he'd been. She could have come after and seen the baby.

Chris fell to his knees in front of her and tried to get her to speak to him, but she was despondent. Jett had never seen Scarlett like this. She'd been downtrodden before, but she always came up with a plan, something to look forward to, a way to fix it in her mind. Never had she looked so hopeless.

She pushed at Chris, who fell down on his backside. "Go away! Chris —"

"Don't you dare start again, Scar? I'm not hearing any of it," Chris shouted back at her.

She shook her head, her hands up helplessly, "Please. I can't do this," she wailed again. "It's not fair. I can't fucking stand it."

Jett sucked in a breath; she'd officially hit rock bottom. Aside from her dropping the glass, she was weeping into her hands as Gigi entranced the other half of the room. Everyone around her, though, was as still as statues.

She buried her face in her hands. "I would do *anything* to have this. *Anything.*"

"Snap out of it. Quit feeling sorry for yourself. Plenty of women can't have children, Shug. You think I give a rat's ass that you can't have kids? I don't. I love you anyway."

Chris shifted back onto his knees between her legs as she sat on the couch and she gaped at him for talking to her that way. Jett let out a nervous chuckle. The guy had a point. Chris reached around to his back pocket and Jett's mouth popped open. Chris pulled out a ring and held it up to Scarlett. Her eyes bugged out as she slapped her hands to her mouth.

"One or a half dozen, I'd adopt kids from Africa, China, whatever, as long as it's with you. We'll Bradgelina that shit and get one from everywhere. I love you, Shug. Since you've come back, I feel as though I've had a new lease on life. Everything is better with you. I don't even care if you want to move back to this palace straight out of a medieval fantasy. I'm down for anything. Just as long as it's with you. Marry me, Shug. You make me happier than any man has a right to be."

Scarlett was shaking so hard Jett could hear her teeth chatter. "Are you sure?" Her brow knit and Jett cursed internally.

Chris caught it too. "Whoever made you think you were unworthy of the same happiness of everyone else has a world of hurt coming their way when I find them. Of course I'm sure. I wouldn't have been carrying around this ring for the past two weeks, waiting for the perfect moment. I definitely wouldn't have asked Hawk for your hand when we were back last time."

"You did?" she asked, and her eyes lifted.

Big mistake. Her face crumpled. Jett would've given his right arm for Slate to not have been there at that moment. She rubbed her finger where a tiwaz tattoo was and looked back at Chris. Jett thought he'd seen that tattoo before.

"Okay."

"Okay?" Chris asked with a hint of a smile in his voice.

She knit her brows again and searched his eyes. "If you're sure."

"Oh, for fuck's sake, Shug. I can think of a dozen men who would kill to be in my skin right now." Chris took her left hand and slid a ring onto it.

"Okay," she said again and Chris pulled her face to his.

Jett blew out a breath he hadn't realized he'd been holding. He saw a staff member passing by and shouted for her.

"Champagne and glasses. Bring a few bottles. We have to celebrate," Jett called, and the girl nodded.

Jett wanted to be the first to congratulate them. Scarlett and Chris were all over one another on the couch. Jett cleared his throat, and they broke apart. Chris rose to his feet and Jett embraced him. Jett took Scarlett's hand and pulled her up and into his arms.

"Congrats, baby sis."

"I'm mortified. I thought I had a grip on it. That was so selfish of *me* — I'm sorry. Congrats to you, Jett. She's gorgeous." She hugged his side.

Her tan face was flushed, and her eyes were watery. "Not exactly like you can choose exactly when you have your mental breakdowns. You're forgiven. No one has a right to be this happy. I want it for you, too." She gave a wan smile, and Jett left her side to go to Amethyst's room.

CHAPTER

TWELVE

My body was still trembling when everyone started hugging me with their glasses of champagne. Chris had proposed. I hadn't seen that coming. It would have to be a long engagement because I had no intention of getting married before he graduated college. Married *again*. I'd be a polygamist like Jett.

Chris's proposal was exactly what I needed to hear and done in his own personal style — with lots of cussing. The Straumrs had even congratulated me and spoke with Chris, which I appreciated since when last they met, Chris had decked Ash.

It was a procession. Hold baby. Get champagne. Kiss Scarlett. Shake Chris's hand. Next.

Quick came up and hugged me with a dazzling smile. "Now *that* was a proposal." I smiled and hugged him back.

"Thanks, Quick. Sorry I haven't said *hi* yet. I've been busy having a nervous breakdown," I said with a self-deprecating smile.

107

"Long overdue," Brass said from behind him.

Quick moved aside and Brass pressed his body along mine. Normally, not a big deal, but now I knew what our bodies felt like undressed when we did that. I laughed nervously as Brass brushed his lips against my cheek.

"Do you think your fiancée would let me make love to you again before you tie the knot?" I could tell he was teasing, but my whole body heated for several reasons.

"Brass," I rasped.

"Enough of that," Chris said playfully, only deepening my blush.

Brass chuckled and took Chris's hand. "I can only assume you meant me as one of those that would kill."

Chris smiled in return. "One of the dozen." He nodded.

I made a face. Not something I was comfortable with them joking about. *Ever.* I felt him before I realized who was next. Slate's body thrummed when he got close to me. Oh Gods, was he going to hug me?

He did.

"Looks as though we shall both be married soon," he breathed into my hair.

"You're speaking to me again?" I breathed through my mouth so I wouldn't inhale his scent. I would do whatever it took not to be swept away by him.

"I was never not speaking to you. Are you happy?" he whispered.

I exhaled shakily and was afraid to take my next breath, knowing it would carry his scent. "Don't take it out on Brass. I can feel the distance between you. I'm trying. That's what counts."

"You don't love him."

It wasn't a question.

"I devote myself to him fully. It's the most I can give him." I dropped my voice. "My heart's not mine to give. I wish it listened to me sometimes so it wouldn't always hurt so much."

I stepped back from him, letting my arms fall to my sides, and he reluctantly let me go. Even after everything, he still wanted me. We were gluttons for punishment. He moved on and shook Chris's hand, but didn't say a word. I hugged Amber and noticed she had a glass of champagne, which shouldn't have made me cheerful, but it did. She lingered when she hugged Chris, rubbing her breasts on him, and I rolled my eyes. Chris chuckled when I took his arm and drank our champagne.

We stayed another two days before going back to Chicago. I spent every day with Amethyst, Cherry, and Jett. Word had spread about mine and Chris's engagement. Well wishes were coming in from the Tios and Lera even sent over a basket of wines and cheeses which Chris and I spent an afternoon drinking and eating stinky cheeses off crackers.

Pearl threw a small party for us on the balcony behind the palace knowing we wouldn't do it ourselves in Chicago, and we introduced Chris to leather pants and the surreal Tidings music. By *we*, I meant Cherry taught him to dance. Like my language skills, I would never be very good at the dances without a great deal of practice. The men in my life made my night by making sure they swept away me.

All the redheaded Tios swarmed the torch lit balcony for dinner and dancing. Brass was spinning me around to the music when I felt a tap on my shoulder. Brass cocked an eyebrow, and I checked to see who my next partner was.

"May I?" Slate rumbled, and Brass gave him a warm smile.

"Of course," Brass said smoothly and held my hand out for him.

"Please do me a favor and take my betrothed off my hands for me so I can dance with my wife," Slate said, and my eyes widened.

Was that a joke?

Brass's smile deepened. "Aye, aye, captain."

I wore my hair up more often as of late; it reminded me less of Tidings. My metallic gold chiffon gown swirled as Slate moved me.

Four minutes.

I only had to be in his arms for the duration of one song. He led me effortlessly along, knowing how to guide my body.

"Makings amends?" I asked, unable to withstand the quiet between us.

"Taking advice from a woman wise beyond her years. She gives so much and asks for so little; I believe this one concession can be granted," Slate said without looking at me.

"Thank you," I whispered, and he slid his eyes to mine.

"I was selfish."

"I already knew that."

He gave me a rueful grin. "I only thought about myself. I did not care to think how much it hurt you to leave. Not only myself, but your family. Jett had said it enough. It had not sunk in until Gigi was born. I am sorry, Scarlett."

"I could never stay mad at you," I whispered and looked away.

"I thought I was not alone, walking here by the shore, But the one I thought was with me, as now I walk by the shore, As I lean and look through the glimmering light — that one has utterly disappeared, And those appear that perplex me."

My heart twisted in my chest. My tender Slate. How many apologies would it take to make his pain go away?

The goodbyes weren't easier the second time. They were worse since I had to say goodbye to Gigi, too. Thankfully, Brass and Quick weren't there to witness what a mess I became and Indigo had the bright idea to let Tree sit in my lap for the ride to the airport. It was a slight comfort, but it helped.

When Chris and I arrived back in Chicago, I told him we should wait a little while before telling everyone about the engagement. Officially, we'd only been dating for a few months, and questions about if I was impregnated were low on my list of my priorities. He agreed without hesitation.

CHAPTER 13
JETT

JETT

To: Scarlett Tio ScarlettSunset@Sunsettravels.com
Are you coming to the wedding? We won't blame if you don't. Pearl wants to know.

Jett

To: Jett Var JettSetter@VallaU.com
Do you think it would be appropriate? Part of me thinks not. Real wife

THERE WHILE MARRYING SUBSTITUTE BABY-MAKING WIFE. THAT ACTUALLY SOUNDS LIKE IT SUPER SUCKS.

SCAR

TO: SCARLETT TIO SCARLETTSUNSET@SUNSETTRAVELS.COM
SAY NO MORE. BIG FAT NO, TELL THEM TO SHOVE IT. CAN'T SAY I WOULD COME EITHER.

JETT

TO: JETT VAR JETTSETTER@VALLAU.COM
BIGGEST POSSIBLE SIGH EVER. CHRIS THINKS WE SHOULD GO, THAT IT WOULD BE GOOD FOR SOME CLOSURE. HE KNOWS ME TOO WELL. SOMETIMES, HE SHOULD JUST PRETEND LIKE I'M PERFECTLY NORMAL AND READY FOR A HEALTHY RELATIONSHIP.

SCAR
P.S. I'M NOT AND ARE NOT. WE STILL HAVEN'T TOLD HIS PARENTS WE'RE ENGAGED. I'M THE WORST FIANCÉE EVER.

TO: SCARLETT TIO SCARLETTSUNSET@SUNSETTRAVELS.COM
I'LL TELL PEARL THAT'S A YES FOR TWO. DO YOU WANT TO BE IN THE WEDDING PARTY? EVERYONE ELSE IS.

JETT

TO: JETT VAR JETTSETTER@VALLAU.COM

Not in a million gazillion years. I'll sit in the back, in black, with a veil and kerchief. You'll know me by the mutterings, "Why me? Why me?".
Just kidding, sooo happy for them.

Scarlett
P.S. They need a sarcasm font.

"They're coming." Jett pushed away from the computer and turned to Slate, who sat next to him in the technology lab.

Jett had never seen Slate in the technology lab. It might've been his first time there. Slate was torturing himself. They'd read through Scarlett's blog about how great it was living this fit lifestyle with her live-in boyfriend. She had social media up the wazoo — just thinking about managing it all hurt his brain. Lots of diet tips, workout tips, yadda, yadda, yadda. There were links to the magazines they'd been in and pictures. At least a hundred pictures of the two of them. The ones on the blog were candid. The two of them at the gym using one another as gym equipment and one of them, Chris must have taken it, of Scarlett in an oversized Chicago Black Hawk's shirt, sitting in bed typing on her laptop.

It looked like something she did often, her bare legs crossed in front of her, blonde hair piled sloppily on her head. You could see Chris's legs stretched alongside their bed. It was the picture she used for her profile; her blogging away. It was an intimate look into their life together, and Slate had said when to stop scrolling and when to keep going.

The magazine photos were as bad. Airbrushed and nearly naked in every single picture, looking like a couple of celebrities with sculpted bodies to boot.

Jett didn't know why Slate had randomly asked to find out if Scar was coming. Jett thought it was an excuse to come into the technology lab for his true purpose of seeing Chris and Scar together the way they really were outside of Guardian influence. They looked like a normal, blissful, myopic couple.

Another email popped up in his inbox. "What is that?" Slate pointed to it and Jett opened it.

"Another email from Scar," Jett answered, not entirely comfortable with Slate reading over his shoulder.

They were his private conversations with Scarlett, where she was free to open up because she didn't have to say the words out loud. She let a little of her pain trickle through and stopped acting like everything was fine.

To: Jett Var JettSetter@VallaU.com
Is the other wife pregnant yet? Did they move out of the Sumar palace?
Scar

To: Scarlett Tio ScarlettSunset@Sunsettravels.com
No and no. They are moving out the week before the wedding. A wing is being prepared for them.

Jett

To: Jett Var JettSetter@VallaU.com
Is it petty of me to be satisfied? I think you guys will have to come visit me while she's pregnant. I can deal with a lot, but not that. Sigh. Do you think I should elope? Chris would be down. He's already mentioned it. I wouldn't do it in Tidings anyway, maybe Vegas? You'd like Vegas. Chris and I went last weekend, just for fun. I'll post pix on the blog soon. :D
Scar

"Eloping would be a bad idea," Slate rumbled, and Jett pursed his lips.

"I'd go to Vegas for her," Jett muttered.

To: Scarlett Tio ScarlettSunset@Sunsettravels.com
Vegas, yes. Elope, no. It is petty, but I won't tell anyone. The wedding is at the Dagr Palace. Do you want a room there?

Jett

To: Jett Var JettSetter@VallaU.com
Um, no. Having to see them at breakfast after their honeymoon night. Pass. Thanks. On second thoughts, I will not go to the ceremony. Sorry. Turns out, I'm not that big a person. I've bent as far as I'm going to and I've got to draw the line somewhere. Chris will get over it. How are Brass and Slate? Slate promised to play nice. I feel pretty terrible about coming between them. AGAIN. Chris has never mentioned it once. He made comments in front of Brass and they laugh like it's some sort of private joke. Cache holes.
OH! Can we either steal some clothes for the wedding or could you pick something up for Chris so I don't have to take him shopping? Thanks! Cherry said he looked hot in the leather pants, so maybe a pair of those with something blue like his eyes? Have Cherry help you. How's my niece? You need a digital camera so you can send me pix. Daily.

Scar

Jett sat back and looked at Slate. "No ceremony, not surprised. So, how are you and Brass?"

Slate cocked his brow. "Getting there. He fucked my wife. Not sure what she expects. He is not the least bit remorseful."

Jett snorted. "You knew how they felt about one another way back when. Just think of it like this. He got her for three nights. You had her for one and a half months. Chris has already been with her four times as long as you two were together. I think Brass is the least of your concerns."

"We speak. We have not come to blows in a couple of weeks." Slate gestured with his hands, like, *what more do you want?*

To: Scarlett Tio ScarlettSunset@Sunsettravels.com
I'll put Cherry on it. No ceremony. Yes, party. Got it. Brass and Slate are better (Still can't believe you did that). G is good, gorgeous like her mama. We'll have your room ready for when you arrive. See you in a couple of weeks.

Jett

To: Jett Var JettSetter@VallaU.com
Trust me. I have no idea how it happened. There's always been this tension. The only time I had to tell Brass no was when I was with Slate. Between you and me, I came close to cheating on Ash one night with him. Alas, he shot me down hard. I didn't even know he liked me THAT way until I was on rousen cause I could smell it on him ALL THE TIME. Brass said he thought Chris only invited him to stay because he was hoping Slate would find out. Brass and I were just too drunk and stupid to see that. Oh well. What's done is done. I had the "I never do this" conversation. Ugh. Never EVER thought I would. Brass said he knew I'd only been with Slate and Chris. That didn't make it any better. One day, I'll have to ask Cherry about the etiquette of those situations, not that I would do it again. OMG, Chris teases about another girl, but he never would unless I started it. Brass was the only one who had done it before. He said he'd had two women. As if I didn't have enough on my plate, I felt a twinge at that.
Thanks for the vent. I don't talk about this stuff.
Scar

"Satisfied?" Jett asked, crossing his arms.
That had officially gotten awkward. If Slate wasn't here, he would've

leant her advice. Told her about the etiquette, but not with Slate glaring over his shoulder.

"Three men." Slate sniffed. "I have been with fifty *times* that many women." He paused. "Explain to me why three makes it worse."

Slate folded his arms over his chest and Jett shut down the computer. "Because she loved you. She loves Chris differently, and I'm sure she has a love for Brass. You never cared much for ninety percent of those women. Maybe Scar, Lera, Lynx, and Amber. That's three. Scarlett doesn't give herself carelessly, so you know she wanted to be with them. Has Brass been with many women?" Jett asked.

"Twenty or so," Slate rumbled.

"Maybe that bothers you. I got a feeling for Chris. I'd say he's in the teens. Gods, to count how many people you've been with on fingers and toes again." Jett jutted his jaw out arrogantly, "Scar always had a problem with the women you'd been with. With fewer lovers, it makes her more special to them."

"It does not. How do you decide who cherishes her more?"

Jett threw up his hands. "I don't. Do you want me to help you set up an email? You could write her yourself," Jett offered.

"No. This was enough," Slate said and walked away.

CHAPTER

FOURTEEN

Slate and Amber's wedding loomed like storm clouds. Suddenly, the wind picked up, and it was raining.

I showed up fashionably late. The Dagr palace had a Romanesque style, groin vaulted ceilings with Corinthian grey stone columns, and marbled tiled. I wore black. It was my private joke with Jett. No veil, though. Chris looked handsome in black leather pants and a black satin waistcoat and a black and blue paisley ascot over a white shirt. His baby blue eyes popped against his tan skin.

Amber's colors were canary yellow and sage green. Yellow snapdragons hung in curtains around the grand ballroom of the Dagr palace. The tables covered in sage damask cloths had seats tied with canary sashes. A pale blue clad staffer stopped and stared at us.

"The ceremony is this way," she said, and my stomach flip-flopped.

"I thought it'd be over," I squeaked.

"No. There was an issue with the groom. Come."

Chris started walking and took me with him. I wouldn't have even of gone if Chris hadn't made me.

The long hall had golden back seats that lined the two sides with a white runner down the center. More snapdragons hung from the ceiling and arched vines lined the path to the front. My heart lurched when I saw my family gathered outside the doors. The women dressed in draped satin yellow dresses that reminded me of a fairytale princess and the men wore matching yellow waist coats.

They saw us coming and my cheeks heated. Chris had helped me pick the dress. It wasn't one of mine; it was one Lera had chosen for me. Black, clingy, and cut across the shoulders with heavy boning that gave me an hourglass figure and propped my breasts up to my chin.

Tawny and Gypsum spotted me first. I gave an awkward little wave. "It's running late. Go ahead in."

Jett and the girls saw us. Amethyst did not look like she had given birth four weeks ago. Chris and I started giving hugs. We had gotten in late, on purpose, so we had a legitimate reason for missing the ceremony, so we were only now seeing everyone. Steel gave me a one-armed hug as we moved past. Quick, Indigo, Brass, Garnet, and Hunter — who was Amber's brother, all said their hellos as we pushed to the front. There was another blonde man who looked rough around the edges, who must have been her younger, yet taller, brother.

Jett's eyes were as big as saucers. "We're running late. Are you going to stay?"

"Might as well, we're already here," Chris said, and I felt the color drain from my face.

"Leave, Scarlett. You do not need to be here," Brass whispered from behind me.

My stomach churned; acid turned into molten lava as I contemplated watching Slate marry Amber.

... I don't know what to do. If I run screaming, I'll hurt Chris's feelings...

"If he does not know you are not over, Slate, then he is blind." Brass's breath puffed at my hair.

... I can't run from my problems...

"Self-preservation."

While Brass tried to talk me out of torturing myself with some cruel and unusual punishment, Slate turned to see what the commotion was and met my eyes. Everything I gave up boiled down to today. So tell me why I wanted someone to save me? To interrupt the wedding and say that they couldn't be together because Slate and I... he was my swan, or black vulture. We mated for life; we belonged together. Maybe he was the black vulture, and I was the swan, whatever. It wasn't supposed to be happening. It felt impossibly wrong.

"Congrats," Chris said, shaking Slate's hand.

"I did not think to see you until later," Slate rumbled.

My voice was gone. I could only smile and nod. It wasn't a natural smile. It didn't touch my eyes, and it hurt my cheeks to plaster on.

"Hey, Shug, let's not disrupt the ceremony any more than necessary." Chris pulled me forward.

Slate's fingers glided over my arm, and he pushed something into my palm. "Say it now," he whispered.

Chris led me down the aisle and I stared open-mouthed over my shoulder at Slate. *You are mine and I am yours.* I turned back around as Chris led me to the front of the hall. I spotted Hawk, Sparrow, and Pearl at the very front and skidded to a halt.

"I can't sit up there."

Eyes were being drawn to us as I dug my heels in. "Then we'll sit here," Chris said with a reassuring smile.

We found empty seats in the middle of the hall and I shut my eyes, putting the emerald ring over my right ring finger. The cathedral windows that spanned the back of the hall shone light over the guests that faced it. They set a band up on the left side with all the usual unfamiliar instruments. I hung my head and let the sun warm my skin.

"You okay, Shug?" Chris asked, and I nodded. No way I was chancing my voice.

The music started and I let my mind drift.

Self-preservation.

I wasn't sitting as a guest at Slate's wedding to another woman. I was on a picnic with Quick and Indigo and Slate. We were laying on a blanket by the River Mani, laughing and smiling. Then, we were making love in the cool river's water under the hot Thrimilci sun. He told me he could hear incredibly well, and I tested him.

"I love you, Slate," I whispered, knowing not a soul could hear me.

He had screamed it back at me. It was the only time he'd ever said the words. *Just breathe.* I thought the words were like a mantra. I heard people moving around me, music playing, but I was blind, deaf, and especially dumb to it all.

Memories pulled me deeper.

Slate revealing the nursery after a big blowout; the place where he'd planned for our children to sleep and play. It was a sea foam green walls and teddy bears. Bookcases filled with stories to read to those children. He'd had it all done for them, the wing, everything for us.

If you don't fight for what you want, no one else will.

My mother's voice echoed in my mind.

I was in love with Slate. Nothing either of us could ever do would change that for me, not while my heart still beat and probably well after it stopped in my cold, dead chest.

I shot to my feet. I had to stop the wedding. When I opened my eyes, everyone else was standing too, and I watched Amber and Slate walk back down the aisle.

I was too late. It was over.

The guests were clapping and smiling and I felt so violently nauseous that I pushed past the guests on the other side. Chris called after me, but if I stopped, I'd collapse into a ball of misery.

CHAPTER 15

JETT

Jett had seen the look on Scarlett's face as Chris led her down the aisle.

Panic.

When he'd walked down the aisle, he'd seen Scarlett with her head hanging and eyes closed, but she was smiling. Gods, he hoped she wasn't having another breakdown. When it had come time to bind Slate and Amber together, Slate had been staring at where Scarlett was sitting. They had only tied yellow and green ribbons around their wrists in a binding ceremony. It hadn't taken long.

Then they were marching back down the aisle. He saw the commotion off to his left and saw Scarlett, pale as death, pushing her way through guests to get to the side aisle. Chris was trying to follow her, but she'd knocked down some poor man in her scramble. The doors had opened and Scarlett had disappeared.

Jett came out through the main entrance of the hall and didn't bother telling anyone where he was going. He ran down the hall and heard another set of footsteps behind him. He turned the corner to see Scarlett fleeing around the end of the hall, and he ran even faster to catch her. Brass ran alongside him as they almost fell over themselves, turning down the hall she'd gone.

She was crouched in an alcove hidden in the shadows. Jett wouldn't have seen her, but it was hard to miss the sound of her dry heaving. Jett slowed and sat down beside her on the cool marble tiles. Brass knelt in front of her and pushed her hair away from her face.

"*Shh*. It's alright. Hard part is over," Jett murmured.

"I'm *living* the hard part," she said, her body retching. "I wanted... to stop it." She sobbed and coughed and Brass took off his ascot and *called*, dampening it and handed it to her. "I love him. Gods damn me to hel. I love him so much. Take me home, please. I can't be here."

Jett felt his eyes burn, and he clenched his jaw. "We'll take you to the bathroom. Get you cleaned up. If you still want to go, we'll take you home."

"Go on ahead. I have her. If Chris asks, tell him she had stomach cramps. He will understand," Brass said.

"What if he asks who she's with?" Jett asked skeptically.

"With me, of course. No reason to lie. You will be missed. I will not."

Jett got to his feet and helped Brass straighten Scarlett out, and he lifted her into his arms. She fell limply against his chest, his ascot pressed to her mouth, eyes closed as he walked down the hall with her. Jett looked at the floor. She must not have eaten. There was nothing there unless she incinerated it.

He drew a fortifying breath. Whatever Slate said as she passed him made her doubt everything. As if Jett didn't know the real reason Slate had wardrobe issues was because he *wanted* Scarlett there, or rather, wanted her to stop it. What that confession must have cost her when she was clinging tooth and nail to the new life she was trying to make for herself.

It was over. The hard part *was* done. Slate Dagr, in the eyes of the Guardians, was married to Amber Lodda.

"Where is she?" Slate had come charging around the corner and into Jett.

Jett grit his teeth. "Don't worry about it. Go tend to your Guardian wife. Leave Scarlett alone. What did you say to her? You had to make it even *more* difficult. What *exactly* was wrong with your waistcoat, brother?"

Slate's face grew stony as he got in Jett's face. "Tell me where she is. *Now.*"

"*Never.* I'd hate to punch out a groom on his wedding day, but in your case, I'll make an exception." Jett spat.

"Is she with Brass?" Slate asked, scanning Jett's eyes.

"Yes." Slate looked past Jett like he could see them together. "He's not interested in bedding her right now, if that's what you're concerned about. She's not interested in bedding *anyone* right now. You shouldn't have made her watch."

Slate furrowed his brow and turned towards the wall and punched it so the wall cracked and rested his head against it.

"I hoped..."

SIXTEEN

Brass handed me a glass of water as I sat slumped on the couch in the powder room of the Dagr palace. He'd helped wipe my face free of runny make up and handed me tissue after tissue until I could form words without sobbing again.

He sat down next to me and unbuttoned the top buttons of his shirt and pulled his hair back in a leather strap. It was getting long.

"Better?"

"No," I muttered, feeling ashamed of myself.

He took the glass from my hand and placed it on the floor. "Shocking. Going through with all those plans. In your mind you are benevolent and wise, but putting it to practice, a completely different story."

I sighed. "Wise words. You must think I'm pathetic. *I* think I'm pathetic."

"No, Scarlett. I think your heart and mind wage a daily battle and some days one wins, on different days, the other."

Brass was blowing a cool breeze over my hot skin and lifting the hair at the nape of my neck. "Do you think I made the right choice? Letting him go?"

Brass rubbed his lips together. "You two are still very much in love. No one has ever said doing the right thing was easy. I think you did the unselfish thing. Who's saying if it was right or wrong? It is all a matter of perspective. Is it right to bring children into a loveless marriage for the sake of having children? Or is it right to tear two people apart who would die for one another? Is it right to stay with someone when you know you cannot meet their needs? Or that when you are together, you put their life in danger?"

I waved my hand. "Okay. Okay. I get it. I'm damned, no matter what I do."

"Will you stay for the rest of the wedding?" Brass asked and leaned back next to me.

I shifted so I could lean into him and soak up the comfort he offered. "I suppose so. Being the bigger person and all that. I think I trampled a man, though. When I apologize, I'll recognize him by the stampede marks on his back." Brass chuckled, and I sighed, resting my head on his shoulder. "How did you know I was getting stomach cramps?"

"Chris was thinking about them when you trampled that man," Brass teased and I shifted my head to smile up at him.

"No healing in Chicago."

"Do you want me to delve?" Brass offered.

"Gods, no. I can't take any more bad news today. Will you save me a dance or two?" I asked, looking up at him.

His stubbled chin brushed my forehead as he kissed it. "However many you wish."

Brass led me back to the wedding, and I waved to Chris, who was dancing with Cherry. I sat with my back to the head table with Ama,

Shale, and a few other Shadow Breakers. Ama made sure I got good and drunk. The only times I made it out onto the dance floor were when Chris dragged me out and again when Brass brought me.

Chris accepted my cramp excuse; I told him it was bad, so we needed to go home in the morning. He agreed and told me to schedule a doctor's appointment because they were getting worse. I put his mind at ease and said I would. Chris was dancing with Amethyst when Ash slid in next to me.

I choked on my wine.

"I find this ever so amusing. I could not marry you because you are a desolate wasteland and now your savior abandons you after you gave yourself to him, heart and soul, for another woman. He gave you the same reason, did he not? Scarlett Tio is to be used, not kept." He leaned forward so his words spun from his mouth into my ear. "Do you think she will conceive his heir for him tonight? Such a shame to waste this body. You know where to find me if you need someone else to use you for a good romp."

Ash glided away, leaving me speechless. I stood in a daze and crossed the ballroom to find Chris so we could leave. I'd had enough celebration for one night.

"Miss Tio."

I turned to find Orion Vetr's blue hooded eyes focused on me. "Orion. How are you?" I slurred.

"Better than you, my dear. May I escort you home?" The older gentleman stepped to my side and took my arm.

"My home is in Chicago now, Orion. If you have a magical way to get me there tonight, I would be the most appreciative person on the planet. Do you have a way to get me home tonight?"

I was drunk and obnoxious and hated myself. Orion's mouth quirked.

"Not tonight, I am afraid. If I could make a way available to you, would I be able to ask a boon?" Orion pondered.

I cocked my head. "I won't write a blank check. Do people still write checks? Is there a bank note or something here? What's the catch?"

He chuckled, and I wondered what I'd said that was so funny. "If... unsettling news should come to light about me. I need you to be the pragmatic voice of Tawny. She is high spirited and short-tempered. I am told you are the one to see to make hard choices." Orion looked past me and I, like an idiot, looked at him.

Slate and Amber sat at the head table and were kissing. She looked stunning in her strapless ivory dress. My heart seemed to implode, and I staggered, standing still. Orion caught me under my arm as I knocked over an array of dishes onto the marble floor. My head swam.

"Come. Think about it. I will take you to the portal." Orion left with me and I stumbled along, trying hard not to trip through my blurred vision.

CHAPTER 17
JETT

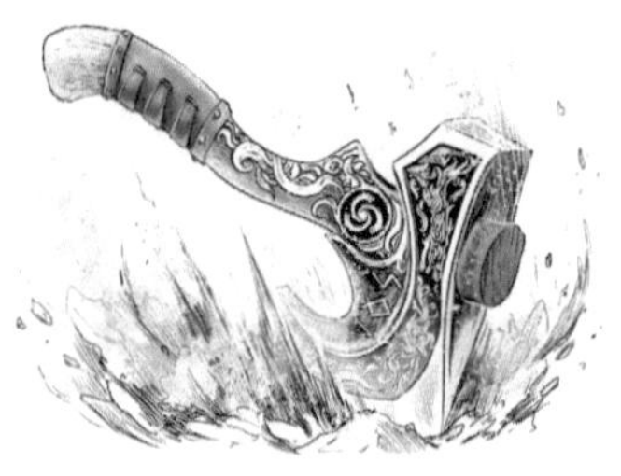

"Orion Vetr took her home. He's Tawny's grandfather." Jett told Chris, who looked deep into his cups.

The wedding party sat around the dance floor as the staff cleaned the ball room. Amber leaned against Slate, sliding her fingers over his wedding band. Not Alder's.

"I heard she was stumbling drunk. That she knocked over one of my guests during the ceremony. She was probably drunk even then." Amber sniffed. "Every time I see her, she is drunk or drinking."

Chris chuckled and so did Tawny at a looked they shared. Jett would have laughed too, but he was too busy being angry. Chris stood and slapped his thighs and stretched his arms high into the air.

"I'd better get back. She doesn't like to sleep alone." He turned and then stopped, remembering something. "I should say our goodbyes now. She wants to leave first thing in the morning. She's been getting sick; we're making her a doctor appointment when she gets back. We'll keep you posted." Chris's face etched with concerned as he furrowed his brow. "Anyway, it'll be a while before we come back again. Football starts soon and she won't come back without me. Sorry. Adios."

Chris waved and slung his waistcoat over his shoulder as he walked away. Gypsum got up with him and they left the ballroom together.

"Did she tell you she wouldn't be coming back until — *what?* Yuletide? When does football season end? Why do I feel like this is a dirty secret?" Tawny folded her arms, and Steel leaned into her to whisper in her ear.

Jett had told Steel that Scarlett wouldn't come back while Amber was pregnant. It would appear Scarlett was already making up legitimate excuses of why that would be. Tawny's face fell, and she grimaced down at her shoes.

"I fiddlesticking hate all this sugarfoot!" Tawny shot to her feet and stomped her feet as she left the ballroom.

The staff was watching Gigi for the night. It was the first night alone with the girls since Gigi had been born. Jett had made many plans in his mind, but now he wasn't feeling amorous.

Steel got to his feet and bid everyone goodnight. Amber stood and smiled down at Slate.

"Come, my love. Let us make you an heir," she said with a sultry smile and Slate rose to his feet and wrapped his arm around her shoulders.

She beamed in triumph.

Brass kicked the chair he had been sitting in and Jett jumped out of his skin. Brass's amber eyes were molten as he pressed his lips together, looking like he had much to say, but bit it back.

He held up his ring finger, the tiwaz tattoo, and Jett remembered where he'd last seen it. There was no way Slate knew about it, but Brass looked like he was ready to spill the beans.

"For her. I should never have come," Brass said.

"You bonded her?" Slate asked in a growl.

"*We* take all the pain with the pleasure and *we* sacrifice. Success through sacrifice is the tiwaz rune. I could not think of a better one for her. I bonded her and then I tricked her into a binding ceremony. We are hand fasted. Ask me if I feel the least bit guilty about it. I should be with *her* tonight and not *here*. I should have made her come to Ostara. Not a mistake I make twice," Brass spat and kicked another chair that crashed into a table.

He turned around, leaving them all dumbfounded. Indigo scrambled to her feet and Quick stood with her.

"Get over yourself, Regn." She cursed before she chased after Brass.

Quick sighed and sank back down to the floor and grabbed a carafe of wine. "Freya's burly boar, I cannot believe he bonded her... Hand fasted! Spinel is going to shit a brick. Scarlett got under his skin. He is acting like..." Quick shut up short and gulped his wine.

Like Slate.

Maybe Scarlett made men go just a wee bit crazy. It would explain a lot. Amber urged Slate forward, and he followed. Jett hung his head and held his breath. By the Mother, having a daughter had made him soft. Amethyst ran her hand down his back and he clasped Cherry's hand in the other.

"Your sister is a good woman. She'll marry Chris and they'll be happy. You'll see," Amethyst reassured him.

Jett nodded, but he didn't believe it.

CHAPTER 18

INDIGO

"It's no secret you haven't been seeing anyone."

Brass stopped his brisk walk to look back at me with an irritated glance. "I see a woman every other month in the patron rooms." He glanced away and picked up his walk again.

My heels clacked over the cobblestones of Valla as I tried to keep up. "You have sex. You're not dating anyone. We all know why."

He stopped again and shut his eyes, as if my presence profoundly aggravated him. I circled around his front and set down my flowing satin dress skirts. The style in Valla during the summer months was that of my mother's home island. Thrimilci fashion was light and breezy on the island of perpetual summer.

"She hasn't been responding to my emails. It's been a month!" I pleaded.

Brass sighed and grabbed my wrist before I could step back. It wasn't difficult to see why Scar had chosen him as her first lover. He was an excellent blend of warmth and safety while being fantastic looking. He stroked my hair during the evening rush just after classes in the middle of the road.

"You have a half year left before you may leave this place. Go with Chris and Scarlett and further your education. Get away from your grief and live a different life." He whispered into my hair.

I took a shuddering breath. Gods' cursed mind reader.

"Fine, but that doesn't help me now. I can't go to Chicago while I'm in classes. *You* can," I said, taking a step back.

Brass sighed again. "And if you go, you might never come back."

I grudgingly nodded.

"I have my team to think about, but I will see if I could go."

I scrunched my face. "That's not good enough. Something's wrong. She wouldn't go this long without talking to me. What if she's hurt? What if the Stygians found her?"

"What if Slate's wedding made her need a break from us all? Give it time, Indigo. She is safer there than she ever was here."

Brass skirted me and disappeared into the crowd.

I growled in frustration and stomped my feet like a child. My tantrum was far from over when I saw a man leaning against the alley way standing smugly still and watching me. I brought my ire his way.

"You're stalking me now?" I snapped.

Silver bit into a shiny red apple and slurped at the juices. "No. Doing a job. Watching a grown woman throw a fit because she did not get her way."

I growled in frustration again and took a step forward to slap him, but stopped myself. It was exactly what he wanted. I hadn't been paying any attention to him or his advances, and goading me into a fight would make me speak to him.

I rolled my eyes and stomped down the road towards the portal gate. Silver trotted to catch up and walked to my side.

"Get out of here, Regn. Where's your girlfriend?" I asked snidely.

"Not my girlfriend, Dove."

"Never ever call me Dove again," I ground out without stopping to look at him.

The portal gate was ahead, and I'd never been so relieved to reach it. Portal gates were from a time when Guardians were elementals and the five islands were one. When Mother Nature's Guardians worked as one, striving for balance in the world. Now we squabbled over power, each family plotting on their home islands.

White light swallowed me whole and the sensation of falling forward rushed over me. We traveled at the speed of light through the portals until we reached our destination with a mere thought.

Silver came out on my heels in the Valla U portal room, bumping his chest to the back of my head. I narrowed my eyes at him and he held up his hands, but his sensual mouth held a hint of a smirk. I would slap off his face.

"I sleep here too," he said in his defense.

"Stop following me. I'm serious," I said, feeling defeated.

Silver's rich brown eyes were flecked with gold and he appeared to want to...

"Get over yourself, Regn," I sniffed.

"They hired me to tail you. I am doing my job."

"How much? I want to hire you too," I said, folding my arms.

It was Silver's turn to look dubiously at me. "Go through Lera. I may not take independent contracts. At the very least, ask my captain."

I sniffed derisively. I'd talk to Slate when Thrimilci froze over.

"Why? What kind of job do you have for me?" he asked cautiously.

"Not a job. I will double whatever they paid for you to stay far, *far* away from me," I snapped and spun on my heel away from him to storm from the room.

Pearl or Jett. One of them must have set him on me. My uncle Jackal may have too. He kept asking me to his classroom for lunch because he was concerned with my behavior. I stuck to myself. There was no *behavior*. They wanted me to find a husband. That was all. I had no interest in husbands.

Silver's hand wrapped around my wrist, snapping my arm taut. "Hey!"

The halls weren't exactly empty, but most of the tyros were at lunch in the great hall. Silver and the other Shadow Breakers were all adept *callers* of shadow. He pressed us against the stone wall and wrapped us in darkness.

"Let me go, Regn," I spat.

"You need a little release, Dove," he breathed, ducking his head down to me.

"'Quick' Silver Regn — single-handedly giving release to half the women in Tidings. Fine, but make it quick, *Quick*." I turned around, resting my forehead and palms against the stone.

Silver rested his head on the back of mine and breathed. "You have one of the sharpest tongues —"

"You've never complained about my tongue before," I interrupted.

He sighed, ruffling my hair, and traced the seams of my dress with his hands. I didn't know what I wanted him to do. I said my biting comment to push him away, but pushing the notorious youngest Regn away was no easy feat.

"Truth. It is capable of a great deal of pleasure."

He seemed to lean towards me, ignoring my jibe as he slowly bunched the fabric of my dress in his hands. If I was going to stop him, it had to be now.

"Garnet not quite cutting it these days? Or is it another one of your blonde nitwits I have the distinct pleasure of being lumped in with?"

He dropped my dress and spun me around so my back slammed against the wall. I craned my head back to look up at him. It took a lot to get him angry.

"You told me to stop coming to your bed! You started locking your doors and when I came anyway, you shouted and —"

"And you went running right into Garnet's arms."

His fingers coiled like he wanted to strangle me. "You told *me* no."

He did not know how many men I'd been with; Sterling and Silver. Sterling's father and Silver's mother had been siblings, but the Hausts didn't recognize the Regn sons as a part of their family. Their mother had not entered a formal marriage with their father and she became pregnant at fifteen. If it was not for Silver's illustrious grandfather, it would've permanently shamed the Regn.

There was, of course, Rikke, but the Wemic scout didn't technically count as a man. The jaguar hybrid had kept me company after my mother died, before anyone else knew she was my mother. I could open up to him without the repercussions that would have come if I confessed my secrets to a Guardian.

"No? Well, this must be a first for you," I said, trying to sidestep around him.

He knit his brows and slowly lowered his head, his eyes scanning mine before his nose rubbed up against mine. I tried not to breathe him in as he canted my chin up.

"Let me back in. You cannot push us all away. You grow colder every day. Bitter," he whispered. "I can help. I want to." He breathed.

I had to get away before he could place one of those kisses on my lips. I'd never get away.

I shoved him back with both hands, and he staggered, blinking at me. "You think you can improve my life just by having sex with you?" I scoffed. "Get over yourself, Regn."

I fled down the long hall in the dimming lights of the sconces until I was far enough away that I could breathe again. Too late. His scent was on my skin. I needed to take a shower.

The day had been a waste.

CHAPTER 19
JETT

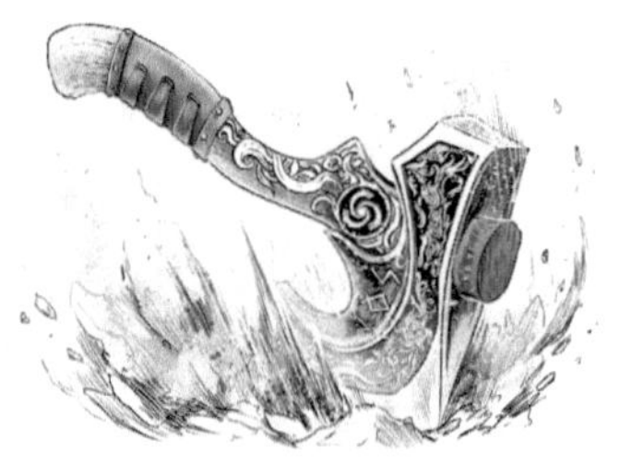

Two months had gone by and Scarlett had not replied to any of his emails. Indigo confessed that she and Scarlett had emailed one another every day and she hadn't responded to her either. Jett had never been on a plane, but he was seriously thinking about risking it so he could show up on her doorstep and demand to know why she hadn't communicated with them.

Pearl and Sparrow were having secret meetings, whether they were discussing Scarlett or the new couple living at the Dagr palace Jett wasn't sure. Everyone was concerned that something bad had happened to Scarlett. She'd dropped off the face of the earth.

Last week, the blog was gone. She hadn't been updating it anyway, but at least Jett could read the words his sister wrote and find comfort in them. Slate had been too proud to ask, but he kept an ear open when he had dinner every Sunday at the Sumar palace.

Tawny wasn't speaking to him and apparently, neither was Brass. Again.

There was no undecided team. You were Team Scarlett or Team

Slate. Slate didn't stand a chance in hel. It wasn't his fault. He was doing exactly what Scarlett had plotted for him to do.

"I'll go. She won't mind if I show up unannounced." Tawny offered as they ate lunch at Valla U.

"We don't even know if she still lives there. She's disappeared," Jett said about the blog and the emails.

"Perhaps she and Chris eloped and do not wish to be reminded of her past," Amber said.

Tawny growled at her with a snarl. "Whenever you think about her, stop. Her name, or any nouns in place of her name, such as *she* or *her* — whatever."

Tawny glared at her, daring her to say another word. Amber only rolled her eyes and continued to eat her lunch.

"Try to be nice to Amber," Slate said dismissively, but Amber preened.

Jett wished they'd go sit somewhere else. He was sick of seeing Amber's face. Only four more months and they'd only see her on Sundays. How could he have ever of thought she resembled Scarlett?

"I will go. She might not want to see family. I am neutral," Quick offered.

Indigo snorted. "We all know your way of comforting, Regn. You'll go see my sister alone when I sprout a set of antlers and become a Faunelle. What about Brass? Chris likes him, Scarlett likes him. He's always taking care of her. If something is wrong, he'll make sure she gets better. I vote for Brass. As it always should have been." Indigo's powder blue eyes slid to Slate, and it surprised Jett to find hate there. "I asked him last month, and he told me to wait. I think he'll go now."

"Well, I always vote for Brass, too," Tawny said, raising her hand.

Quick rolled his eyes. "Who is against Brass? Does he even *want* to go?"

"You're joking, right? He loves her. They're basically wed," Indigo said, plainly eating food off her plate.

"I do not see what is so special about —"

Tawny interrupted Amber with a slap to the table. "I know you were not speaking about *her* again."

Amber folded her arms across her chest and looked at Slate, who shrugged. She huffed and went back to her meal.

Quick groaned. "Frigga's sweet grass. I will ask Brass. He has never left Tidings except when he went with Scarlett the first time."

"Went where?" Slate asked, forgetting himself.

"He walked her out into Rhode Island. She was having second thoughts or some nonsense. I do not know why he bonded her if he can read her mind. Seems like overkill. No one wants to know a woman that well."

Indigo threw food at him, and Tawny slapped his arm, making him chuckle.

"It's on his wedding ring finger. He had fasted her. Put two and two together, Silver. Honestly, how are you two related? That is what Guardians do in lieu of marriage vows. I don't think she knew that when she did it, but Brass certainly did. He wanted to marry her the only way he could before she left, possibly for good. Brass is long lived, Chris isn't. They'll marry in sixty years if Chris is healthy, forty if he's not," Indigo said with a smile.

Jett quirked an eyebrow at her. "You've put a lot of thought into this. Do Brass and Scarlett know about your plans for their wedding?" he teased, and she laughed.

It'd been a long while since Jett had seen his sister laugh.

"No, but all they need is the right push. If Chris hadn't come along and Brass went to visit her, I bet they'd be together already. Say Chris dies in sixty years. That still leaves at least twenty years for them to live in wedded bliss. I bet she'd move back to Tidings for him if it came to that. Mark my words."

Quick snorted. "I will write it on my calendar. Sixty years from now... attend Brass's wedding." He feigned writing into the air, and Indigo threw more food at him as he dodged. "If I did not know any better. I would say you have a crush on my brother." Quick said, and Indigo gave him a sly smile.

"Maybe I do. What's it to you?"

"Nothing," Quick spat.

"I thought not." Indigo returned to eating and Quick frowned.

It had been going on for too long. They needed to sleep together again and get it over with. Slate's face had darkened, and the muscle leapt in his jaw.

Too long.

TWENTY

Pizza for dinner again. I was turning into a hermit. I was trying my hand at writing and painting like my mother used to do and usually ended up browsing meme websites, doom scrolling video clips, and laughing at stupidity. My life had gone down the crapper.

My buzzer sounded, and I grabbed the cash for the pizza man. The local pizzeria that I'd eaten at with my mom was still living in analog, but I wouldn't have it any other way.

I was wearing two-day-old dirty grey sweats and a Blackhawk's shirt Chris had left behind. I hit the buzzer and heard the door open. My greasy hair sloppily knotted on top of my head and mismatched fuzzy socks. I hadn't gone to my new gym in a week. I hadn't gone that long without working out unless someone had died.

I unchained my door and threw back the dead bolt. "Just a second," I called as I put the dollar bills in my mouth to open the door.

The dollars floated from my gaping mouth, and I took a step back. "What are you doing here?"

Slate filled my doorway. He wore jeans and motorcycle boots, with a black cotton 'V' neck and a rucksack slung over his shoulder. He dropped the bag inside the door and closed the door behind him without taking his eyes off me.

"I thought you were the pizza man," I mumbled.

Slate knit his brows.

"It's a man who delivers pizza to your house."

"Where is Chris?" Slate's nostrils flared, and I knew he was catching the scent of my apartment. That was in shambles.

I started cleaning. I straightened piles of paper and carried dirty dishes to the kitchen. Slate followed me and I fidgeted.

"What are you doing here?" I asked again.

"He moved out?" Slate asked.

His long wavy mane didn't have its usual beads and fetishes, but it still tumbled down to his shoulder blades. His thick lashed silver eyes followed my every move. My apartment never seemed so small.

I crossed my arms and Slate's eyes went to my bare finger.

"You should leave. I'm very busy," I lied.

"Yes. You seem busy with this *pizza man*," Slate said dubiously.

"Slate. What do you want? You can't show up unannounced. I know your wife can't possibly know where you are or is she in that bag you brought? Why did you bring a bag? I never gave you my address. How did you get here?" My eyes were wide, and I heard the buzzer. "Excuse me. That's my pizza."

He shifted, but I still had to brush him as I slid past to the living room. I picked up the bills I dropped and opened the door, shoving them at the delivery man and taking my pizza. I spun around and the box bumped into Slate.

"Gods, move over. I know my place isn't huge, but you don't have to be *everywhere*."

"Jett gave me your address. I arrived by plane, and taxi. Amber does not know where I am and I brought a bag because I plan to stay until you are well again," Slate said, picking up a bra I'd left on the couch.

"You can't," I said, putting the pizza down on the coffee table.

"Why is that?" he asked, sitting down on my beige microfiber sectional.

"Because... Chris won't like it," I spluttered.

Slate kicked off his boots and crossed his legs at the ankle on my coffee table. "I do not need to be Quick to know that is a lie. When did you dump the poor sap?"

I scowled. "Why do you assume I dumped him? Maybe he dumped me because I've clearly lost my marbles." I gestured to my filthy appearance and grubby apartment.

"No man would leave you willingly, Rabbit. How long ago?" Slate asked with a smile curving his full lips.

I sighed. "Are you hungry? I don't have much, but there is this pizza."

"Please," he said with a nod, and I went into the kitchen to grab plates.

I also cleaned it, wiping counters and shoving dishes in the washer. When I returned, I brought back with two bottles of water and plates. I handed Slate one of each and set my own on the table. Slate chuckled.

I scowled at him. "Does my misery amuse you?"

Slate's face softened, but his eyes glittered. "No, Rabbit. You can use *calling* with me. I will not report you to the authorities."

I gave him a side eye and started *calling* and had my apartment picked up in a few minutes. Aside from the bedroom, but I had no intention of letting Slate see it.

"Before you relax. I need you to send Jett a message. Your family is worried about you." Slate nudged my laptop next to the pizza with his foot.

I sat down in the corner of my couch, far away from Slate, and picked it up. "Should I let them know you arrived in one piece?"

"No. They do not know I am here either. I did it on my own. They think I am on a mission for the Shadow Breakers." Slate confessed, and I pursed my lips.

"I don't find it reassuring that no one knows that you're here. What do you think is going to happen? I'll just lay back and take you? Be your khoraz here away from your wife and you can go back when you're through with me? I'm telling them you're here because nothing is going to happen between us and it's not good to lie to your loved ones," I said reproachfully, and Slate lifted his pizza free hand in surrender.

"Do what you must, Rabbit. I came to see you back on track, nothing more."

I narrowed my eyes at him and opened my computer. Slate watched me, fascinated, and I fidgeted. Why was he looking at me like *that*?

To: Jett Var JettSetter@VallaU.com
I'm alive.
Scar

I didn't have to wait long for a reply. It was like Jett was sitting there waiting for me to write him. I narrowed my eyes at Slate again. I didn't know why I didn't rat Slate out, but I should have.

To: Scarlett Tio ScarlettSunset@Sunsettravels.com
It's been nine weeks, Scar! You could've been dead! We're sending someone to check in on you. No arguments.
Jett & Tawny

To: Jett Var JettSetter@VallaU.com
I'm depressed. It happens. Chris and I broke things off. Tell you more later.
Scar

"Hey!" I shouted as Slate plucked the computer off my lap and read my emails. "That's private!"

I accidentally clicked out of the window, and my screensaver popped up. I gasped.

"No, Slate. Please!"

I felt frantic. He was never ever supposed to be here and if he ever was; I had no reason to assume he would ever be interested in looking at my computer. He held my wrists as the pictures played on the screen before him. I slumped to the couch and yanked my hands away.

I forced myself to keep looking as Slate watched the slide show.

I surprised him in the first one — shirtless, and a sheen of sweat glistened on his body. His cheeks were flushed, and he was in our big white bed. The next picture he was coming towards the camera, he looked like he was pretending to growl at the picture taker. He was definitely naked.

The next picture was of me. Quite a few of me are of me. I was naked and laughing. My hair was wild as my assailant was obviously above me, tickling me. I kept them because I loved to remember how happy I was and knowing that if it happened once, it could happen again. There was a picture of me from below. You could see the length of my naked body in the shot, and we were under the blankets. The look on my face was very come hither.

The next was one of Slate and me kissing. It looked like the best kiss ever. We were both fighting smiles and looked completely devoted to one another.

A *PLAY* button popped onto the screen and I dropped my head, already knowing Slate was going to play it. I'd lost count of how many times I'd watched it. So far, the pictures had been cruel and unusual torture; the video was worse. He pressed play.

It was me giggling like a madwoman. I turned the camera around so it faced Slate. The white sheet pooled around his waist as he leaned against our headboard, looking completely sated. I interviewed him using some corny reporter tone.

"Say something to the video, Savage Storm. Your fans want to hear what your secret is to your undefeated standing."

Slate laughed, rich and hearty.

"Be scary, very scary, and sex, lots of sex with the undefeated female champion. She keeps me on my toes."

He growled and grabbed the phone away. I was on the screen now. I looked shy and sexy, with just fiddlesticked hair that was only a little flattering.

"You are recently married; how can your fans expect this to affect your performance?"

"Well, Mr. Reporter... actually, you're pretty good looking. Don't tell my husband, but I think I'm going to have to call it off so I can get into your pants."

I leapt forward on the screen.

"Whoops, not wearing any. Even better!"

Despite the phone being dropped and forgotten on the floor, I could still hear myself.

"I love you. Love, forever and always. Yours, mine, the world's — for all time."

The screen went back to the first picture, and the slideshow started again. I reached over and snapped it shut, then snatched it out of his hands. The bathroom beckoned and locked the door with a false sense of security. I would not cry. That was all I'd done lately; my bedroom floor was littered with tissues.

Slate rapped on the door with his knuckles.

"Not that I'm ungrateful for your concern, but go back to your wife, Slate. I don't need you here." I turned on the sink and splashed water on my face.

"Take a shower while you are in there. The pizza can wait," Slate said through the door and I glowered at it.

I took off my soiled clothes and jumped into the shower, letting the warm water wash over me. I'd colored my hair back to its normal light golden blonde. The blonde contrast looked good in the photos. My natural color suited me.

Fifteen minutes later, I was clean and free of superfluous hairs. Something I'd neglected for weeks. I tied my robe around me and opened the door to find Slate leaning on the door frame, his hands holding the top. He pushed off when I opened the door and I smelled something burning when I went into my room.

"What's that?" I asked, changing into a pair of black yoga pants and a hot pink tank top. I even put a bra on for once.

"Chris's shirt," Slate replied as he stalked from the bathroom.

I opened the bedroom door, and he offered me a smirk as he sat back down on my couch. "Tell me what happened with Chris. You seemed a good match."

I searched for his tone of sarcasm and found none. We weren't talking about my creepy photos when I sat on the couch. I ran my fingers through my hair as I thought about my answer. Slate handed me a plate with a slice of pizza.

"Thanks. He's great. I gave him his ring back. I can't marry him — that's what it boils down to." My appetite was gone.

"Why is that?"

"You really want to talk about my lack of love life?" I asked, making a face.

"I want to hear everything you have been up to, Rabbit," Slate said, sliding his arm around the back of my couch.

I sighed. "Not much. After I came back from Tidings, I realized I would never fall in love with Chris no matter how good he was to me and I was being selfish keeping him around because I was content with him. He didn't take it well. He still calls, wanting to get back together. Working together was too hard for him, and me if I'm being honest. I deleted my blog because we loaded it with pictures of us. That's it. I have money saved up, so I'm living off that so I don't have to bug Pearl for a handout. It's modest living — easy to maintain."

"You have been alone for two months?" Slate asked, leaning forward.

"No," I said, shaking my head. "I have Tree."

She was sleeping at the far end of the sectional blissfully unaware of our intruder.

Slate sighed as much as a man like him would sigh. It was more like a gust of breathy air expelled from enormous lungs enough to force a sailboat out into the ocean.

"I liked it better when I knew you were being taken care of."

"It's not up to you and I take care of myself just fine. You're not needed here, Slate. There's nothing here to save. I'm showered, fed. What else do I need to do on your checklist for you to leave?" I asked.

Slate knit his brows. "You are in a foul mood. You have not been rude to me... it has been so long I do not remember."

"You're invading my space. This was a Slate free zone. I had no memories of you in it! Now you've ruined that." I pouted, turning back to my pizza.

We ate in silence until the pizza was gone and I put the box in the kitchen before returning to the couch. "What else? Let's get this over with. What more do I have to do? I contacted the family. You want me to get a new job? I can. I haven't been ready, but I have a decent resume. Want me to go to the gym. I will leave right now."

Slate exhaled deeply. "Can I stay the night?"

"No," I snapped.

"Then can you show me to the nearest motel? All of those things you mention sound good. We will start there," Slate said, reaching for his boots.

"No! No! Tell me what will satisfy you and I swear, I'll do it so you can go home," I protested, feeling anxiety bubble up.

"Do you know how long it has been since the last time we made love?" Slate asked, his hair slid in front of his face as he pulled on his boots.

"The first Friday in February in the bathroom stall at headquarters. Is this pop quiz time? My memory isn't as good as yours, but it's still decent," I rebuked.

Slate lifted his head with a smirk. "Amber is not pregnant."

"No one asked," I snapped.

"You do not have to. I see the question in your eyes."

"Not yet, you mean. She's not pregnant *yet*. You'll have to excuse me if my heart doesn't bleed for you."

Slate lunged across the couch, and I yelped, sending Tree scrambling into the bedroom. He pinned me against the microfiber fabric, his body flush to mine.

"I think you are in a foul mood because it has been too long, Rabbit." Slate purred, hovering above my face.

He stretched my arms above my head, and I clenched my jaw. "Get off me."

"You bonded Brass."

My eyes widened a fraction. "We needed to get hold of one another when I was in trouble. It was when we were together. You saw every inch of me. The only thing I had to hide it was the ring."

Slate's lips curled. My answer had pleased him immensely. His eyes slid down to my cleavage and I tried to make my breathing more even. He reached down with his teeth and pulled out my necklace. I'd stopped wearing my silver torque and Yggdrasil necklace, but I always wore my stone pendant necklace. Alder's ring slid over the swell of my breast and Slate looked down at it.

"I made a mistake giving this back to you."

"You don't need it anymore. You have a new one." I told him and he held up his bare hand, flashing me his love rune. "Your love rune is more than adequate," I ground out.

Slate breathed heavily and moved off of me. I sat up and rubbed my ribs. I slid the ring off and placed it on his knee.

"It's yours. I would never give it to someone else anyway. You can stay tonight, but tomorrow you have to leave." I told him and got up from the couch.

"Come with me, Rabbit. Look in the bag."

I looked down at the bag and chewed my lip. I bent down to it and unzipped it. All of our gear. I didn't know he got this past security at the airport, but I didn't ask.

"I have a mission in Mabon. They've spotted Karkinos there. You wanted to come with if I went, here I am."

I took a deep breath. "Okay."

"You will come?" Slate asked.

I nodded. "I will, but you can't come back here. This is my sanctuary away from you. I need you to respect it."

"Only if you invite me next time." Slate agreed, and I made a face.

"Make yourself at home for now. I'll get you some blankets." I walked into my room and got blankets and pillows from the closets.

I came back into the living room, and Slate was stripping. "What are you doing?" I spluttered.

He stood in his black boxer briefs and that's all... in my living room. "I left my shorts on, Rabbit."

"Don't you have a shirt or pajama pants?" I said, trying to focus on the blankets in my arms and not on what filled those two small shorts.

It *had* been too long.

Slate leveled his eyes at me. "You have seen me in much less than this."

"Half a year ago!" I tossed the blankets at him and stalked into the bathroom.

I brushed my teeth and found Slate waiting on the other side of the door again. He slid past me into my tiny bathroom and picked up my toothbrush. He brushed his own teeth with it and I gaped at him.

"You are determined to insert yourself into my new life, aren't you?" I said peevishly, and he smiled.

I growled and went into my bedroom and locked the door behind me. I shoved all the tissues into the wastebasket and the dirty clothes in the hamper. Anxiety made my mind wander once I got into bed. Slate was in Chicago. He'd flown here for me because of Karkinos. I wasn't buying that for a second.

My bond with Slate entered my mind like a wrecking ball, and I groaned. That was a dirty, rotten trick. It was unspoken that we wouldn't activate our bond anymore. Neither of us had since we separated, but it was alive and well in my mind, as if I didn't already know his feelings.

Pleasure bloomed in my stomach, and I gasped. *Slate.* It coiled and tightened deep in my loins. Two months was a long time when you were used to it multiple times a day. More so when you were a former rousen addict and a khoraz. My hands fisted in my blankets as I panted.

By the Mother, why was he doing this? I fell out of bed and scrambled to my feet as another knee buckling wave shook through me. I unlocked my door and opened it.

"Stop that right now!" I shouted.

He was on my living room couch. I would not look that way.

"Doing you a favor. You can thank me later," he said roughly, and I shut my eyes as I gripped the doorframe.

He was doing it as I spoke with him. Had he no shame?

"I will *not* thank you. Your wife will not thank you. Stop it, now," I cursed.

"If you wish," Slate purred, and I slammed the door shut behind me.

I laid back in bed and squeezed my pelvis tight. *Gods,* that was feeling good. Now I was achy and anxious. I'd be twice as grouchy in the morning. I punched my pillows and pulled one over my face and screamed into it.

The door opened silently. "I heard what you said during the ceremony. I thought you would stop it — counted on it."

Slate detached from the shadows and entered my bedroom. "Impossible."

"I told you my hearing was good, Rabbit. I can pick your voice out in a crowd." He took another step into my room.

"What are you doing?" I asked. I hadn't moved from where I laid on my side facing the door.

"Sleeping in your bed. The couch is too narrow. We have a long day ahead of us." Another step.

"You can't. It's my bed," I said.

"I realize that. What happened to your doctor's appointment? Are you well?" Slate asked, and I squeezed my eyes shut. "What is it?"

"You don't want to know. Trust me, Slate," I squeaked.

"Is that what triggered all of this?" he asked.

"Everything. Me hiding away from the world? Yes," I said thickly, and Slate quit his slow approach and angled right for me.

I threw up my hands. "Please don't! By the Mother, Slate, if you ever loved me, don't!" I shouted, but something etched his face with concern and worry, even fear.

He held my wrists as he delved into me, and I started shaking. Slate's chest rose and fell heavily.

"No," he whispered.

I was all cried out. I cried for weeks after that doctor's appointment. Chris drove me and refused to leave until I faced whatever was going on with me. We'd broken up that following day when my brain had processed the news. It had nothing to do with him and everything to do with me.

"I found out when I got back," I said numbly, and he released my wrists.

"Chris said you had been feeling sick, with cramps, that you were going to see a doctor. That is when?"

"Yes."

Slate rose from the bed and paced. "No, Scarlett. No."

"I know!" I shouted back at him.

"That is why you are hiding here? You did not want one of us to find out? Does anyone else know?" Slate asked as he paced, which was really more of a stalk.

"I have only left my apartment for groceries and to quit my job. I haven't spoken to anyone. Nothing changes. What's done is done."

"Nine weeks, Scarlett. I have been living with *her* for nine weeks. You are telling me that nine weeks ago you could have conceived? That all of this has been for naught? How long since your last healing?" Slate's voice sounded as disbelieving as mine did.

"The last time anyone *called* with me was Tawny's birthday. Maybe three months," I whispered. Slate squatted on the floor and put his fists to his head.

"Scar," he breathed; his muscles flexed in his back.

"I *know*," I whined.

I did. I'd been dealing with it for two months.

He stood up so fast it gave *me* a head rush. He turned to me and stalked towards the bed. Slate threw back the blankets and climbed in.

"Slate. You can't. It isn't right. I don't want to be this person," I whispered roughly, and I knew he wasn't hearing me.

I'd never seen him look so sad. Amber made him miserable, but she was his choice, not mine. He hated his life and didn't feel like he had control of it anymore. Now we found out it was all for no reason. We had just needed time.

He hovered above me, weighing how much we'd enjoy it against how angry I'd be that he seduced me. His lips pressed firmly together as he narrowed his eyes at me.

"You can sleep in my bed tonight. We'll leave in the morning," I said, and he scoffed.

"I say I stay here. With you. We will come back with a bairn and —"

I pressed my finger to his lips. "I don't want to fight. Let's just enjoy tonight. We'll leave tomorrow for tomorrow."

He kissed my finger, and my stomach flipped. Slate slid next to me and tucked me against his body, snaking his arm around my hip to rest against my heart.

CHAPTER

TWENTY-ONE

 Mabon was beautiful. The leaves of perpetual fall bloomed in their rich scarlets, ambers, and golds. The landscape was full of lush rolling hills, interrupted by the occasional protruding boulder. Haust castle sat on a hilltop like an old grey Medieval historical landmark. Moss-covered stone ridges connected the grey stoned roads to through the hills and over the occasional stream. I loved it there.

I'd loved waking up next to him even better. Running to the grocery store, making him breakfast in my little kitchen while he leaned against the doorframe watching. Eating together on the couch watching garbage television and his scent permeating my skin. Therein laid the danger of Slate.

Slate's face was tight on the plane. It would've been amusing if he hadn't looked so completely petrified. I *called* and put him to sleep, which he didn't thank me for when he woke up. Pretending that he was big bad Slate at all times was just fine with me. We took the portal from Rhode Island straight to Mabon. It was like old times.

153

Our path led away from the castle, past the trolls and the fairies too, unfortunately, but Lera's contact was a Centaur, so I could see them. Slate had told me to activate my bond when we arrived. I had missed having the reassurance of his presence in my mind.

We started walking towards the Centaur village. It was a two-day walk; I was really counting on getting a ride back from them.

Slate kept bumping into me. He wasn't really made for strolling, and I kept shoving him back. He would laugh playfully and eventually bump into me again. We stopped for lunch on a boulder and I ate an apple I'd pulled from my pack and tossed one to Slate. He gave one of his rare cheek creasing smiles and for the millionth time I wondered why me?

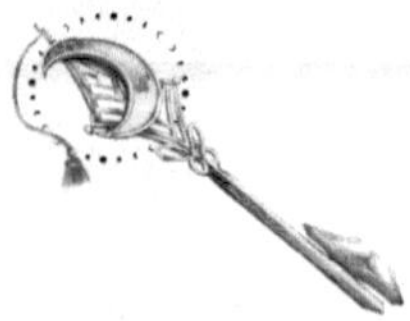

We entered the forest before nightfall and kept walking until my feet wouldn't carry me anymore. Slate hunted as I set up camp. He came back with a pair of rabbits and set about skinning them. I was glad one of us knew how.

I pulled out my roll after dinner and laid down, pulling my cloak up around me. I didn't start a fire. If there was something unsavory in the woods, I didn't want it knowing there were only two of us. Slate chuckled and laid down next to me, tucking me tight to his body.

He was so much lighter. It was breaking my already broken heart.

The sky was lit by a brilliant red dawn. I peeked out from under my hood and Slate's body was molded to mine. Anyone could've walked up to us. I gave a rueful smile and quickly stamped out my joy. I was only borrowing him; every second I was with him would make it that much harder to leave later.

We ate a quick breakfast and started out again.

It was a cool fall morning; the sunlight shone through the riot of leaves as we walked ever towards the Centaur village. Slate had started his routine of nudging me as we walked and I debated kicking him since shoving him wasn't working. I might as well try to move a mountain.

The sun was high when we stopped for lunch. He took off as I wandered towards a brook I could hear in the distance, thinking I might catch a fish. I had little experience with fishing, but I could shoot a thin blade of air better than most.

The brook wasn't deep, and I saw several trout looking fish in the waters. I bent down to catch myself a couple.

"Who comes to the wight's waters?"

I fell face first into the brook and swallowed a huge gulp of water before I pulled myself out on the other side. I'd know that voice anywhere, though I hadn't heard of it since Tawny's wedding.

"Mom!" I tried to scream, my voice strangling. I looked around frantically for her. "Mom!" I called again.

"We do not know this, *Mom.*"

I choked on a sob. Did I die?

"Dad?" I croaked.

I was on my feet looking around, my heartbeat in my ears so I could hardly hear anything else.

"We do not know *Dad.*"

"It's me, Scarlett. Oh please, I can't see you. Where are you?"

Panic laced my voice. Cold seeped into my skin as I shook. I had to be dead.

There was a creaking and the rustle of leaves, but it wasn't one leaf, it was thousands of leaves. I fell to my knees in the mud and looked up at the tree before me, shifted so two faces appeared to look down at me. I made some incoherent noise as the faces of my mother and father came into view from the bark of the enormous tree.

I gaped as my mind tried to process what I was seeing. At the oak tree's base, as thick around as an elephant, was one mossy stump that bent and curved to form two trees as a female and male body. The branches of the tree formed their limbs, moss and knobs in the bark made their faces. They faced one another and could shift enough to see me. They looked human, but obviously not, as thick waves of leaves formed my mother's hair and the form of my father's chest etched in the bark.

"Mom." I sobbed. "I miss you so much. I've given up the love of my life for nothing! It's such a mess. I thought I was doing the right thing, but all I needed was time." I buried my face in my hands and sobbed.

"Do not cry, night's child," my mother said, and I felt her branched arm brush my head. "Love makes fools of all of us. You are no exception."

"Then I am the biggest fool of all," I cried. "Are you... happy now?"

"We know only our love for one another. Love transcends life," my father said, and I cried harder.

They were together in death in a way they could never be in life, so why did I feel so gypped?

"I didn't have enough time. We didn't get to be a family. Mom, you never met Gigi. She's the most beautiful girl you've ever seen. Jett is such a good father; you'd be so proud of him." Tears streamed down my cheeks as my voice warbled. "I think Indigo is having a hard time, but I promise I won't let her be lonely forever. I'll fix it."

I didn't think it was possible to feel so empty and long so bad for something. Their faces watched me with friendly, open bark smiles and I knew they did not know me at all. I wanted to build a house right here in the woods and never leave. I'd be the crazy witch who lived in the woods and talked to trees. It was okay, I could totally do that.

I got to my feet, my pants soaked from the brook and mud, and trudged over to the stump. I threw my arms around it as much as I could and cried against it. The Mother had given my parents such a magnificent gift, but they had lost their memories and still found love in one another. Their love was so strong they were two souls in one being. Their tree limbs embraced me and I wanted to crawl into their branches and stay there until I died. I didn't care.

"The Mother needs you, child," my mother said.

"I don't want to leave you. Mom, you don't know how much I miss you. Managing my life is a full-time job and shouldn't be left solely to me. I'm terrible at it. Come back and help me," I sobbed.

I just wanted her to make it better, fix it for me like she did when I was little. We'd go inside and bake cookies and she'd tell me what she thought I should do as we sat around the kitchen table in our tiny house.

"Mother is in peril," my father said.

I pulled away and looked up at the tree faces. "I'm sorry, what?"

"The Mother's power is waning. Something powerful disrupts her life. You must right it. Balance it, Guardian," my father said.

I shook my head. "I'm not a Guardian."

"You and he are keys." My mother's warm voice said as she gazed past me.

I turned and saw Slate on our side of the brook, staring at us.

I turned back towards the tree. "No, that's not possible. What could we possibly do to fix the Mother?"

"We do not know how, only that you must," my father said.

"Well, that doesn't help at all. Can't you call her up or summon her and find out? I'm not good at fixing problems, I only make them worse!" I shouted angrily at the tree.

No, I wasn't responsible enough for this. I had no clue what I was doing.

"Go now, Guardian, and remember our words. Love and balance. Help the Mother."

My parents' tree forms shifted back together, my mother gazing up adoringly into my father's face as they held one another and froze like statues.

"No! No! No! You can't leave me again!"

I beat on the tree trunk with my fists and they didn't seem to notice me. Whatever made them sentient was gone.

Dry heaves raked through me, and I felt Slate's hand on my back. I gagged in the most unflattering way, but I didn't care. I felt him *call* and my stomach settled and my hands healed from where I'd bloodied them on the tree. He wrapped me in his arms and I pulled my arms into my chest as I bawled against him.

Becoming a wight allowed my parents to come together, but in exchange, everything else — forgotten. Why did it have to be one or the other? Would that make them miss us? Would they be miserable, stuck to the soil as they were remembering we were out there and unable to reach us? I liked to think that erasing their minds made them happier. They certainly seemed so.

Slate smoothed my hair back with his hands and cupped my face. "These are not your parents; they are the Mother's wights. Their fate is to help balance the land here and do her bidding. They do not know you; they do not feel emotions for us. Think of this tree as a headstone, but you have one who can speak back. You can always visit and hear their voices; it is a good thing as long as you do not expect too much."

His eyes were gleaming as he looked at me. I knew I was filthy. Mud clumped on me. My face was full of snot and tears, but when he looked at me, he saw all of me, not just my appearance. He saw down to the heart of me. I couldn't stand his love right then. I pushed him away and stalked over to the brook and bent down, splashing water on my face and wiping the mud off my pants as best I could.

I didn't need to look at Slate to know how hurt he was that I'd pushed him away. I had too much in my head. Panicked and sad, delirious and confused, and for fiddlestick's sake — who knew the human body was capable of so much pain! I wanted to faint just to make it go away.

I dried my hair and pants with my *calling* and picked up my pack from across the brook. It disoriented me when I turned to look at Slate.

"Which way?" I asked hoarsely. The lump in my throat was so big it surprised me I could get words past it.

He walked towards me and crossed the brook to stand in front of me, his handsome face furrowed with my pain he must have felt through the bond. "We should rest. We could talk about what happened. There will be other times to look for Karkinos. We could go back to the palace and tell Jett and Indigo, and the others about this place," he said soothingly.

I thought about it for a split second, but I couldn't go sit in my room and cry. I needed to do something productive. He slid his hand into my hair and tilted my head up as he searched my eyes and lowered his mouth to mine. His lips were so soft and he smelled like cloves and sun burnt leaves and the cool wind. My eyes shot open.

Gasping, I stepped back. "This is part of your prophecy, isn't it? If I don't stay away, you die. If I stay away, I die inside every day and Tidings with it!" I shouted before I started running in the direction I thought I'd been going in before.

"Scarlett, wait!" I heard him curse, but I didn't stop.

So many lies! So many secrets!

I ran blindly, hoping I was going the right way. The sun was still high. I had only been by the wight that was my parents for a short time.

I ran up a steep hillside and slipped at the top. There was nothing to grab but leaves burgeoning trees as I slid off the side of the hill onto my stomach. Hidden stones and dried twigs scratched at my skin before I free fell onto the ground. My feet hit first and thankfully I remembered to go loose and bend my knees.

It still jarred me and I laid on the dirt path as leaves floated down over me for a moment, trying to work my ankles until I heard snorting. I knew that snorting from Tribal Relations class. Minotaurs. Or there was bison in the forest. What were the Minotaurs doing on Mabon? They lived in Elivagar, and unless they were with a Guardian, should not have been island hopping.

I scrambled to my feet and stood face to face with a Minotaur camp. I had fallen over a cave they camped about twenty Minotaur in. They spread out facing me, looking as surprised as I was to find one another there.

I summoned my diplomacy as I slid my pack off my back, just in case.

"Greetings. Do you happen to have a Guardian escort?" I asked in my most official sounding voice.

A round of snorts and deep belly laughs. At least I thought they were laughing. It echoed from the cave as they spread out. I was reversing. It was not good.

"Should I take that as a *no*?" I asked, arching an eyebrow.

I was crouching now, waiting for who would attack first. They were surrounding me.

"Stay a while, Guardian girl," said a ram human hybrid.

"No thanks, busy, busy, busy. I'll be on my way if it's all the same to you."

I spotted a red clay portal gate behind them deep in the cave and my eyes shifted back to the approaching Minotaurs. I couldn't leave that gate. It had to be destroyed.

The ram shook his head. They had on black cuirasses and fur vests with hide skirts belted on by thick leather. They wore no boots over their hooves.

The ram shook his head. "I do not think so, I am afraid. See, I have camped here for two weeks and we ran out of playthings." He gestured to the side of the cave and I almost vomited.

Five bodies, human bodies, tossed aside like yesterday's garbage. Women — judging from the small frames and length of their hair, but their bodies were at different stages of decay. Carrion had been at the corpses, making it impossible to tell from a distance. I covered my mouth unwittingly, and they charged.

I went full elemental.

They couldn't touch me with their hands, but they could with their weapons. I was fire embodied and fighting for my life, incinerating all those around me. Another menacing body came out of nowhere and I knew Slate has joined the fight.

I had to get to that portal.

Slate distracted them long enough for me to wriggle under a few bodies and I *called*. The earth opened up beneath the gate as the ground shook, protesting against my unnatural strength. The gate fell through the crack and I closed it, smashing it to bits, showering dirt and leaves around us.

I heard a roar and turned as a massive bull charged at me, but he didn't hit me. He slammed a nix torque around my throat and my elemental power winked out. I screamed wide eyed as my fingers touched the torque.

Not again! NO!

I fought through my panic and sprung my blades, disemboweling the bull as his hands sizzled from grabbing my fiery throat.

Slate was ripping the Minotaurs to shreds. They were retreating into the cave. They must not have seen me there, or that I destroyed their portal. I stabbed them from behind, making sure I hit every organ that would ensure a slow, painful death for what they did to those women.

Blood sprayed me and I looked like the red harbinger of doom.

I grabbed my pack off the ground and slung it around my shoulders and threw myself into the thick of the fighting, careful to stay away from Slate as he indiscriminately tore apart flesh. Even in the gory mist of blood, his skill was incredible to watch. The fear that should have infused me was absent. They had asked before me if I had a death wish and it had been a resounding no until that day.

We faced the final two, who weren't looking nearly as cocky as they had when they were facing me down. With one swipe of his blades, Slate decapitated one and the other one scattered.

"Scarlett!" he growled as I turned to chase down the second one.

The trees were a blur as I whizzed past them and after the final Minotaur. It turned to make a last stand, seeing as he wouldn't be able to outrun us. I grit my teeth as he launched up off my feet, and I yanked my pack over my head, letting it drop.

Slate lifted me as one might a doll and boosted me forward as my knives flashed. I grit my teeth, feeling like a human rocket. With the momentum of my body, I drove my blades into its skull. I watched my blades burst through its bone and flesh to explode out its scalp.

It fell back, pulling me with it.

I huffed as I got to my feet and put my foot against its face, pulling my blade with a sick sucking sound.

I panted; my blood was pounding through my veins as I looked around for more. Slate and I were the only ones left.

We looked at each other, our chests heaving. He had countless wounds on his torso and his arms. His charcoal shirt was a second skin wet with blood. I wondered if I looked as grisly.

My mind had fled me, my only thoughts were to kill and now that it was over...

I looked Slate over and I could see the same look reflected on me. I felt it through the bond. We charged towards each other. I retracted my blades as I leapt into his arms and we collided. I wrapped my legs around his waist, kissing him like a woman who had been drowning and he was my air.

Mine. All mine.

Mine forever.

Mine for all time.

Our kisses were frenzied. My mouth opened as far as it will go as he slid his tongue into it. We fell to the crispy leaf covered ground with a grunt and he tore off my clothes with his blades. My blood made my body thrum, my nerves were alive and raw. The bond ricocheting our lust off one another until it was all-consuming and the only thing I could think of was having him inside me, filling me. I brimmed with need and the want to release.

We were both panting when he ripped my underwear off. Scraps of the fabric clung to my legs as I spread my thighs for him. Dirt and leaves stuck to my hair. All that my mind registered was Slate and his body and my need.

I pulled his face down to mine as I guided him into me and gasped.

"Ah!" I cried as he plunged into me.

Waves of pleasure crashed over me. I was sinking into him; his pleasure was my pleasure, and it was exquisite. I scratched at his charcoal shirt as he drove into me again and again. My head thrown back as I moaned, matching his thrusts.

The sweet ache built until I was drowning in it. I screamed as I clenched around him with embarrassing swiftness. The rapture crashing through me in a burst that made my ears burn and my toes tingle threatened to render me incoherent for the rest of my days.

Slate howled when he shuddered into me. My body is limp beneath him. My eyes had slid closed, and I was ready for a nap.

The pent-up sexual frustration with the rush of the fight. It'd been six months since that bathroom stall in the prep room. I was high on blood lust and, *well*, lust and now I was coming down hard.

Did I just have sex next to a dead body with a married man?

Better to save that for later.

My brain had put up a sign that read *Sorry, we're closed.*

Slate was kissing along my neck and pulling on my nipples with his teeth. I opened my eyes and looked at him.

Slate in all his bloody bronze glory.

"Torch," he purred if Slate was the kind of guy who purred.

"Shh," I said, resting my head back in the dirt.

He chuckled and got to his feet. I groaned as he pulled me to mine and I bounced into his chest.

"We have to get to the Centaur tonight. I do not want to risk camping out here if there are more around."

I nodded against his chest. We had to let someone know there were Minotaur in the woods of Mabon. I doubted this was the only group. What had they been waiting two weeks for? We should have taken a prisoner to question.

I looked down at myself and started. My cloak was still on — we had ripped the rest of my clothes from my body. I had scratches all over my skin from where Slate had gotten a bit carried away. Someone wounded Slate as well, and blood was drying on his visible skin. He reached up and removed the nix torque from around my neck.

I ran my hands over my face and they came away bloody. Or maybe they were already bloody, and I just made my face bloody?

Slate took my hand and grabbed the pack I'd dropped before I flew through the air, impaling the Minotaur. I walked behind him, appreciating the view, since processing what had just happened was not on the agenda. Walking nearly naked through the woods was not what I had planned to do today either, though, so I guessed there was a first time for everything.

A river ran a little way away from the mouth of the cave. They had probably camped there, so they would have fresh water. It wasn't very wide, but it looked deep. I took off my cloak and kicked off my boots while I unbuckled my blades.

Slate was already in the river getting the blood out of his hair when I reached him. He was magnificent, his sculpted chest shown above the water as his long hair dripped water down his face.

He was glowing. I was in awe of him.

I dunked myself and washed my hair under the water, trying not to stare at him. It'd been a long time since I'd seen him that way and it made my heart hurt. He could feel that.

The cold water refreshed my memory. I remembered why I always wiggled my way out of it. Suddenly, I felt like an idiot. Sex only muddled everything. Sex with Slate turned me into putty for him to mold. I scrubbed my skin with my nails as Slate floated over to me.

"Having regrets?" He looked amused, but I felt the nervousness in my head.

Him nervous? I scoffed internally.

He had nothing to be nervous about. He was a God among men and shouldn't even exist on our planet. Some artist rendered what sex, darkness, and prowess had created, and Slate broke from the mold.

"I just had sex with my married ex-lover drenched in blood a dozen feet away from a dead body. My mother's life wasn't example enough. I need to destroy my life in exactly the same way for myself," I said, ducking in the water so my breasts hid.

"You are my wife. We will sort out the rest when I get back," he said somberly as he placed his hand on me and healed me. I returned the favor.

"You don't get to pick who is your wife for the moment. We're not interchangeable. If one isn't up to par, you can't switch her out for a new one," I said caustically, running my hands over my wet hair.

"*You* pushed for this. I never wanted you to leave. I begged you to stay, not to run. You had no faith!" Slate rose in the water to shout at me.

"Don't you think I realize that? I could have avoided all the pain I put myself through and been with you this entire time! I might've been carrying your child even *now* if I had stayed. You don't think it's eaten away at me for the last couple months? I thought I was being noble, putting your needs before my own. It turns out that I really *am* a neurotic little rabbit! I gave up everything for no reason!" I shouted back at him, slapping the surface of the river. "My greatest regret is letting something so amazing slide right through my fingers instead of holding on for all I was worth!" I curled my fingers as if I could still hold on to what we were.

Water ran in rivers down his body, his wavy hair curled when wet. He hadn't put his beads in yet, and it clung to his hard pecs and back.

"Amber has to go," Slate rumbled, and I shook my head with irritation.

"Everyone told you not to choose that girl. Did you have to get engaged so soon?" I regretted my words as soon as I said them.

Slate roared in frustration, his neck cording, fists slammed into the water. "You..." He pointed at me. "You told me not to sacrifice for nothing. I was doing as you bade me! I will not stay with her, Scarlett."

"I was wrong! Is that what you want to hear? I was wrong about all of it! You were right. I had no faith. I rushed into it. What else do you want me to say?" I shouted, getting to my feet, so the river ended just below my chest.

"How much longer do you think I have to live? My fate grows close. You are my mate. Our paths are the same. We are meant to travel this road together," he said, coming closer.

"I won't watch you die!" I screamed and turned to the shore.

My eyes widened, and I covered my chest with a hand, but Slate charged forward and stood before me, blocking me with his body as we pulled clothes from our packs. I didn't bother with undergarments. I needed something to cover me — pronto.

One Centaur stamped its hooves. "No need to dress on my account, Scarlett."

He was what I thought mermaids would look like, with his long golden blonde hair that fell to his waist and stunning blue eyes and tanned skin, muscled from everyday activities.

"Lewt. I'm glad it's you. This is my... Slate. You might remember him from the last time I was here." I walked over to Lewt and he scooped me up like a baby and gave me a hug.

A low growl announced Slate's displeasure, and I smiled internally. "He's probably angry he forgot to piss around you." Lewt chuckled and set me down on my feet easily.

Lewt had arrived with nine other Centaurs. We had given them a pretty magnificent show.

Slate stalked behind me, fully dressed now. "I have been expecting you."

"You're Lera's contact?" I asked. It was a small world.

"Yes, we came here to clean out this den and saw they had done it for us." He gave me a look that asked, *you two?* I nodded.

"It would seem the only thing left to do then would be to bring you back to the village," Lewt said with a curl of his pink lips.

"That's exactly where we were headed," I said, and walked over to my roll to collect my pack.

So ten Centaur saw us shouting naked in a river like a couple of heathens. I could feel his bunch of angry emotions like a knot in my mind that I had distracted him enough not to see them approach. I slung my pack over my shoulders and raised my brow to Slate, who glowered.

"It'd be faster if we rode," I said, and he narrowed his eyes and slid them to Lewt.

"I have legs to walk on. I will meet you there," he growled.

"Don't be difficult. You have a wife to get back to and I have a new job to find. I don't want to waste any time."

Slate leveled his eyes at me. "I am not going back without you."

Lewt trotted forward expectantly, and I reached up as he slung me around to his back effortlessly. I leaned forward and wrapped my arms around his male torso as I tried not to squeeze too hard with my thighs, just like riding a bike.

Slate growled in his throat.

"Jealous man?" Lewt asked, looking over his shoulder.

"Possessive. But the feeling isn't exclusive," I said with a wry smile.

Lewt chuckled and started forward and I squeezed around him so I wouldn't fall off, not like a bike at all.

The other Centaur surged forward with us and soon we were galloping through the woods, whatever path that would have led us there forgotten as the hoof falls fell all around me like thunder. I rode on Lewt's Palomino back and gazed out at the other Centaur and realized I knew a few of them.

Hute, the black-haired stallion that Indigo had rode galloped on Lewt's right-hand side while Fert, the only female Centaur I'd seen until now, was just behind us, her long brown hair flowing free in the wind, a tiny scrap of fabric covered her human chest. Even Goep was there with his thick Clydesdale body and flowing chocolate mane. Tawny had had a blast riding him last year.

There was no way *not* to make that sound dirty.

Pressing my cheek to Lewt's back, we zipped through the woods. I forgot how thrilling riding with them was, but exhausted. It took all of my energy just to hold on. We didn't speak as he hurtled through the trees. He might hear me, but I wouldn't be able to hear him with the wind beating at my ears and the thunder from their hooves falls.

The ride would make up a lot of time. If we could find Karkinos first thing, then we should make it back home in less than two days. Slate would be back with his public wife in less than a week. The thought made me bury my face in Lewt's back, pretending the tears were from the wind.

What we would have to do when we reached Mabon's town went through my mind. We would have to report what we found, including the women's bodies, so their families could have a little closure. I wondered how many other camps hid in the woods.

TWENTY-TWO

Hours after night had fallen, we arrived at the Centaur village. Torches lit the small wood homes and a few humans milled about around the little cabins. There were only a handful of Centaurs, most of which were entering the village as we were. I knit my brow; I didn't think humans lived with the Centaur.

We reached the outskirts of the village, and Lewt swung me over his shoulder. My feet hit the leave covered ground, and I smiled at him gratefully. I was also grateful to be off his back. My fanny pack was killing me. Lewt arched an eyebrow at me and I gaped as his horse half merely shrunk into his back as he grew shorter, his front legs turning into thickly muscled men's legs.

The Centaurs could transform into humans, and he had very human parts.

I averted my eyes, finding the night sky very interesting for the moment. Someone behind me removed my pack, and I turned. Slate had apparently deemed their nudity as a sign that it was acceptable. I widened my eyes at him and his lips curled as he pulled on his pants. I caught Fert and the other female Centaurs admiring his firm backside, and I scowled at him.

"Why are you naked?" I hissed. "How did you get here so fast?"

His smirk only broadened into a smile. I turned to Lewt and looked towards the sky again.

"Is this your clan?" I asked.

"Yes, the five clans split up the hillside, but close enough to walk to as a human. We do not show Guardians this side of ourselves." He gestured to Slate with a nod, who was pulling on pants at the moment. "We can keep your secret if you can keep ours." Lewt said, and my eyes flitted from the sky to his. I saw respect there.

There were crates set up alongside the entrance to the town. The Centaurs grabbed clothing as they made their way in. They handed out simple rough-hewn trousers and long tunics with moccasin type slippers. Everything was adjustable to accommodate the varying sizes of their frames. There were separate crates for women. I glared at Slate, daring him to look at the naked women as they rummaged through the crates, pulling out either a more fitted version of the men's clothing or long sleeve shift dresses of the same fabric.

A dressed Lewt approached and waved us forward. "You can stay in our guest house. We knew you were coming, so it is prepared for one," he explained with much too much glitter in his eyes.

"Thank you," Slate rumbled next to me.

"Why bother changing into humans at all? Why not stay Centaurs?" I asked, finally succumbing to my curiosity.

"Space. Our other form takes up a lot more space. The homes would have to be larger. This way we conserve our forests instead of tearing it down to make more room for ourselves." Lewt explained and led us to a small cabin.

Only the necessities. Small bed, a little square table with two unpolished seats, a washbasin, and a little round mirror that hung on the wall. Oh, and a chamber pot. I hated chamber pots. The bed was long, but narrow and the only way we'd both fit on it together was if I laid over Slate. The sweaty Scarlett blanket special coming right up.

I put my pack down on the table and lit the candle that rested atop it, then thanked Lewt, who gave me a bright smile. "At first light, we will take you to the shore. Karkinos was still there as of this morning. We have stew left over from dinner; I will have someone bring over two bowls."

"I will collect them," Slate said as he followed Lewt out.

I frowned. Why wasn't I privy to the man talk?

I peeled off my pants to find the inside of my thighs a little red from chafing against Lewt's sides. I poked my head out of the cabin and found Fert walking with the other females, bowls of stew in hand.

"Fert!" I called out, hiding my lower half behind the thin door.

Fert turned and strode over to me, dipping her bread into the stew. "Guardian. How may I be of service?"

There was that air of being a dominant female among animals that made her just a little haughty and challenging, but I ignored it.

"Do you have anything for abrasions?" I whispered, but the women behind her tittered.

Fert looked overwhelmingly amused, but didn't laugh. "Yes. I shall send it right over."

"Thank you," I breathed, relieved.

I had planned on sleeping in my clothes, but since Slate had torn apart my only other change of clothes, I had to settle for my shirt, panties, and a pair of fluffy socks I'd brought. Sometimes, it was the little things.

A tween girl brought over a jar of ointment, which I thanked her for and carried the jar over to the bed. I laid down and looked down at my red inner thighs and noticed it climbed higher, probably on my backside too. I sighed; we were going to do a lot of riding tomorrow. I hoped the ointment worked magic because I was going to need it. The idea of asking Slate for healing my sore fanny pack was mortifying.

All that constant chafing for hours had rubbed my skin until it stung. I should have worn better pants; my cloak would work for the ride tomorrow to ease the sting. I hoped that would work. I took the top off the jar. It smelled lemony and cool.

The door swung open and Slate filled the doorway, stew in hand. He gave me a quizzical look and closed the door behind him with his heel before setting the stew on the table.

"What are you doing?" he asked, fighting a smile.

I had closed my legs and sat up, looking guilty.

"Nothing. All that riding..." I trailed off and tried not to appear mortified.

Slate laughed, and it was delicious — making him smile that rare smile that creased his cheek. Warmth bloomed in my stomach at the sight of his joy, even if it was my expense. I pouted and got to my feet.

He raised his hand to heal me, and I jumped back. He leveled his eyes at me, and I nodded. His warmth filled me and I knew he was delving as he healed. He shut his eyes and sighed.

"Still whole?"

"A fertile womb, Torch," he replied, and my cheeks heated.

I skirted his body and sat bare bottomed on the wood chair. The stew smelled like potatoes and tomatoes with beef, veggies poked up from the thick orange brew, and I ate greedily, sopping it up with my bread.

"Hungry?" Slate asked, sitting in the chair cross from me.

He looked like a grown man in a child's chair. His presence filled the tiny cottage, his electricity charging the air.

"Famished. There was a distraction during lunch," I said dryly as I finished my stew.

He had brought in two mugs filled with some sort of hot tea; I guzzled it down with my supper.

I crossed to the washbasin and filled it with water before splashing my face and attempted to rub my teeth clean with a finger. I looked at myself in the mirror. My hair was a tangled mess. Tomorrow I'd braid it. I finger combed through it and turned around to find Slate already in bed. His clothes were neatly thrown over the back of the chair. I took a quick inventory of the items and my cheeks flushed.

"I never tire of seeing you blush," he said in a low sensuous growl I felt in my toes that only made me blush deeper. "Come here."

Our bond was still active, but I didn't need it to decipher the look in his eyes. With those two words and those beckoning eyes, I was pliable in his capable hands. I stood in front of the stuffed mattress with its knitted blankets.

"Just because we did earlier doesn't mean I will again. It was a momentary lapse in judgement. Nothing has changed," I said stupidly, and he quirked a dark eyebrow. "You know what I mean." I climbed into bed.

Everything had changed. We could have been together if my doctor's appointment was just a few days before. I stopped protesting.

We fit if he laid on his side against the wall. Slate shifted his body, so he leaned over me. He smoothly crossed over my leg and pulled my body to the center of the narrow mattress. I narrowed my eyes at him and he held up the jar and smiled, the hard planes of his face softening just a little.

"I'm already healed."

"This will prevent more chafing."

It could have been a lie. With no knowledge about rashes or balms, I was at his mercy.

His hands slid up the sides of my thighs until he reached for my magenta boy shorts. He hooked his fingers into them and pulled them lower, slowly, as the pads of his fingers caressed my skin. He bent my legs as one into the air, pulling them off my feet from where he kneeled. They dropped to the floor, and he parted my thighs to either side of him. My skin prickled.

He was making a pretty good argument to accept his care.

Slate scooped out the lemony ointment from the jar and pressed his finger to my inner thigh, lathering it on. I reached my hand over and untied the leather strap from his hair, letting it fall in glossy waves to the side of his shoulder.

How did he make rashes sexy? That shouldn't have been possible.

Slate finished putting it on my thighs and crawled up me until his face was even with mine, his weight supported on his extended arm. I felt him hard below my belly button.

"I do not think you will need this," he said as he untied the lacing of my shirt. He leaned me forward and pulled it over my head.

My hair fell around me in a cascade of light golden-brown waves. The candlelight flickered, casting our shadows on the wall, its pumpkin scent mingled with the smell of fall that hung heavy through Mabon.

My hands went to my chest, and he pushed them softly away as he kissed my breasts, sucking gently on their peaks as he made his way up my throat. His breath was hot and heavy on my skin. I turned my head to kiss him. *Ugh,* I loved this man. His chest was hard beneath my fingers, silk over steel. I ran my fingers over the crease between his pecs and down his bronze abs, down to below his belt line.

He stopped me and broke our kiss. "Not yet." He breathed. "I have not finished with you."

I squirmed beneath him as he fell back on his heels. He stood erect, long, thick and hard in his lap and my mind turned to mashed potatoes.

"Turn over." He commanded, and I obeyed, his powerful hands guiding me, which was good since my legs had a slight tremble to them.

I laid on my stomach with my head on my crossed arms as he ran his hands over my shoulders and down my spine and I got the feeling he was memorizing the curves of my body. Every beauty mark, every single nuance. It caused me to shiver in delight.

Slate scooped more lemony ointment from the jar and ran his finger along the curve of my backside, his every move gentle and precise. A moan hummed in my throat and I felt Slate's will power crumble. He leaned forward, the weight of his chest curving with my spine as he tugged on my ear with his teeth.

"I will be gentle." He promised, and I moaned in ascent, I didn't care how I got him as long as I did.

He pulled my hips up, so I rested on my hands, my back arching, and he moaned before he was in me. Slate pushed my legs closed and slowly eased inside me, careful not to smack his hips against my ointment covered skin.

His love, passion, and his lust bubbled over into me; his pain was gone. I'd done that. He *seemed* lighter after a lifetime of secrets and hiding. Having the truth of himself out in the open must do that to a man.

Slate's movements were deep and slow inside me, the delicious tension building with his adagio rhythm. I was coming apart at the seams.

"Faster," I rasped.

"The balm…" he said in a low, grave tone.

"*Idon'tfuckingcare.*"

It came out in a rush and he moaned as his fingers gripped my hips tighter with one hand and grabbed my hair with the other, wrapping it around his wrist and pulling my head back so I was almost sitting in his lap. I felt his leg muscles tense and his skin slapped against me, holding me still as he drove into me, faster and harder.

I exploded around him, crying out his name.

"*Fuck*, Scarlett." He ground out as he held me tight against him, lifting my body as he rubbed his hips against my backside.

We collapsed in a heap on the bed, his body on top of mine, our bodies slick and sticky. I shifted underneath him and moved to the side so he could roll onto his back. He opened his arms so I could lie against him. I took a moment to appreciate the view.

His black hair fell across the pillow. His hard muscled body had more defined muscles than I knew numbers. Slate's face was relaxed, his long lashes almost touching his brow as his grey eyes peered out at me, the hard panes of his face free from tension. I crawled along the length of him and rested my chin on my hands as I gazed at him after I pulled the blankets over us.

A small smile played on his full lips. "What is it?"

"I rarely see you without all your fetishes." His hair was a glossy midnight hue that looked almost blue in the sunlight.

I leaned forward and pressed my lips to his and nuzzled my cheek to his jaw. He hadn't shaved it today, so there was already short blue/black hair poking through.

"I like it. I can't imagine not liking any way you looked."

"Are you flirting with me?" he growled, sending shivers through my weak body.

I reached up and ran my fingers over his face. He had high cheekbones and a straight masculine nose that had a small flat spot on the bridge. He had a chiseled jawline. His eyes framed in those thick, long black lashes that belonged to a prettier person, not the virile man beneath me.

"You feel better," I said, running my fingers over his lips.

"I do," Slate said gruffly and kissed my fingertips.

I leaned over him and rubbed my cheek against his eyelashes.

"What are you doing?" he asked as he blinked, making his lashes brush against my skin.

"Whatever I want. Hush now. Just let me be weird." If I was breaking all the rules, I'd do what I wanted.

He grabbed my waist and pushed me higher so my head pressed against the wall and my chest hovered in front of his mouth. He buried his face in my breasts.

"This is what I want," he teased.

He brought me back down to his chest. "I'm exhausted." I murmured as I rested my cheek against the ridges of his muscles.

"Sleep then, wife."

"I thought you were going to say wench." I murmured dreamily, and he chuckled.

"Wench as well. Sleep well, wench. I expect two helpings of this in the morning." He squeezed my backside.

He pushed my hair to the side as he stroked my back.

"Scarlett."

"Mm?"

"Do not scamper away. I am done chasing." He murmured, and I held my breath, grateful we deactivated our bond.

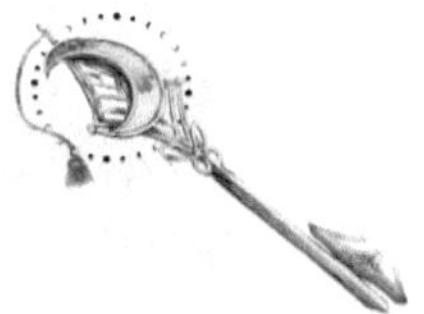

Slate got his first and second helpings of wench that morning.

Calling, I had done a quick rinse of my body and dried the floors. Slate watched with never ending amusement, but then he liked the heady smell of our sex on him. I liked it on him too, but *this* girl wanted to be fresh and clean. I couldn't disappear into the wild like he would do in the next hour.

I thanked the Gods that I remembered my deodorant as I swiped it on. I could do without a lot of things; toilet paper and deodorant are two things I never wanted to do without. I brought my own TP on this trip just in case. Sometimes, you had to think ahead.

He looked pleased as punch and perfectly sated as his eyes followed me around the small room. I was done getting ready, Slate was nowhere near it since he was still naked in bed, his arms folded behind his head, one long muscled leg stretched from under the blankets, when someone knocked on the door.

Slate made no move to cover up, so I opened the door to find Lewt, golden and stunning in the morning sunlight.

"*Um*, Slate will be just a minute." I explained awkwardly, but the cabin was small so Lewt could see Slate's bare leg through the crack I'd opened with the door.

The door swung open further, and I realized Slate was standing naked behind me. "Five minutes. We will meet you at your home," he said before closing the door, but not before I caught the quirk of Lewt's lips.

He knew exactly what we had been up to this morning. The aroma was in Slate's very skin. The cabin carried the scent, too. He walked away and pulled on his clothes on. I turned from the door to stare at him.

"I know what you're doing."

"What is that?" he asked, feigning innocence.

"Are you going to advertise our sexploits to every male who has ever been remotely interested in me?" I asked, crossing my arms.

He looked up at me from buttoning his pants, giving a rakish grin.

"Yes," he said as his teeth snapped back together, looking like the cat who caught the canary.

I narrowed my eyes at him. "Well, I guess I'll have to do my best to keep you from having much to talk about," I said, plopping down on the bed.

I didn't see him move. He was on me, pushing me back into the mattress, his hands sliding over my chest. His lips curled at the knowing effect our skin touching had on me.

"You think you will be able to withhold it now?"

His smile deepened as he pressed his hips into mine. Freya's burly boar! The things this man's body did to mine should be illegal. I was going to look into that.

I didn't want to fight. We could argue until we were blue in the face later. We'd made our bed, now we had to lie in it and deal with the consequences.

He lifted himself off me, pulling me up as well. His face was suddenly grave, making butterflies beat in my stomach.

"Do not sleep with Brass again." His gunmetal eyes bore into me and my cheeks heated.

I dropped my eyes and busied myself with straightening the room.

"I need to hear you say it," he whispered.

I walked over to him and wrapped my arms around his waist, the blades of his belts crossing his chest hard against my arms. "Slate..." I cooed. His hand rested atop mine. "I'm still in love with you."

He turned in my arms, so I craned my neck to gaze up at him. His expression was wary as he asked. "Is it that hard to give up?"

I cocked my head and gave him a small, rueful smile. "One thing I know for certain is that when we are together, I don't want another man's bed."

He kissed the top of my head.

We both knew I hadn't said the words. I wouldn't make promises I didn't know if I could keep.

I packed away the rest of my things and Slate walked us over to Lewt's cabin. Lewt was there waiting for us at a long table that could seat ten people. It was plain roughhewn, like everything else here. They lived simply and as close to nature as possible.

Lewt's cabin was easily the largest in the village. Being a clan leader, he most likely had it for meetings and such. He didn't seem like the type to value material things. He beamed a smile our way as he stood, and I smiled back before we reached the table. We sat and an attractive blonde woman brought three bowls of porridge with pieces of apple out.

Slate acknowledged her with a nod and his eyes swung to Lewt. "Rest well?" He asked with an irritating glint in his eyes.

"Very. Thank you for your hospitality." Slate said with a delicious curve of his lips.

This was a stupid game.

"Will we be leaving after we eat? I hope I can ask you for a favor. I know you've done so much already."

"Yes, we shall. Anything for you, Scarlett."

I couldn't tell if men always taunted one another, or if it was something to do with the animal in the men I knew.

I spoke before Slate could insert something inappropriate or cut to the chase and whip it out and pee on me. That would not be cool.

"I could really use a ride back to Mabon's town center. We have to alert the local Guardians to what happened and get those women's bodies back to their families."

I'd see those bodies in my nightmares for years to come.

"Of course. Will you need a ride, Slate, or will Scarlett be the only one to ride me?" Lewt asked, humor etched on his mouth.

I pinched my lips, wondering how Slate was going to react to that.

Slate surprised me by laughing. "I think Scarlett will be the only one on the back of one of your pony boys."

"Too fast for you?" Lewt asked, grinning.

Slate scoffed, and I felt like I'd missed something. "We shall see." Slate raised his eyebrows at Lewt.

Oh, fun. I'll be stuck on Lewt's back while these two have their pissing contest.

Nope.

"I don't mean to be indelicate, but should I catch a ride from someone else if you two are racing? Maybe Goep?" I asked, finishing my porridge.

The Clydesdale looked built for a steady trot, not a breakneck speed racer.

"No." They both said at the same time.

Yikes, okay. This was something beyond me, undoubtedly testosterone driven.

We reached the shore within in an hour. Slate won the race, but I judged it unfair since Lewt had to carry all of my extra weight. That pleased Lewt immensely, while Slate's expression was sour. I did not know how he got everywhere so quickly… him and his secrets.

Karkinos was right where it was yesterday. I could see only the tops of the dark jagged towers from the shore, but it was what I was the day of my father's funeral. Slate's face was smooth. It was bad.

"It's been here how long?" I asked.

"Just under a week. We have seen it here in that exact spot before," Lewt said, a grimace marring his golden tanned face.

I stood on the shore, my hand blocking the sun next to a naked Slate and Lewt, Hute, and Goep in Centaur form. I had to warn the others.

"Let's head back. Lewt, we should talk."

Lewt nodded, sensing my resignation.

He scooped me up, and I slung my arm around his neck. I ignored Slate's frustrated look before he disappeared. We started back towards Mabon.

On the way, I explained what happened with the Wemic and the Jorogumo. I urged him to unit their clans just in case. The village could not withstand a herd of Minotaur raiding it in the middle of the night. Everything would burn to the ground.

Lewt looked grim while we walked, but not shocked. He carried me in his arms for hours even while he galloped. My thighs thanked him. I still ended up riding for six straight hours until we reached Mabon. I sat on my cloak, but after so long, it didn't matter.

I gave Lewt a hug and promised to visit again under better circumstances and waved to Hute and Goep. Hute asked after Indigo so I tried to let him down easy for her. The black-haired stallion took it well. Slate reappeared and said his goodbyes to the Centaurs.

"Are you coming into the castle with me?" I asked Slate.

"Why wouldn't I?" he asked, furrowing his brow.

"Just a question," I said, rolling my eyes.

We were walking along the path when Brass sprung up in my mind. I put my arm out.

"Slate, Brass is here," I said anxiously and turned to him, wide eyed.

A muscle leapt in his jaw. "Your *bond* with him?"

"We have only used it once, the night I left. It activated when I fought Mirage a second time. Never *ever* were we to use it again. Something is wrong," I said, feeling my panic rise.

Slate cursed as he saw him heading straight towards us. Slate cursed.

"What is it?" I asked, trying not to wring my hands.

"Amber." He cursed again. "When we fought the Minotaurs, it bloodied our hands."

My heart lurched, and I covered my mouth. "Oh Gods, Slate! They know!" Slate walked towards me and I held out my palms. "Stop, just go. They are probably together. Do you realize what we did to them?"

Brass would have felt everything I felt.

"Do not scamper, Rabbit."

There was an edge to his voice that never used to be there when he spoke to me. It sounded like desperation.

"Please. Don't let them see us together. Go. I'll take care of the Haust." Against my better judgement, I closed the distance between us and kissed him deeply, "I love you, Slate." I breathed before I took off at a run, knowing he would easily catch me if he tried.

I started towards the imposing shadow of grey stone that housed the great family that ran all of Mabon, Brass and Slate's biological family.

Were they the ones who wanted to harm Slate?

I'd have to ask another day; one look behind me to where Slate had stood on the other side of the grey stone bridge told me he had taken off as soon as I started moving.

Something about that hurt.

My thighs chafed something fierce as well as my fanny pack as I walked uncomfortably to the castle. I should have had him heal me before we went our separate ways. In the dark, the castle looked unwelcoming and foreboding. Its drawbridge was down, so I could cross its murky moat. Moonlight shone through its parapets along the flat roof slit for archers.

I shivered and took a deep breath; crisp autumn air filled my lungs, fortifying me.

Slate. How could I be so oblivious to the most obvious things?

Guardians detailed to the Haust house wore deep chocolate-colored cloaks trimmed in gold with a gold jumis embroidered on the back. The barbican of the castle was empty except for the guards. It looked like it was used to marital troops.

The Guardians saw me approach, and I tried not to walk bowlegged and raised my chin in an attempt to look like I knew what I was about. "My name is Scarlett Tio. I need to speak with the Haust. It is a matter of grave importance," I said. "I'd like an escort."

The Guardians gave me a once over and did a silent communication before one of them waved an arm at me without speaking and led me through the studded heavy wood double doors.

Now *that* was a castle.

I traveled back in time to when a Grand Inquisitor questioned witches. The castle was a blend of high cathedral stonework and old-world wood crafted trim. One thing was certain, whoever designed the great families' homes way back when he had a certain view for each island and really stuck to it, nothing was half done. If a king descended the stone stairs in a red robe trimmed in snow leopard fur, I'd say, 'Greetings, your highness' and give him my best curtsey without a second thought.

They spread fringed rugs across the stone floors, with rugs even covering the stairs. I felt bad for their staff, or servants. They probably had servants.

The Guardian led me to a first floor sitting room. I passed under the cathedral's arched doorway and took a seat on a high-backed brown leather chair.

Like everything else in the castle, even the furnishings had an old world feel to them. The chandelier was a ring hanging from chains to the ceiling, lights resembling candles lit the dark room. I kept feeling like dust should cover everything, but there wasn't a speck to be found. Now I was *really* feeling bad for their cleaning lady.

The door opened, and I got to my feet. Peak Haust entered the room with Sterling, Quartz, Ash, and Diamond. Ash started leaning forward in his seat before recovering, and I pasted a smile on my face. Peak had an identical one, his light green eyes observing me. I wished I had something cleaner to wear.

"Miss Tio. Please sit. You are not one I would expect to grace these rooms. Did you not leave Tidings some time ago?" Peak said, gesturing to the seat behind me.

I sat and tried not to wince when my skin touched the stiff upholstery too quickly. "I did."

They sat in the surrounding chairs. Diamond looked decidedly ashamed, probably about her best friend being with my husband, but so did Sterling. He wouldn't meet my eyes. While in contrast his sister Quartz, the blonde beauty, had a smug smile on her lips, her eyes sparkled. Ash's handheld hers and I tried to ignore them.

"To what do we owe this unexpected visit? Would you like some tea?" Peak asked.

Now that I knew Peak was Slate's uncle, I could see the resemblance, the same bronze skin, the same glossy midnight hair. Peak's had more curl to it, but his eyes had thickly framed dark lashes too. I could see Brass's resemblance too; I thought, feeling disgusted with myself and Tidings's inbreeding.

"No, thank you. I am in a hurry. While traveling through your woods, I was attacked by Minotaur. A camp of them, to be exact. Mutilated human bodies were with them. I dispatched them, but I believe there may be more and that your people may be under attack."

Peak also shared the same long, dark lashes Slate had. "Dispatched? Where was the camp?"

I filled him in on the details. "I wasn't alone, otherwise I would not be here today."

"Who were you with? Your fiancée?" Ash asked. I really didn't like the smugness in his tone.

"Another Guardian. He went ahead to Thrimilci to inform my family."

"Miss Tio, while I appreciate your tenacity, I see no reason to call in the calvary. It was an isolated incident. I will have the bodies reclaimed and we will investigate the event. How do you suppose twenty Minotaur arrived on my island unnoticed?" Peak ran long fingers along the silver that streaked through his black hair.

"There was a portal gate. I destroyed it."

Quartz snorted and flipped her long honey blonde hair. "*You* destroyed a portal gate?"

I narrowed my eyes. "I did."

Sterling's violet eyes flickered to his father. Why did he look so anxious?

"Interesting. Well, thank you for informing us. I am sure you could understand our preoccupation during this delicate time," Peak said, picking invisible lint off his knee.

"Delicate time?" I asked, confused.

"Planning my heir's wedding and my daughter's." Peak gestured to the surrounding couples.

Poor Indigo. I knew all too well the pain of watching the man you love marry another woman.

"I've taken up enough of your time. I'm sorry about the late hour."

I crossed the room and shook Peak's hand, surprise crossing his features so quickly I thought I'd imagined it. His nostrils flared and his eyes seemed to brighten, but then it was gone.

I inclined my head to the others and left the room. "I shall walk her out," Sterling said and hurried after me.

Once we were a safe distance away, Sterling pulled me into another room.

I crossed my arms and looked at him as he hit the energy plate for lighting, a trickle of his *call* to lightning providing enough to light the room for as long as he needed. We were in an enormous library with beautifully crafted shelves that stretched from floor to ceiling all the way around the room, a librarian's wet dream. They must have been collecting books for centuries. The painted ceiling depicted the tree people, leshys with humans, creating the first Guardians.

Sterling's boyishly handsome face looked anxious. "Indigo knows I must go through with this marriage."

"No sugarfoot, Sherlock," I snapped.

"Sherlock?"

"Forget it."

Sterling sighed; his dark eyebrows drawn down over his violet eyes. "It is politics. I love Indigo, but my family does not approve of yours and my mother is Willow Natt, Delta Natt's sister. There is no way they would have let me marry her."

I knew who his mother was and her relation to my stepmother. "But she was good enough to sleep with all these years?"

"My father arranged it with her mother." He let out a long breath.

"You should have stopped it as soon as you started sleeping with Diamond."

I understood why he didn't. I could see in his eyes he loved Indigo; it just wasn't enough. He was right, of course, his family would never allow it and if he did it anyway, he risked becoming like Jett, having to live away from the land that was rightfully his. Indigo would do it for him, though.

"I know. I really love her," he said, his voice breaking at the last word.

He must have been having a seriously off kilter day for him to be speaking so much to me and about such personal business. Sterling and I had hardly ever spoken when things were good. Things were hardly good and if I had to guess, he was feeling overwhelmed about their current wedding planning.

"If I catch you trying to sneak around with her and ruin her reputation *and* her chance at getting over you, I'll hunt you down, Sterling. I think you're a good guy, but don't cross my loved ones. I don't want bad blood between us."

"You may not always feel that way Scarlett, I have not always been a good man. I try every day to make up for it," he said cryptically.

Sterling stood in the center of the room, looking lost. I almost felt bad for him. I could have been him if Ash had got his way and we married, no love between us. He may have lusted after me, I may have even done it myself a time or two prior to our breakup, but that would never turn into love. Slate was living what Sterling would go through. Misery.

Looking at Sterling, I saw my father and my heart broke for him, too. "Good luck, Sterling. I mean that. Sometimes, though, all the money and power in the world can't bring you happiness."

Although he'd torn out Indigo's heart and stomped on it, I crossed the room and embraced him. It wasn't pity; it was empathy and even though I'd startled him at first; he seemed to understand and his stance loosened.

"Your friends kind of suck, so if you need to bend someone's ear in private, come find me."

It was the only solace I could offer him.

He would lose Indigo; I would do my best to keep her away from him myself.

TWENTY-THREE

It was raining when I left the Haust castle. I pulled my mother's cloak out; bits of blood and mud crusted over it, but I put it on anyway and pulled the hood up, feeling downtrodden.

With the wight my parents had turned into and their warning, along with the threat of the Minotaurs raiding the Centaur village, I was feeling beyond overwhelmed and, of course, there was Slate.

Every inch of me was aching and tired, and the rain soaked me to the bone. When I found Brass waiting for me under one of the larger stone bridges, I climbed down the hill and met him where the stream ran under it.

He stood with the sheets of rain pouring down around him, his amber eyes hard. I reached for his hand and he drew back.

"You are better than this." I pulled my lips between my teeth and waited for him to continue. "Is your happiness more important than hers?" he asked softly, and I found it hard to meet his gaze.

"Did she know it was me?" I whispered, looking up at him through my lashes that a drizzle had caught on.

"No. She only knew he was sleeping with someone. She came to the Sumar palace and asked for help to find him. I was looking for you. I was not sure what island you were on. She was with me when Slate met us near the gate. Amber was extremely upset."

"Brass, under normal circumstances, I never would have done this," I said in a measured tone.

"*Please,* tell me what justifies it in your mind."

Lightning flashed, and Brass's amber eyes looked unusually hard. I took a step forward and held out my right hand for his. He offered it and I placed it on my stomach.

"Delve." I whispered, and I felt his warmth flood through me.

Brass shut his eyes and some of the anger faded. "I am sorry, Scarlett."

"I'm sorry, Brass. I didn't think yesterday —"

"And this morning," Brass said, pressing his lips into a firm line, and I dropped my eyes and nodded.

"I hope you weren't doing anything, *um*, that would have —"

"Made *coming* awkward?" Brass offered with a dry smile.

I winced. "Yes."

Brass blew out a breath and wiped the drizzle from his face. "I was eating lunch for the first time. It happened so fast Ama stared at me across the table. Food fell out of her mouth. I would say that was awkward. Last night, I was alone in bed. I knew it was you and I thought you would seek me out. Then I realized you did not know it was active. I believe you would not have done it if you had known."

I wiped the water that trickled down my face. "I wouldn't have, I promise. Are you cold?" I asked, noticing his dark honey cheeks were red.

"Yes, but I have never felt what you felt for me like this. I read it in your mind. This is different. I can *feel* you." Brass watched me and I couldn't stop the butterflies in my stomach.

"We can deactivate it. I need to go home to Chicago, anyway. I knew this... bubble would burst. Honestly, I'm surprised he left so easily," I said, shaking out my hood.

Brass averted his eyes, but I could feel him as he could feel me. He hadn't told me everything.

"You're the only one who doesn't lie to me. You always tell me the truth, even if I don't want to hear it." I pleaded, stepping closer, so it forced him to look at me.

"Amber found out she was pregnant today. She told him when —"

My head swam. The last thing I remembered was my body jerking when Brass caught me. The rain poured cool on my face and lightning flashed as I looked up at the bottom of the bridge.

"That is why I will come with."

Brass and I had sat arguing in my rental car for the last hour since I came to. He'd taken off my damp clothes and laid me down in the back seat until I came around. He'd changed into Slate's American clothing, which I found disconcerting. The pants were a little long, but otherwise they fit him. A leather strap pulled his hair back at his nape as he sat next to me in the passenger seat.

"I'll be fine," I lied.

"Hi. I am a mind reader. Brass Regn, remember?"

I scowled at him. "Sarcasm doesn't suit you."

Brass leaned his head back against the headrest and groaned. "You are being difficult. I know you are not working, Chris, and you are no longer an item, and until Slate came to see you, you had not showered in days."

I held up my fingers. "Two! Two days. Everyone is a critic." Brass turned to me, placing his hands on the center console.

"If you are well in two nights, I will leave. I swear it."

I sighed, "Two nights. If I'm showering, eating, and a functioning adult, you'll go? No hassle?"

"No hassle," Brass agreed.

I turned the key in the ignition and started towards T. F. Green Airport.

CHAPTER 24
JETT

To: Jett Var JettSetter@VallaU.com

Chris and I broke up shortly after the Midsummer festival. I deleted the blog; we centered it on us both and since there's no us, it makes little sense to keep it. I regretted that decision, so I revamped it. Sorry it took me so long to reply. Things have been hectic. They featured the original magazine Chris, and I in contacted me when they found out I stopped blogging and asked if I wanted to write regular articles for them. I accepted; I work mostly from home.

BTW Brass is here. Yup. No joke. If you check out the blog, he's in it alive and well. Tell Quick to keep his panties on. What started out as two days has turned into a week, we'll see when he decides it's safe to leave. Don't ask. Could you please let Quick and the other Regn know he has taken up cuddling with Tree on my couch? They are welcome to come collect him. He eats everything and forces me to workout every day. Thanks.

I hope everyone is well. Send Gigi my love, give her extra snuggles for me.

Scar

P.S. I already know about Amber. Send them my best wishes.
P.P.S. Minotaur in Mabon — Whhaaa?

Jett frowned at the screen. That answered *that* question. Quick paced behind him at the computer and Slate leaned back in his seat next to him.

"Not even a note? He did not activate his bond, so I would know where he was, nothing. He shacked up with Scarlett? This whole time? It has been a week!" Quick growled in frustration.

Jett couldn't blame him. It aggravated Quick that Brass hadn't come back after he left with Amber to find Slate. Then Amber had revealed that she was pregnant.

It was bittersweet. Jett was happy Slate would be a father, but it was with the wrong woman. Brass must have told Scarlett, that was probably why he had stayed after they had asked him to go check on her. Now Scarlett wouldn't come to visit, not until the baby was born and maybe not even then. Jett didn't want to have been Brass when he'd told her.

"They're not shacked up. We asked him to check in on her. I know Scar, she sounds irritated that he is hounding her, not like a person who is lazing about in paradise. You know your brother better than that," Jett said, pulling up the blog.

"Let me see it," Slate said, putting his forearm on the back of Jett's chair.

Jett withheld a grimace and hit enter. Quick hovered above him and Jett thought again that they needed to figure out how to do this stuff themselves. The blog popped up and Scar was right. She revamped it.

Only one picture of Chris mentioning that he was her friend. There were now a dozen pictures of Brass and her. Slate went rigid beside him.

Pictures were not an accurate depiction of what life really was. It was a single moment in an imperfect life and the ones Scar put on her blog were no doubt the best ones she'd taken.

"She found a new workout buddy," Quick said dryly, and Jett clenched his jaw.

Jett scrolled through; it'd only been a week since Brass had been gone. They'd gone to the lake and Grant Park. There were candid pictures of them at both places together. They were in swimsuits and sunglasses, laying on towels with big beaming smiles in the one of them at the lake. It didn't look intimate; it looked friendly, but it was Brass and Scarlett and there was a thin line there. In another picture was Brass sleeping on her couch with Tree, snowy white, and curled on the side of Brass's face. The caption read; *I think Tree is in love.* Brass had obviously taken a photo of her for her new profile picture. It was Scarlett sitting in her swimsuit from behind and her hair piled on her head with her sunglasses on, and all you can see of her face is her profile. She looked beautiful, yet sad. There were a few pictures of her and Brass working out together, similar to the ones she had of her and Chris, but more of a silly nature than intimate.

Slate looked like he wanted to punch the screen. Jett had never found out who Slate had been with in Mabon. He couldn't think of any girl Slate would have been interested in there, but Amber had said he was having an affair. That she had felt it through the bond. If Scarlett ever found out, she'd freak.

"Tell him to get back here. She is a grown woman. She can take care of herself," Quick snapped.

"Quick, I'm trying very hard to ignore how you are speaking of my sister, but you are pushing it," Jett said slowly and Quick sighed.

"Gods, Brass has done nothing like this. She might be a witch. Look into that."

Jett felt his lips quirk and typed.

Hausts are doubling their guard. The Centaurs have joined clans, it's all anyone is talking about.
G is good. Getting bigger every day.

Jett
P.S. Sorry baby sis.

To: Jett Var JettSetter@VallaU.com
Don't sweat it, I'm not. Chris and I were great as friends. He wants more. I can't give it to him. Whatevs. Of course Brass is happy, he lives rent free, and has me cooking and cleaning for him. What man wouldn't want that? Ugh. It's cool. It's nice to have a friend around right now. He probably reads that in my mind. The bastard. No idea how long he plans on staying. He's getting stir crazy, talked about taking up the gym on their offer to let him train people while he gets his certification. Ba ha ha! Could you imagine Brass training people at the gym? I have to remind him he can't bring his daggers everywhere. "No, Brass. You won't need to stab anyone at the beach." :D
He likes my car. I'm teaching him to drive. Which is awesome. I'm finally better at something! Sigh. Between you and me, I love Brass. He's put everything aside to make sure I'm better.
Scar

Jett didn't move. He wasn't sure what Slate would do. It was his own fault for reading over his shoulder. He shouldn't even be doing it.

Quick fell into the seat opposite Slate and wiped a hand over his jaw. "I do not know what to say," he murmured. "I have told Brass to run off with a girl before. To have some fun. To not be so fucking responsible and selfless all the time. Never did I think he would. And not with another man's wife." Quick's face was full of disbelief.

Slate stood slowly and pushed in his chair. "Invite her to Keen's wedding. He wanted to see her, and she likes it there. Let her know he is marrying Tika next month."

"She won't come," Jett said.

"She will. The Wemic mean a great deal to her," Slate said before walking away.

The door shut, and Quick took his seat. "Do you think she loves him?" he asked.

"She loves him. If anyone could break the hold Slate has on her, it'd be Brass."

To: Scarlett Tio ScarlettSunset@Sunsettravels.com
Keen is marrying Tika. He asked if you would come to the wedding next month. Most of the family is going since he's the chief's brother.
You in?

Jett

To: Jett Var JettSetter@VallaU.com
Count us in. Send the details.

Scar

TWENTY-FIVE

"You're wearing holes right through those clothes. I don't want to hear it. You can pay me back."

I drove to the Harlem and Irving Plaza with Brass, who was reluctantly letting me buy him clothes. He had been wearing the few items Chris had left behind and Slate's outfit. I was doing laundry for him every other day. It was more for me than for him.

Brass caught women's eyes wherever we went. I hadn't minded at first, but slowly it had grated. I knew it was bad when he ducked his head and rubbed his lips together. Every once in a while, a woman's naughty thought would make him blush, and my blood heated.

Brass came out of the dressing room in a pair of distressed jeans. It was a coed dressing room and girls were stopping to ogle. My eyes widened, and I hopped to my feet. I started pushing him back into the dressing room.

"Brass, you can't be shirtless in public unless we are at the beach, or a pool, or a place where you see other shirtless people. I think the old lady had a stroke," I whispered in a rush as I shut the dressing room door behind me.

Brass looked down at me with a smile curling his lips. "Perhaps you should have specified. It is a changing room, after all. What is the difference if I am half dressed in here than there?"

I gestured to the door, spreading my arms wide. "*Privacy*. This isn't Tidings, you can't walk around half naked. Here. Try this one, it's stretchy, so... it'll stretch."

Brass picked up the heather grey shirt. "We have these in Tidings. I believe they are called shirts," he said sarcastically as he pulled it over his head.

I fought a smile as he ran a hand over his hair and held up his hands.

"Good. You'll look good in anything; we're just making sure they'll fit," I said, picking up the items he'd tried on and draping them over my forearm.

It was a hot August day, and I'd wanted to take Brass to a concert at Grant Park that night. We'd gone once before and had a great time. I wanted to treat him while he was outside of Tidings. There wasn't much to do for leisure there. I had worn a pair of denim shorts and a flowing floral racerback. I plaited my hair around my head to keep cool with my beads and fetishes throughout.

The jeans Brass had been wearing fell against my sandal, and I straightened. "I'll take these to the spot. The sitting spot, where I'll wait. Whenever you're done, I'll be there." I sidled along the wall to the door and groped blindly for the handle.

Brass laughed. "You have seen me in *much* less than this."

My cheeks heated, and I found the doorknob and swung it open. A blonde woman in her early thirties was passing by and she stopped in her tracks. She raised her brows and gave Brass an appreciative once over. I slammed the door in her face.

"Put your clothes on. We're leaving," I said, crossing my arms and facing the door.

Brass's hands braced against the door as he leaned down to my ear. "I believe you're jealous."

I pinched my lips together. "I'm not jealous. That was disrespectful."

Brass moved his hands away, and I waited until I heard his pants zip back up before I turned around. I opened my mouth, and he cocked his brow above his glittering amber eyes.

"You may leave, Scarlett. I am not finished," Brass said, and I blinked at him.

I licked my lips and left the dressing room with his clothes in my lap. He'd dismissed me. What's more, I had been rude to him and he had every right to dismiss me. I folded the clothes he'd tried on in my lap as I waited and tried to not feel like an idiot.

Brass exited the dressing room a few minutes later and smiled at the young girl working at the counter as he dropped off a few of the items. He handed me the others, and I stood.

"These will do," he said and strode forth.

My mood plummeted at the thought that Brass might be mad at me. For all my griping, he had been my saving grace after finding out about Amber's pregnancy. I would've easily gone *three* days without showering without him.

I paid for the clothes and we headed to the grocery store to restock the fridge. I was used to running errands with Chris before Brass started squatting at my place. When I'd moved out, Pearl had paid my rent up for the year, my utilities were cheap and I didn't go out. Groceries were my big expense, especially since Brass had moved in.

I pushed the cart as we walked along in silence. He hadn't spoken to me since the dressing room. The squeak of the wheels is the only sound between us. We would have the concert at the park tonight so we wouldn't have to talk then either.

"Do you want me to make something for lunch or to eat out?" I asked as I opened the freezer door, plucking out chocolate ice cream for me and strawberry for Brass.

"We can eat at home," he said absently, and a strange flutter happened in my chest.

Home?

I knit my brows as we walked, trying to ignore all the two interested glances Brass received from the opposite sex. Was he letting off some kind of pheromone today?

We unloaded the groceries together. I folded his clothes on my bed into neat piles before putting them into the dresser drawers while he put away the groceries. I came into the kitchen to help him.

"I put your clothes in the left half of the dresser. It's been empty since Chris moved out, anyway. The jacket we bought is in the bedroom closet and I put your toiletries in the bathroom. Now you won't smell like vanilla anymore." I said, smiling as I opened up the cabinets above the sink. "What are you hungry for? There's leftover chicken. I can heat it up and make sandwiches or wraps? We can put it in a salad too if you like," I offered, pulling out plates.

"I am not hungry for food," Brass said close behind me.

"What do you want, then?"

My kitchen was tiny, but it suited me just fine. I glanced over my shoulder at him, furrowing my brow, unable to discern the tone of his voice.

Oh.

I snapped my head back to the counter with the plates still in my hands and gently placed them down. There was nothing to preoccupy me with. My mind searched for ideas to give me time to think while Brass stepped up behind me. I could feel him lower his mouth to the nape of my neck and gently press his lips to my sensitive skin.

His breath tickled the fine hairs, and my skin prickled. He pressed a second kiss to the side of my neck and my eyelids slid lower. I licked my lips and slowly turned around. Brass's plump, defined lips puckered, his amber eyes soft and inviting. Brass placed his hands on either side of me and I tilted my head back, placing my hands over his.

"Every man that gets involved with me ends up hurt. They hate me afterwards. I'm afraid I'll lose you." I whispered throatily and drew a fortifying breath.

"You could not push me away if you tried," Brass responded. "I am your friend foremost." There was a protracted silence until he spoke again, the air wrought with tension. "Other than him, do you think you will care about another man more than you care about me?"

My breath hitched, and blood pounded in my ears. "No," I said, swallowing. "What if I want nothing serious? I've just had three back-to-back engagements. Repent in leisure and all that."

"Try not to overthink it, Scarlett. Perhaps I only want to sleep with you." He quirked a brow, and I blushed, but didn't avert my eyes.

It was my greatest shame how selfishly I clung to Brass. I could deal with everything else I'd done that was deplorable, but wanting Brass was my deepest, darkest secret that he had just drawn out of its shadowed corner and thrust out into the spotlight.

"Perhaps I only want to sleep with *you*," I said, and he smiled slow and sexy and my mouth went dry.

No small amount of anxiety ripped through me. It petrified me I would lose him. Losing Slate had left this gaping hole in my heart. I could lie, give excuses, and pretend with my family, but Brass never tolerated it. He was the one who made me be honest with myself. I could always count on him for the truth. Every reason I cared for him was why I had wanted him to be the first man I had lain with. If he were to go the way of my other relationships I'd had with men and demand more than I could give or push too hard so I ran away sabotaging things.

This was *Brass*. This wasn't some random guy I'd been seeing.

Chris and I had started out as friends too until I developed feelings for him. My feelings for Brass were already in place, I never let myself touch upon them because there was Slate. He was the suit of armor I wore whenever I met someone. They had to penetrate through him to get to me, but Brass had been there with him. My love for Slate was a hopeless, desperate thing, while what I felt for Brass was a seedling. Its tendrils reaching for the sunlight, bright green and begging to be watered.

"You and me? We're complicated, aren't we? It wouldn't just be today or tomorrow. People would be... upset."

Playful banter time was over. This was the truth, and it held me back. I was still in love with Slate, the desperate rotting thing that it was, it was there and it may always be there.

Brass's eyes were hooded as he looked down at me. "I know where I stand with you. I know where *he* stands, and what that means for me. I acknowledge and accept it, Scarlett. I always have. When I asked if your happiness was more important than hers, I did not want you to be *un*happy. Only to think through what you were doing. No one waits for me. I am all yours."

My eyes slid down to his lips and back up to his eyes. Why was I so nervous? Part of me felt like I was going to vomit. Brass and I had kissed and done *much* more. It felt different. I suspected that's why Brass was waiting for me to make the first move.

My arms lifted, and I slid my palms up onto his chest. I ran my fingertips along his collarbones and to his neck. He closed his eyes and his lips slightly parted as my fingers tips grazed the side of his neck and into his hair. I pulled the leather strap, letting it fall free. I ran my palms down his stubbled jaw and ran the pad of my thumb over his lips. He opened his mouth enough for his teeth to graze it, and a thrill shot through me.

I pulled his face down to mine and slanted my mouth over his. The small thrill turned into a tidal wave.

Brass hadn't let go of the counter; he pressed closer so his body molded to mine. His lips were soft. Brass's hands gripped my waist and lifted me onto the counter. I didn't break contact with him for a second as I wrapped my legs around his waist.

Cinnamon and spring rain.

I could feel the callouses on his hands as he ran them up my thighs and over my hips. Our kisses were deep and passionate, like the man. I found myself breathless as he kissed down my jaw and down my throat. My breathing grew rapid as his hand skimmed under the fabric of my shirt.

I held my arms up on instinct and he drew back with a chuckle as he gripped the hem and pulled it over my head. I wrapped my fingers in his hair and brought his face to my chest. My head hung back as he planted open-mouthed kisses over the swell of my breasts. He pushed the cups of my strapless bra lower; his mouth pulled my hard nipple into it and my body bowed with a gasp. My hands flew to the counter and hit the plate I put there, knocking it into the sink and shattering it.

He chuckled when he tried to pull away to clean the mess and I held him firmly to my skin. His lips were dark pink and beginning to take on a swell from our kissing.

"Your bond is active," he said breathlessly, and I let go of his head.

I held up my hand and to find I'd cut it on one of the plate shards. Blood trailed from my palm over my fingers. Brass took my hand, chest heaving and not from anything I was doing, and rubbed my blood on his finger before healing me.

I sucked in sharply. His mind was so different from Slate's. There was this simmering of rage in Slate at all times. There was only a calm sort of serenity in Brass amidst the passion and love.

"By the Mother," Brass whispered, and I concurred.

We searched one another's faces. If I looked half as wanton as Brass, we might not make the concert tonight. Brass lunged at me, yanking my clothes off as I tried not to fall off the counter, giggling like a lunatic.

I used my *calling* to tug off his new pants when I sat naked before him and he pulled his shirt over his head so quickly I was sure it would catch on an ear. It was still falling to the floor when he crushed his lips back over mine. His palms cupped my backside roughly, moving my hips against him, and I felt frantic. I peppered his neck and shoulder with kisses and pulled on his thick, dark hair. He moaned, and I sucked air in sharply as he shifted my hips, pushing into me.

Making love to Brass made me feel like he had mapped out my nerves and memorized them as his hands, mouths, and other appendages maximized even the slightest touch. He was in my head, using his talent to bring me to the precipice of my pleasure, over and over.

I strove to return the favor using my own talents.

We wandered around like nothing happened when we went to the festival. We walked to the different stages to listen to my favorite bands.

Brass didn't mind the crowd of thousands as long as I stayed near. There was this strange awkwardness for me that wasn't there before.

I didn't know where we stood, or if it was a onetime thing again. Before that day, Brass and I had had three nights together over nine months. It had been three months since our night with Chris. Would we go another few months acting like we were just friends?

We were both in a good mood when we left the park and took the train home. Brass thought the trains were disgusting, but then, who didn't? It wrinkled his nose until we emerged from the platform and walked to my car.

He drove home, and I readied for bed after him like roommates.

Tree sensed my mood and padded over to my lap. She was enormous. The size of an average cat was at only seven months, with the promise to keep growing. She was such a lover. I was only a little envious that she preferred Brass's company to mine.

I wore my favorite grey racerback and shorts when I crawled into bed. I only had one air conditioner in the bedroom window. If I shut my door, the other rooms would become sweltering. It was a hot day. I laid awake listening to the hum of the a/c. Brass hadn't made a move to deactivate our bond, so he knew I was awake since he was.

After we made love on the counter, we took it to the floor. Then I *called* my robe over and finished making us sandwiches. He dressed before settling on the couch, waiting for me and that had been that. I didn't know what to do or say.

It was *Brass*.

Angrily, I kicked off the blankets, startling Tree, and padded over the wooden floor to the living room.

Brass laid on his stomach in the red boxer briefs we'd bought earlier. He turned his head on the couch so he faced my way.

"Can I help you with something?" Brass said in his smooth, deep voice.

I crossed my arms with that fluttering in my chest, spreading to roll over my body. He was purposely giving me a hard time. He just confirmed it.

"It's cooler in my bedroom," I said petulantly.

Brass rolled over. Velvet dark honey skin over his hard packed muscles. He ran his hand over the 'V' that led south, drawing my eye, and I *felt* his amusement.

"Is it? That's interesting," Brass said with glittering amber eyes.

I sucked in a deep breath and crossed the carpet to stand over him. He folded his arms behind his head, watching me with a slight quirk to his lips, made for kissing.

"Are you hot out here?" I asked, keeping my arms folded.

He gave a little shrug, his biceps flexing. "Are you hot in there?"

I bit down on my lip to keep from smiling at the big jerk. "You're determined to make me work for it, aren't you?"

"Work for what, Scarlett?" Brass purred.

My hand whipped out, and he caught it around the wrist. He was quick, but I already had my fingers curled around my goal. His lips parted, and I watched his nipples harden.

"I want you in my bed, Brass Regn. You have a debt that needs to be paid. Did you think I would let you live and eat here for free forever?" I shook my head, clicking my tongue. "I take my fee in flesh."

I'd never spoken that way to Brass, and his eyes seemed to blaze. He released my wrist, and I took a step back, moving my hand from between his legs. When he stood, he dwarfed me as he stalked my way.

"Let it never be said a Regn did not pay his debts," he purred, and I squealed as he chased me all the way into the bedroom.

He caught me and spun me around to my back and kissed me sweetly as I giggled.

"That wasn't so hard, was it?" he purred.

CHAPTER 26
JETT

To: Jett Var JettSetter@VallaU.com

Sorry for waiting until the last minute, but we won't be able to make it out. I hope that doesn't put you guys out too bad. Maybe we will make it out for Yuletide? Brass wonders if there are any messages for him. We can Skype when you get this.

Scar

"Yuletide? In four months? Yes, I have a message for Brass. What the *fuck* is he doing? Has he left Tidings for good?" Quick's voice has risen dangerously high in his incredulity.

Tawny pursed her lips. "Go to her blog." She urged, and Jett pulled it up.

They had a regular viewing party huddled around the computer today. Indigo sat to the other side of him and Slate was behind him. Indigo and Tawny both knew how to use computers. They could've handled it instead of him.

Indigo laughed, not her usual perky laugh, but a darker, more knowing one when Jett scrolled through the blog.

"We can look at this later, Tawny," Jett mumbled.

"Show us," Slate growled and leaned so close his brother's hair fell over his shoulder.

Jett frowned at the love rune that dangled near his ear and continued to scroll. It'd only been a week and a half since their last correspondence, a lifetime to Jett since her disappearance. She'd been writing every other day. There were more pictures and four new posts. Quick bumped into Indigo as he leaned closer into the screen and she hissed like a cat.

She had a new profile picture. They must've really enjoy going to the lake. It was a black-and-white photo; Scarlett was leaning back against Brass's chest with a shit-eating grin on her face and Brass was kissing the top of her head, looking away from the camera. Jett assumed they were at the beach because he was shirtless and she had what looked like a bikini top on, but you could only see them from the chest up. Brass banded an arm around her, so his palm was over her heart.

They'd been going to museums and a concert; she talked about some shopping trip they'd taken. There was a little about her new job and links to articles she'd written.

More pictures.

They'd gone to Navy Pier with another couple, some people they knew from the gym. There was a picture they'd taken of the four of them and two more. Jett tried not to smile. One was of Brass and Scarlett from behind, holding hands and she's pointing to something at a kiosk. The other looked like it was at the end of the night, Brass and

Scarlett's silhouettes in front of fireworks. They were definitely kissing in it.

The title for that post was *A New Dawn*. Jett read the first few lines.

Not counting my chickens just yet, but there's something to be said for a man who has your back through the thick and the thin. Who sees you at your darkest moments, shrugs and tells you he loves you anyway.

Now, if only I could get him to stop trying to get me to run away with him...

"*Fuck*," Quick said in a breath.

"I knew it," Indigo beamed.

Tawny sat back and looked thoughtful. Slate seemed frozen in place, that or he read slowly or worse, he was rereading it to make sure he'd seen it right the first time.

CHAPTER

TWENTY-SEVEN

The sound of Skype calling roused me from where I leaned against Brass in our bubble bath.

"What is that noise?" he grumbled.

"I think Jett is calling. Come on. It's the least we can do." I wrapped my robe around me and padded into the living room.

I woke the screen and clicked the *Accept* button. I couldn't help to smile like a crazed person. Indigo, Tawny, Quick, and Jett hovered in front of the screen, fighting for space. I waved excitedly to them.

"Hi! I've missed you guys!" I said in an unnaturally high voice.

"Good, come back then," Quick said, sounding irritated, and I gave him a small smile.

"Soon. Things are well here. Working, working out again. How's my niece?"

Jett was talking about Gigi when Brass came around the computer and plopped down beside me. Jett ducked his head and Quick cursed.

205

Tawny's and Indigo's faces were beet red, and I heard a deep growl like an animal. I knit my brows and realized what had happened.

"Brass!"

I couldn't catch my breath. I was laughing so hard, so I pushed Brass's towel between his legs and fell over laughing so hard my ribs hurt.

"There's a camera there. They can see everything," I said between giggles, and Brass rubbed his lips together as his cheeks reddened.

He ran his big hand over his thick, damp locks. "I think she only tells me half of everything on purpose so she can be better than me at some things. It's so few. I like to humor her," Brass teased and stood, giving me a peck on the lips before going into the bedroom.

I was still laughing and tucked my wet hair behind my ears. The four of them were staring at me through the computer screen. Quick's mouth was open and Tawny was trying to mouth something on me.

"Were... were you in the *bath*?" Quick asked.

I opened my mouth and realized how Brass and I looked to them. I licked my lips. We'd just kissed in front of them like we did it every day, and we did.

"*Um*, yeah. So what's up, guys?" I tried to change the subject.

"Did he just say *it's*?" Quick asked.

I gave him a dry look. "He's adopting the language quirks. *It's* not a big deal. Did you only want to call to talk about how much Brass is changing, because he's not? A dialect change is not the end of the world. Neither is a bath."

Brass crossed the room, now in pants, and sat down next to me, sliding his arm on the couch behind me. "Quit giving her a hard time. She isn't holding me hostage here. If anything, it is the other way around."

Quick pursed his lips. "Come back for a visit."

Brass chuckled as he pushed my wet hair over my shoulder. "What for? I have lived there all my life; this is my vacation."

"She is your vacation?" Quick asked, bewildered.

Brass cocked his brow. "She is not my vacation, Silver," he said, his voice dropping. Quick stared at Brass, and he chuckled. "Silver, I cannot read your mind through the computer. Any tongue lashing you wish to give me will have to be said aloud."

"Get back here! What are you doing?" he shouted.

I shifted next to Brass, and he pulled me closer to him on the couch. "Enjoying life, Silver. If it means that much to you, we can come back for a quick visit. We'll not hear anything said about our living arrangement. What you see is what you get."

Quick blew out a breath. "So, this is a thing now?"

"A thing..." Brass muttered.

I put my hand on his thigh. "We take it day by day. I know I don't have the best track record. Today, it's a thing." I looked to Brass, whose amber eyes glittered at me. "Today, we're together. One day at a time."

Brass's hand slid over my cheek and down my back.

"I think it's fantastic," Indigo chirped.

"So, you'll be here in two days?" Tawny asked.

"Looks like," I said, and anxiety pooled in my stomach.

"Is there anything you're not telling us?" Jett asked.

I looked at Brass, who looked at me. "Yes, but we are waiting before we tell anyone."

"By the Mother, you did not propose did you?" Quick said, groaning.

Brass smiled at me. "Not yet. If I asked now, she'd run away. I've seen her do it enough to know when to push and when to let her go. You're happy with the way things are, aren't you?"

"Very." I agreed and leaned forward to kiss his lips.

The computer screen toppled sideways, and I sat forward as the camera displayed the room. Slate straightened and balled his fists. Jett pulled Tawny onto his lap and rolled over onto her. Slate wreaked havoc in the technology room. He tore entire tables that were bolted to the floors and threw them crashing into computers. Jett lifted his head towards Quick, who was guarding Indigo with his body. Tawny's head ducked under Jett, and her hands were over her ears. The deep roars Slate bellowed as he demolished the room brought tears to my eyes.

The door slammed, and there was a crash. Smoke and debris floated around the tech room. Jett moved off of Tawny and helped her to her feet. She looked around in disbelief.

"How?" she asked, bewildered.

Quick tried to help dust Indigo off, particularly her chest region when she slapped his hands away, making him chuckle.

"Is it broken?" Tawny asked, walking through the demolition.

Jett spotted us and righted the computer. "Here."

"If Brass comes back with her, shit is going to go down," Quick said, taking Indigo's hand despite her protests and helping her over a half-broken table.

"Brass knew that when he slept with her the first time. Slate should pay more attention to his pregnant wife and less to whom Scarlett is with. What was he even doing in here?" Tawny snapped.

Brass had found my hand and squeezed it.

"They're still on," Jett said, hardening his chiseled features.

"I didn't know he was there," I explained, and Jett waved his hand dismissively.

"He shouldn't have been."

"Should we not..."

"No!" the four of them yelled.

"He'll get over it," Jett said, offering me a smile.

"See you guys in two days," Indigo said as the computer died.

I turned to Brass, who pulled me into his lap. He opened my robe and took liberties with my body.

"We knew this would happen. Better this way than when we get there. Now he knows." Brass said, lowering his mouth to my chest.

I nodded and rubbed his head. "Do you think he'll hate us forever?"

Brass pressed his lips together. "Perhaps for a time, then we will have to reach out to him."

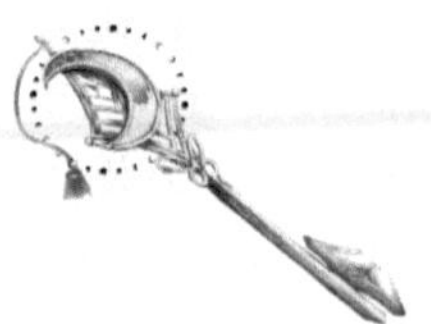

Brass and I had a double date on a dinner cruise the next night with the couple from the gym. He had never been on a boat. Brass had never done many things we'd done lately, and I was happy to show him around.

We stood at the back of the boat leaning on the railing with his arms wrapped around me and I breathed deep. Cinnamon and fresh spring rain.

"You are introspective tonight," Brass said in his smooth, deep voice.

"Hmm. I don't want to go tomorrow," I told him, leaning against his chest.

The breeze swept up my dress, and Brass kissed my cheek. "You don't want to see him."

"I'm dreading it. You saw what he did to the tech room. I've come between you two before and now I've done it again, ten times worse this time. He's hurting, he doesn't get sad when he's hurt, he gets angry." I sighed, "One thing. That's all it took to completely mess up everything."

"You know what I miss most about Tidings?"

"Besides the unpolluted air? What's that?" I asked.

"The stars," he said, gazing up at the dark sky.

"What about your niece and nephew?" I asked, and he sighed.

"Them too. Our family is very close, not unlike yours," Brass said and ran his hands over mine.

He brought his mouth down to mine. I kissed his lower lip and then his upper, and he smiled. My nose burned as I nuzzled into his chest. I felt a fluttering in my chest and I finally understood what it meant.

"I hope to find out," Brass whispered into my hair.

"Hmm?"

"If you can be in love with two men."

My whole body tingled as Brass held me close.

"Shug? *Uh*, Scarlett?"

I drew back from Brass and peered around him. "Chris. Hi. How are you?"

It couldn't be more awkward. Brass stood beside me and didn't make a move to put an arm around me or anything. I took a step towards Chris, and he strode up to me and gave me a hug. It was one of those hugs that involved his whole body rather than just the arms. I bit down on my lip and dulled my talent; Chris's emotions were rampant.

"I'm good." Chris drew back. "Brass. Hey man." Brass stepped forward and took Chris's outstretched hand.

"Chris, good to see you again," Brass said politely.

"Small world, huh?" Chris said as the wind off the lake ruffled his chestnut hair.

He'd stopped calling me right around the time Brass moved in. He looked good, but then, he always did.

"How long has this been going on?" Chris asked, shoving his hands into the pockets of his khakis.

"Few weeks only," I said, and he looked relieved.

Chris must have thought I cheated, and the thought made me sick. "Cool. Cool." He said nervously and his baby blue eyes settled on me.

Brass cleared his throat. "I came down to see what happened after the two of you ended things. She holed up in the apartment after she quit her job," Brass said with a smile. "I think your date is looking for you."

A short blonde with super high heels looked annoyed Chris was standing so close to me. He looked over his shoulder and seemed to remember her suddenly, and laughed.

"Right. I better get back. It's still really new. She doesn't trust me yet." Chris gave me a killer smile, and I returned it.

"I doubt putting in a good word for you would help," I joked, and he laughed.

"No, I better keep her away from you. She's seen our magazine spread. That's how I met her, through that photographer. You're a high bar to be held to."

Brass stepped up when the silence stretched and offered his hand to Chris again. And shook it before he walked back to the blonde.

I made a face at Brass.

"Did you have to make me sound like a kicked puppy?"

"You bewitched that man. You have that effect. It was a small boon for his anguish." Brass took my elbow, and we went back inside.

A trail of broken hearts, Quick had said.

CHAPTER 28
JETT

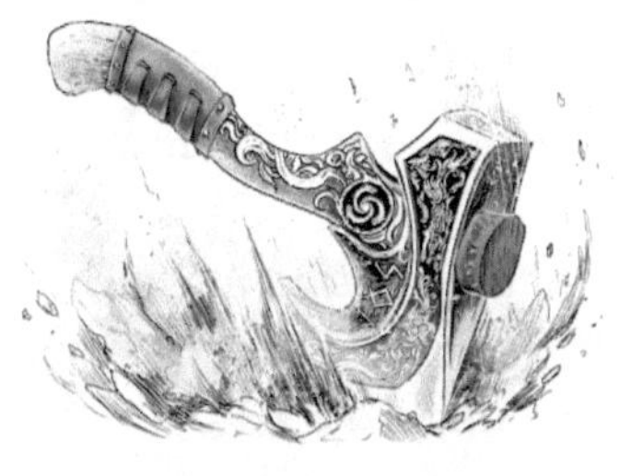

"We'll need a buffer. You've got to come." Jett told Quick.

"Yeah, yeah. I know. I invited Ama and Shale to join us as well," Quick said at lunch.

Brass and Scarlett were getting in tonight and they were leaving for the Wemic in the morning. Tawny followed Slate and Amber with her eyes until they sat across from them. Tawny was trying to be nicer since Amber was pregnant, but it was a laborious process.

"What secrets are you telling?" Amber asked.

Jett hated the sound of her voice, but he especially hated that she looked so much like Scarlett — a cruel reminder in front of him every day of what should have been.

"Brass and Scarlett are coming in tonight. We're making traveling plans," Jett said, focusing on his pasta.

Cherry patted his thigh under the table, and he gave her a weak smile.

"We should come over for dinner." Amber noted and looked at Slate, whose upper lip had lifted in a sneer.

"No."

"*Yes*. Scarlett was so interested in when we would conceive. She will be pleased to find we succeeded."

"She already knows." Indigo said with an edge to her voice.

Jett sighed. "When I spoke to her, she said to send you her best wishes."

Tawny grumbled under her breath, and Indigo snorted. Likely, nothing nice.

"Perhaps you can all come to our palace and have dinner there? I am sure she would like the nursery." Amber chirped, pushing her strawberry blonde hair from her face.

Tawny's fists balled, and Jett cleared his throat. "Maybe another time. She was sick the last time she was back. Most likely it was nothing serious, but she may still be unwell. Best to keep things light for now."

Amber nodded disappointedly and Jett's eyes slid past her to where Ash was gliding up from the bench and coming their way. Jett jutted out his chin arrogantly and waited for the Straumr to come.

"I saw Scarlett's *blog*," Ash said with glittering eyes.

"So?" Indigo snapped.

It shocked Jett. Indigo tried not to side against her old family and friends, but Scar had changed all that.

Ash smirked at Quick, whose face grew harder by the moment. "I told her Dagr dumped her as I did because of her fruitless body. It would appear your brother does not care that she is a damaged waste."

"Liar! You've not gotten close enough to her to say that!" Tawny shot to her feet, wielding a butter knife.

"Truth," Quick muttered and Ash smirked.

"At *his* wedding. She was all alone. Even the myopic didn't want to be near her." Ash said in a low, measured tone.

"At Slate's wedding?" Tawny looked ready to cry. "What is your problem! She was always good to you, better than you deserved. They attacked her at *your* sugarfoot palace. It's your fault! She shouldn't have even been there that night." Tawny turned to Slate. "That's *your* fault." She snarled, and Indigo caught her hand.

Ash hissed, and Jett swung his head. "One more word, Straumr and I will render *you* damaged waste," Slate growled.

His wrist blade sprung and aimed at Ash's groin.

Amber's eyes went wide. "Slate, stop that! He's the Prime's nephew."

"Try me," Slate growled, and Ash took a step back.

Slate retracted his blade and went back to his lunch, and Tawny sat down.

"Like mother, like daughter. That bastard child deserved what it got." Ash sneered and Jett and Quick both *called*, pinning Slate to the bench.

There was only one thing Jett could think to do. He revealed his talent. It was a ridiculously useless talent, but it distracted.

Every muscle stood out in Slate's body as he tried to *call* against them. He *was* the patriarch of the Dagr line. He couldn't get thrown out of Valla U.

"Get the fuck off me." He ground out and Jett sliced his head once to the left as he summoned what he called Divine Beauty.

"What was he talking about? Scarlett was pregnant?" Amber asked, perplexed, as Jett's skin became luminescent and he glowed.

He was irresistible. He felt the moment Slate stopped struggling, enraptured by his appeal. It didn't matter, man or woman of any background. They were all attracted to him.

Jett grunted as hands pulled him off the bench. His Divine Beauty was slowly fading, and he tasted blood in his mouth. Cherry was giggling from his side, so that was not who was pressing her pillowy breasts to his chest, trying to meld their bodies into one. Tawny's thin hands firmly gripped Jett's black shirt as she kissed him deeply from where she straddled him.

She was a lot stronger than she looked. She'd grabbed his legs and yanked him under. Jett was not a small man; he'd slammed his mouth on the table's edge and blood smeared over Tawny's wide, swollen mouth. She blinked big hazel eyes dazedly at him as his influence over her dissipated. There was a lingering effect from the talent. Her lush chest heaved as she tried to control herself even with Cherry and Quick ducking their heads down to see what had happened.

Jett tentatively reached up from where he laid on his back to wipe his blood from her lips and she opened her mouth, sucking his thumb between her lips, her tongue sliding along it.

"Steel is going to be so mad at you," Cherry chided Jett, but Tawny thought she meant at *her*.

Her rhythmic sucking of his thumb stopped and Jett grit his teeth. Tawny pulled back and let out a little yelp and then another when she tried to scramble away, and whacked her head on the underside of the table. Her creamy porcelain thighs peeking out from her caftan uniform from how she'd rucked it up while she ground against him.

Slate and Amber looked under the table where Tawny looked like she was about to cry. Jett sat up as much as he could and made placating gestures to her as he tried to cover his lap.

"It's not your fault. Ask Slate. He probably wanted to make out with me, too." Jett told her as her soft lower lip wobbled.

"I don't..." She sought Cherry's smiling face. "I'm so sorry."

Cherry held out her hand and Tawny reached for it carefully, wondering if Cherry was going to sock her for molesting her husband. The two girls got along very well; Cherry had filled Tawny's need for a friend since Scar had left them. Tawny took it, disentangling herself from Jett's legs after she'd been sitting over.

Jett glared at Slate and Quick, daring them to make a comment, but they both smiled knowingly as Jett adjusted himself. He should have pulled his thumb out of his uncle's wife's mouth. That was not cool.

The whole interlude had lasted under a minute.

Jett rolled out under Tawny and Cherry's feet and dusted himself off before sitting back down on the bench. Cherry licked her finger and swiped at Jett's lips with one hand, and grabbed his lap with the other. Jett grunted but made no move to stop her.

"I think you enjoyed that," Cherry whispered.

Jett bent to whisper his apology when he noticed a gap on his other side. "Where's Indi?"

No one was paying attention to what Indigo was doing. She'd climbed off the bench and followed Ash back to his table. Jett cursed when her hand cocked back and she slapped Ash, coming up in his blind spot.

The table erupted, and Jett saw Sage get in her face and Sterling come between them. Sage's pale face was red as his features tensed with what were undoubtedly harsh words. Tawny was already up and running around the table to where they stood and took Indigo from Sterling with great effort.

Reed Tio, the disciplinarian and their great uncle, stood in the aisle and crooked his finger to the two girls. Indigo held her head of corn silk hair high as she shrugged Tawny off and followed Reed from the dining hall. Indigo had been different for months; things had gotten bad rapidly after Scarlett left. Now she was probably going to get thrown out of Valla U.

Quick stood slowly and followed them with his eyes, and Jett sighed. The only one who had her crap together was Tawny, but that was because Orion kept her as close as possible. There was no room for her to trip up without him being there to save her.

She marched after them with a determined look on her doll-like face. He'd seen that look on Scarlett's face. If they were going to throw Indigo out, Tawny was going to give them a fight with the Vetr heir.

Jett was glad she was gone. He would have to apologize profusely to Steel. His angelic little wife could suck the paint off a wall. Jett made a face, adjusting again, and gave Cherry an apologetic smirk.

"First, we fix things with your sister. Then, we go to your bedroom and we come up with a way to persuade Steel to let me spend the night with his wife," Cherry said, arching her brow at Jett.

Under different circumstances, Jett would've laughed.

"Steel is going to kill me for letting her touch me... at all," he groaned.

CHAPTER

TWENTY-NINE

I wrung my hands, and Brass took them in his. "They will not be there. They live at the Dagr palace," he said for the third time since we left the airport.

We had taken a cab to Colt State park instead of renting a car. The cabbie dropped us off at the gates and we dragged our luggage through the gates that were framed by the two sculpted bulls. If the cabbie thought it was strange, he didn't mention it.

Brass and I stood side by side as we looked at the tree portal. We were in the same spot we'd been in when I left the first time.

"Kiss me. I need a good one," I breathed.

"Do I sometimes give bad ones?" Brass teased and my mood lifted a fraction.

Dusk had fallen, and the sky was a riot of vivid reds and blues. Brass took my luggage from me, setting it aside, and laid me down on the grass covering me with his body.

"*This* is what I wanted to do to you when you left that night." He whispered and slid his hand under my skirt.

"Someone could see," I whispered, but my hands were already unzipping his pants.

He pushed my denim skirt up around my hips as Brass lowered himself to me.

The blue faux starlight of the Sumar portal room would always remind me of my first day arriving at Tidings.

When Brass and I came through the portal, we found the room empty. The others would likely be ready for dinner and packing their rolls for tomorrow.

We found my old bedroom prepared for us and we put our luggage in the closet and went downstairs to meet the family for dinner. I didn't want to change my clothes; I liked that Brass and I wore American clothing. He wore a white light fabric button down with the sleeves rolled up to expose the Yggdrasil necklace at the hollow of his dark honey throat. His jeans hung low on his hips; we were a little matchy-matchy since I wore a white racerback camisole. We could have been going to a beach wedding.

My wedge heels clacked on the tiled floors of the palace; I came to a stop before we turned the corner into the informal dining room. I could hear the murmuring of voices. Brass slid his hand into mine.

"Slate and Amber are here. I wanted you to know before we go in. Amber knows you were pregnant before. There was an altercation with Ash. Come. There's more." Brass cupped my face and looked into my eyes.

I nodded again and released his hand. "Should we?"

"We are who we are. We do not change for them. They accept us or they don't."

"But you saw…"

"It is inevitable," Brass said and molded his lips to mine.

We turned the corner into the room as one and Brass kept his hand at the small of my back. With my abilities muted, I forced a smile and started greeting everyone around the table. There was a somber mood to the room I didn't understand.

Quick was the first one to us who gave me a noncommittal hug and stared at his brother, who only tried to cover his lips with his hand as he nodded. Quick was looking him up and down like he'd never seen him before.

I hugged Gypsum, who took Tree from me and started. His burgeoning zoolinguist abilities could be extremely strange. Gypsum's olive face lit and dimples sprung into his cheeks. He was getting so tall, his straight sable hair threaded with copper beads as long as Slate's now. His eyes flitted down to my stomach and to Brass and me. I kept moving as Brass spoke to him.

Indigo gave a smile that looked as forced as my own.

"We need to talk."

I knit my brow. "Of course."

Pearl stood and embraced me fiercely, planting a kiss on my cheek. "You look radiant, darling. I received your letter. I am sorry things with Chris didn't work out. He was a nice young man. I see you have an escort. Good evening, Mr. Regn," Pearl said, and Brass took her hands as he kissed her on both cheeks.

"Good evening, Matriarch Tio," Brass said with a warm smile.

I walked around the table and gave Steel and Tawny hugs; Tawny squeezed me like I would bolt if she didn't hold me in place.

"I kissed your brother. It was terrible. He has a talent; did you know that? It's like your manipulation talent, but a million times stronger. Even Slate and Quick said they wanted to kiss him. I'm sorry they're here. Amber is either a complete bitch or really thinks you give a sugarfoot about their baby."

I shut my eyes and breathed, trying to process her deluge of information. "I do care about it, Tawny."

She drew back and looked at me. "You look fantastic. Getting lots of sun?"

I nodded. "I enjoy writing articles at the lake and Brass thinks it's funny we all get half naked and ignore each other even though we sit five feet away." A small smile played on her wide mouth.

"He looks *great* in jeans."

I dropped my voice. "He looks even better out of them."

Tawny giggled mischievously and my mood lightened a little more. "I know. I saw." Her fair cheeks reddened, and I laughed.

I'd forgotten about that. Brass was right behind me and gave her a hug while giving me a rueful smile. That man was always in my head.

The girls were up next and Gigi was still awake just for my visit. I hugged Jett with one arm as I held my niece.

"*Ugh*. I could just eat her up. Look at those eyes! You are in so much trouble, Jett."

Jett beamed down at his daughter. "Look at those lips. They're bigger than her face. Just like yours." He chuckled, and I swatted him as I bounced.

"Brass, look at my adorable niece." I said over my shoulder and Brass lifted Gigi from my arms.

"Those lips. Poor girl will suffer her aunt's good looks."

I pursed my lips playfully at him and turned back to Jett.

He reached up and pulled a blade of grass out of my hair, cocking an eyebrow.

"Someone must have been mowing their lawn," I mumbled.

"Lie," Quick countered, and I narrowed my eyes at him.

Jett embraced me again. "It was her idea. We're trying to be nice."

"It's okay, Jett." I told him with a tight smile.

My palms were sweating as I hugged Cherry, and I cocked my head. "Cherry — are you?"

Her cobalt eyes widened, and she looked to Jett. I spun to my brother, who leveled his eyes at me.

"We haven't —" He started, but I squealed and hugged him again.

"Oh! Congratulations, Jett. Amethyst, Cherry. All of you. Oh, I'm going to cry." I fanned myself with my hands as tears welled in my eyes.

I had let the cat out of the bag and everyone moved about the table congratulating them. Amber approached me and I felt Brass slip the gift bag into my hand. My stomach turned into a burning pit of bile when she embraced me and rubbed her stomach.

I held out the bag and tried to smile, but I kept feeling it slide into a frown. My face was doing a weird twitching thing I couldn't control.

"I heard the fantastic news. You must be thrilled. I made you a little something for the nursery," I said, swallowing against the lump in my throat.

She beamed and took out the canvas I'd painted. It was a whimsical painting of a merman sitting astride a Centaur with the solar cross of the Dagr sigil in the sky and a lion hybrid with a black beast.

"What is that?" she asked, frowning.

"A barghest hybrid," I explained, and she grimaced.

"It is hideous."

My cheeks heated with inexplicable anger. "He is *not* hideous. It's just a painting... for fun."

Her smile lifted, and I felt the slyness of it. "I heard you lost a child. That must have been awful. Here, you can touch Slate's and mine."

Someone cranked up the temperature in the room a hundred degrees as she gripped my hand and put it to her stomach. My hand went to my mouth to stop the bile that flooded it.

"Delve," Amber said with a hint of annoyance.

Brass grabbed my hand away from her, and I sucked in a deep breath. My whole body felt feverish and slick from sweat. We were playing some weird tug-o-war. I patted him and raised my hand again and delved. I'd never done it to Amethyst while she carried Gigi, but I could feel the life inside Amber. Like something extra bright and innocent in her midsection.

Brass steadied me with a hand on my back and I felt him *call,* stilling my roiling stomach. He went utterly rigid.

I swallowed. "That's amazing. Sorry, I've had a busy day with all the traveling."

Brass led me back around the table at a snail's pace because I was close to fainting. His fingers were rubbing my skin. He was so stiff I frowned at him.

... What is going on with you?...

"Whatever happened with your doctor's appointment?" Jett asked, distracting me from Brass's response, and the heat in my face returned.

"Everything was well," I said and continued to walk around the table.

Amber sat back in her seat. "Did it have to do with your condition? You cannot have children at all?"

Brass's irritation flared. She *was* a bitch. She'd taken premeditated actions to torture me.

"*Could* not," Brass said.

I didn't look up as I hurried to my seat and gripped Brass's hand so he'd shut his trap and sit down next to me.

... Not now!...

"We have to talk," he said in a whisper.

... Right now?...

Brass grunted.

"*Could* not?" Indigo asked.

"Yes, that's why I went to the doctor," I said to Amber as Slate took his seat next to her.

"Did Chris change his mind about wanting to have children?" Amber asked, feigning an apologetic smile.

I poured myself a glass of water and drank deeply. "We saw Chris last night. He is seeing someone new. I'm happy for him. Do you have anything stronger than water?" I asked with a self-deprecating smile.

"Truth," Quick said, and I gave him a gracious smile.

"You said *could*. Past tense," Indigo insisted.

I didn't care who watched as I dipped the edge of my napkin into my drink and dabbed at my forehead. Indigo passed me a carafe of white wine that Brass held hostage in his fist.

"Perhaps you should lie down. I will bring dinner up," Brass whispered, and I laid my palm on his forearm.

"I just need a minute," I breathed.

"Scarlett, you do not look well, darling," Pearl said with concern etching her face.

"Hot flash or something." I laughed nervously and turned to Brass.

... You can't be weird. Only I can be weird right now. I need you...

I piled food on my plate and grudgingly stared at the wine Brass moved out of my grasp.

"How did you know Cherry was pregnant?" Jett asked.

"My sense of smell is sensitive to certain things. Her hormone levels — I can smell it on Amber too," I said, choking on her name.

Slate was looking at the painting, and his eyes slid to mine. My heart lurched, and I looked away.

"Thank you for the painting. I especially like the barghest," Slate rumbled, and I flashed a smile, keeping my eyes averted.

Amber tittered. "Do not act like strangers. I do not mind if you give him a congratulatory hug. We made a *life* together. We should celebrate it with everyone."

Slate glanced at her out of the corner of his eye, and her smile slid a little.

"No," Brass whispered, and I gave him a look, getting up anyway.

"Are you going to ignore my question?" Indigo asked peevishly, and I snapped out of it.

"When I said the doctor said it was good, I meant the erosion was gone." I shrugged and rounded the table.

Jett's fork clattered to the table. "You can have children?"

"I can," I said, and Jett sprung up, sending the cream upholstered seat flying.

I was only a few steps away from Slate when Jett picked me up from the floor. "Thank the Mother. Dear Gods, my daughter has made me soft." Jett said as his big turquoise eyes gleamed. "I am having a strange day."

I giggled as he sat me down on my feet and watched him try to open his eyes wide to dry them. "The pressure is off you now, Indi. I can have Tios too." I told her with a smile and she did, in fact, look relieved.

I could see it in her posture and knit my brows. Something was up with her. Jett held his hand up as we always did when asking to delve, and I smiled. I'd never tire of hearing that I healed. Brass was carefully rising from his seat in my periphery.

Jett put his hand to my stomach and recoiled as if burnt. I gasped, staring at him.

No. I knew I healed. Whatever ever he saw was wrong!

"What's wrong?" Steel called, getting to his feet.

Jett's turquoise almond eyes were wide as he lowered them to mine, scanning them. I heard Gypsum get to his feet, and he embraced Brass.

"Congratulations!" Gypsum shouted, and Tawny squealed.

"What?" I asked, feeling dizzy.

Quick's neck looked like it hurt as it whipped from me to his brother repeatedly. "Let me see!" Quick demanded as he almost ran around the table.

Quick out his hand to my stomach and his eyes flew up to mine. "Twins!"

Tawny squealed again, and I retreated. Brass met me at the end of the table.

"What?" I repeated and turned to Brass.

The heat was sweltering. Bile splashed in the back of my throat.

"Twins," Quick said again and sank down into a vacant seat.

It happened in a blink. One minute Brass is putting his hand on the small of my back and the next I saw Slate launch across the table and I threw myself over Brass. Slate collided with my chest and I heard it crack as we went down. More than one person was screaming.

Slate swung over my head and Brass swung back. I was finding it hard to breathe and wheezed with every breath.

"Scarlett!" Brass growled and Slate started blinking down at me, realizing his not just straddling Brass, but me as well.

Slate leapt off me, his bronze features etched with horror. I was still wheezing when Brass disentangled himself from beneath me. Slate moved, shrugging off Quick and Jett, and helped Brass lay me down.

"Get away from her, you great big oaf!" Tawny screamed.

Slate's face hardened, and he set his hand to my stomach, delving. Brass's palm was over my chest where the pain was and my breathing came easier. I sucked in a deep breath as the faces of my family hovering above me.

"They are okay," Slate's voice was thick and his words slurred.

Brass's head snapped up to his. Brass had a bloody nose and the skin under Slate's left eye was swelling. I lifted my hands to them both and *called*. They looked back down at me.

"I'm okay? I have... oh my gods!" The edge of panic shot through my voice.

Brass watched with a clenched jaw as Slate rested his hand on my stomach again. He nodded and held it there. I looked to Brass.

"Did you know?" I asked in a pitch only meant to be heard by dogs.

Brass turned his head once, and I exhaled. Tawny and Indigo were shouting at Slate, and Brass sighed.

"We never need healing. I *called* to your stomach and felt... life."

My head swam, and I held my hand to it.

"Give us three a moment, please," Brass asked.

Amber protested, but Tawny snapped at her and she stormed off. Pearl and Quick lingered, but she took his arm and led him away, closing the door behind them. Brass stood and helped me into a seated position. Slate's hand was still on my stomach and his head hung, hiding his face.

"I am going to walk away. I will be right down the hall if you need me," Brass said to me. He looked to Slate, who had lifted his head with a knit brow. "Neither of you deserves what has happened."

Brass strode from the hall and I followed him with my eyes until he disappeared out the opposite way the others went. Slate and I were alone.

"I am sorry, Scarlett," he said in that same strange tone.

"It's okay," I managed a gentle tone. "I'm sorry, too."

Slate pressed his lips together tightly, and I got up. He held me there, and I stiffened as he laid down on the floor and put his head in my lap with his hand still on my stomach. He was *calling* the entire time. Slate nuzzled my stomach with his face, and I squeezed my eyes shut as tears fell.

"Give me a moment. That is all I ask."

I saw he was wearing Alder's ring again, and he freed his hand long enough to slide the emerald ring from my necklace and onto my ring finger. My throat hurt from suppressing my cries.

I knew what he needed. It's what I needed at his wedding. To know I was causing him that much pain tore me apart. I took a shuddering breath and spoke through my sniffles.

"We live in Mabon. In a cottage deep in the woods so we can have privacy. I am ambassador for the Centaur and you for the Wemic. Right now, though, we lay before a fire after having made love and you rub oils over the great swell of my stomach that carries your twins. A boy and a girl, Lark and Wren. They'll have dark wavy hair and flawless bronze skin. Wren will always try to keep up with Lark, who is constantly getting into mischief. We'll have another two or three, maybe another girl and two more boys. Sea, Alder, and Brass for the uncle who spends far too much time hanging around the cottage."

"And ogles their mother," Slate rumbled, and I smiled tightly as my tears ebbed.

"Who ogles their mother," I agreed with a nod. "We'll spend nights in a big white warm bed making love as our cottage full of children sleeps and work as a team to raise our extensive family. Uncle Jett will always try to drop off his children so he can be a lech with his wives, and Indigo and Quick will conveniently show up for visits at the same time, every time."

Slate made a noise deep in his throat that sounded like contentment.

"Tawny and Steel will only have two very bossy children who come over with their uncle Gypsum and bring him woodland creatures demanding to know what they're all thinking, to which he will always reply, 'Put me down.'"

Slate kissed my stomach and my hand stilled on his head. "I cannot live this way. You were my hope, and I have lost you."

I ran my fingers along his jaw and he shifted to look up at me, cutting me to the quick. "You'll live, Slate. You'll live for your unborn child, who needs a father."

He sucked in a deep breath and exhaled slowly, "I am sorry, Scarlett."

I nodded woodenly and swallowed. "I didn't know, Slate. Honestly, I wouldn't have come. I could leave now."

"No." Slate turned again in my lap so he could face my stomach and placed his hand on it. "What I would not give to be him," he breathed.

Brass rounded the corner, and I raised my head to him. His face was soft and sad, having read everything we'd thought and discussed. I'd never seen Slate so vulnerable, and I found it unnerving. He was a dim shadow of himself and my heart was heartbreaking.

Brass offered his hand and Slate shut his eyes. "I always knew you would have her. I had only wanted a few years before that. If it has to be someone else, I am glad it is you."

I pulled my lips between my teeth and stifled a cry.

... Close your eyes...

Brass sighed and shut his eyes. Slate shifted in my lap to face me and I bent my face to his and brushed my lips against his in a soft kiss.

"You are a good man and you will make a wonderful father." I whispered against his lips and he breathed me in.

I moved away from him, and he sat up. Brass opened his eyes and took my hand, lifting me up, and offered it to Slate, who shook his head and got up on his own.

Brass bent his knees to look into my eyes. "I can't pretend I'm not happy, Scarlett."

I held his hand over my cheek. "I never thought I would have children and now I'm having two. *Your* two." I smiled a little. "I'm not unhappy, Brass. I'm... conflicted. You're amazing and you'll be an amazing father."

"*But* you're still in love with Slate and wanted to have his children, too," Brass added, creasing his brow.

I let out a shuddering breath. "Can't I have both?" I laughed nervously and Brass pulled me to him, wrapping his arms around me.

"Maybe, love. One pregnancy at a time," he said, kissing the top of my head.

We watched him walk away before the others returned to finish dinner.

Dinner spanned the incredibly excited to the totally disheartening. Slate had not returned and Amber had gone back to his old bedroom alone. She'd felt outdone by my miraculous return to the fertile lands, and doubly so when the fact that I carried twins came to light. Cherry was hardly three weeks along and so no one else could know. We were in the same boat and I felt a camaraderie at being pregnant at the same time with her. Tawny, while excited, felt left out.

As Brass and I readied for bed in the gorgeous pearlescent bathroom I loved, Indigo peeked her head in and joined us.

"Did you mean what you said about coming to stay with you for a while?" She asked, picking up her toothbrush.

My bangs had grown out, and as I tucked them behind an ear, my golden waves fell down to the waist of my ivory nightie. "Of course." I told her, sparing a glance for Brass, who gave a nod.

She ran her teeth over her pink lower lip. "They expelled me from Valla U today."

"What happened?" I demanded, and her powder blue eyes grew fierce.

"Ash. He went too far, so I slapped him. I wish I had waited until after lunch so it wouldn't have been in front of the provosts. Moon was there, too. They didn't have a choice." Indigo's corn silk hair slid over her shoulder and I frowned sympathetically at her. "Tawny was impressive. She invoked the wrath of Orion and convinced him to come to the university with Pearl and Sparrow to change the provosts' minds, but they could not do so."

"So that's it? You don't get to be a Guardian?"

"They're letting me take the Ragnarök, but there's no one to train me and —"

"Silver will do it. I will go to headquarters before our trip back and clear it with Lera. I should check in on my team, anyway," Brass said.

His team. I'd made him a captain. I'd completely forgotten.

"No, I don't want to be a burden on him. We can barely stand to be around one another as it is," Indigo said running her fingers along the bathroom counter.

"Not another word. Consider the matter closed. You can train with my team if nothing else." Brass gave her a warm smile, and I felt her mood lift.

We said goodnight and went into the bedroom.

"There's only one thing left to do," he said, kicking the door shut behind us and wrapping his arms around me from behind.

I felt awful. My initial reaction had been so distressed. I was ecstatic to be pregnant. Twins! Brass was the kind of man made for being a father. He would shower our children with love.

"Oh? What's that?" I asked as he marched me to the bed.

"To marry," he said, kissing my cheek.

I froze and turned in his arms. "That's not funny," I said curtly.

Brass released his hold on me and sat down on the bed. "I know you said a blood vow to Slate. Scarlett, I have to tell you... When we bonded — that ceremony with the ribbons was a hand fasting. We're essentially married *as long as love lasts*. If I can get Slate —"

My eyes widened in incredulity. "What are you saying? That you're going to ask Slate if he can... I do not know what you're saying. You're going to ask him if we can marry?"

Brass leveled his eyes at me. "It's not completely unreasonable. You are carrying my children and we love one another, even if you're too afraid to say it."

"No. I'm happy about how things are. It's been two weeks, Brass!" I said, scoffing.

"Right. You must have been in season that first time. Is there a different reason you don't want to be with me, Scarlett?" Brass asked and my heart dropped.

I crossed the room from where I paced and held his head to my chest. "None. I boldly demanded you give me your body my first time for a reason. You've always been special to me, no matter how I tried to deny it." He wound his arms around my legs. "I just can't do that to Slate. I've hurt him so much already. Children are enough for me. We're together. That's what is important."

He hid his disappointment well. I would always be in love with Slate, and he would always be my husband. Acting like we never happened and marrying Brass hurt too much to contemplate. Things were better than I could've hoped for, as they were.

An idea struck me, and I loaded Brass's arms up with pillows and blankets. I smiled impishly as I led him through the halls.

"Where are you taking me?" Brass asked for the sake of asking since he knew perfectly well we were going to the balcony.

"I want you to sleep under those stars you miss. You might even get lucky if you wish hard enough on one of them."

Brass waggled his brows at me as we walked out onto the balcony.

CHAPTER 30
JETT

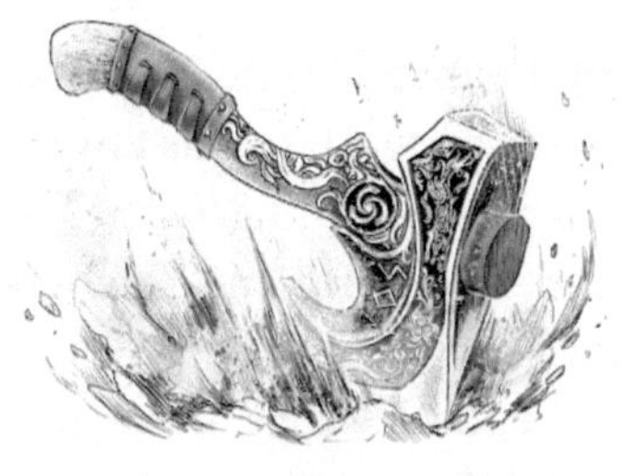

"This is deeply disturbing, even for you."

Jett walked up on Slate, who sat leaning against the wall of the hall. Through the glass door was the semicircle balcony that rested above the falls. Jett had looked out the window to check out what Slate was watching, and he'd almost fallen over himself trying to get away from the door.

Brass and Scarlett had laid blankets down on the grey stone in an apparent makeshift bed, complete with pillows. Brass was lying on his back with Scarlett, wearing nothing but a satin nightie that had slid off her shoulders, straddling his lap. It wouldn't have been as visible if the moon wasn't full. Since it was, you could see every nuance of her facial expressions, the way her skin shadowed, where his fingers gripped her backside as she moved.

Was Slate insane?

"Come. We'll fall into deep cups. We're going to be fathers. Our children are going to grow up together. If you have a boy, your son may court my daughter when she's thirty... forty years old."

Slate's palm rested on the clear glass door as he watched his close friend and wife make love. "I never should have broken my rules."

Jett slid down the wall next to him, keeping his eyes away from the door, but he could see movement in the corner of his eye. "It is better to have loved and lost than —"

"Stow it. Nothing good has come of it," Slate rumbled.

"Where's the girl you had a fling with before you found out Amber was pregnant? I don't condone cheating, but since technically you cheat on Scarlett with Amber, I don't think Scarlett will mind if you take a siesta for a day. We'll watch over Amber and —"

"It was Scarlett."

"Huh?"

"When you agreed to ask Brass to check in on her, I flew out that night and went to her apartment. I was with her when I was in Mabon. She was the one who went to the Hausts while Amber told me the news. It was always Scarlett. Do you still believe she would not mind?" Slate asked dryly.

He wiped a hand over his face and shook his head. Slate had been out of sorts since Amber told him about the pregnancy. Slate was always the one who was going to suffer the worst when this thing with Scar ended. Jett had promised himself he'd be understanding and be there for his brother for whatever he needed him for.

Now, Jett thought it wasn't just Amber's pregnancy that broke him, but having Scar slip through his fingers a second time. Her and Brass...it was the beginning of a lifelong relationship. One look at them and you wondered why they hadn't been together all along.

Slate rose to his feet and Jett clamored up. He didn't want Scarlett to see him sitting there alone like a pervert. The door to the balcony opened and Brass entered the hall in his loose linen pants and bare feet.

Jett looked between the two men as they faced off, unsure of what he should do. Scarlett must have passed out after their lovemaking.

"I knew you could not resist watching after her," Brass said wryly.

"You fucked my wife and got her pregnant," Slate ground out.

Brass held up his hands in surrender. "Guilty on all charges. I have a favor to ask."

Slate took a step towards him, and Jett raised his hands between them. "You won't win her back by killing the father of her children."

Slate's jaw clenched, eyes flashing. "You dare ask me for a favor?"

"I want to marry her," Brass said simply, and Jett winced.

Slate threw back his head and laughed. It was wicked and sent a shiver down Jett's spine.

"Not a chance. Does she want to marry you?" Slate asked, pointing out to the balcony.

Pain laced his words. If Jett could hear it, so could Brass.

"No, but she'll come around. It's you. It's always been you. She doesn't want you to hurt. She'll never settle down with me unless you give your blessing." Brass told him plainly.

Slate looked out the door. "I cannot."

"Cannot or will not?" Brass pushed.

Slate's silver eyes snapped back to Brass. "You broke our bargain. I will die with her oath, and she can never say the words to you."

Jett sucked in a sharp breath. Brass nocked up his chin and ran his thumb along it nodding.

"We can make a new bargain."

Slate's face was expressionless as he waited for Brass to continue. Jett checked outside to make sure Slate's demonic laughter hadn't given her night terrors, and she dove headlong off the balcony to escape it.

"I've always been prepared to share her. I feel as though I am already. You're always there in the back of her mind, constantly worrying about you. She wants to have your children." Brass said, meeting Slate's eyes.

"She is carrying yours," Slate growled.

Brass nodded. "She won't always be."

Jett groaned. Another crazy bargain. Wonderful.

CHAPTER
THIRTY-ONE

After making love to Brass on the balcony underneath the clear Thrimilci night, Brass had pointed out the constellations to me and told me we were in the Atlantic ocean. How had I not known that? Honestly, when people start telling you that you're not quite human and there's a whole side of yourself that would be dissected and tested for science, you just roll with it and see where it leads. I didn't think it would lead to earth. Maybe another realm of existence.

"You miss it."

"What?" he'd asked.

"All of it. I'm sorry I forgot about your team."

"I would rather be with you," he'd said, but I wasn't completely convinced.

"They're not mutually exclusive," I murmured, and Brass shifted me in his arms to search my face.

"Spell it out for me."

"Indigo needs me and..."

"Slate."

I bit my lip. "Brass, I've never seen him look like this. It's like he grew harder and harder and this whole pregnancy with Amber and me... he looks miserable, but a dangerous miserable. Like he might do something stupid. Regardless —"

"You want to return to Valla U?" He'd asked.

I nodded. "Not really, but both my mother's daughters can't *not* be Guardians. I hadn't known how hard this was going to be on Indi. With Sterling getting married, she's withdrawn. Cold. Gypsum is just getting weirder every time I visit."

"And you believe you can fix them?"

"I can try. I'll pack up my things when I get back, but keep the apartment since it's paid until next February. You belong here. You're only in Chicago for me, and if I'm here, then we can be here together. Not married, but together... hand fasted,"

Brass's naked body rolled over me and his hair fell to the sides of his face as he looked down at me. "You want this?"

I nodded and ran my fingertips over his bearded stubble. "I don't want to have the twins in Chicago. They're Guardians. They belong here, too."

Brass ran his hands in featherlight strokes along the inside of my thighs. "You'd have to do the Ragnarök challenge..."

"Amethyst did it. With you waiting at the finish line, if I'm injured, I know you'll take care of me. I'm worried, but not enough so that I'd let it stop me. Maybe I can find some armor that has a hard place over the stomach to protect them." I chewed my lip. "When will you know their sex?"

Brass gave an impish grin. "Soon." His hand slid higher and my back bowed.

"Good, I want to know it. I'm getting excited."

"I can tell." He purred.

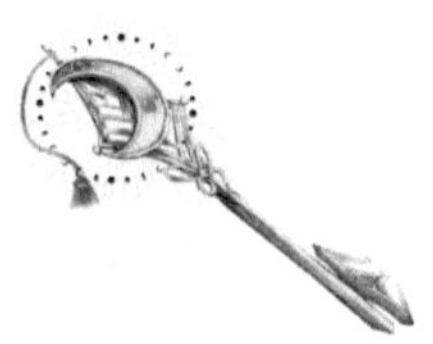

Staff kept their eyes averted as we walked the halls barefoot and half clad, the blankets and pillows piled high in our arms. Amber was storming her way down the stairs when we passed her.

"Are you going today?" she asked without preamble in a petulant tone.

"*Um*, where?" I asked, holding a pillow over my thin nightie.

She rolled her eyes, and I took a steadying breath.

Must not slap Slate's other wife.

"To the Wemic. Slate does not want to jeopardize the baby, so he asked me to stay. Cherry is staying as well. What about you?" Her big blue almond eyes glared at me accusingly, as if this was some grand orchestrated plan.

"You do not have to go if you wish to stay," Brass offered.

"I didn't fly all the way in from Chicago to sit in a palace. I'm going to Keen's wedding."

Brass's brows rose. "Your choice, Scarlett. We're going, Amber."

She whirled around us and continued down the stairs in a flurry of anger. Brass pursed his lips.

"She thinks you did this."

I rolled my eyes. "It's not like I don't have you here with me. What does she think is going to happen?" I held my hand to my stomach and wished I could delve into myself.

Brass smiled warmly at me, and heat unfurled in my stomach.

He freed a hand and held a finger to my lips. "I know."

I gave him a grateful smile in return, and we walked to our room.

It felt good to be in my gear again. Brass had gone to headquarters without me and I slipped into snug khaki pants and a white tank top with my seax on my thigh, belt of blades around my waist, and wrist blades buckled on, I wrapped a thin white scarf around my neck to cover my head later.

Everyone was at breakfast save Brass and me as I sat on Pearl's right in Hawk's old seat as we ate. She couldn't stop smiling at me. Her emerald eyes glittered, and a weight felt like someone had lifted it from my shoulders.

"I was going to wait to announce it when Brass came back, but I'm too excited to wait —"

Quick interrupted me. "Do not tell me you are engaged again."

"Silver!" Indigo admonished.

I sucked on my teeth and waited until my anger ebbed. "We're not getting married, Quick. Thanks for that by the way, though you should encourage me to get engaged to him since it seems to be the fastest way for my relationships to end," I snapped.

Quick looked properly cowed as Tawny, Cherry, and Indigo shot him daggers.

"As I was saying —"

"He got you all buggered up; it was a safe assumption," Quick defended and my cheeks heated.

"Silver, please, darling. Manners," Pearl said, and he winced.

I grit my teeth. "We're moving back. If Moon will let me, I'll go back to Valla U and complete the last challenge. Brass has offered to train Indi, so she'll be prepared for it. He's at headquarters now, smoothing things over with Lera."

"I will speak to Moon while you are away. When would you be returning?" Pearl asked.

"I'd need a week to settle things in Chicago. So, two weeks from now."

Pearl gave me an impish smile, and I looked dubiously at her. "Will Mr. Regn be joining us?"

I could've really used a rock to crawl under. "*Um*, not officially. My old room is fine. If we take that step, it will be in Ostara."

"You have talked about moving in with our family?" Quick interrupted again.

"By the Mother, let her finish."

"Thank you, Steel. Yes, Quick. Surprise, surprise! Two people see one another and talk about the future. It's perfectly natural." I rolled my eyes dramatically and noticed Indigo.

"Indi? I'm keeping my apartment until next spring; we can go back anytime."

She gave me a bright smile. "Happy tears. Sorry, I see how that could be confusing." She giggled nervously, "I'm glad things have worked out for you after everything. It gives me hope."

I gave her a sympathetic smile and leaned towards her to hold her, and she clasped me back. "I think things look better than they are, Indi. They are slowly getting better, though; these babies are a blessing I didn't dare pray for. I'd have them on my own if I had to. I want them so bad," I whispered in her ear.

"You wouldn't have to do it on your own," Indi whispered back. "Twins."

I smiled and withdrew. "Twins. I'm probably going to get as big as a house," I said, pulling a chuckle from around the table.

"Brass won't mind as long as you have his healthy babies," Jett said, smiling smugly, and I shifted in my seat.

"I doubt he would," I said thoughtfully.

"When did you find out you healed?" Jett asked.

I rubbed my brow, noticing the blue morning glories were taking hold of the entire north wall. They added a sweet floral scent to the ornate room.

"Chris made me go to that doctor, so two days after Slate and Amber's wedding." I dropped my eyes.

That had been a massively terrible week.

Pearl rose and started saying her goodbyes. "Travel safe, my darlings. By the time you return, I will have your room ready at Valla U again." She kissed the top of my head and strode from the room in a swirling green chiffon.

"So... when did you and Chris break up?" Jett asked.

I made a face at him. "We broke up the following day. I wasn't in a great place; it wasn't Chris's fault in the least. He helped me through a really rough time."

"And you never saw him after?" Jett prodded.

"By the Mother, Jett. I saw him three days later at the gym and I quit because it was too hard for him to work with me. We saw him again two nights ago while Brass and I were on a dinner cruise."

"A dinner cruise! That sounds romantic. At Navy Pier?" Tawny beamed and asked about the night.

"And Brass came to your place nine weeks later, four weeks ago, give or take?" Jett asked.

"Jett. These aren't Chris's. You can ask me flat out. It's easy to keep track of." I said dryly, "I doubt anyone else here can count, aside from Tawny and Indigo, without taking off shoes and socks."

Indigo beamed. "You're in good company."

Quick's face was beet red. I was sure he knew he was only the second human man she'd been with, but maybe I'd been wrong.

"I wondered myself." Quick admitted.

"A little wondering hurts no one. Brass is the father."

"Truth," Quick said, shaking his head in disbelief.

"Any more questions, Jett?" I asked with a small smile.

Jett nocked his jaw up and sucked on his teeth. "Brass came to you four weeks ago. You're two weeks along. Happened pretty fast."

"All it takes is once," I retorted.

Jett's face split into a grin, and I made a face at him. "What are you smiling at?"

"Truth." Quick said absently, and I stuck my tongue out childishly at Jett, making him laugh.

"You are a terrible liar."

I fought a grin. "I know. That's why I don't do it."

"Truth," Quick said again.

"What is she lying about now?" Brass teased as he walked into the informal dining room.

He'd taken to wearing fewer beads threaded through his hair and keeping it knotted at his nape. A piece had fallen free and grazed his dark honey cheek bone as he strode past the table to where I sat at the head. He leaned down and kissed my cheek, and Indigo made a move to give him her seat.

"No thank you, I only wished to confirm that Lera has given her approval, and she says you are welcome back as her delegate." Brass smiled down at me. He arched his brow and looked around the table. "Good morning. I see she has told you already."

Everyone rose from the table since we were done with our meal. Jett shared a look with Slate, whose eyes I'd been ignoring all morning. Amber had been pouting beside him. She'd return to the Dagr palace after we left.

The rest were already leaving the dining room when I looked between the three of them, trying to understand their cryptic talk. Brass put his hand to the small of my back as I stood.

He took my hand and nodded at me or them. I wasn't sure. "All in good time, Scarlett. I promise. Nothing bad will come of keeping this one. You have my word."

I sighed. "Men and their secrets." I shook my head and slid my eyes to Slate, whose lips curled a fraction.

I skirted Brass and left the room. They could speak freely now with all their secret talk; I wanted nothing to do with it, even though it was about me. I trusted those three idiots implicitly, which probably made me the grandest idiot of all.

CHAPTER 32
JETT

Slate paced on the other side of the table. Jett was glad Scarlett took the hint and had left them alone. Brass waited until she was far enough away that she couldn't pick up on their emotions before he'd began again.

"The baby in Amber's belly is yours, Slate. Apparently, she caught on to you trying to drug her after laying with her." Brass told him wryly.

Slate shut his eyes for a moment. "I had hoped she laid with another."

Jett scoffed. He'd been in denial that first week. Now he understood why. There was no way Slate would've wanted to go back to Amber after being with Scarlett in Mabon. That Scarlett would have an affair surprised Jett — sort of. Slate had asked Brass to scan her mind and figure out if he was truly the father.

Jett dry washed his face. "So you two come back, kind of live together, kind of date and you claim the kids? Is she planning on doing the Ragnarök?"

"No!" Slate stopped in his pacing.

Brass quirked his brow. "It is not up to us. She wants to do it, so she shall."

"I will not have her risking her children's lives. She can take the test at another time." Slate's jaw clenched.

Brass held up his hands. "You act as though I've plotted this. It fell into my lap and I have been trying to fix things. I want to be with her. — yes. I would do anything to accomplish that as long as it made her happy. You're not thinking clearly because you want it all back. Too much has happened, Slate. There is no going back. You should be glad you are doing the Ragnarök with her. This way, you can make sure she is on your team."

Jett's brows lifted. He hadn't thought of that.

"Scarlett, Indigo, Quick, and you. I'll take Tawny, Cherry, and convince Cyan to team up with us. This could actually work out better," Jett said.

Slate rubbed absently on the jade love rune. "That will work."

"You're going to have to try not to push too hard while you're at Valla U together. Control yourself," Brass said and Slate glared.

"I can control myself, Regn. When I cannot, it is because an intruder has worked their way into my stronghold, stealing what is mine."

"She's not yours anymore."

"She is my wife and mate. She's *mine*."

Brass shook his head ruefully. "You held too tight. She needs to be free. She belongs to herself. I am only allowed to share with her. The sooner you figure that out, the happier you'll be."

AMA AND SHALE met them at the Thrimilci portal gate. It was a fifteen-foot-high mosaic arch, done in whites and blues. Spiraling ironwork below it radiated from a blazing sun and below that, an iron patch work door. The shimmering white roads of the town's crowded heart with people out and about in traditional chiffon gowns or sleeveless V neck linen tops common to Thrimilci.

Thrimilci was the island of perpetual summer. The Sumar palace rested atop the cliff side that hundreds of white adobe styled homes slanted down with royal blue roofs. Its Moroccan style domes of gold and blue that capped the turrets stretched into the clear blue sky. The Mani and Sol Rivers met behind the palace that created the falls below the balcony.

Jett pulled up his scarf as he walked alongside Slate. Quick was on his right. Brass and Gypsum were deep in conversation just behind them. Steel walked along, watching Tawny as if the sun rose and fell with her. He'd forgiven Jett, but looked tight around the eyes when he said it wasn't a big deal. No one better touch his perfect little wife.

Gypsum wanted to know if Brass could read the minds of animals. He couldn't, Brass couldn't hide the amusement at Gypsum's curiosity. The youngest of their group would start at Valla U in the coming year.

Scarlett walked between Tawny and Indigo. Amethyst walked beside Indi while Shale and Ama floated about joining whatever conversation interested them at the moment. Ama could read auras, actual colors around people. She'd been frowning every time she'd looked at Slate.

Shale and Ama loved a Shadow Breaker baby. They were ecstatic about her pregnancy. Jett liked to see Scarlett looking back to normal. Her hair was back to its natural color, she'd grown out her bangs, she was still into her fit lifestyle, but she hadn't lost her soft curves. Too many Guardian women crossed the line between tight and hard. Amethyst had always been willowy, tall, and slender. She'd put on a little weight since having Gigi and Jett couldn't have been happier. Her svelte figure had some meat to it for once.

They walked the flat desert lands without so much as a single tree between the random oasis to shade them. The girls were not fond of popping a squat out where everyone could see them, but you did what you had to.

It was early evening when they arrived at the undulating sandstone hills they called the red hills. They'd reach the Wemic by tomorrow afternoon. As the sun fell, the desert grew cooler. It never dropped below eighty in Thrimilci. Jett snapped out his roll and Amethyst moved to his side. Steel unfurled his and Tawny's next to Jett.

Jett watched Scarlett unroll hers. Brass finally left Gypsum's side. Before he could put his roll next to hers, Slate snapped his out with a flourish and laid it down close to hers. Scarlett's turquoise almond eyes widened and her face lost its color. She looked up to Brass, who pursed his lips to fight a smile and unrolled him to her other side. Slate had no intention of giving them any privacy or making it easy on them. Jett approved of Slate's actions.

Indi scowled when Quick laid him down next to her and he gave her a broad grin that usually worked on the ladies. Indigo was over it. She rolled her eyes and sat down, folding her arms around her knees as Gypsum got a small fire going.

Freya's burly boar. It was going to be an uncomfortable outing.

He watched Scarlett sit down carefully on her roll to face the fire between Brass and Slate; her knee was a few short inches from Slate's. She looked at his knee as if it had conspired against her. Scarlett looked like a wee child between the two big men.

Tawny and Amethyst prepared dinner. Gypsum pulled at the leather throng around his neck, Ama and Shale lying next to him. It was a panpipe, hardly bigger than his palm. He played a tune, and Scarlett laughed.

"Chief, when did you become a musical?" she asked, her full lips parting into her drop-dead gorgeous smile.

Gypsum looked embarrassed by the attention. "The animals like it. A few months back, I picked it up."

She looked at the fire and absently ran her fingers over something under her shirt. "I guess I've missed a lot."

"All the more to experience now that you are back," Ama chirped with her endless optimism.

The perky, buxom blonde leaned against her lover and much less curvy counterpart. Shale smirked. Jett was worried about her penchant for rude remarks. No one wanted to hear her opinion on Scarlett and Brass, and she looked like she itched to say something.

Gypsum played the flute-like instrument as they ate their meal of dried meat and bread. They seasoned it well and brooked no cause for complaint. Quick had moved closer to Indigo, and she wasn't withdrawing from him. His palm that held his weight rested behind her back so he was leaning towards her. Jett couldn't tell if their arguing was becoming part of their foreplay or if Quick liked. She made it a challenge for him. Few women turned down Silver Regn.

CHAPTER 33

INDIGO

Loneliness had gotten the better of me when Silver slid under the thin blanket. The way Sterling had looked at me as I walked with my things to the portal room after Reed reluctantly expelled me was salt in the wound that had been festering for months.

Four more months left until the love of my life married his betrothed.

Silver's deft fingers slipped through my hair, braiding it, and the action alone made him hard against my backside. As he moved, I inhaled his patchouli sandalwood scent that would stick to my skin for days.

At least it seemed that way.

He'd been trying to get back into my good graces on and off for months. Silver kept getting distracted by this girl or that one. His attempts to win me back failed miserably because he couldn't accept that I wouldn't stop seeing Sterling. Silver could share my bed when we were both in the mood. I enjoyed having him in it. What I didn't like was the inevitable fight we would get into when he asked me to stop seeing Sterling.

It never failed.

We'd gone off and on for a while now and it always ended the same. That was the definition of insanity, wasn't it?

Silver *was* insane if he thought I'd try to be exclusive with him. He and Slate were both well-known womanizers around Tidings. Slate had only stopped sleeping around because Scarlett tamed him as much as a man like him could act tamed. That had only drawn more women to him. There would have been even more if they'd known he was a Dagr.

Leeches. Parasites.

Silver ran his palm over my hip, pressing me tighter to him, and kissed my ear. The man had talented lips; I'd give him that. Oh, who was I kidding? He had talented everything. It'd be sad indeed if he wasn't from all the experience he had.

"Turn around, Dove," Silver whispered.

I felt the blood rush to my face. "Don't call me that," I whispered harshly to him for the umpteenth time.

If someone ever heard him call me that, they'd ask what it meant.

I could hear the satisfied smile in his voice. "*Dove*. No reason to be ashamed. Your cooing makes my cock hard," he purred.

The fire hadn't died out yet, but something about the outdoors got everyone all riled up. Poor Scar wouldn't be enjoying Brass's company because Slate had laid down next to her. Scarlett had watched on with horror as he turned on his side and fixated on her as she tried to go to sleep. Brass had gotten the crumby end of that deal for certain.

I reached behind me for Silver's belt and unbuckled it before I pushed down his pants. He cursed.

"Not like this, Dove," he said with no small amount of irritation.

"I don't want kisses, and flowers, and promises. I want your body. You can give it to me, or not, Silver. No one is forcing you."

I regretted my harsh words even before I said them. I liked Silver. He made me laugh, devilishly handsome, and he was sweet to me. A score or more of girls would kill to have Silver trying to force them into a relationship.

Silver took my hand out of his pants and rolled over. I sighed. I was mean to Silver. Sterling would never have accepted my tone. The difference being, Silver always came back.

I rolled over and slid my hand over the corded muscle of his hip that made that 'V' shape I loved to trace. Silver made no move to stop me as I slid further still until I gripped him in my fist. I slowly stroked his satiny skin until he stilled my hand with his and turned around.

His chocolate brown eyes usually held a bottomless pit of mischief and arrogance, but whenever I hurt his feelings, he gave me this inexplicable look like the one he gave me now. I realized every time how much I cared about him. I rued that I did. Without a doubt, I was part of a half dozen girls who thought she was special to the illustrious Silver Regn.

He was waiting, probably for an apology I wouldn't give him. I brought my hand up to his anvil like jaw and he shut his eyes, taking a deep breath. I *called,* lifting my hips, pushing my pants down to my ankles, and pushed my suede boot off so my khakis hung on one leg. We rolled, and I parted my knees to either side of him.

I went back to my original goal of pushing down his pants and he lifted his hips so they bunched halfway down his muscular thighs. "Do I make it difficult for you to be sweet?"

He was looking at me again when I raised my eyes. I adjusted the thin blanket over us and slid my stomach down to his as I guided him into me. I muted the moan that sprung to my lips and rocked my hips with my stomach flush to his, so we had a modicum of privacy. That campfire was still flickering, and anyone who bothered to look would see us.

By the Mother, when was the last time I let myself lay with Silver? Four months ago, at least. Right after Scarlett left and everything turned to crap. Garnet started hanging around with Amber and I read the writing on the wall. I had to fight for Sterling. I wouldn't fight for Silver too. The decision to force him out of my bed was a preemptive strike.

Silver's hips moved undermine as he slid his hand into the hair at my nape. He could be so predictable. Silver pulled my face down to his and brushed his lips against mine until I parted my lips, willing him to deepen it. He gave that smile that had drawn me to him in the first place and the acid in my stomach churned.

I loved that smile. Loved to hate it most days.

He gave it away like candy to his staunchest admirers. It was a meaningless expression when he'd shared it with so many. He rolled us over and pulled the thin blanket with us. I leveled my eyes at him. He knew better. I didn't like him to have control. Once we got started, I was more amenable to letting him do as he wished, but this didn't qualify. We hadn't fooled around in months. He was taking advantage.

He leaned down to kiss me, and I turned my face. Two could play at that game.

Silver needed to feel like every girl he was with loved him. He needed all of their passion for them not to put limits on him. I couldn't grant him that. All I had were limits. My limits guided everything in my life. It was the only way I could do it and not hate myself. I was in love with Sterling, but the only man they had seen me with in public as anything more than a friend was Silver. There was so much of me that resented it. It didn't matter that it wasn't his fault.

He could be on top, but he wouldn't be kissing me. It was one or the other. Silver's face hovered above mine, waiting for me to turn back, and I glared at him from the corner of my eye. He sighed and contented himself to burying his face in the crook of my neck and thrust deep. My fingers dug into his taut backside.

His full, soft lips kissed along my throat, and my eyes rolled back into my head.

A warning should come with his kisses.

They were drug inducing. Causing more hallucinations than boomers. One could actually believe she was special. That she could be his only lover. As if there was any possibility of a future with him. That she could fall for him.

"*Ooh, ooh.*" I moaned as I felt my insides clench around him.

Silver could keep going forever if he wanted. He'd proven it to me on more than one occasion. He took advantage of my lack of lucidity and roughly claimed my mouth. His bearing changed, now triumphant, confidence infused his movements. He was never in a short supply of confidence; a little humility wouldn't kill him.

"Let go," he whispered huskily against my lips.

You let go; I thought peevishly as the self-proclaimed master of the multiple orgasm elicited another finger-curling-breath-quickening-loin-clenching response and he swallowed my moan with his gifted mouth.

Silver's breathing grew shallow, and I pushed him back with my *calling,* catching him with hands of warm air as he shuddered. He sunk against me when his body stopped shuddering, and I sent his seed out into the sand.

"I hate when you do that," Silver said thickly next to my ear.

My eyes slid closed; I was exhausted. "I hate when you climb on top, or when you kiss me, when you know I don't want to. You'd hate for me to wind up pregnant. I didn't bring any tea. I had no intention of sleeping with you."

Silver rose to his elbows, and I could feel him looking down at me. "Lie. Must you be so cold? Do not take whatever he did out on me. I am not your punching bag."

I opened my eyes, narrowing them at him. The low light from the fire cast his face in shadow. Several cold rebukes came to mind, but I let them go. I would want to Silver to share my bed again on this trip. I *could* be nice if need be.

"Did I hurt your *feelings*? I'll make up for it tomorrow night."

Maybe not nice.

Silver leveled his dark eyes. "I would tell you to get laid, but apparently that works neither."

He rolled off of me and I straightened out my pant legs under the blanket and pulled back on my clothes and kicked off my other boot. Quick turned on his side away from me but didn't move his roll. I sighed.

I didn't understand Silver's soft spot for me. I knew it existed and somehow every molehill became a mountain. He didn't ask for much. I just had a problem giving him anything. Getting kicked out of Valla University was the topping on a terrible year that was far from over.

I shifted to my side and wrapped my arm around his waist. I slid my hand under his shirt and traced where I knew his tattoos were. They had healed so smoothly there was no telling where the black jagged Celtic marks were, but I had memorized them. I knew that two inches to the left of his navel; it curved up over his hard abs, that an inch from the crease between his pecs just above his nipple was another thick curve that circled round to his collarbone.

"Are you okay, Silver?" I whispered, and he sighed.

He shifted on the roll to look back at me and held my hand so I wouldn't draw it back and let it fall over his hip. "I am. You are not, Dove. It is okay to be upset about getting thrown out of University. You can vent to me, not at me."

All the caustic things I wanted to snap at him, and I swallowed them back. He pulled me so his body laid flush to mine.

Classic Silver. Such a short memory. I rested my cheek on his chest, breathing him in and held him tighter, allowing him to hold me back. It was kind of nice to be held. I'd never spent the night with a man before Silver. Sterling had been engaged to Diamond for years, and if anyone caught us together, it would have been catastrophic. It was bad enough everyone knew without seeing.

"Kiss me," he coaxed.

I squeezed my eyes tight and drew back from his chest, and he lowered his mouth to mine. His kisses had a dizzying effect. Drugs, I tell you. It was on his lips. The deeper the kiss, the farther I fell. My heart pounded, a swelling feeling blossomed in my chest, and my skin tingled.

His kisses left me vulnerable. A condition a Tio woman couldn't let herself be in. A curse befell us. All the Guardians knew it. Tio women were never happy for long. Something always went wrong. Scarlett had never gotten that memo.

"You never told me you had only been with one other," he whispered.

I never should have let that slip. Now he would think he was special to me. He was very good looking; he required no effort, and I knew he had a penchant for one-night stands. That was why I had taken him back to my rooms the night Diamond came to her masquerade. He wasn't supposed to get attached. He wasn't supposed to bring his clothes and toiletries, even his Gods' cursed toothbrush, to my rooms. I wasn't supposed to seek his company.

"Rikke, the Wemic scout too." I told him, hoping it would burst a little of his bubble.

Silver was a hard man to deter. "The first human man you chose as a grown woman." He whispered, and I nearly rolled my eyes.

"I chose Sterling first," I murmured, and he deepened his kiss.

"You were just a girl then. Now you are a woman."

I fought a smile at his assessment. The world revolved around Silver Regn, as he saw it.

I was ready for him to take me again, I'd let him do it anyway he wanted. Silver drew back and rubbed his nose along mine.

"See. Not so bad, Dove," Quick purred.

"Are you going to help train me with the Shadow Breakers?" I asked.

"All business? You are not supposed to know about us. Let us pretend you do not. Yes. Of course. Will you be surly every day or only most days?"

"Most days." I admitted, and he kissed the tip of my nose.

"Truth. I will look forward to the days you are not. Why do you put yourself through this? End it now before he marries. You are miserable and bitter; you will end up like Canis."

"Don't concern yourself with what I do outside of our trysts. What about your brother? Are you ready for him and Scar to come back together?"

Quick blew out a breath. "Not talking about your other lover, are we? Number one? Will I always be number two? Second in everything?"

"I'll not discuss him with you. Yes, I am upset with him."

Silver slid his hand up my side to my breasts and dipped a finger into my neckline. I gave a little; he gave a little.

"To be honest, I am rooting for Slate to make a triumphant return. Brass is my brother and I love him to death, but Slate is just as much my brother. Brass could indisputably find another woman that he could love and she would in return. Slate has shown interest in two women — Cordillera and Scarlett. That is not for a lack of trying, either."

"Silver, she's pregnant with Brass's twins. Slate doesn't stand a chance."

It hurt me to be blunt about Scarlett's situation with Silver. He had this... mushy side I'd never known was there until we started sleeping together.

Silver lifted his head, and his gaze slid past me. "I do not know about that."

I shifted and Silver moved me, so I laid away from him and he tucked me to him, letting me be the little spoon. He couldn't resist kissing along my throat as I watched. Brass laid asleep on the roll and Scarlett sat a little way off next to Slate, facing the way to the Wemic away from camp.

"Sterling said Scarlett was in Mabon. He said she came to the Haust castle. It makes little sense, but he was adamant."

"What did you say?" Quick said, leaning over me.

"Shh! Gods, do you want to wake the entire camp? I said Sterling-"

"I heard you. Amber found Slate in Mabon. Remember when all of those Minotaur had killed those village women? That was when Brass went to Chicago."

"Okay... So, what?" I asked peevishly, and he made an exasperated sound.

"Slate and Scarlett in Mabon at the same time. Amber said Slate had an affair. It was with Scarlett. Slate is still in the game."

I twisted in Silver's arms. He smiled down at me. His dark hair was always perfect. It was irritating. He kept it short, with the top long and styled like he was from the roaring twenties. I raised my hand to his hair and mussed it up, and he pulled my hand away.

"Freya's burly boar, Indigo. There is no need for that."

"Leave it, Silver," I said, pulling his hand away from his hair as he smoothed it to the side. "I suppose I felt bad for Slate now that everything he wanted she has with someone else. Your brother is a good man, though."

Silver's eyes glittered down at me. "Try not to sound like you are in love with him. It wears on me."

"I'm not in love with your brother. Don't be ridiculous."

"True. You sleep with me and you hardly *like* me," he said with his eyes flitting between mine.

He didn't say a *lie*. "I like you enough." I told him, and his lips quirked.

"Say it for me, Dove."

"No. I don't like to. It's stupid. I don't know how you ever got me to play your ridiculous game, anyway."

"I will remind you how." Silver lowered his mouth until it brushed over mine.

My eyes slid shut as I lifted my chin and his tongue slid against mine. Yes, that's how. His drug induced kisses.

"I love you, Silver." I told him against his mouth.

He smiled and drew back. "You are right. It is a stupid game."

Silver laid back down behind me and laced his fingers through mine. You couldn't give him an inch or he'd take five miles.

CHAPTER
THIRTY-FOUR

Slate had made it impossible for me to relax. He stared at me while I tried to sleep, so close I could feel that familiar draw tug me to him. My only concession was that Brass appeared more amused than upset by the entire thing. Then I'd felt the bond spring up and my eyes shot open.

That bastard.

He'd looked at me with those silver eyes reflecting the moonlight two feet away from me and nodded to follow him. He stood and soundlessly he walked a little way off. I gently *called* into Brass to make sure he was in a deep sleep so I wouldn't disturb him and took his arm from around my waist before following Slate.

He'd sat in the sand near the camp. I turned around to see if any of the others were up and I noticed they all were raunchy debauchees. Gypsum, Shale, and Ama were gone and blankets moved in familiar ways from Jett's end, Tawny's side, all the way to Indi's. That was surprising. The way she'd been speaking to Quick, you'd think she hated him.

"Sit," Slate said as I got close.

I did as he bid with the overwhelming feeling like I was going to vomit in the pit of my stomach. "It's not okay for you to activate the bond like this," I whispered and he pulled me towards him.

I huffed out a breath, but didn't move when he forced me to lean against his chest. At least I was sitting on the sand and not in his lap. We'd gone over this before. Might be not right, despite how he acted. He wrapped his arm around my side and delved with a shaky breath, and a low groan pulled from my throat. He was more than miserable, but then he'd *called*.

"Are you mad at me?" I asked.

"No, Torch. Never. On the contrary, I am... at peace. You have everything you wanted... for once."

"Not everything," I murmured.

I could feel Slate's eyes on the top of my head. Slate sighed, and I tried desperately not to breathe him in and failed. The scent of cloves and a crisp fall wind permeated my nostrils.

"In the dark, it is hard to tell which one of us has been more broken. With you, I had a torch to guide my way."

I turned towards him and felt my heart lurch. I couldn't move back. Brass shouldn't trust me with Slate.

"Slate..."

"Tell me."

"I..."

"I need the light, Scarlett."

He was still *calling* against my stomach. "I love you. Forever and always. Yours, mine, the world's, for all time," I said through a shaking sob that bubbled up.

His eyes slid closed, and he lifted his hard face to the night sky. "Thank you."

I laughed nervously, "What for? For ruining your life? For causing you more pain than any one person should endure? Or marrying you, abandoning you when times were tough, or for planning to raise children with another man? Don't thank me. Curse me. Curse the day you ever set eyes on me. I am a horrible, foolish girl who has no right to your love or forgiveness."

My throat hurt. My nose burned. I could no longer see through my bleary eyes and Slate sighed.

"You are my wife. My mate. What is there to forgive? You are my Torch."

His voice had this soft quality to it that disturbed me. I hated it. I wanted him to roar, to pin me to the sand and shout at me. He looked at me with intense, clear grey eyes and I took his strong jaw in my hands and leaned forward. My lips met his, and the world disappeared around us. The bond deactivated, and I sat back on my feet.

"I'm pregnant, Slate. They're not yours. I carry Brass's twins. Just like my mother before me, I had an affair with a married man I can't be with. I'm a monster because there was a small part of me that hoped they were yours, but they're not. What's worse? I'm *happy* to have children with Brass. I don't know what to do with all this love I still have for you and Brass is so understanding he makes me want to strangle him sometimes. He should be furious with me. I hate that you're having a baby with Amber. I hate her and this poor innocent soul that I also kind of love because you're its father and I will forever hopelessly be in love with you." Slate wiped my tears with his thumbs.

"Brass asked me to let him join in our blood vow," he whispered, and I gasped.

"No. I told him no," I said, feeling frantic.

"Come, lie back down. We need to sleep," he said, lacing his hand through mine. "Everything will right itself, Scarlett."

I wouldn't say he'd looked better. He looked like hell. For good reason, too. He rose, and I walked alongside him and back to the rolls. I slid back underneath Brass's arm and Slate rolled on his side towards me. We stared at one another for a long moment before I extended my hand. He shut his eyes and slid his arm out to lace his fingers through mine, gripping it tightly, and he *called* again. My eyelids instantly grew heavy.

CHAPTER 35
JETT

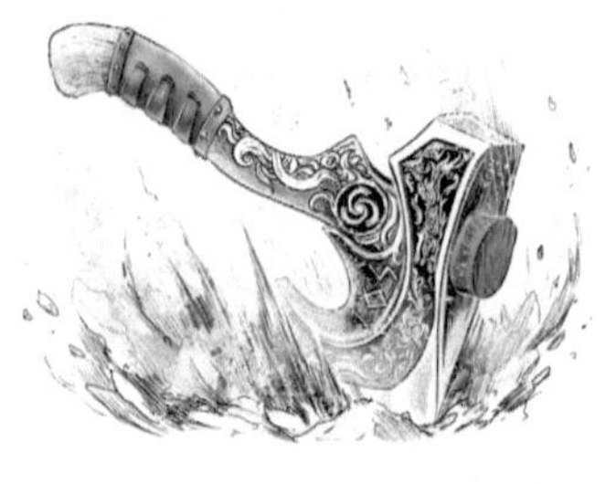

"They can live like us. Amber is a problem, but... everyone dies."

"Amethyst!" Jett started.

She rolled her mocha shoulders and smirked with her wide mouth. Amethyst was the diplomatic one. She did the right thing by Guardian tradition. She didn't talk about assassinating a greater family wife.

"Maybe I should pry their fingers apart so no one else sees it," Jett said, grimacing at the way Slate and Scarlett's hand laid in the sand between them, clasped eerily, reminding Jett of rigor mortis.

"Too late," she said and nodded to where Quick was speaking against Indigo's ear from where they laid spooning.

"There are worse things than having two spouses. I love both my husband and wife in equal measures. Though I loved you a little less when I was in labor with Gigi," Amethyst teased.

Jett leveled his eyes at her. "You think Slate and Brass would... share her?"

Jett looked to where they laid on the ground again. If Slate was two feet closer, he'd basically be sleeping with them. It was a close call.

"Brass has already." Amethyst was quick to point out, and Jett wrinkled his nose, making Amethyst laugh. "She is your sister, after all. Maybe she likes the idea of having two spouses. You certainly do."

"Slate won't share her, and they aren't like you and Cherry." Jett made a face and Amethyst doubled over laughing.

"No, they are not."

Amethyst's laughter woke the other two groups out of their slumber. Tawny stretched from where she rested atop Steel, who ran a hand over his tan face and down Tawny's back. Jett bet she was forgiven without a second thought. She turned mid-stretch and met Jett's eyes, which she immediately dropped and her fair skin flushed.

It would be awhile before they could face one another without that awkwardness.

Slate stirred and didn't let go of Scar's hand. Brass rolled away from Scarlett stretched his limbs. She shivered despite the warmth of the morning and flexed her fingers. Her eyes shot open, and she slowly retrieved her hand. Slate watched her retreat and sit up next to Brass, who had seen the interaction.

"Where —" Tawny asked when Gypsum, Shale, and Ama rounded one of the low hills.

She pursed her lips and set about picking up her roll. Scarlett decided sitting there was too awkward and got to her feet to start on breakfast. Indigo disentangled herself from Quick with great effort and helped her.

Jett narrowed his eyes at Quick. Everyone had been in an odd mood last night and had coupled up. Everyone except the tense threesome that Scarlett had going on. No one had gotten laid there.

Gypsum looked around sheepishly as he sat down, carrying his roll. The future patriarch of the Sumar looked guilty. Shale's long sheen of raven hair fell over her tiny taut shoulder as she put her things in her pack, her up-tilted dark eyes squinted in the bright sun. Ama was as bubbly as ever, her low-cut shirt showing an expanse of bosom on her petite frame. Not that Jett was looking.

Scarlett had been so intent on making breakfast, it was finished within minutes and she stood wringing her hands as everyone finished putting their things in their packs. Jett was coming around to

Amethyst's thinking. Amber was the problem. What could they do about that one?

He shook off his hostile thoughts and went to Scar's side to help her pass out the oatmeal with pieces of dried apples and spiced with cinnamon. She gave him a grateful smile, but her face was tense.

"You okay?" he asked in a low tone.

"Hm? Me? Yeah, *um*, no. I wish I could designate someone else to make all my decisions for me or someone who could talk me out of my stupidity, but I'd probably just do them behind their back."

"Regretting your decision to move back?" Jett asked with a knowing smile.

She smiled ruefully. "Is it that obvious? I know it's cowardly, but..." She leaned in as she passed him one of the collapsible bowls. "I'm ashamed to say I don't think I can stay away from Slate. There's too much... there. The problem is, I love Brass. I don't want to lose him." She ran her hand through her caramel waves and started. She'd said more than she'd intended to, and Jett wondered if she'd ever actually told Brass she loved him. "I'm as bad as you. I didn't mean to have feelings for Brass. Things were easier in Chicago. They happened so quickly... it snuck up on me."

"Love him, or in love with him, baby sis," Jett asked pensively as they leaned close together.

"In love. I have been... I knew I was falling for him... before. Chris wasn't like this, and it's scaring the crap out of me..."

"Because of Slate."

"Because of Slate." She nodded. "I knew before I left that there was something unexplored with Brass, but I couldn't do that to Slate. I don't know why I thought it would be any easier now. It's even more complicated..."

"Because of the babies?" Jett urged.

She knit her brows and her turquoise eyes flitted between his. "Yes. This is so complicated I don't know if I'm coming or going anymore."

"You will not be pregnant in Chicago, Scarlett. I forbid it. Do what you must, but you're not going back. Do you think mom was happy going at it alone?" It was a low blow, but it had the desired effect.

She dropped her eyes. "Gods, no. She was miserable and got very good at hiding it. Jett, not now, but I have something important to tell you about Mabon... and mom."

They passed out breakfast and a silent communication passed between Indigo and her as Indi followed her to sit between Amethyst and Indi, so neither Brass nor Slate could be near her. They'd done it so innocuously it looked as if Indi had simply chatted her up when she gave Amethyst her bowl last.

The two men followed her with their eyes to where they sat, and Brass chuckled. Did Scarlett not realize that whenever she had tried to get away, one of those two had found her? Unless she was planning ongoing to a foreign country or Antarctica, they'd find her, and possibly even if she went that far, too.

"How did everyone sleep? It is a glorious morning, yes?" Quick said, stretching his arms high above his head and taking Scarlett's vacated seat.

Indi glared at him over her oatmeal, and he flashed her a smile back. The dynamic there was too ridiculous.

They broke camp later than expected but made up the time with a brisker walk. Scarlett looked ready to sprint away and stayed carefully between Tawny and Indigo, occasionally falling back to talk to Ama and Shale about returning and training Indigo. Ama looked a little too excited about training with Indigo.

The desert turned into red dirt canyons that carved the earth into craggy crevices with its own underground water supply. When they reached the red canyons that the Wemic called home, a dark figure appeared from a shadowed area and trotted towards them. It made straight for the group. Indigo froze and Scarlett nudged her with a hip. Quick made a face next to Jett.

"The Wemic scout," he muttered.

"Guardians!" Rikke shouted as he raised a clawed hand.

His vertical pupil scanned us in his lime green eyes as he gave a feline like a smile from his black furred face. He clasped his clawed hand to the back of Slate's head and they met foreheads. He did it to all of them until he reached Indigo, whose ear he nipped making her blush bright red.

"We have been expecting you. Come, the celebrations are about to start. Congratulations," he said, turning to Slate and Scarlett.

Rikke patted Slate on the back and hugged Scarlett but held her out, sniffing the air. "That is not your scent."

She looked like she would vomit. "Slate is married now, Rikke. You can congratulate him. I am pregnant, though, so thank you. One of Jett's wives is pregnant, too," she said with her face burning with embarrassment.

"Are you angry?" Rikke asked and Brass stepped forward.

"Embarrassed. Brass, I'm with Scarlett," he said, holding out his hand.

Rikke's eyes widened, and he looked at Slate. "Rikke. This is a surprise."

Slate patted Rikke on his back. "A story for another time. We are here to celebrate Tika and Keen."

Ama stepped up to Rikke with a glint of interest in her eyes, and Quick sniffed. He reached forward and grabbed Indigo's hand. She yanked at it, but relented and let him pull her to his side. Rikke noticed the interaction and a feline smile parted his black lips.

"Indigo, you have taken a mate?"

"No."

"Yes."

Quick and Indigo said at the same time. Rikke's pupils dilated as he looked at her.

"Your scent says he —"

"Okay. I have. Shouldn't we hurry?" Indigo's tan cheeks blushed, and she pulled her scarf higher over her head to shadow her face.

THIRTY-SIX

The village was beautiful beyond my wildest dreams. Big white blooms hung in threaded garlands all throughout the town. The path down the center of the town was littered with petals. I stared openmouthed at the red clay Wemic adobes and how they had gone to great lengths to decorate for the wedding.

"The people Pearl sent did all the work. Tika is beside herself; she is pleased. Careful, her hugs are fierce," Rikke said with a wink of his lime green eye.

Wemic were everywhere, dressed in the finest clothes, which were white, very revealing dresses. They were all so happy and I turned my empath abilities up to bask in it. Wemic wore flowers tucked behind their ears and tucked into their hair. Some had even made wreaths for their heads of the white flowers.

We reached the village center, and a lion patterned male turned towards us and his face broke out into a well-practiced smile. His fawn-colored fur paled as it tapered to his stomach and, under his chin, white

261

underlined his gold eyes. White swirls adorned his body, and they pulled the front of his long light brown hair back and tied fetishes throughout it.

When I saw him, and I broke out into a run, a cheesy grin spreading across my face. Keen had run towards me too, his smile widening when he saw how happy I was to see him. I slowed when we neared, but he didn't and he swept me off my feet, swinging me around. Laughter exploded from my lungs as I tossed my head back.

"I enjoy seeing you this happy," he purred before he closed his velvety lips over mine. "One last time before my mate catches me," he said conspiratorially, and he set me on my feet.

I wiped tears from my cheeks. I did not know why I was crying. My entourage caught up behind me. "Enough of that, Keen, or I will tell Tika," Slate said with a smile on his face as they met foreheads.

Keen raising his brow and looks over his shoulder, "Good thing she was not here to see. A congratulation is in order."

"To you as well, my friend," Slate said, clapping a hand to Keen's shoulder. The Wemic were all taller than average men, but not taller than Slate.

"About the baby as well. Congratulations, you will make a strong father," Keen said, squeezing Slate's shoulder with a clawed hand.

Nervous laughter bubbled up from me. "He's married, Keen. I'm with Brass." I gestured over to Brass, whose eyes glittered with amusement. "Sorry. Keen and I have a unique relationship. I promise no more kissing."

Brass introduced himself, and Keen weighed and measured. "Your baby?" Keen leaned forward and sniffed the surrounding air with a flat cat like nose.

Brass's dark honey face turned to mine and his amber eyes apologized. I gave a nod. Keen was too nosy for his own good.

"Yes," Brass admitted

Keen chuckled. "Shifters brand their mates. They have claimed you for some time, Scarlett. I am shocked he would let you lie with another man."

"I am having a pup of my own," Slate said in a low tone.

"You mongrel!" Keen admonished.

Brass wrapped his arm around my shoulders, and I gave his hand a squeeze. I'd been keeping my distance all morning, after the awkward-ness of last night.

... I kissed Slate last night...

"I know he activated the bond," Brass murmured as he kissed my temple.

Of course he did. He knew all of it.

Slate never wore white; it reminded me of our big white bed. His long wavy mane had dozens of braids with silver Celtic etched beads threaded through it with five carved fetishes. A single jade love rune, and four ivory pieces, a jumis, a sun, starburst, and solar cross. Haust, Sumar, Tio, and Dagr - by the Mother how dense I was. It was right in front of my face the entire time.

I wore my own fetishes, a starburst identical to Slate's, a jade canine that I'd stolen from him, a pearl from when we visited the Merfolk for the first time, and two beads, one ebony, one bronze from Brass. Indigo wore my turquoise tree of life fetish in her hair these days. It was our father's sigil.

Keen walked away and embraced me again. "I am sorry. I thought you two would mate. My apologies."

"We did," Slate rumbled, and Keen held me at arm's length and looked between us and laughed.

My gut felt as though it'd been punched and I smiled weakly, I pointed to Brass, "Scarlett's boyfriend." I pointed to Slate. "Scarlett's husband."

Gypsum wore copper beads in his hair that was now down to his chest. He made a face at me. Slate seemed to swell at my announce-ment, ignoring everyone's stunned expressions.

"Amber," Ama whispered and scoffed.

"Who is this Amber?" Keen asked.

"Slate's wife," Quick replied as he stared at me. He didn't look surprised either. Had Slate already told everyone? "So boyfriend?"

I rolled my eyes. "Is *lover* preferable to you, Quick?"

"No," Slate growled, and my cheeks heated.

"Companion?" Brass offered, and I frowned.

"Therefore, I don't want to label it. More than friends, less than... married," I said, looking up to Brass.

He scratched the side of his nose with a finger and hid a smile. "Labels do not change a thing for me."

"Agreed. So now that that's cleared... I have something else I need to tell you." I looked at Jett and Indigo.

"Gods, Scar. What else have you been hiding?" Jett asked.

"Nothing! I haven't been back in a while and it's... disturbing."

Jett ran a hand over his close cropped dark blonde hair and his turquoise almond eyes met mine. "Well?"

I licked my lips. "Maybe Steel and Slate should join us... privately. It's personal to us."

Indi frowned. "Just say it. Silver will torture it out of me, anyway."

"I hardly call it torture," Quick said, mood perking.

I looked up at Brass, who gave me a nod. "It's about mom and dad. While we were in Mabon, I came across a tree. An enormous tree. It started talking to me... mom and dad are a wight."

They stared blankly at me, and I looked to Slate for help. "I saw it. They do not remember who they are, only that they are there to protect the forest and pass on the Mother's word. It intertwined them in one tree."

Slate described exactly what we saw without telling them what the tree had said. I wasn't ready to address that yet, and the others gaped in disbelief.

"What the fuck, Scar? You tell us a month later?" Jett was pissed and I couldn't blame him.

"What did you want me to do? Amber came looking for him. We had activated our bonds during our fight with the Minotaurs and she *knew* he'd been with someone. If I was there, I might as well have been holding up a sign that read *I fiddlesticked your husband!* Then I found out she was pregnant. I felt like a monster! Ask Brass, I was evil, even to him for the first... I don't know..."

Whoops. They hadn't all known about Mabon, but they did now.

"Around two weeks of trying to kick me out," Brass offered.

"I'm telling you now. I can show you where they are when we get back, I promise. It might not help, though. It hurt like hel that they had no idea who I was."

Tawny held Steel, who just learned his sister was a tree. His intentionally tousled dark blonde hair was messier than usual. His turquoise eyes, identical to Jett's and mine, looked watery in his tan face. Steel looked like an American poster boy with a swimmer's body. Tawny had her arms around him, offering her comfort.

"At least they're together now," Steel said, clear and firm.

Keen cleared his throat, and we all shuffled around, ashamed of the scene we were causing. "Babies and marriages are cause for celebration, no matter the parentage. We have much to celebrate. Thank you for coming to my wedding."

This was why I loved the Wemic.

It's where I came to get a grasp on what really mattered and to clear my head. It's where I went when I grieved after my mother's death. I should have come back after my father's too, but they had addicted me to rousen and were under Slate's care. I couldn't be far from him then.

We continued on into the Wemic town to the three guest adobes they reserved for Guardians and called dibs. There were three beds to an adobe and nothing else. They stuffed them with feathers and wool if we were lucky, straw if times were tough. These were good times. Tawny and Steel took the first one with Jett and Amethyst. Gypsum, Ama, and Shale took the second. Indigo gave me a questioning look, and I shrugged as I led Brass to the third.

"What are you doing?" Indigo asked, putting a hand to Quick's chest as he followed her in.

"Am I spending the night with you or not, Dove? I can find somewhere else to rest my head tonight," Quick said, looking down his nose at her.

She clenched her narrow jaw, but kept it shut as she continued into the adobe. Quick walked in with a victorious smile. I met Indi's eyes and mouthed *dove,* and she grimaced with a shake of her head.

Brass scooped me up under my arms and laid me down on the feather mattress before climbing on top of me. Quick groaned, which we ignored, and Brass slanted his mouth over mine as his hand ran over my bent leg at his hip.

"A full day," he murmured.

"It's a miracle we made it. Are you angry?" I asked him, running my fingers tips along his stubbled jaw and into his hair.

"No, Scarlett. I do not blame him. He would not go down without some kind of fight, and I do not expect you to fight him off every time. I seem to remember a certain someone doing the same to him. I can see now why he did not like it," Brass teased with twinkling amber eyes.

"Tonight, when everyone is drunk on chang'aa, we can sneak back here and steal some time alone," I whispered and he smiled so brilliantly, it almost made my eyes hurt.

"I will hold you to that. I —"

Brass cut short when a shadow darkened the doorway and came into the small adobe. The second bed was vacant and Slate tossed his pack on to it as I tried to scramble up from under Brass.

"Did Shale and Ama kick you out so they could have their wicked way with Gypsum?" Quick asked with a wicked grin of his own.

"I want to be close to my wife while I can," Slate said, lifting his grey eyes to where I sat smoothing my hair next to Brass.

I wanted to object, to tell him to get lost so I could lay unabashedly with Brass, but I had seen that look on his face too many times before. Challenging and predatory, he was daring me or anyone to deny him so he could tear them apart. No one would get between him and me.

... Now what?...

"Now we change and celebrate," Brass said, sliding off the bed.

His lips pulled up at the corners as they all started undressing. Indigo had given me a sympathetic look before Quick covered her with his body as she changed into the loin cloth top and skirt traditional to the Wemic. I sighed and picked mine off the floor before spinning around and facing the clay wall. Naked Slate and Brass was not how I envisioned my day. I pulled my shirt over my head and my body gave an involuntary shiver as my hair tickled my back. Brass stood at the foot of the bed across from Slate.

Everyone in the room had seen me in the buff at some point. I didn't know why it had grown into an issue. My hands held the bra before deciding to clasp it again to tie on the top of it before removing it. I looped the piece around my neck and to cross it over my breasts. My hands reached behind my back to tie it when invisible fingers popped off my bra and knotted my top on. I started and held the piece to my chest when I realized it was Brass trying to help me without touching me. I looked up to give him an appreciative smile when I saw he was completely nude.

He laughed richly as I dropped my eyes. Guardians and their lack of modesty. I'd gotten as bad as they had, but then I went to Chicago and Chris had brought me back to my senses. It didn't matter if your gene pool was the crème de la crème, naked was naked and some things should be private.

I tied the skirt around my waist before removing my pants and underwear and folded them neatly, hoping everyone else was clothed. As much as loincloths allowed. I had my own beaded belt that weighed down the swaths of fabric. Slate tossed one to Brass, who caught it without looking, and my mood sunk to the floor.

What was I doing coming between them?

I stood and smoothed down the fabric. The top covered little, and I didn't have the thin layer of fur the Wemic had to cover my exposed stomach, which felt vulnerable now that I knew two lives resided in there.

Brass smoothed his hair back, his dark honey arms bulging as he knotted it at his nape.

My stomach was as flat and toned as ever. No sign there yet.

"By Ragnarök. We will look into getting you specially made armor," Brass noted and looked at Slate.

This was going to be a group effort? That was news to me, but it did not disappoint me. Brass moved so he could rest his palm on my stomach and I felt him *call*.

"Okay?" I asked.

He gave me a lopsided grin. "Okay. Your stomach has settled."

Slate's electric hum glided closer, and I stiffened as he held up his hand. I nodded without looking, and Brass took a step back. Slate's rough, calloused palm scratched the soft skin of my stomach and heat flooded me.

"Your hands are rougher. Training more?" I asked, chewing on the inside of my cheek.

If there was a more uncomfortable position to be in, I wasn't aware of it. As my true husband felt the lives of his best friend's unborn children, my boyfriend watched leaning against the wall with no intention of leaving and easing the slightest bit of awkwardness.

It was the theme for the trip. Awkward. Horribly awkward.

Slate made a noise in his throat, part moan, part hum in ascent. My skin prickled beneath his hand and the thin fabric couldn't hide the other involuntary responses from my body.

"Spending as much time away from my sham wife as I can," Slate rumbled.

I looked down at him, his long thick lashes fanned across the hard plane of his cheek as he stared at my stomach as if he could see the babies.

"Have you taken a paramour?"

My question made my ears ring. Why I would torture myself with his response was like the way he insisted on sleeping in the same adobe with Brass and me. We couldn't help ourselves.

He lifted his narrow grey eyes the color of the sky during the winter snowstorm to mine and let his full lips curl. "No, Torch. Having one pregnant errant wife and a pregnant sham wife is enough."

"Forget I asked," I said, stepping back and away from his palm.

"There is no one else. There would not Amber if —"

I sucked in a breath sharply. "Keen said it was a three-day event. I'm going to find out what they have planned for the women today."

I hurried past them both as I half trotted from the adobe. Slate couldn't finish that thought out loud. I liked him touching my stomach and taking an interest in *them*. It fed something... maternal in me.

"You certainly do not look pregnant," Shale immediately said when she saw my exposed stomach.

"Everything alright?" I asked, settling in on my knees. Shale looked grumpier than usual.

"Ama wants to sleep with every Wemic in sight. I am on my monthly and do not wish to be pawed, literally," Shale snapped, and I was sorry I asked.

Quick made a disgusted face behind Shale's back, and Ama thumbed her nose at her. "Cordillera will commission you a special maternity outfit for your competitions. I see... black leather one piece with a spot cut out for your stomach," he said obnoxiously, squinting as if he could see into the future.

"Gods, you're a fanny pack."

I crossed my arms and saw Slate and Brass emerge from the adobe. No one was bleeding, so it was a success. I got up and started towards the painting adobes.

"Hormones!" Quick yelled after me and I debated going back and stabbing him with my seax.

Tawny, Indigo, and Amethyst were already in there getting painted.

"Red," I told the cheetah girl, painting the swirls over my skin.

She tittered and said something in Wemic that a vaguely understood as, "White when with pups."

I groaned and nodded. I hadn't thought of that. The men came into the adobe and Slate eyes widened slightly at my paint color. It was as much as a shout from another man. White was for married couples, or if you were pregnant, I now knew. Quick, Shale, Ama, Gypsum, and Indigo were in and out in their blue swirls. Brass sat down and asked for red. They reserved it for warriors or older married couples. They allowed him to wear it. Naturally, Slate chose white. It was the first time I'd seen him in anything, but the blue and I knew he did it intentionally, as did Brass by his cocked brow.

I rubbed the emerald ring that hung from the chain around my neck. It was something I did absently. I pulled it off and slid it into my right hand. I supposed it was foolish to keep it around my neck. Slate wore my father's ring as his wedding band. I wondered how Amber felt about that.

A beautiful tigress entered the painting of adobe, white swirls over her striped fur. They plaited her long, black sheen of hair down her back. She scanned us until she found me.

Tika's golden eyes lit up. "Scarlett! I did not think you liked me, but when Keen said you would attend our wedding, I knew I was wrong. Is today not beautiful? The growers made such wonderful decorations, they will speak of our wedding of for ages! Thank your grandmother for me. Is what Keen says true? You and Slate are mated?" She gushed as she held my hand. The Wemic painting around me looked as irritated as I felt.

I wanted her enthusiasm to infect me. Trapped in the adobe with Brass and Slate was not helping my mood any.

How long did it take to draw a bunch of swirly things, anyway?

"Slate and I... mated." I told her carefully, "I will let Pearl know. They did a beautiful job." I told her, trying not to sound as sullen as I felt.

She beamed. "The men will hunt all of today and tonight we shall eat what they caught. Tomorrow, we shall do our *raqs sharqi* at dinner, and the next day we wed!"

"I'm sorry, what is *rock son Cherokee*?" Tika doubled over in laughter, and I stared at her dubiously until she regained her composure.

"You are funny. *Raqs Sharqi* is the dance we perform for our husbands." My blank stare told her just how much I knew about this dance they were supposed to be performing.

She held her hands out, "I will teach you my dance and we will do it together! It will be better for both of us. Oh! The looks on their faces when we perform it. We will have to practice all night."

I groaned internally as I watched Tika nearly skip away. I found her happiness irksome, and my grumpiness was unwelcome. They finished painting us and we met with the other who were already drinking around the fire being built.

Slate was poorly hiding a smile, and Brass pursed his plump lips to the side.

"I don't think I like the two of you smiling. It makes me nervous."

"They have painted you and Slate white. Tika thinks you are getting married," Brass said, and I blinked in confusion.

I opened my mouth and shut it. I was stunned.

"It is a reasonable assumption here. You're both in white. Mated — you marry." Brass shrugged broad, muscular shoulders.

My nostrils flared as I drew in a breath and I went the way Tika went when Brass caught my hand. "Whoa. The sister-in-law of the chief is arranging a joint ceremony as we speak with the chief's wife. It would be a grave insult to disrupt their wedding."

"Brass, you can't be serious," I said, dropping my tone.

"Honestly, I don't see the difference. You will still be in my bed at night. This is just for show." Brass said, shaking his head.

"We are already wed," Slate said pointedly, and my stomach flipped.

I shook my head. "No. I already act like I'm not married once, I won't do it, *er*, twice. This would be sordid even for us, and I think we know sordid." I twirled a finger to include the three of us.

Brass sighed. "I didn't say this was a dream come true, only that it would be an insult if you backed out."

I knit my brows. "Brass, I think you have too much faith in me," I whispered.

Brass reached up, tucking a lock of hair behind my ear. "They're only words."

"It's a symbol," I whispered, fully aware that Slate was next to us.

"Whatever you wish," Brass said, cupping my face.

I gently pulled away and ran my teeth along my lower lip. "I'd have to kiss him."

Slate laughed, and he gave one of those rare cheek creasing smiles that softened the hard planes of his bronze face. "Torch, a single kiss is not the problem here."

"I don't have a dress," I said feebly, and Slate gave another rare smile. "On one condition."

"That is?" Brass asked.

"We can switch to another adobe."

Slate frowned. "If that is what you want, Torch."

He walked away, and I regretted my request. "I only asked because you shouldn't have to go through all that and have to face him first thing in the morning. I didn't mean so we could..."

"You don't have to explain to me, Scarlett. I know. He will be fine. This way, we both get what we want. Thank you for thinking of me," Brass said, and he kissed me for the first time all day.

I sighed. "One more time."

Brass chuckled and kissed me chastely before following Slate to go on the hunt.

THIRTY-SEVEN

The others took the news of our mock wedding well.

"Why not? You deserve one ceremony in your life. It's not like you're not already married. Frigga's sweet grass. This is insane," Tawny had said, shaking her head.

Their loved ones spent the entire day telling stories of the couples' story and adventures together after the men got back from the hunting party. The men were all stinking drunk and Slate plopped down next to me. I didn't think Slate, and I had any cheerful stories to tell, most of ours being more like horror stories, or done in private. The Wemic were having a hard time encouraging us to join in the storytelling. It was difficult when they had so many funny stories about Tika and Keen going back to when they were cubs together.

Jett stood, to my surprise, his jug of chang'aa sloshing as he held it up. "I thought the first time Scar and Slate met was the morning I introduced myself to her as my brother. It turned out that he accosted her in a bathroom and cajoled her into giving up a kiss under the mistletoe. I knew that something was different about his feelings for her. He didn't plan on disappearing before dawn. He'd found someone to wake up next to."

My mouth popped open, and I forgot to raise my jug and cheers when Jett sat. I met Brass's eyes over the crowd.

... This is the worst idea ever. Remind me again why I'm doing this...

Brass blew me a kiss, and I gave him an apologetic smile.

... Somehow this is your fault...

He smiled warmly and inclined his head.

Slate sat at my side, the pseudo blissful couple that we were. He'd put my emerald ring back on my ring finger and fire burned in my belly. Tawny stood on wobbly legs. Chang'aa was basically firewater and much stronger than anything they had in Thrimilci.

"I don't have a single memory that doesn't include Scarlett. In order to understand my neurosis, I should give you a little background." She held up three fingers. "How many boys Scar had kissed before meeting Slate? There was a three-year gap between the third and Slate. To say that she was inexperienced would be a drastic understatement. In comes Slate. The anti-Scarlett. I warned her off, told her what a bad idea he was. She listened until I saw them unguarded together. She lived in a place called *Denial* and she frequently visits there when Slate is concerned." Tawny snorted and met my eyes. "No one could look at him the way she did and not know the truth." She sighed and raised her jug. "To all those hopeless romantics."

The Wemic cheered.

Brass stood and my already pounding heart twisted. "I helped Scarlett... go on vacation. When it came time to go, feeling as if she had no other choice, she was still loathe to go. I could read her mind. She kept waiting for him to show, praying silently he'd appear and force her to abandon her plan. She never would have stayed for me. I asked her to. I still think if he had shown she never would have left, but she had laid her plans well and he had been —"

"One minute," Jett interrupted, clearly as drunk as the rest of them. "I waited. He came through the portal less than sixty seconds after you left."

I held my breath, waiting for the pain to ebb. Less than a minute.

Sixty seconds and my life would be completely different. Sixty measly seconds.

Indigo stood, "I don't know if anyone knows of the one and only time Slate told Scar he loved her..."

My mind wandered as Indigo retold the story of the river and even spoke fondly of Quick, or Silver, if you asked her. They didn't understand that every time Slate called me Torch; it was his way of telling me he loved me.

I should have risked the insult. Keen would have forgiven me. Reski, the chief, sat with his wife, Nata, the beautiful tigress and sister to Tika. The lion man had an impressive mane of golden hair and golden skin. Wooden beads hung from his mane of hair; scars crossed one of his golden eyes, white fur underlined. He, too, had a white chin under his muzzle and a lighter stomach. Red paint covered his cheekbones down to his jaws and on his forehead into his hairline.

Their middle brother, Nekee, looked more like Keen, but never smiled. They had dipped his hair in red and plaited. Red paint covered his jaw down to his collarbones.

Tikee was a lynx hybrid, his fur the longest of the other Wemic I'd seen. Ears long and high on his head reddish brown and spotted fur sticking straight out. He was taller and burlier, with a great booming laugh.

Keen and Tika sat next to them, not having to feign their blissful mood. My mood had soured like spoiled milk in my stomach on a hot summer day. I was going to vomit. Slate slid his hand on my lower back and I felt him *call* to soothe me.

"Thank you," I whispered inaudibly, and he brought his hand back to his knee.

Quick stood, but Brass quickly grabbed his elbow, pulling him back down, sending people into a fit of laughter. Whatever story he had to tell about us would not involve clothing.

Tika stood, and my eyes widened. How could she possibly have an anecdote about us? "I noticed the change in Slate when Scarlett accompanied him to our lands. Mostly because whenever one was not looking at the other, the other was looking at them." She laughed prettily as well as a few other people. "Now that Slate was training me when he visited, what *was* a secret was the last couple of times I came for one of our sessions. I found him and Scarlett together and they were both always so angry with me for interrupting them. I am glad he has found someone who can match his rage." She drank from her jug, and I tried not to scrunch my face.

I did not have rage. Sure, every once in a while, Slate and I had drawn knives on one another and spared, but we never really did any damage.

Though... I couldn't imagine Steel and Tawny pulling knives on one another.

The night stretched on and everyone fell deeper into their cups. I needed Brass to bring me back. He met my eyes over the heads of our group and got up. I walked around the canyon and doubled back behind the guest adobe. I didn't have to wait long before Brass stumbled his way back there. He was just as drunk as the rest.

"Kiss me, Brass," I begged as I pulled on the strings of his loincloth, making it fall to the red dirt.

He gripped fistfuls of my hair and smashed his lips to mine as he spun me around so my back hit against the gritty adobe wall. His hands pushed away from my top, from my breasts. I winced as he gripped them firmly and pushed my loincloth to the side.

The back of my head slid against the adobe as he picked me up under my backside and drove into me. I gasped and wrapped my legs around him. My nails dug into his shoulders as he moved into me. His tongue whirled around my outstretched throat. I said those two words as if they came from someone else's mouth and Brass moaned huskily as he thrust harder and deeper.

My insides coiled. I needed that with Brass.

The day had left me confused. Was I Slate's wife? The mother of Brass's children? Was I meant to be with either? Or was it worth the pain and frustration that all three of us experienced being near each other?

I let go of my emotions and let the mindless pleasure wash over me. Brass deserved me to only think of him while we were together. I couldn't think of much past how good he felt inside me. My coiled muscles clenched around him and my arms tightened around his neck as I moaned.

"*Scarlett,*" Brass breathed as he shuddered into me.

He held me there as we panted and he set me on my wobbly legs as I leaned against the adobe and *called* to clean myself. Brass picked his loincloth off the floor and tied it around his waist. His upper body glistened in the moonlight and I saw the scratches along his shoulders. I raised my hand, and he looked down at his shoulders and smiled.

"War wounds," he said breezily and leaned in to kiss me.

I gave him an impish grin and healed him, anyway. "Let's not rub it in."

"I did not think you would want to while we were here. I am glad you did," he said and tilted my chin up so he could kiss me deeply and I wrapped my arms around his waist.

Brass and I never had such rushed uninhibited sex. We always made love. I needed his unbridled passion, but it was just as off as the whole day had been.

"I'm so confused, Brass. All I know is I don't want to lose either of you, but I can feel you both slipping through my fingers with my indecision."

"Becoming a polygamist, are we?" Brass teased.

I gave him a dry look as he dusted my sticky skin off. "I love you, Brass..."

Brass's eyes glittered, and he held his finger to my lips. "But you're in love with him. I know Scarlett and I'm still here."

"Why did you want me to do this? You knew how hard it would be on all of us, yet you still pushed."

"Testing you, perhaps. Maybe I think you deserve the ceremony you never got out here in the middle of nowhere. No one will find out. Closure. Who knows? Maybe I do not know why I pushed. Perhaps Slate is my brother and I love him and he loves you and some part of me hopes you'll leave me, so I do not have to be the one who came between you. Maybe I did not think it through at all."

Brass gave me a rueful smile, and I nuzzled against his chest. Cinnamon and spring. I ran my fingers along his scattering of dark chest hair until he drew back.

"I will meet you in the adobe. I have to find a dark shadow to relieve myself. Too much chang'aa." He joked and gave me a quick kiss before walking off.

I straightened my top and righted my skirt behind the adobe. Movement in the shadows caught my eye, and I pressed against the adobe wall with my teeth against my lip in case I needed help. I'd activate the bond for Slate.

The shadow detached, and I froze.

The barghest hybrid. Seven feet tall and rippling with charcoal bunched muscles, it had long pointed ears that would have been in the place of human ears with three sets of horns protruding from its head. One set like tusks curved from its jaw, a set curled slightly from behind its ears that were very short and the third set curled like a ram. Its short snout flared above teeth as long as my fingers. The beast man had black hair that hung from its head, held back by its series of horns. Its eyes reflected the moonlight back at me as it prowled closer.

The primordial need to flee infused my body, but Slate had been right: I was a rabbit. I froze instead, knowing if I ran, he'd catch me. He wore a loincloth tonight, but we'd spent enough time together to know that thing never stayed on long. The animal the rousen had created within me made my nostrils flare as I picked up his scent and took a shuddering breath.

It stoked the eternal fire inside me that never quite died into a fury, despite having just been with Brass. I pulsed between my legs and a noise that was no part of a human moaned in my throat. It spread its lips in a fiendish grin with a mouthful of sharp fangs.

"More?" it rasped, sniffing the surrounding air.

He towered over me, and my knees went weak. I shook my head in negation and its grin grew sinful. His eyes shone with that predatory air that let me know, under no uncertain terms, that I lived at his leisure. He could tear open my throat like paper. My every breath was a gift he bestowed.

"His scent is on you," it growled and my breath caught as he lowered his mouth to my throat.

My skin tingled and felt heavy. His sharp teeth nipped at the thin skin of my throat, its tongue slid out coarse and wide and my eyelids fluttered.

"I want you, mate." It rasped and took my hair in its massive claw to pull back my head.

I was panting, trying to find a coherent thought. "No more."

Slate once told me barghests mated for life. He didn't warn me that once mated, I would feel an inexplicable attraction to it I struggled wildly to overcome.

"You tell me *no*? Deny me *mine*?" It growled.

I was turning into a puddle. "Things have changed." I breathed.

It licked up my face and back down my throat. Its sharp teeth nicked me, and I gritted my teeth as it sucked down hard over the wound. My nipples turned into hard pearls against the thin fabric that hid them until the barghest hooked claw tore the end that looped around my neck and it fell free.

My arms were heavy at my sides as its mouth roamed over my unveiled skin. Touching and tasting as I drew ragged breaths. Thoughts just out of reach nagged at my mind as it wrapped its entire mouth around one of my soft, sensitive breasts and suckled. I whimpered with need, hot and slick under my loincloth, pulsing from the beast man's mouth.

"You want me." It rasped as it dragged its fangs over the underside of my swollen breast.

Yes, I thought, but shook my head. It chuckled with a husky darkness that said it knew better.

"Your body wants me." The beast rumbled deep in its chest as if it possessed a part of its throat no human did.

"But my mind knows better. It's not just about me anymore." I managed two complete sentences until it rose to its full height and I shut my eyes against it, fully expecting it to roar in my face as it had on previous occasions.

"About the whelps then?"

I nodded, and I felt it lean against me, its clawed hands wrapped around me almost gently, or as gently as a seven-foot tall, three-hundred-pound beast with razor sharp fangs and claws could manage.

"Do I scare you, mate?"

"No. Sometimes. When you lose your temper," I whispered.

I frowned. Was that a line from Beauty and the Beast? It could've been. This was no tailcoat wearing prince, though. The barghest was a primitive intensely sexual beast with three things in mind: the 'F's,' feeding, fighting, and fiddlesticking.

"Would you have my pups if you knew they could wind up like

this?" It rasped and I blinked, opening my eyes and trying to peer up at it.

He stood too close and held me too tightly for me to see his face. "Are you asking me to?"

"I am asking if it would be so bad."

The conversation had thrown me for a loop, but if we were playing the hypothetical game, I'd bite. He hadn't killed me so far for sleeping with Brass. Why kill me now?

"Depends."

"On?"

"Are you born with those horns, or do they grow later?" I asked stupidly, and his whole body jerked with sudden laughter.

It boomed across the canyon and I wondered if anyone would come running to check out the devil from Legend cackling in the shadows.

"Later. One does not shift until they come into manhood. Only the boys, not the women. There are no female barghests," he rasped.

His horned head lowered again as he started licking, softer this time, over my skin and down to my stomach, where he seemed too content to nuzzle its face without goring me with one of its horns.

"If it had happened, then I don't see why not. I wouldn't be afraid of it, though it would be hard to control as a teenager, I imagine," I said after some quiet contemplation.

My wits were returning slowly, and I wondered how we had gone down this tangent or why Brass hadn't come looking for me. The beast nudged my breasts with its snout and seared my skin with wet kisses.

"You are my mate. Barghests mate for life. I will not play with another. You will have my son and he will be barghest," he said and rose.

I objected to that nonsense when he took a step back, placing his arms to either side of me against the adobe.

"Do not scamper, Rabbit. I will catch you." It rasped and my heart leapt into my throat.

The beast's fur drew into its bronze flesh. Its horns melted into his scalp, his snout shortened into a man's full mouth and a straight symmetrical nose that would make sculptors weep. He shrunk six inches and his cawed hands turned into rough man's hands.

My chest rose and fell with shallow breaths as I blinked at Slate. His eyes were still glinting silver, like the beast's in the moonlight. Not human eyes. Those grey eyes that sometimes flared to silver. No human eyes reflected light. No human made the sounds he made in his throat or could make love like he did for hours on end. Part of me always knew something dark and dangerous lurked beneath Slate's surface, and now I knew what. Keen said he was a shifter. A barghest shifter.

"Slate?" I panted.

I could still see the residual emotions from the beast in him. He wasn't the Slate I knew yet. He nodded once, and I reached down for my top with shaking hands.

How many times had the barghest shown up out of nowhere, four? Five?

"Your son. He would be like you?" I asked, trying to tie the scrap of fabric around my chest like a bandeau top, but my fingers moved clumsily behind me.

"He would, Torch. That is why I never wanted children. I am a man most days, other days I am a beast. When you are young, the change comes quickly and you cannot control your anger. Anger, passion of any kind, becomes an issue, so you teach yourself not to feel it. I did well until you came to Tidings," he rumbled and closed the space between us, stilling my hands from my top.

"You... had sex with me as the beast. You... we... you branded me. That first night you met me as the beast when you bathed me with your tongue, you were claiming like a little kid would a piece of candy."

His mouth quirked at the analogy. "You are mine. My mate."

"You didn't think I should know this before we said the marriage vows? Or what about after I was pregnant the first time, Slate?" I cupped my breasts to cover them.

"I would have eventually. I am now, Torch. Do not act like it is a mystery revealed. I came as the beast to our bed, or would you fuck a tribesman in our bed?" Slate asked, arching a brow.

I raised my own and beat against his chest. "You bastard! I was on rousen! I would have slept with anything then and you know it!"

He caught my fists and yanked me towards him, lowering his mouth to mine and pressing me tightly to his body. My bare chest smashed against his as I struggled against him.

"Enough!" I shouted, pushing away. "I was with Brass —"

"I saw."

"You watched?" I asked, appalled.

"You did not hide it." Slate said in a growl, and my heart lurched.

Slate's memory was as good as a time capsule. He'd never forget what he saw.

"Why would you do that?" I squeaked; my voice was thick.

"To remember. You have made your choice; you choose to lie with Brass. Now I can make my choice." He took a step towards me and I slapped him as hard as I could and his head snapped to the side.

"You think you can seduce me whenever you want? Like I'm some plaything for you and your friend. I'm done with both of you. He knew, I know, Brass knew you were this beast. I bet he knew you were watching. He's too smart not to know, and he knows your mind. He would have felt you and he let you watch, anyway."

I fastened the knot between my breasts and hoped that would do until I got into the adobe. Slate grabbed my arm, but I yanked it back.

"Don't touch me." I hissed, my elemental power burning in my eyes like hot coals as I stalked off.

CHAPTER 38
INDIGO

Silver gripped my hips, and I lowered my mouth to his. I was breaking all the rules, anyway. Might as well indulge in a few steamy kisses. One day, when times were good, I'd see if Silver could bring me to climax with just his kisses.

I bet he could.

"*Ooh, ooh,*" I moaned against his cheek and he stiffened beneath me with a few hard thrusts.

I laid my head against the crook of his neck and he kissed my nose as he ran his hands down my back. A shadow blocked out the moonlight in the doorway and I shifted my head to see who it was while trying not to pant.

Scarlett, looking worse for wear, her chest was heaving as she gripped the front of her top that had ripped somehow. Her face hid in the shadows.

"Brass," she called in an accusatory tone.

The darkness lifted in the far bed and my eyes went wide and I looked at Silver, who shrugged with a wicked grin. "You knew he was there," I whispered harshly, and he kissed my nose again.

"He does not get off on watching. He was giving us some privacy. I swear it," Silver whispered, and I gave him a doubtful look.

"Scarlett —" Brass got up from the bed with the thin blanket wrapped around his waist and approached her like a wild animal that had wandered into the adobe unintentionally.

"Save it, Regn! You knew it! You knew what he was! And he was watching." She choked out the last word, but she wasn't crying. She was raging. "You knew he would confront me tonight. My friend *first*, right? You're cousins. He said it was a male thing. Are you a barghest too?"

"No, just a mind reader. It was not my secret to tell. I knew —"

"I've known you both for a year and a half and no one thought that might be an important detail? I don't even care what he is, I care you conspired to hide it." She accused, stabbing her finger like a knife towards him.

Brass was taking cautious steps towards her. "He is not entirely himself when he is like that. Less and more. Not prone to rational reason. He was my friend first."

Scarlett went rigid. "I'm glad you said that. I hope you both will be very happy together."

My mouth popped open. It could only be about one person. Silver winced visibly, and I shifted my hips so he slid from me. They had forgotten about us for the moment, but they'd remember soon enough.

A massive shadow appeared behind Scarlett and she turned as if she sensed it. Brass stepped forward, so they trapped her in. Her head whipped between Slate and Brass.

"Come to bed, Scarlett. Sleep on it. We can all speak more in the morning." Brass took another cautious step forward.

I saw now why Brass was being so cautious. Her eyes had been closed. She wasn't raging; she was seething. Her eyes weren't her eyes anymore. She turned into an elemental. Seeing Scarlett so furious instantly ignited me as the cold gripped me, I turned into the water. Silver gasped as his hands slid through my body and I drenched him. Brass and Slate looked our way and Scarlett took advantage. She raised her hands and flipped them. She moved out of Slate's way as his body flew past her and into the center bed. It pinned Brass against the far wall and she turned as if nothing had happened and her pack flew into her outstretched hand before she left the adobe.

I leapt up in my elemental form, a crystal-clear version of myself completely made of water with ice-blue eyes.

"What did you do?" My voice came out with this echoing quality that reminded me of an underwater cavern.

"Indigo, put some clothes on!" Silver shouted as I sprung from the door and skidded to a halt.

Scarlett was walking with Tika, who was speaking animatedly next to Scarlett, who was back to calm collection as she sauntered to another adobe with the tigress. My anger ebbed. Scarlett was okay, and I went back into the adobe.

Silver was covering himself with a hand as he dried the bed with his *calling* and worry etched into his normally arrogant face. The corner of my mouth lifted and my elemental form slipped. Silver held his hand out to me, and the wet blanket flew up around me. I bit the inside of my cheek as I wrapped it around my body and stamped down the unwanted warmth that seeped into me.

I helped Silver dry the bed as Slate and Brass spoke in low tones. She dropped them from the moment she'd strode away.

"You two cocked it up. Cannot say I am surprised by the way you have both been carrying on. It is confusing as it is. Add in you two, and a pregnancy... you are lucky she did not incinerate you both," Silver said, and I gazed at him from under my lashes.

"Do not listen to him. He is trying to stay in her good graces," Brass said and Silver narrowed his chocolate brown eyes at his brother.

"And I am right. Your timing could not be worse. Now she is supposed to remarry Slate? Ha! Good luck. Normally, you would send Brass in to butter her up. Too bad he has tangled himself in this web," Silver said, as he straightened the dried blankets with one hand and continued to cover himself with the other.

I laid back down and spread out the blanket I had wrapped around me so Silver could join me. He *was* in my good graces at the moment.

He'd earned his spot, possibly for the next day as well. Silver laid on his back and I tossed my arm and leg over him as I rested my head on his shoulder. Silver's arm slid over my hips, and I traced his tattoos with a fingertip as I closed my eyes.

"I did not think she would be this angry," Slate rumbled, and something gave me a foul taste in my mouth.

"Lie," I said, and Silver looked down at me.

Slate sighed. "It could have been worse."

That felt fresher, cleaner, and more honest.

"Truth," I said, and Silver smiled down at me.

"I do not recommend trying to be like me. A lie every so often is a good thing," Silver said, as he planted a kiss on my forehead.

I heard someone approach the bed, and I was very aware of my nudity. Brass kept his eyes averted as he rubbed his lips together.

"May I try something, Indigo? Would you touch my hand for a moment?" Brass asked.

Silver drew his brow down. "What is this?"

"A test of sorts. Please?" Brass asked, and I slid my hand from Silver's tattoo and touched Brass's big hand.

... She will forgive me. I cannot let this prophecy take me before I can give her my son...

... Now go away, Brass. I plan on being up a long while with my Dove and you two idiots are killing her mood, which is good for once. Thank the Gods. If I catch either of you looking...

... You can hear us. Can't you?...

I gasped. "I can. Silver!" I admonished and slapped his chest.

"Ow! What did I do now?" Silver asked, taking my wrist.

"You told Brass you call me Dove," I whispered, and Silver laughed.

"He would read it in my mind, anyway."

"You're thinking about it right now! Stop thinking, Silver!"

Brass smiled. "She can absorb powers. We will have to see how long they last. This is a bad adobe to read minds on. I am sorry about that."

I gasped again and sat up, looking at Slate, whose silver eyes bore into me. He sat up under the blankets with his back against the wall.

"You're barghest," I breathed. "The one Scarlett painted for Amber. She didn't know it was you."

"I thought she did. She turns a blind eye when confronting things that concern me," Slate rumbled wryly and I felt that fresh feeling again.

"Truth," I said. "That's what people do when they're in love. They don't see what they should, what's obvious to everyone else. I wish I could say I'm shocked to find that you're really a beast, but I feel like I already knew."

Slate scoffed and Brass went back to his bed and slid under the blankets, folding his arms under his head and let the loincloth fall to the floor. Slate scooted down and laid in bed as Brass did in silent introspection.

... Want to put these new powers to use? You will know my every thought...

I dropped my voice low. "What if your thoughts stray? It's bound to happen, Silver."

Silver turned his body towards me and kissed me deeply, making my thoughts seem far away.

... I do not think of anyone else when we are together. Let me prove it...

"By the Mother, this was a rotten idea," Brass murmured and Silver smiled as he opened his mind up to me.

My eyes slid shut as his thoughts came at me a mile a minute mixed with Brass and Slate's. Slate's made me want to recoil as if burned while Brass's left me feeling warm, yet sad. They both loved Scar. I didn't understand how they could stand to be near one another, knowing they competed for the same woman.

... Because we are brothers...

THIRTY-NINE

Tika had saved me from running away from my problems.

"I saw you sneak off, and I thought now would be a good time to teach you the *raqs sharqi*," she'd said when she saw me walk out of the adobe.

Her vertical eyes were bright with a joy I felt no more, and I couldn't say no to her. I mustered all of my energy and stayed up for hours in the little adobe, shaking my hips around and twirling as she showed me. All my time training really paid off; I could follow direction well, pick up easily, and I was in the best shape of my life.

I woke up with my arms around Tika and her arms around me. It was awkward because she slept naked. My eyes shifted around for an escape before I disentangled myself from her. I headed to the lake we'd swam in on our last visit.

When I stepped out of the adobe, the village was still. *Not a creature was stirring, not even a mouse.* I knew where it was, so I grabbed my towel and headed there wearing my grey racerback and matching shorts barefoot, but with my seax strapped to my thigh. I wouldn't be out and about without it.

What I needed was some time to think. I walked deeper into the red clay canyon and followed the small stream that led to the ravine. It opened up to a lake. The same lake that I had first been intimate with the barghest. Slate. Amber was likely growing a little barghest baby boy — a prophet too, to boot.

I stripped off my clothes and dipped my Mod About You pink painted toes into the gritty water. I'd wondered why the barghest hadn't taken me when I'd offered myself up on a silver platter that night. Now I knew, not only was I inexperienced, but if he'd slept with me in that form, he'd have been stuck with me for life. Slate had waited until I was on rousen to sleep with me in that form. Once I was his khoraz sex slave.

We were married. We'd been married since December and it was September! Never once had he hinted at it. I would have remembered.

The hot Thrimilci sun warmed the cool water, and I floated in the deeper depths, gazing up at the cloudless sky on my back. All different fish swam beneath me. The more frightening, the deeper you went. It was darkest near the canyon

Water splashed over my face as someone swam nearer, making waves. I righted myself and hoped they weren't swimming under the water. Jett did the breaststroke as he made his way over to me and I sunk down to my chin, hoping the water was murky enough to hide me.

"Come here often?" he said, bobbing up in front of me.

Droplets clung to his close-cropped hair, and he ran a hand over his chiseled features as he smugly smiled at me.

"Jett, I'm so naked right now," I said, leveling my eyes at him.

"Yes." He feigned concern. "That would make two of us."

"You are the most inappropriate, brother. Stay over there, I'll stay over here," I said, sweeping my long hair from my face.

Jett smacked his full lips together, making a face. "I have seen you nude so many times it does not shock me as it had, darling sister. Where are your leading men? Baby's daddy or husband?"

"Slate told me he was a barghest, showed me. I didn't know. I have tunnel vision for that man."

Jett's turquoise almond eyes went skyward, and he sucked on his teeth. "Yup. It was bound to happen. He has been sloppy since he met you."

He floated on his back and I decided to join him rather than risk catching an eyeful. "He told me his son will be one, too."

"Yup. Don't worry. Orgasm equals first turn and not by yourself or Slate would've turned at ten." He chuckled at his own joke. "When Larn'ra took Slate, she didn't count on him being barghest. That was an interesting endeavor. None of the Merfolk tried to take him since and he's gone back to their lands a few times."

"Lera knows too, and Quick..." I continued.

"And Hawk, Pearl, Sparrow... Gypsum knows because when you were captured, he shifted in front of him. I don't know if you've seen your old wing, but he broke it all down to kindling. It's empty — save the nursery, which I suppose now you'll have to add a crib to when you move back in," Jett said nonchalantly as he floated alongside me.

I sighed. "Jett. I'm going to do this on my own, I think."

"What happened to Brass?" Jett blew water from his mouth. "We'll support you no matter what, but I don't think it'll be any easier if you're alone."

"I've jumped from one guy to the next. I could use some alone time."

"Don't beat yourself up. You're not a serial monogamist. You're an attractive woman who has men lined up to date her. If you leave Brass, another will try to court you. You may be pregnant, but you're a Tio. A *fertile* Tio. Seems to be in the genes," Jett said, sounding self-satisfied. "You really think you can stay angry at Brass or Slate?"

I sloshed in the water. "No. Jett, how does it feel to love two women?"

"Complicated. It takes total honesty — even admitting if you're jealous. Relationships ebb and flow. Sometimes, I feel closer to one more than the other. It's the same for them." He looked pouty. "Thinking about trying to cajole Slate into sharing you? Brass might, he has already, but Slate is not the sharing type." He lifted his head up to gauge my reaction.

"Gods, no. The two of them would team up against me. Besides, Slate is married to Amber." I chewed my lip. "I miss him — *us*. Loving someone this much and totally loving yet another person is selfish. My heart is a whore."

The morning swim was what I needed to rejuvenate. My head was clearer. For all the good it did me. I was turning into Tawny with my hot-tempered flare-ups. Slate was barghest. It was one of a half dozen secrets he'd revealed since Yuletide.

His real heritage, his actual birthdate, that he was a shifter and a prophet. The barghest mated for life. It was the only thing keeping me from flipping out again. He'd only slept with me in that form and if what he said was true, he wouldn't ever be with another as his barghest form. It was strangely flattering. What was stranger was that there was an animal inside me that responded to his barghest form. It was undeniable. I wanted to drop on all fours and raise my rump ever since that first time. Last night had tested my will power and I would have failed if he hadn't shifted into his human skin.

On the walk back with Jett, he'd told me how honored Chief Reski was that Slate was marrying the granddaughter of the ruling family of Thrimilci in their humble village. I wondered what Reski would make of things if he knew we'd said blood vows at my father's funeral, just the two of us out on the pillar that held the Var castle. Looking back, it suited us. Slate and I didn't follow the rules. Ash had been right. It had been wonderfully romantic. Now it was one of many steps I'd taken to ensure my current miserable position.

The village was coming to life when we arrived, just in time to see a snow leopard Wemic man leave the adobe Ama, Shale, and Gypsum had been in with the cheetah twin girls grinning when he passed us on their way in. Jett and I shared a knowing look, and I froze when I saw Slate and Brass eating breakfast together around the ashes from last night's bonfire. They watched Jett and I as we went our separate ways and he gave me a kiss on the forehead.

"Try to relax, baby sis. This is a vacation. Have your wedding with Slate, pretend time has reversed and you've gotten a second chance.

What happens here, stays here and at night, climbs between the sheets with Brass. Nothing needs change, it's a show. You're only acting. No one is asking you to feel."

I gave Jett a look that must have been pitiful from his expression of sympathy. "I can't *not* feel with those two."

"Then try to keep them both. The worst they can say is no," Jett offered in complete sincerity.

I made a face and ran my hand through my partially damp hair. My skin was a deep tan from all the time I'd spent in the sun in Chicago and now in Thrimilci. My golden-brown hair was blonde at the ends. I *did* like how lean my legs looked with the darker tone, and I used it to my benefit as I strode over to Brass and Slate, who sat eating in their loincloths.

Already rich deep tans, the two men looked even darker than usual sitting there hardly dressed at all. I held my chin up imperiously as I addressed them, keenly aware that I wore nothing under my grey racer-back and shorts. Brass was murmuring to Slate; amber and silver sets of eyes followed me from under dark brows.

My arms crossed below my chest. "I haven't thought it over entirely. I'm angry, but I do not know what to do with either of you."

Slate regarded me with gunmetal eyes, making me feel about the size of an ant. "Do what you wish, wife. Is that not what you do, anyway?"

My brow twitched.

"We are supposed to wait out your ruling?" Brass scoffed with a dry smile. "I can think of a score of women who would be grateful to be in your position. Can you, Slate?"

"A score at least," Slate rumbled.

I pinched my lips together. They were turning the tables on me. How dare they! For a dozen other reasons, but most clearly, I would never be a polygamist with those two men to gang up on me.

Did Brass's mouth quirk? I narrowed my eyes.

"I can see you both have your heads up your fanny packs. Savor one another's company while I spend my time with people who don't lie, manipulate, seduce, or coerce me," I sniffed and turned on my bare-footed heel as I walked off.

"You could not even spend time alone then," Slate called after me and my step faltered.

I started towards the little adobe I shared with Tika; we were going to make skirts for our dance after breakfast. She claimed the skirt made all the difference; I was skeptical, to say the least. The distraction was welcome and I would hide out with her as long as she'd let me.

Keen's adobe was on the other side of the path decorated in swirling white patterns as Tika's was, white floral garland hung across the roof like a thick blanket. None of the flowers had wilted overnight. Whatever skills the growers possessed must have allowed them a longer shelf life.

I ate breakfast with Tika and her sister, the chief's wife, Nata. The two tigresses were in spectacular moods that I found increasingly annoying. All my cranky remarks met with giggles and smiles. I wanted to fight someone. I needed to get out some aggression, but I had a terrible feeling that none of my previous sparring partners would risk it given my, *um*, condition.

My skirt suffered my ill temper instead with the repeated stabbing of the needle and thread I wielded like a blade as I attached the red, purple, and yellow dyed fabrics to the waistband to match Tika's. They complimented a sewing ability I didn't know I was capable of, as we finished the skirts by attaching topaz gemstones around the belt line.

I had to admit; they were beautiful, in a belly dancer way. When we tried them on, it hung low on my hips, the strings of topaz drawing your attention. The swaths of fabric reaching my ankles covered more than the loincloths they wore, but were more sensual, especially since the heavy belt made it look like my hips swayed dramatically as I moved.

We beaded more topaz together to go over our bikini like tops as a heavy necklace that draped over my breasts. Nata nodded and clapped when we practiced our routine for her.

"Tika, you look so beautiful! Keen will be thrilled. It will not disappoint Slate, Scarlett." The chief's wife said, grinning her feline like smile.

There were moments where you could forget they weren't human just a regular woman and her sister discussing the upcoming nuptials, but then they smiled and their long teeth were visible in their mouths that only slightly resembled muzzles and you remembered they had a dangerous animalistic beauty that could never be mimicked by a human.

CHAPTER 40
JETT

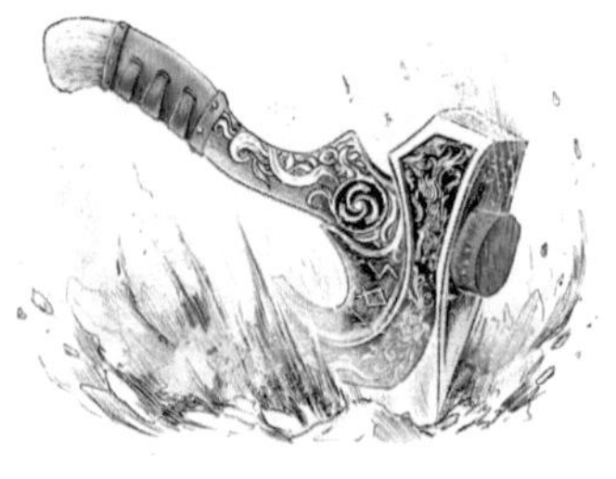

Indigo had been unusually sweet to Quick. Quick had been especially receptive and idly he wondered if it was the start of something. They sat down together after they'd helped grow more flowers for the wedding tomorrow and helped preserve the blooms that hung in long, looping garlands through the village.

Night had fallen and while Indigo's half-clad form was pulled between Quick's outstretched legs to feed him dinner over her shoulder with her fingers, Jett pulled Amethyst into his lap similarly. They rarely spent time alone, so the trip was a rare occurrence in their three-way marriage.

Jett saw Scarlett briefly before lunch after their swim in the lake. Her open smiling face was absent as she pinched her lips together and walked with purpose to where the platters of roasted venison, nopals, and peppers they spread over a bed of spinach. Slate and Brass were staying close. It had to be a part of a grander scheme since staying away from her offered them no advantage. It was good to see them together again, as it should be.

Scarlett hadn't cast them a single glance as she collected two meals and walked back to the adobe they had confined her and Tika all day. Keen had intersected her and put a familiar hand on her slim waist. Her face had contorted into a smile the moment he spoke. He captivated her undivided attention and Jett suspected if she'd been Wemic, Keen would have had no competition if he'd wanted to court her. The temperature seemed to drop as they spoke animatedly before she continued on, and Keen sat down beside Slate after getting his own lunch.

"Tika is determined to make Scarlett a Wemic. They are performing the *raqs sharqi* together." Keen's smile was feline like. "What will your wife say about you performing the rights with another?"

Slate eyes held an air of smugness and frustration. "*Scarlett* is my wife. This is a vow renewal."

"She does not act as though she is. Her scent was of Brass *and* your barghest form. I was not aware she did not know," Keen prodded, and Slate put down his plate.

"Scarlett should not make decisions concerning herself," Slate rumbled and gave Brass a side-long glance.

Keen left in that eternal optimist way he had. "Tika has a surprise for her. A dress Nata has been making the last two nights. My brother's wife is a talented seamstress. Scarlett has been greatly honored. If only she had been Wemic..."

Slate raised his brows above glittering grey eyes. "Her suitors have enough competition without you."

"I would not call it a competition. She wears your ring, carries your brand. Your blood is her blood."

Slate smiled sarcastically. "Someone should tell Scarlett that."

Brass chuckled, and Jett shook his head, tuning out the men. The dynamic between Brass and Slate was a strange one. It wasn't that Scarlett was with Brass. The problem was that right now; it was Slate's turn. Brass wasn't supposed to be with Scarlett until later. They'd planned the whole thing last fall. If someone else would be with her, according to Slate, it would be Brass. Chris had been an unforeseen obstacle neither of them had been happy about, but they'd righted it in time.

Slate had been furious when Brass inserted himself into Chris and Scar's relationship. He came around quickly enough, and they set the plan into motion once more. As far as Jett knew, Scar did not have the faintest clue about the two men's agreement to share her. Not that Slate had wanted to share her at all, and once Brass had moved in with her, things had changed for him as well. Neither of them wanted to share, but they knew if they worked against one another, they'd only push her away.

What kind of wrath would she call down if she knew Slate had only married her *after* Brass had agreed to wait until Slate's prophecy came to fruition before seducing her? It was why Scarlett slept with Slate in the first place. Him showing her the wing he'd had built and proposing. If Brass never agreed to step back and care for her after he died, Slate would never have been comfortable proposing.

Keen sat next to Slate, who elbowed him in the ribs as Tika and Scarlett sat down on the cushions arranged for them across from the bonfire of the men. Slate's eyes were already on her. She fidgeted as she sat down, avoiding the silver barghest eyes that reflected the firelight.

She subconsciously placed a hand on her toned stomach as she sat

Reski, the Wemic chief, sat to the other side of Keen looking every bit the lion king he was with his majestic mane of fawn colored hair falling around his face held back with a red and white band across his forehead. The middle brother of Reski and Keen sat to the chief's right with Tekee.

"This is sure to be a good *raqs sharqi*!" Tikee said, holding his orange and white furred belly.

The Wemic men let out hearty laughs. Slate's face stayed smooth.

Tawny, Indigo, Ama, Shale, and Amethyst moved to sit around Scarlett as her band of bridesmaids trying to expect her every need. Which was none, since she spent most of her time giving Slate a run for his money with her brooding abilities. Tika had her own group of attendants that smiled and laughed high and unabashedly while teasing Tika about Keen and speaking of things, the only things the closest of friends would know. The vibe of the two groups was in complete contrast.

Jett, Steel, Quick, Brass, and Gypsum sat with Slate. Jett and Quick traded raunchy jibes, making Steel and Gypsum laugh and blush at the same time. Brass would occasionally laugh, but his amber eyes swung to Scar more often than not.

The drinking began in earnest after dinner, jugs of chang'aa passed out around the crowd. Scarlett looked miserable, drinking water out of a terracotta jug with a blue band around it, signifying its non-alcoholic contents.

Music played, and Tika turned to Scarlett. "*Raqs sharqi* time."

Her tigress face was bright and Jett thought he saw Scarlett look towards the heavens.

They went into the adobe to get their ribbons of fabric that they held in their hands while they danced. She didn't look nervous, as Jett thought she would be to dance in front of the entire tribe for Slate. It had definite potential to be humiliating.

Scarlett followed behind Tika as she led the way to the bonfire in front of the men. Scar's face relaxed as she stood before them, noticing that the men who surrounded Slate as his quasi groomsmen were all familiar faces.

Tika stopped five feet out from Keen, and Scar did the same with Slate. The groomsmen, Jett included, smiled as they looked up at her. Her eyes slid to Brass, who rubbed his lips together, and Slate, whose face was smooth, but his eyes locked with hers.

The steady bass of the drums started, and it was time to *raqs sharqi*. She stood with her chin held high and her chest slightly bent forward and my arms raised. The light red fabric held high and then the dancing began. Scarlett's face smoothed. He'd seen that face before when she competed with the Shadow Breakers. She separated herself from her emotions and almost looked like a different, colder person.

Tika and Scarlett were two people with one mind, all of their movements synchronized. They started out slow; the drum beats were steady as their hips made circles, their fingers extended gracefully, their arms extensions of the graceful movements their bodies made. Their bodies rolled slowly and someone played an instrument that *chinged* every time they hit it. The base picked up and their swaying hips punctuated the beats. They twisted and lifted as they danced around. They faced each other, and the beats slowed again as they rolled our bodies until they stood mere inches apart, the fabric in their hands sweeping around one another, the movements suggestive.

It filled the canyon air with tension and wood-smoke. Scarlett wasn't looking at Slate, much to his annoyance. Her body glistened with sweat from the desert heat and the close bonfire she danced before. Jett sat beside Quick, behind Brass, who sat opposite Keen at Slate's side. Tika was as tall as Scarlett with a similar shape, though hers was covered with sleek striped fur, but when they danced in perfect rhythm the two young women weren't a Wemic and a human. The swerve of their hips and flow of their limbs were a seduction. They enticed their future husbands to their beds with their every move.

The base picked up, and they turned back to Keen and Slate, and while her eyes rested on him, they saw through him. They started to shimmy and shake, the topaz clicking as their bodies moved, their hands raised to best display their hips and stomach as they moved. They were raw sensuality. Scarlett threw up an arm, extending her leg forward with her toe pointed, her torso bent, and the music stopped.

Scarlett's stomach muscles flexed with her panting when the Wemic clapped. She smiled when she looked at Tika. She beamed back at her and then at Keen to gauge his reaction. Scar's smile fell when she turned to Slate. Whatever she saw there made her lick her full lips and look at the others. Gypsum and Steel clapped with red on their cheeks. Quick was leaning back on his palms with a smirk. Jett didn't need to be a mind reader to know he was wondering if she would teach Indigo about those moves. Scarlett's turquoise almond eyes fell to Jett's, and he saw how hard she was playing at not caring. He gave her a big thumbs up and gave her his proudest smile. The corner of her mouth tugged up in a lopsided grin.

Tika pushed at her back to get her moving. They went to the adobe and came back freshened up in the plain loin clothes and went to their spots by the women. The girls all lean forward and complimented Scarlett, judging by the self-conscious smile on her face.

Keen was being teased by the men who surrounded him while their group sat in an uncomfortable silence. Quick leaned into Jett's shoulder and dropped his voice pointlessly since Brass would have already read his mind and Slate could hear a pin drop during a hurricane.

"Who do you think she will go to tonight?"

"Whomever is smart enough to apologize first?" Jett sipped from his jug, watching Scarlett watching the men past the bonfire.

CHAPTER

FORTY-ONE

"I shouldn't have met you here. It's the day of my vow renewal. It feels wrong to spend the night with you," I said, with Brass tying my loincloth back around my waist.

He'd found me on my way back from relieving myself. Brass hadn't said he was sorry, but I could *feel* it. I didn't want to go to the adobes, and I didn't trust him or Slate at the moment, so I took him deeper into the canyon and up to where Keen and I had gazed out at the stars many times before.

Brass was a passionate man. Everything he did in life was done with his best effort. Once he'd told me dating was hard because women would think of other men even in passing. That shouldn't have been possible. When you were with Brass, he was warm and genuine, not to mention incredibly sexy.

We'd been up late with Brass showing me just how sorry he was and how much he enjoyed my dance with Tika. Thinking about it as I readied made my insides squirm deliciously, and I bit down on my lip to keep from smiling like a loon.

"I take that as a compliment," Brass said in his smooth, deep voice.

I glanced at him over my shoulder as he smoothed his hair back into a knot at his nape. Big dark honey biceps bulging as he tied it. I turned to him and ran my nails over his back and around to his chest, letting them run over the ridges of his body.

"Last night was amazing. Every night with you is. I'm an incredibly lucky woman," I purred and sighed. "What about tonight?"

I held my hand up in the early morning light; the emerald glowing brighter as the rays of light shone through it. Brass's hooded amber eyes looked down at me.

"It is your wedding night. I imagine you will be with your husband."

"I don't understand you two. I can't turn it on and off. Be with him, be with you, act like if you were with someone else, it wouldn't bother me. What is going on? I feel left out of the loop, but somehow in the center."

Brass turned me around, and we started walking back into the canyon. "Slate is your husband, I am your... boyfriend, as you say. If Slate had his way, he would be the one to have you. He does not want to share with you. I do not want to share with you either, but there is unfinished business between you. I would rather you figured things out now rather than we find ourselves in a mess later. Scarlett, I know you are still in love with him. You are having children with me, but you won't reveal the handfasting. You realize we are married? Do you know what you want?"

We reached the bottom of the canyon, and I stopped to look at him. "I do. I want to rewind time and to have never of left him. There is no regret between us. On the contrary, I selfishly wish I had two lives to live so I would never have to be without either of you. On the other side of that coin, I am almost glad that everything happened because I get to be with you. I don't have any answers — just a bottomless well of doubts and questions. I wish I knew what the best thing for me was and someone made the choice for me. How can I raise our children when I can't even make a single decision?"

Brass tilted my chin up and kissed my lips. "A swim. I promise to keep my hands to myself, mostly."

Brass laced his fingers through mine, and we began our trek to the lake.

As soon as we came into sight, I was swarmed. I gave Brass a wave goodbye as they carried me into one of the painting adobe's getting prepared. I couldn't help but notice Brass's smooth look when they carted me off. A man conflicted.

I didn't have time to worry about Brass when they unceremoniously stripped me and the Wemic went to work as I tried to maintain a modicum of modesty. It was an uphill battle. Ama and Shale went to work removing any hint of hair that they felt shouldn't be there, leaving me feeling prepubescent while Tawny brought in a white dress. Everyone seeming completely unfazed by my nudity except for me.

It helped that Tika was just as nude and being equally violated as the Wemic prepped her as well. We underwent plucking, scrubbing and oiling before they styled our hair and dressed us in loose tube-shaped garments. Tawny and Indigo wanted to do my hair, and Ama insisted on doing my makeup.

"What's this?" I asked, as Tawny held up the dress she'd brought in.

"Nata made you a dress when she heard you didn't have one. It's in the Thrimilci style, not the Wemic." Tawny said as tears glistened in her eyes.

I was speechless.

I held Tawny's hand as I stepped into my dress.

My wedding dress.

Butterflies set flight in my stomach as Indigo clasped the dress at the center of my back. I hadn't seen many mirrors on my visits to Wemic lands, so when I turned around to find a floor length one in front of me, it took me a second to realize I was looking at myself.

Tawny and Indigo had curled my hair into big voluminous loops, part of the front pinned back away from my face where a crystal sun hung on a silver chain that dangled on the center of my forehead. Three strands of crystals hung just off my shoulders of the empire waist dress that led to a heavily beaded center that connected just under my breasts where the beaded belt started out narrowly and grew wider the closer it came to my sides. The fabric didn't start till just above my breasts in an inverted 'U' shape. The skirt was silken folds of fabric so light it was like wearing folded clouds.

I barely recognized myself.

"Oh, Scarlett," Amethyst said before breaking down into tears. I wrapped my arms around her. "If only your mother could see you right now."

"Mom would not miss it; she is here with us in one form or another," Indigo said from my side.

I swallowed hard and let myself be hugged by my closest friends and family and the most important women in my life.

"Are they ready?" Came a guttural voice from outside the adobe.

I looked at Tika, who was fanning her face to keep her tears from falling but was otherwise ready. She turned to me and met my eyes; I gave her my best smile. She looked beautiful. Her white floor length dress was of fabric that *swished* when she walked and tied behind her long dark hair that was braided down her back, small white blooms tucked all along them.

She nodded and Indigo held open the curtain covering the door, the Wemic attendants going with them. My cheeks heated and something much larger than butterflies beat against my insides.

"I know you and Slate are over, or whatever, but I'm so glad you're getting a wedding ceremony." Tawny wiped a finger under her red-rimmed hazel eyes.

"I can't believe this is happening," I said, feeling like the few bites of cactus pear I'd eaten wanted to make a return.

My bridesmaids started filing out one by one, alternating with Tika's girls. Ama met with Gypsum, Indigo with Quick, Tawny with Steel, Jett with Amethyst, and finally Shale with Brass. When it was just Tika and me, we moved closer together like magnets, finding our nerves more tolerable than being closer together. We didn't bother with soothing words. The comfort of one another's presence was enough.

The music grew louder, and we heard the shuffling of feet and we knew it was time. Tika's father, who was a huge jaguar man, dropped the curtain hanging in the doorway and took her arm, leading her out first. She gave me a reassuring smile. I returned as she headed out with me right behind her.

Once we were out, someone *called* and white flower petals fell like feathers from the sky. I couldn't help but look up in amazement at how beautiful the scene was. I had to remind myself it was my wedding. Somebody should have pinched me.

I gazed forward and saw that the space beyond the bonfire had split into two sections. Down the center of the path, flower petals fell like snowflakes from the many garlands that hung overhead. Wemic stood to either side of the path. Our bridal party stood off to the side. Girls in both parties wore simple white dresses while the men in our bridal party were shirtless with white linen pants, which made them seem almost overdressed to Keen's loincloth wearing men.

I had forgotten how my feet worked and felt an arm slide through mine and Jett appeared on my arm, starting me forward. A lump the size of Texas formed in my throat as my eyes watered and I gave him a grateful smile. A grand arch made up of a blanket of more white flowers was our destination, and under that arch was Slate.

He took my breath away.

My heart skipped when I saw him standing there. They plaited his midnight waves in dozens of narrow braids that formed one larger braid down his back. His usual beads and fetishes threaded through it. He wore loose white linen pants and a sleeveless linen 'V' neck.

I had never been more nervous, but when my eyes met his, the world around us faded into the background. The faces turned towards me disappeared, the musicians' beats faded and it was only the two of us. As we moved closer, the smile on his bronze face grew until creases appeared in his cheeks and I felt my own cheeks hurt from how wide my smile was.

Jett stopped in front of him and shook his hand hard once before passing my hand to his. Slate's touch was electric, the draw I felt towards him pulled taut. We stood lost in one another four minutes until we heard people cheer. Keen and Tika were married.

I unclenched my fist and touched my father's ring on Slate's finger.

The two big men had had the same size hands. My hands trembled as he closed his over mine again. Our eyes locked.

"My name is not my own, it is borrowed from my ancestors. I must return it unstained. My honor is not my own. It is on loan from my descendants. I must give it to them unbroken. Our blood is not our own. It is a gift to generations yet unborn. We should carry it with responsibility."

We chanted the blood oath in unison. We could only say it as a marriage vow with one another. The blood oath we'd sworn at my father's funeral prevented us from uttering the words to anyone else. I wouldn't want to.

What Brass and I had differed from what Slate and I had. I wouldn't want to marry Brass the same way if it had ever come down to it. At the moment, that was the farthest thought in my mind.

Slate didn't wait for me to move. It wasn't a church kiss, that was certain. He pulled on my hand hard, so I crashed against him and he slid his hand into my hair, kissing me deeply.

I was helpless to him. My husband. *Slate.*

When he released me, he smiled against my lips before turning to the crowd. I felt lightheaded and heavy at the same time as I saw my friends and family smiling and clapping, some even crying.

We met Keen and Tika in the middle of the path and we faced our friends and family together. The crowd grew louder and Keen threw up his clawed hands,

"Now we feast!" He grabbed Tika's hand as they ran down the aisle.

Slate turned to me and reached for my hand. He looked younger than I'd ever seen him, his eyes bright as we ran down the flurry of flower petals being thrown over us.

My version of heaven changed every few months, but it seemed to revolve around the same people. That moment was my new heaven.

The Wemic lit the bonfire and platters of food floated around the people. Slate and I sat with Keen and Tika, members of our bridal party, sitting around us on cushions as we ate. I couldn't stop smiling. Slate had never smiled wider, and it was contagious. Every time my eyes met his, I was astonished anew at how visibly happy he was, and in public.

We fed one another with our fingers, and I didn't think we'd stay late at the reception. The attraction between us demanded physical satisfaction. He felt it too. Every time he looked at me, his eyes glinted.

He grabbed my hand and dragged me out to where the Wemic were dancing.

The Wemic didn't have an equivalent to slow dancing, so when we got onto the dance floor, Slate picked up the train of my dress and pulled me close, his leg between mine as he guided my hips with his hands. It was the first time we were sort of alone all day. The Wemic around us are busy moving with their own partners. I saw all the couples out there with us. Quick was dancing with Indigo, and Brass and Shale were even dancing. Ama was in the crowd with Rikke, who I had been told she had seduced with Shale the night before.

Slate's mouth was at my ear, his breathing uneven, when he whispered, "Can you dance for me tonight like you did last night?"

I burst into laughter. "I didn't think you liked it. You didn't even smile."

I could tell he fought the urge to pick me up when he said, "That is because another hundred behind me could see what my wife could do. I thought I would have to fight them off."

I bit my lip and look up at him through my lashes. "Say it again."

His lips curled. "*My wife.*"

I pretended to swoon, rolling my eyes up to the sky and placing my hand on my head. His laugh was rich when he wrapped his hands around my waist, pulling me back up.

"Can I cut in?" Jett asked. Amethyst smiled at Slate and offered him her slender hand.

"Of course," I said, shifting to Jett.

Jett smirked as we attempted to dance to the Wemic rhythm. "So... you look happy."

"It's my wedding day," I said dryly and sobered. "How's Brass doing?"

Jett shook his head. "Good, all things considered. Those two have probably worked out all the kinks and you are being manipulated into doing whatever goal they've set in the grander scheme of things."

My jaw dropped open, and he laughed.

"They aren't that clever, baby sis," he said and pulled me closer.

I danced with every single one of my male relatives and Quick before I reached Brass. I gave him a nervous smile as I approached, and he slid the fabric of my sleeve between his fingers.

"I'm jealous," he said without preamble.

"When tonight is over, it all ends. I promise," I said.

"Don't make promises you can't keep," he said, and pulled me close so I leaned against him as we slow danced with everyone else moving to a much faster beat. "This wedding is much more like the one Slate envisioned for himself, not the one at the Dagr palace, right down to the woman."

"Do you hate me right now?" I asked, hooking my arms around his.

"No. I hate him at the moment, but in two days, when we are back in Chicago, it will be a distant memory. Yesterday we were together. Tomorrow we will be together. Today we are not."

I looked up at him, and my forehead creased. Did that mean he would seek another woman? Not knowing would bother me, but imagining him with someone else would be worse. With great effort, I let it go.

Brass and I were dancing far closer than a married woman should dance with another man when irritated emotions wafted to me, followed by rage. Brass stopped moving, and we looked around. My heart lurched dangerously when my eyes settled on the strawberry blonde hand fasted wife of my husband.

"Slate!" Amber called out; her blue almond eyes bright in the bonfire's light.

Hawk ran a hand over his silver hair, looking exasperated, and spotted me with Brass. Amber disappeared, and I followed her with my eyes to where she found Slate, who stiffly held her as she showered kisses on him.

"By the Mother. between you and me, Amber is very spoiled," Hawk said, standing next to Brass and me. "She whined nonstop until I agreed to bring her." He looked to the heavens.

"What a surprise," I said numbly and felt Brass give me a reassuring squeeze.

Slate was looking over the heads of the dancing Wemic, searching me out. I felt leaden as I looked away. Hawk ran the back of his finger along his trim goatee.

"You look lovely, Scarlett. You didn't get married yet, did you?" he asked uncomfortably.

Brass would have to ask Hawk before we had permission to marry. Already, I was regretting my return to Tidings.

"I'm already married," I breathed.

I turned to face Brass with my scalp prickling. "Let me say goodnight." He gave me a nod, and I reached up on my tiptoes to give him a quick kiss, not caring who saw and turned around without waiting for his reaction.

"It will only take a second," I said, holding up my index finger. I trotted over to where Steel and Tawny sat with Reski and Nata.

"I just wanted to say goodnight. And thank you for letting us get married here Reski, tonight has been... magical," I said, plastering a smile on my face. Tawny stood and hugged me fiercely.

"You deserve a little happiness. I am glad it came together for you," she said, her long dark tresses brushing my cheek as she hugged me.

I didn't have the heart to tell her Amber showed up.

Reski and Nata stood, and he wrapped his arm around her thin shoulders. "We are happy too. Our tribe has always been on good terms with the Sumar. This only binds us closer. My wife and sister-in-law, thank you for all your contributions to the festivities. You are always welcome here," the chief said, smiling, Nata nodding beside him.

I forced another smile and crossed the dance floor to where Brass waited. Keen and Tika stood with Slate and Amber at the other end of the dance floor. Hawk had found a flustered Gypsum, and Brass pulled me close as we walked back to the adobe.

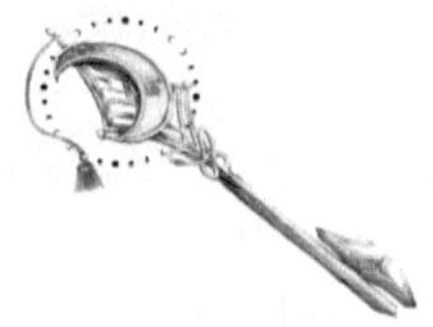

I COULDN'T SLEEP. I turned in his arms and found that despite his even breaths; he was wide awake. My chin tilted up and kissed his defined lips. His hands tightened around me as he sucked in a sharp breath.

"I have to go to the bathroom."

He guffawed, watching me amusedly, "Already the mystery is gone? I was told it would happen when you married, but I assumed that meant if I was the groom." I made a face at him and leaned over to kiss Brass.

"I love you. Keep the bed warm for me," I said, standing up and giving him a wry smile.

"I'll never get sick of hearing you say that," he said, trying to keep things light.

He grabbed a fistful of his shirt that I wore and pulled me close for a kiss. "Take your seax." He pulled my seax from under the bed and sat up further, pulling my leg so he could buckle it on.

I watched him do it and balanced myself by placing my hand on his head. "Brass. Today was more than I'd ever wished for. I'm glad I got it. Thank you. I'll never deserve you. You know that, don't you?" I said, chewing the inside of my cheek.

"I'm the first and I'll be the last man you lay with, love. Everything else is just a footnote," Brass said, pressing a kiss to the inside of my thigh as he curled around the bed to grope me.

"I really have to go now," I said before rushing out of the adobe and narrowly missing his hand swiping at my bottom.

I hurried along the canyon, skirting the bonfire, and decided peeing in the canyon instead of in town would be a better idea. I couldn't hear any music and I figured the party was over. We had left a couple of hours earlier and it had still been in full swing.

I squatted unceremoniously against the wall and relieved myself. I did a little shake before standing and headed back up the canyon wall.

The scrape of someone walking made me freeze in place and look around, shrinking against the wall.

I looked away from the village and saw nothing. Then I heard a single scream. I'd heard that scream before. I'd heard it sound just like that in a screech of horror.

Indigo.

When last she loosed a bloodcurdling scream, it was when someone had thrown my mother off the Vetr castle balcony. *No. No. No.*

Screams filled the air, and they were coming from the village. I felt the cuts forming on my feet as I ran, my toes stubbing all rocks on every other step. The village came into view and I saw them.

The Jorogumo are attacking the Wemic. I didn't stop running and my feet hit something that sent me flying.

My face slid along the canyon floor as I skidded. I knew it was bad when the blood immediately filled my mouth and I sucked harshly at the burning sensation over my cheek. The side that skid on the ground was raw from where the skin scraped away. I got to my feet and held my stomach, but it didn't hurt. I searched out the source of my fall and let out a wail. Amber and Slate's baby in her womb, her throat slit and her eyes like mine, staring up at the starry sky. She must have been coming out to relieve herself, as I did. Her blood was still pooling, which meant it must have happened just after I passed the spot not five minutes ago.

A blood-curdling scream ripped from my throat when the ice-cold torque snapped around my neck with pain that brought me to my knees. I couldn't *call,* I couldn't shift. I tried over and over and I couldn't reach it. A maniacal laugh sounded from behind me and I struggled to my feet. Nirrin and his cheetah brothers prowled around me. I moved to stand.

"Little Guardian girl, I told you we would continue this." His vertical pupils are wide in the moonlight. "We thought she was you. We could not have her go alerting your mate. Slate does not stray from his type, it appears."

I clenched my teeth. I didn't like Amber one bit, but she didn't deserve to die.

"If you're going to kill me, there's no need for the dramatics," I ground out, backing until looking for a way to reach my seax without them noticing.

I hadn't seen Nirrin in my last two visits to the Wemic. The cheetah scout had threatened me before, and Slate had stopped him both times.

His laughter chilled me. "If only it was that simple. Get her," he said simply.

Like it'd be that easy.

I saw a blur of blonde and heard one of the cheetah man's yelp. I grabbed my seax and stabbed the closest one through the stomach before I grabbed Indigo, fighting the pain of the torque as we raced towards the village. She had come for me. I did not know she'd known where I'd be. She was in a daze and wearing a Quick's black linen Shadow Breaker shirt. She reached up and yanked off the torque, her in black, and me in white. I'd accidentally grabbed the shirt Slate wore when he'd traveled there.

We reached the edge of the village saw the slaughter. The five hundred spider hybrid rogues were pulling Wemic out of their adobes and killing them in the path that was still covered in white petals, now turning red from the blood of the Wemic. I searched with my blood pounding in my ears for my family and spotted them fighting outside of the guest adobes.

I saw all of them alive and I almost cried out in relief.

Instead, I ran into the fray with my seax swinging and slicing into Jorogumo left in right, whatever I could reach. Spider-like legs went flying, and I was awash in blood, pulling Indigo with me closer to our family.

"Scarlett, Indigo!" Jett screamed, but they surrounded him and Amethyst, fighting at his side. They were all half-dressed, if dressed at all.

Brass and Quick heard Jett's shout and saw us fighting our way towards them and someone knocked me off my feet from behind. I didn't look behind me, but scrambled on my knees for my seax. They kicked me *hard* in my stomach and I curled around a booted foot as tears sprung to my eyes.

Masked men fought alongside the Jorogumo.

"Pick them up, get them out of here." The man with the black mask ordered.

I spat blood as they threw me over a shoulder. My head lifted frantically, searching for Indigo and someone to help us.

Slate.

His bellow rocked my captor and caused me to fall to the ground.

"Scarlett!" Brass shouted, and I rolled on instinct, narrowly dodging the men wrestling beside me.

I crawled over to where Indigo fell. "Get up!" I tried to shout, but it came out a croak.

I pulled her up, throwing her arm over my shoulder, and tried to hobble closer to my family so I could go back and help Slate. Wemic roared all around me as they launched a counterattack against the Jorogumo.

I glanced over my shoulder and saw Slate being brought down. Three Jorogumo surround him with the masked man and Nirrin. They had nets and something that looked almost like a harpoon trying to drag him down to his knees. I looked between the adobe and Slate. Brass made eye contact and shook his head. Indigo grabbed my hand, and warmth flooded me.

"Be careful," she rasped, and I sent my healing into her.

I let go of Indigo and rushed to Slate's side without waiting for Brass's response. With Nirrin distracted, he wasn't trying to get the torque back on. I stabbed the first Jorogumo while sliding underneath it, gutting it as I went. I came up next to Slate, and he glared at me.

I turned my back to him and started in on the other two, Jorogumo, but my little knife wasn't enough and the Jorogumo seemed to be focused on us. I heard another bellow and Brass broke through the surrounding line.

"Get out of here, Scarlett!" Brass shouted at me while he blew apart one after another of the Jorogumo. "Go to the adobe."

"I can't leave you all to fight alone!" I shouted back as a Jorogumo pincher stabbed through the arm holding my seax.

I held back a cry, so I didn't distract Brass and Slate, but it pulled me close to finish me.

"Do not kill her!" a masked man shouted.

His shout caused us all to drop our guard for a moment. Slate and Brass realized they caught me in its pinchers and tried to turn to help me, but there were just too many.

Out of my peripheral, I saw the third cheetah brother running into the fray towards Indigo. Panic welled up from me and I leaned down for my seax with my left hand and wrenched away from the Jorogumo with a scream. I could see the bone in my forearm, but I couldn't stop even though blackness threatened to swallow my vision from the agony. I had no choice.

Tears poured down my face as I stabbed at the giant spider hybrids around me. I had to get to Indigo. I was almost free of the Jorogumo line heading back towards the canyon when Nirrin and the masked man noticed me. Nirrin lunged, and I braced for the impact. My head hit the ground with an audible crack and I felt my fingers lose grip on the blade.

In my mind's eye, I saw Ama scream and pain flooded through me. Slate roared again, and I grappled with Nirrin, who was twice as strong as I was. I shifted. Nirrin hissed and fell back as I turned into fire and took up my blade with my other hand. Nirrin narrowed his eyes at me before running off.

"*SCARLETT!*" Slate bellowed like a man possessed, and my heart lurched.

He shifted into barghest form and three men had him surrounded with a nix torque around his neck. He must have felt Ama's bond break, and they took him while he was down. My heat twisted again as his silver eyes slid past me. My head whipped around to find Brass sneaking up behind me.

"He loves you, Scarlett," Brass said roughly, and I screamed.

I turned around in time to see the towering barghest give me a dangerous grin and went loping off deeper into the canyon. The three men chased after him with the remaining cheetah brothers and a handful of the spider hybrids.

Panic burned in my stomach, infusing my body with adrenaline. Blood dripped off the fingertips of my right arm and my head pulsed with pain. I struggled to my feet with tears in my eyes and *call* energy out of the air so all I could hear was silence.

I clapped my hands together and the retreating Jorogumo that was climbing the sides of the canyon went flying in a soundless thunderclap that drove them into one another and onto the rocks, causing them to burst open. Their insides showered the earth below in a rain of blood. The shrieks of dying Jorogumo filled the air, and I was the harbinger of their death.

I ran, fueling my fire and burning them alive, and followed the way Slate ran. A blonde blur was next to me dousing the dangerous fires, and I spared a glance for Indigo. She gritted her as she shot frozen spikes of ice through the dying Jorogumo running alongside me.

Indigo has never been the fighting type, but she's there. Filthy and blood soaked, just like me. My sister.

We followed the path of destruction until we came to a low ramp of the canyon wall that led to the land above, with bodies of Jorogumo littered around the bottom. We ran up the ramp like formation and could make up forms in the moonlight far ahead.

"Slate." I tried to scream, but it's barely more than a whisper.

Brass's bond was active. He was okay. Mine was active, I was sure; I wouldn't know what he would feel at the moment. It was a given that panic would be among the emotions felt.

Then a blast lifted the grit into the air around the forms ahead, and they disappeared into it. I pumped my legs faster and Indigo pushed herself to keep pace.

In my mind's eye, I saw Slate hang his head, and then it was gone. The bond was gone.

I loosed a scream, not realizing I *called* as I did it. The ground in front of us as far as I could see rolled roughly as if a giant took an edge of the world like a sheet and shook it out, sending debris flying into the air and knocking Indigo and me back.

My ears rang. I blinked on my back, unsure of what had just happened.

"Scar?" Indigo asked, crawling over to me as small red stones fell over us like a meteor shower.

Dust hung heavy and I couldn't see through the tears. My breath was stuck in my chest. When I finally gulped, it was a haggard sound that caked my throat with gritty red dirt, and I immediately started coughing and hacking as I rolled onto my hands and knees. Minor cuts bled from all over my exposed skin as I shrugged Indigo off me and rose onto the swollen, bleeding feet.

"I have to find his body," I croaked.

Ama's bond. Slate's bond. It wasn't possible. It couldn't be.

The moonlight offered little in the way of a searchlight, but I couldn't leave him out there to be eaten by vultures. Indigo tugged on my arm and I helped her to her feet, healing her. She grabbed my shoulders and shook me.

Her blonde hair was wild around her dirty tan face, the black shirt she wore in tatters, and she was barefoot like me. "Scarlett, what are you saying?"

"I have to find his body. Help me. I can't go back without him."

I *wouldn't* go back without him.

Her eyes flitted between mine, and I felt her *call*. Relief flooded her features, and panic surged through me once again.

"The babies are okay. I would kill you if you endangered them. We would all kill you. I'll help you look as long as you promise to take care of yourself." Indigo was much more stalwart than I would've thought she'd be.

I sheathed my seax on my leg. The black handle of the sword had a carved woman's design and etched in gold. Its scabbard was black and hand-stitched, with gold embossed wings and buckles. It was barely as long as my forearm and wickedly sharp. Slate had bought it for me on my second day in Tidings. All my gear was enchanted so it wouldn't burn when I shifted, including my Yggdrasil necklace I wore around my neck and my silver torque. One for being inducted into Valla U and the other for completing my first year.

Valla U was far from my mind as I hobbled over stones in the direction I'd seen the forms before. The dust still hadn't settled and I couldn't see over ten feet in front of my face in the dark. Indigo trudged to my side; she lifted her black men's shirt to reveal a thin belt she wore with a sheath for her short seax that hung from her naked waist.

"I can absorb other people's powers. I was making love to Silver when I felt those men come into the village. They were Stygian Knights. The ones who escaped the raid. They knew we'd be here, Scarlett. They had planned to take you, me, and Slate. I started screaming when the thoughts came into my mind. I left Silver there without an explanation." She tripped over a stone and I caught her arm.

My tears had stopped as she told me how she only needed to touch someone to absorb their powers. She had Brass's and Quick's and now my empath abilities and I could feel her building up to the inevitable question as we walked on.

"Scarlett, did you feel Slate die?" she asked cautiously, and I grit my teeth.

Crying would help no one.

She nodded beside me, picking up the way Brass did from my mind. "We won't go back until we find him. As long as the babies are safe."

CHAPTER 42

JETT

Ama's funeral was held with a hundred Wemic, which included Keen's brother, Nekee. Keen and Tika had been safely atop the canyon and had come down only when they heard the screaming. Amber had had her throat slit by a Wemic claw. Nirrin, that bastard. They had wrapped her body and froze it so they could bring it back to her family.

It was the third day since the attack. They'd cleared the village of bodies and found enough wood to make pyres for them all. Amethyst and Hawk had grown trees just to be cut down and grown more again. She was resting in one adobe that survived Scarlett's wrath.

Brass left just after the funeral with Quick to find Indigo and Scarlett. Jett had insisted he'd go himself, but with Shale despondent and Amethyst helping make pyres, someone needed to help rebuild the village with Gypsum and Steel. Hawk and Tawny organized the people and grew fresh food for them all so they wouldn't have to hunt while they grieved. There was a great deal of grieving going on.

Jett's throat choked once more, and he swallowed against it. Brass said Scarlett was healthy if dehydrated and starved walking through the desert. They thought she'd come back on her own. They had hoped Indigo would talk some sense into her, but Brass said she was determined. To do what, they weren't sure, but Jett thought it had to do with Slate's death.

Jett thanks every God and every star that Scarlett was pregnant, so she didn't do something incredibly foolhardy like try to join him in the afterlife. He'd seen her face when he'd drawn the attention of the Stygians and gone into the canyons. He'd also seen Scarlett and Indigo take off after him, raining death and destruction down in their wake. Jett doubted that they even knew that they'd single handedly turned the tables of the attack.

His elemental sisters. Fire and water, balancing one another out.

Indigo had doused out most of the fires before she left, but Scarlett had been a loose cannon. He'd never heard of someone using that much air, and he was certain the earthquake he'd felt later was moments after Brass said Slate had died. By the Mother, Slate's bond had broken and Brass and Quick had fallen to their knees. The taciturn Shale had gone from sobbing over Ama's body to downright wailing. There was no consoling her. Even now, Tawny and Amethyst took turns feeding her and putting her back to sleep.

The town was almost running again and aside from the smell of the burnt bodies that hung in the air, Jett had taken the time to wash the dirt off the blood as much as he could. You couldn't tell a battle had taken place that had killed a hundred and four people, including a Stygian so badly burned they couldn't pry off his mask and two hundred and thirty Jorogumo rogues.

Jett was going to wait another few days before going back to Thrim-ilci and telling Pearl that her adopted grandson was dead. Worse — dead and they couldn't find the body. Jett knew if Scarlett didn't come back with his body, then there wasn't one to be found. He knew that's where she had gone and was thankful Indigo had been clever enough to follow her. She wouldn't any harm come to the twins. He was certain of it.

Brass and Quick would force them to come back by any means necessary, and they would give Slate a proper goodbye. In one swoop, the Stygians had killed off the Dagr line with Amber's death. Jett met

Steel's red-rimmed eyes, and he ducked his head again. None of them had spoken since the first day. They did what needed doing without having to ask. It'd become a sort of morbid dance.

Scarlett would come back and she'd need them more than ever. Shale would be a dim reflection of how bad Scarlett would be.

CHAPTER

FORTY-THREE

Swallowing was impossible. My throat was too dry for the motion. I *called* a stream of water into my mouth. *Better.* My eyes felt glued shut, and I slowly forced them open. The early morning sun of the desert made the sky look red. *Like the blood of the Wemic.* I sat up stiffly and stretched. Indigo was sleeping beside me, curled in the fetal position. Her hands tucked under her tanned face; her full bottom lip lowered so her every breath puffed out of her.

I stiffened. We were being watched. Unseen eyes made the hairs on the back of my neck rise in warning.

We had reached a savanna grassland from the desert early the second day of our trek. The long dry grass gave way to shrubs until Acacia and Baobab trees grew up from between the cracks in the ground. We'd curled up alongside a tree and had been so tired neither one of us could stand watch. I could only vaguely recall laying down.

I placed my hand on Indigo's shoulder and gave her a gentle shake. "Indigo, wake up."

"Hmm? I'm up. Did you find something to eat?" she asked, shielding her eyes from the bright morning rays.

We had found some nopales we'd eaten as we walked and with our *calling* we hadn't gone thirsty. We healed one another as we went, and Indigo checked on the babies, the only things that kept me tethered to this world. Two days of only eating the cactus pears and not sleeping until we were dead on our feet. We hadn't found *his* body. Even thinking his name hurt.

Indigo's stolen powers had disappeared the first day we'd been in the desert, but she still had mine from our constant touching. Indigo had stopped asking how far we were going to search. Until we found him had been my only response. Had some unseen predator stolen his body? Had a Jorogumo eaten him?

Best not to think about that.

We lost the trail days earlier. That first night. Still, we kept on.

"Shh. We're being watched," I breathed as I drew my short seax from my thigh sheath.

I wanted to kill something. We hadn't been in the mood to hunt before, but now we were half starved and wanted an excuse to drive my blade into something. Anything. I closed my eyes and tried to pinpoint where or what the being was. Indigo stretched next to me and *called* water into her mouth as she tried to act nonchalant.

"To the left. He doesn't mean us any harm. He's guarded and curious. We're on his territ —"

My words cut short when the creature rose. What I thought was a thorn bush, raised until it was a man. Yet, not a man. Antlers stuck up from his tawny face with long hair that matched his short fur coat. He wore roughhewn pants, and a strap crossed over his chest that held a quiver. A sheathed blade hung from his hip and he carried an unstrung bow as he came towards us.

Indigo and I rose as one. We looked even more wild than he was. The hybrid was half elk, with fetishes that hung from his tall antlers. He was well-formed for a man, with a nose like a deer. I'd never seen a Faunelle, they were native to Thrimilci, but the hybrid was unmistakable.

"Greetings. How does the day find you?" he asked.

One look at us and you knew the day did not find us well. If I looked half as bad as Indigo, it was a miserable day. Because I was in Slate's shirt, I looked the worst of the two.

"In good health. How does the day find you?" I answered, sliding my blade into my sheath.

The Faunelle's round brown eyes scanned our appearance, and I regretted not having ran a hand through my hair before running into the noble tribe.

"Better than you both, it would seem." He gave a friendly smile with flat teeth and my guard dropped some.

"Have you come across any Jorogumo this way?" Indigo asked.

The Faunelle creased his tawny brow. "Jorogumo this far? We have heard of these occurrences, but have encountered none. Were the Wemic attacked?" he asked, speaking English.

He eyed us again, our disheveled appearances taking on new meaning. "Yes," I croaked roughly as I pressed my lips into a firm line to keep them from quivering.

Understanding darkened his eyes, and his white furred jaw tightened. "You are within an hour's walk from my village. Do you have the strength to walk?" he asked.

"We do," I responded and thought Indigo would leap for joy.

We walked with the Faunelle male named Adal and retold the

events of three nights past. He knew the art of listening, never interrupted and once our story was told, asked for details.

The story was told with time to spare during our hour-long walk. How something that changed my life so completely could be explained in less than an hour boggled my mind. Indigo filled in the gaps, and Adal apologized for the deaths on my wedding day. I inclined my head, unable to find my voice.

The land showed signs of fertility and small cultivated farms cropped up before we reached a web of streams. Faunelle had built streams and piled the access red dirt in tiny hills that they built their huts atop. The streams led all the way from a river that led directly to the ocean. We were on the other side of Thrimilci. A half-hour walk to the tip, Adal informed us.

The Faunelle was like the Wemic. Where the Wemic had leopards, lions, tigers, and cheetahs. The Faunelle had moose, elk, antelope, and all different deer. Their children, in fringed roughhewn clothing, pants or simple shift dresses, pulled on Adal's pants and stared openly at Indigo and me.

"You brought us Guardians!" cried a little pudu deer girl.

Adal pulled two small sacks off his belt and handed them to the gathered children. Nuts, berries, and shoots spilled from the bags and the children ran off in fits of giggles. Vainly, I smoothed my hair and ran my hands over my filthy, blood-stained shirt. Indigo was doing similar actions beside me.

Small canoes drifted along the stream, carrying Faunelle and goods between mounds. From the way they openly watched us, I guessed Guardians didn't frequent so far on the island. An elegant tawny doe with long fiery red hair that fell to her hips approached, carrying a wooden staff that's wood twined around to form an oblong cage at the top.

Her thin mouth spread into a smile as she lifted the white wood staff to Adal. "Greetings. How does the day find you?" she asked in a pleasant tone.

Adal's wife, or else would be soon from the way they looked at one another, was very much in love and my heart constricted.

"Well enough, and you?" I asked.

Her smile turned sympathetic. "Very well. Come, you looked tired and hungry."

Adal took the staff, and my eyes widened. "You're the chieftain?"

Adal was a head taller than I was and he looked down at me with a small smile. "That I am, Scarlett. This is my mate, Raud. She will give you fresh clothes and food. We may speak more after."

Their kindness with no hesitation made my nose burn, and I sniffed hard, hiding the beginning of a snivel. We arrived, told them a story that could have been false. They knew we had the power to do serious destruction, and still allowed us to walk among them.

We didn't speak as Raud led us to a small canoe and after we climbed in; she pushed off with a long wooden pole pushing off down the stream. Despite the full night's rest, a lethargic weariness fell over me and Indigo scooted to sit next to be drawing her knees up under Quick's shirt and leaned on me, offering me her support.

The canoe slid onto a mound and we stepped out as Raud pulled the canoe higher onto the mound. We waited with our toes in the brown silt as her long skirt dipped into the water. She wore a high halter top with a cropped stomach that displayed the white fur that covered it. She gave us another small smile as she started towards the stilted hut that topped the mound and gestured towards it.

Bathed and clothed in long haltered dresses with fringe along the neckline, Raud handed us each a plate of cassava bread filled with pistachios and pomegranates coupled with a honeyed mead which I had to decline in favor of water. It was one of the best meals I'd ever eaten. Raud handed us seconds, and we ate with gusto.

Adal walked in and took a seat across from us in the hut at the low table. We sat around on rustic ladder chairs. "Are you feeling hale?" he asked, handing Raud two more sacks and pressing a furry human hand to her white stomach.

Raud smiled lovingly at Adal and took the sacks into a separate room, leaving us with her mate. The chieftain of the Faunelle.

"You seem young for a chieftain," I blurted, and Indigo's eyes widened at my rudeness.

Adal only smiled kindly and set his staff in the hut's corner. "I am. We elect chieftains here, and they chose me a pentad of years ago. The Faunelle are an easy tribe to govern. I mostly devise ways to make our lives simpler, such as increasing the streams to include the outlaying crops. There are few disputes to settle here. May I?" he asked, gesturing to me.

I had grown accustomed to people touching my stomach to *call* and feel the twins, so I nodded without hesitation and Indigo made a face in the corner of my eye. I realized belatedly that a Faunelle couldn't *call*, and he reached for the chain of my necklace instead. My body went rigid as he pulled the chain over my head and inspected the small stone pendant the size of a copper skoll.

"When the Grar Dyr chooses a timi, the shadows of dagr and nott will blend as one against the rising flood. Asamt they will stop tid and decide the fate of the world."

I blinked at him as he went in and out of Old Norse. He reached to his antlers, where a leather strap wound about and untwined it as he spoke.

"May I ask if you carry the Grar Dyr's bairn?" he asked in a respectful tone.

Only one person called it that. My lockbox was back. I shoved any emotions into the box and shut it tight.

"I don't." I said. "But I am pregnant. How did you know?"

The corner of Adal's black lips pulled into a lopsided smile. "The way you looked at my mate when I greeted our unborn."

I dropped my eyes, unable to meet his soulful brown orbs for another moment. "What did you say just now? That..."

"Prophecy. When the Grey Beast chooses a time, the day and night will blend as one against the rising flood. Together, they will stop time and decide the fate of the world. It is an old prophecy handed down from chieftain to chieftain and their mates should anything happen to them. We were told the twins of the Var and Sumar would come in the wake of andlat for the piece."

Adal pulled the piece of leather from the point of his antler and slid off a triangular piece of stone. "This." He handed both pieces back to me. "Is for you. The Mother needs your help. We mean to aid you in whatever you need. They intertwine all of our lives in this. All the world's."

Indigo laughed nervously, clearly uncomfortable with the fate of the world riding on my incapable shoulders. I couldn't blame her.

"That sounds very ominous," she said, putting aside her clay plate.

Adal raised the two stripes of white that were his brows in his tawny face. "Or propitious."

Indigo's tan skin flushed to her ears, and she gave me a rueful smile. "Of course. It's just that... we've been through a lot in recent months."

Indigo relayed the death of our mother, father, my failed engagement and capture by the Stygians until the separation of me and the Grey Beast until she summarized with the telling of his death. Raud had taken a seat next to her mate as I threaded the triangular stone piece through my pendant necklace and clasped it around my neck.

Adal leaned back with his brows drawn down. "Impossible. Grar Dyr is a legend among our people. He would not dispatch easily. His part to play has yet to come. You must be mistaken." Adal said, sounding so self-assured I wondered if I'd mistaken our broken bond.

I wished there was a way I could've felt for him with my inguz tattoo over my hip with the Shadow Breaker tracker traced into the delicate Celtic designs, or better yet, the rune EH on the inside of my lower lip that held the bond between Slate and me.

Slate.

There. I thought his name.

"We were bonded. Twice. I felt the bond snap," I said, swallowing back another snivel.

Adal looked at me skeptically. "He was your mate?"

"Yes." I answered without hesitation.

"Do you carry his son? Grar Dyr is not someone you would mistake." Raud finally spoke in a high feminine voice with a matronly air.

"No, another man's." I said looking away.

I bit my lip so hard it drew blood and the coppery taste coated my tongue. I no longer had to worry about my bond with Slate. More emotions went into the lockbox. I drew it in my mind; silver, like his etched beads, with the jade canine as the centerpiece at the top. A pewter solar cross for the Dagr over the clasp and black leather lined like his old bedroom. There was nothing neat about the inside of the tumultuous box.

"Then he lives. He will find you," Raud said as if it was so simple. "You will have this birth and then carry his."

I clenched my teeth to stop the angry diatribe that itched on my tongue to be released at the casualness of her tone. As if we wandered the desert for fun, as if our expedition there had been for sightseeing or out of curiosity and not because I refused to give up that we would find him or his body to bring home. Adal placed a hand on her knee.

"She means there is no fork to this prophecy until the end. He must be there. If either of you are not, then I suppose we already lost all and we cannot accept that. You both must collect the other pieces and be at the temple to start the works before the others. I do not know who the others are, I do not know what the works are or where, and I do not know who else holds the pieces. There were nine pieces to activate the work. I wish we had more to offer you, but that is all that we know. Time is of the essence," Adal said in a grave tone and it felt as though someone danced on my grave.

The fine hairs all over my body stood even with the warmth of the savanna sun, and Indigo leaned closer in her chair. Her slender body seeking comfort from mine familiarly. I leaned back. We could have been doing it all our lives instead of just the last year.

"As far as we know, Grar Dyr is dead. Are you certain the prophecy wasn't about his uncle or cousin?" I asked and nearly started at how clear and detached my voice sounded.

"A daughter of Var and Sumar would carry his son. That is part of his prophecy, but it is about the father, of that we are certain."

Sumar was easy enough to figure out. It meant summer, but Var? He answered my question before I could ask.

"You are the daughters of spring and summer, are you not?" Adal asked.

"We are," Indigo answered with a sigh.

Raud shrugged as if to say, *well, there you go.*

"Is there any other part of the prophecy that might have some sort of contingent? Should one of us die?" I asked in that same detached tone, as if discussing curtain patterns.

"You come in the wake of andlat — death — you are the daughters of spring and summer. It could have been of you. Grar Dyr chose you," Adal said to me. "There is no other Grar Dyr that we know of, only the one. He made his choice. You carry his son."

In the wake of death. They knew this and still let us in. I never should have returned to Tidings; we always knew I'd watch Slate die. Now the Faunelle were trying to convince me he was alive. If he wasn't, we would lose it all. It was so impossible; a hysterical bubble of laughter rose to my lips. Thankfully, I bit it back.

I had an epiphany. "Indigo, tell me you're certain Sterling isn't barghest."

It stood to reason if Slate and Sterling were cousins even if Brass wasn't, that the violet eyed young man could also be a barghest since Slate had inherited the trait from his father. Lark and Peak were brothers. Sterling was the only other Haust male other than Slate and Peak.

Indigo's eyes widened, having gone down the same track of thinking I had run down. "I don't know, but I'm not carrying Sterling's son. I'm sure of that."

I slapped a hand to her stomach just in case, and when I sliced my head; she let out a shuddering breath. "It would have been Silver's, not Sterling's, if I was," she murmured.

"Grar Dyr has a cousin. The same line that he received his form from has another son. Is it possible..." I trailed off.

Slate had been a prophet; he knew the prophecy. He knew much more than he had told me. Unfortunately, that was nothing new.

Adal and Raud looked at one another, having a wordless discussion until Adal turned back to us. "It is very doubtful. After all, you both are here and you already carry a piece. You will have his son."

I rubbed the pendant Pearl had given after telling me they'd passed it down from generation to generation of daughters until I received it. She'd said it skipped my mother because her life had gone down a different path. I thought she meant because she moved to Chicago. Now I knew she meant because she hadn't had children with Lark Haust.

Pearl might know more about the prophecy than she said at the time. She was more observant and just as secretive as all the Guardians, regardless of her grandmotherly demeanor.

Two pieces of nine with no other knowledge. Like needles in a haystack. My insides churned. I knew where another was. Non're had offered it to me when he first gave me rousen that transformed me into the mindless sex addict I'd become for a short time. He said two nights would earn me the piece; I'd turned him down. The Stygians brought me back, and I'd been there for three. I knew where we could get the third piece.

"You know something. I can see it in your eyes," Raud said with an enlivened look.

I pursed my lips. "I know where I can get a third piece owed to me."

I felt through my bond with Brass that he was coming. I wasn't ready to deal with Brass, but I wouldn't let him wander the desert looking for me. Likely he had someone with him, Jett, Gypsum, or Quick. I wondered how long he'd been coming towards us since he seemed to make excellent time.

"We must leave soon. How long does it take to get from the Wemic village to this one?" I asked.

"A day depending on your stride," Adal answered.

"Our people are coming to retrieve us, so we must leave in the morning. We would like to claim guest rights with you if you could accommodate us? There will be at least four of us, including myself and my sister." I told him, hating to impose any more than we had already announced.

Raud offered a brilliant smile, and I realized she glowed with an inner light that made her beautiful. Not exotic like the Wemic women, but graceful and warm.

"We had expected no less. We have a hut for Guardians alone and will have it outfitted for your needs. You may sup with us tonight and we can have breakfast in the morning. How do you know more will arrive?" She clearly asked for our plates.

"I have a bond with another. He's coming. I doubt he's alone." I explained and thanked her for the meal.

Indigo rose to her feet and ran her palms over her soft beige dress. "We'd like to earn our stay and offer our services in any capacity.

Perhaps we could help with the crops or urge more fish into the stream?" she asked.

Adal and Raud shared a secretive pair of smiles before Raud led us to the door. "As is our custom, you may earn your stay with a chore we deem necessary. Follow me, please."

Brass and Quick came before nightfall. They must have set a grueling pace to get there so quickly and were stumped when they found Indigo and me chasing around the Faunelle children blindfolded after telling them tales of the Guardian history and about the other islands. The Guardian's favorite tale of love, betrayal, and power had made one little doe cry.

"They both died? Dagr and Natt could not apologize and fix it?" she asked after Indigo told her that Natt killed himself after Dagr sacrificed herself in order to stop his mad project that had since then sunk into the ocean.

Indigo gave her a small smile. "They joined in death. They are probably a wight somewhere beautiful in the world, guarding a copse over lakes, souls intertwined together in eternity. Natt died because he could not live without her." She told the little girl.

My wheels had turned then and had flitted away as one girl blindfolded me and we played a game of catch. I called out, and they responded as I stumbled over the unfamiliar terrain. It was eerily similar to how I'd been living my life as of late. I would need to take the blindfold off and stop shrinking away from adversity if I was going to be the person the world needed to save it. The Faunelle's story had come too close to the wight that was our mother and father's warning for me to dismiss. Whether I liked it or not, fate chose me to help or hinder the grand scheme. I hoped to help it.

I came up short when my nose smashed into the hard chest of a man and he gripped my biceps in steady fingers as I pulled off the blindfold. I slid it over my head with shaking fingers, realizing I'd been so focused on finding the children, I'd stop paying attention to Brass's bond.

His handsome face was vacant of emotion. I knew he was keeping it tightly reined in my presence. His amber eyes peered down until I felt laid bare before him.

The children called to me, and I turned my head, grateful to escape from those knowing eyes. "Another time, children. Our friends have come," I said and saw Indigo rush to Quick, who caught her in an embrace that swept her off her feet and pressed his fine lips to hers.

I didn't sigh. There was no need for it. I was happy she'd thawed for him, for now at least. I handed the blindfold to one child, and we walked to Adal and Raud's hut to introduce them. Brass walked in stride with me as Indigo filled them in on what had occurred since we left them.

They told us of the destruction of the village and how Ama had been killed fighting outside one adobe, with Shale defending the door from the Jorogumo that housed the Wemic's infants and children. The Wemic had honored her greatly, as much as they did Nekee, Keen's brother, who had died in the fighting against a Stygian. They had taken only one Stygian down. By me apparently, since he was so badly burned, no one could recognize him.

Brass kept silent as Quick asked all the questions, no doubt because Brass was gleaning his answers from our minds before we could utter a word.

"I am so very sorry," Quick said suddenly, and I drew up short.

"He's not dead." I told them in the same self-assured tone Raud had used that made me want to believe.

I could *feel* the others worry, as if I'd lost my mind. "The Faunelle believe Slate is alive and has convinced Scarlett as well," Indigo confided, and I tried not to let their doubt irritate me.

"Scarlett, we felt the bond break with Ama and then with Slate. You felt it too," Quick said gently, and I picked up walking again.

"They could have skinned him. They had a torque collar around his neck," I said matter of fact.

Another silence. "Even with a collar, no man, even three men, was stronger than Slate," Quick said in that same careful tone.

We reached the steps to Adal's hut, and I led them inside. "They used the torque to render him helpless, and you saw that braid he was wearing. I bet they yanked it taut and sliced the tracker at the base of his skull in one swipe. It would've skinned the tattoo right off."

"Why would they do that when they could simply kill him and put an end to the prophecy?" Indigo asked, trying to push me to face the truth as she saw it.

"I don't know, but then people do a lot of things that make little sense," I said and Brass grabbed my arm.

"That feels like a personal remark. I think we should speak in private," Brass said, and I pulled my arm away. Not roughly, but insistently, letting him know I had no desire to be alone with him.

"I don't think there's anything to discuss. This is the way it is. I value your friendship beyond measure, and that's how I plan to keep it. You can accept that or not. I hope you do," I said, nocking my chin higher.

Quick gave a low whistle and moved past us with Indigo in tow into the hut. I heard Raud greet them as I faced off with Brass.

"I know you are grieving —"

"There is nothing to grieve. Ama, yes. I grieve for Ama and for the Wemic who lost their lives. That's all. I don't accept that Slate is anything but captured as they'd planned to do. It's a trick and I mean to find them with whomever's help I can get," I said.

Brass took a step forward, and I stiffened at his touch. He saw my reaction and stopped moving.

"That is it then? You cringe when I try to touch you? For what, Scarlett? So you can cower behind fairytales because you are punishing yourself for the past? Should we not mourn his loss together? No one understands it better than I do. You know that."

I grit my teeth. He was right, but I couldn't make myself go to him. If there was even the remotest chance Slate was alive, I wanted him back.

"Brass, I love you. I can't accept that he's left me. I made the worst mistake of my life by leaving him and I would do anything to get him back."

I searched his eyes for the hatred that must lurk there after my blunt words but didn't find it. "The night of your birthday, Slate broached me with an offer. He said it was his destiny to be a victim of the prophecy.

He had accepted it and believed he could sire no children, take no wife because of it. Then he met you. He broke all of his rules, tried to win you."

"What offer?" I asked, feeling Indigo's suspiciousness from the hut.

Brass rubbed his lips together. "He saw us together that night and knew there was affection between us. He asked if you would accept him as your husband and if you should carry his child, if I would care for you."

My face was expressionless as I stared him down. "As my..."

"I believe Americans call it a domestic partnership," Brass said with an uneasy smile.

I sucked in a deep breath. "Let me get this straight. Slate asked you to rear his children and care for his wife as he would? Brass that's..."

Horrible, depressing, honorable, selfless — a million things came to mind.

"I was content to be your friend until —"

"Until it was your *turn* because he was dead?" I offered, unable to hide the agitation. "I jumped the gun and left him early, slept with you before you two planned? No wonder you both were so strange." I shook my head.

Their actions had been missing tremendous gaps, but I'd found the pieces. There had been a pact between them for my love.

"He could not allow himself to leave you —"

"Broken? Pregnant? Widowed?" I interrupted him again.

"Mourning alone," Brass said, leveling his eyes.

"I'm more focused than ever. I need a friend, not a lover," I said, steeling myself.

Brass and I faced off in silence.

... How could I ever make love to you again without thinking about him, knowing it's what he planned all along? That he sacrificed himself because we had everything he ever wanted...

Brass dropped his head. "It is hard to compete with him when he's up on your pedestal. We struck a new bargain," he almost whispered, and I waited. "You asked if you could have both and we arranged it so you could. I always intended to raise Slate's children. After you have mine, if he helped convince you to marry me, I would look the other way so you could have his children, too. Saying it out loud to you sounds much worse than when we plotted it," he said with an uncomfortable smile when he saw how appalled I was. "I told you I would be there for you, no matter what. I meant it. Scarlett... we are going to have children together," he breathed.

He lifted his big arms to embrace me, but I withdrew. I couldn't let him touch me. He nodded in understanding and I turned around before I had to see the hurt in his eyes. If Brass held me, the seed of hope I'd cultivated might wither and die. It might tempt me to give up hope and let him carry me off and forget about my troubles. I had to believe Slate was alive.

We entered the hut, and I introduced Brass to Adel and Raud. "Greetings. How does the day find you?" Adal asked Brass.

"Mourning the loss of loved ones," Brass said and asked the same question back.

"Well, thank you. We are sorry for your loss," Raud told him.

We supped with the chieftain and his wife as Adal retold the story he'd told us earlier with our permission, and once Raud passed around mugs of honeyed mead and my water; we took our mugs to the canoe. Adal stirred us down the stream to an outlaying hut and we bid him goodnight.

Quick held Indigo's hand as she stepped out of the canoe. I took his hand after her, surprising him, but I didn't want to risk Brass's touch. The hut was a singular round room with two stuffed mattresses, a small table and two chairs at the opposite end, and a woven rug at the center.

The Faunelle had supplied us with simple shifts to sleep in as well as fresh pants for Quick and Brass. Quick and Indigo started undressing at once and got into the bed barely big enough for them both to fit as I fumbled around in my mind for a suitable excuse.

Brass snapped out his roll without having needed to be asked and removed his shirt before laying down. I slipped out of the fringed dress and into the plain shift before crawling under the thin blanket. It wasn't as hot as it was nearer Thrimilci's town heart, but it was still warm. I knew part of me was being ridiculous, but I needed to clarify things between Brass and me instead of falling into old habits.

Still...

... Come to bed. We slept together in a bed before we were ever together. I'm sure we can now. Please, before Quick sets me on fire with his glare...

Brass rolled onto his back and gave me a blank expression. I beckoned, and he slowly got up from the roll and removed his worn pants before climbing in beside me. I'd gone stiff at the feel of his warm body and my heart thudded loudly in my ears. It wasn't a betrayal of Slate's memory, was it?

No, he was still alive.

Brass's annoying habit of reading my mind was a terrible nuisance as he wrapped his arm around me and held me close as he murmured, "If he's out there, we'll find him. I will be your friend, confidant, or lover. All three if you wish. You do not have to push me away, Scarlett. I will not try to force my affection on you. Your happiness is mine." He whispered into my hair and my fingers gripped around his wrist, holding him tighter to me.

"I'm falling with no end in sight. I love our children already — *you*. He wanted to die because I stole what little hope he had left."

Knowing Brass made me a better person. When I was with him, I felt unworthy of his attention. He was bright and warm and wonderful while I was chaotic and frivolous at best.

His skin smelled of cinnamon and spring. I'd inhaled him deeply enough times to know that when the sun baked his skin, the cinnamon scent became musky and intoxicating as it was now.

Did it make me weak that Brass's arms offered me comfort? That knowing he'd stand by me under any circumstances made me feel as though I stood a chance at finding Slate?

Possibly, but I'd take any strength I could muster in any form I could find it.

CHAPTER 44
JETT

Scarlett and Indigo knelt beside Shale in bed. They'd come back early that afternoon with Brass and Quick. The girls had hugged them all fiercely and gone to where they'd spread Ama's ashes and held one another as they stood in silent contemplation. Then, they'd gone to Shale's side and been there since.

"She's in shock. Isn't that one stage of grief?" Jett asked as he stood beside Hawk.

Quick and Brass shared a look. "Scarlett truly believes Slate is alive. She will not listen to anything else," Brass said, watching the three women through the doorway.

"And whatever Scarlett asks of her, Indigo will do in this," Quick added with a too fond smile aimed at Indi.

The Wemic's grieving was over and the rebuilding nearly finished. They'd leave in the morning and give Sparrow, Pearl, and the rest the bad news.

Jett ran a hand over his face. "She's changed. Harder somehow. Resolute, determined, something. You're sure —"

"The bond broke. We have never felt the bond break unless the person died. The Faunelle gave her hope where there is likely none to be had," Brass said in a sour mood.

One look at Brass and Scarlet together and Jett knew things had changed drastically between them. She wasn't the girl he'd brought back from Chicago. It was Slate's wife. Devoted lover. You were with her or against her. Brass had agreed to be with her only so that when she realized Slate would never return, she had someone to lean on. It was a hard pill for Brass to swallow after they'd been living together for the last month, and Jett suspected sleeping together right until the wedding.

For the Mother's sake, she was pregnant with his children!

Jett knew Scarlett was beating herself up about that more than anything. She thought she drove Slate to sacrificing himself because she'd made this perfect life with Brass. Unfortunately for Brass, Scarlett's self-loathing trickled into him.

Hawk, Gypsum, Steel, and Tawny had come in from their daily work of repairing the village, cooking, caring for their animals, and helping the few crops the black painted Wemic kept so the villagers could grieve without having to worry about the mundane routine. They huddled around Scarlett and Indigo when they brought Shale out.

Brass's brow drew down when Shale's petite form lurked behind Scarlett. A smirk and the obsidian sheet of hair that fell past her shoulders usually softened her handsome, angular face. She wasn't smiling, and her hair was lackluster. She didn't look bedraggled, just not herself. Harder, colder, and determined with that same set to her jaw as Scarlett had.

Tawny clutched at Scarlett, which she stoically endured as she comforted Tawny. "The babies are fine. I'm fine. As soon as Slate returns, everything will be better."

Tawny blinked at her as if she'd cracked, then spun to look at Brass. "Is she...?"

"Sane?" Jett offered with no small amount of sarcasm.

"I'm right here. You can ask me. Things will never be back to normal, but when Slate returns, it will be as close to normal as it can be," Scarlett said, holding her chin high.

"Frigga's sweet grass," Tawny whispered, "You've lost it."

Scarlett's too full lips quirked at the corners. "I've never seen things more clearly; Slate is my husband and Brass is the father of my children. What I've done to them is inexcusable. I can only hope one day they'll forgive me."

Indigo mirrored Scarlett's resolve, but a shadow of doubt clouded her expression, which let Jett know that even though she was standing by Scarlett, she didn't believe Slate was alive. Jett supposed for the sake of the twins, it wouldn't hurt to humor her for some time. Eventually, she would have to face the truth.

When they made camp, Brass silently slid his roll next to Scarlett's and Jett caught him, pulling her into his arms. Jett held his breath as he waited for Scarlett's rebuff, but it never came. Instead, she wrapped her fingers around his forearms where they crossed her waist, seeking solace in his presence.

Gypsum had taken the position to Shale's right during the day and when they made camp had laid down beside her, not quite touching her. There was more than enough grief to go around. Hawk was toting Amber's frozen body around all day and even though he'd set her away from camp, it was like a siren going off of the death and destruction they'd left.

Shale had shadowed Scarlett all day.

"Captain would want her guarded," Shale had said simply, and pulled her scarf lower to shield her skin from the high sun.

Quick had forgiven Indi in a blink for having burst from their bed and, with enough hints from Quick, they weren't exactly sleeping, and gone to find Scar on the night the Wemic were attacked. That wasn't true. The attack was the collateral damage of Slate's capture. Over a hundred Wemic dead for one man.

Who did they think he was, or better yet, what did they think he could do for them?

Tomorrow afternoon they'd arrive at the Sumar palace. That was when things would get harder for Scarlett. Pearl would likely want a funeral for Slate. What would Scarlett do then?

FORTY-FIVE

"He's captured. Not dead."

I kept my expression cool as we sat in Pearl's sitting room in the highest turret of the palace. Our bedrooms were big, but Pearl's room was sprawling. Her massive white bed sat under a recessed arch that was backlit. Ivory silk fabric draped on either side of the massive bed. I sat on an oversized cream couch that was sinfully soft across from Pearl, whose tears streaked gracefully over her high cheekbones.

Brass and Shale stood behind my couch, Indigo and Quick shared the other while Jett paced. Steel stood with blotches of red on his tan cheeks, with Tawny's arms wrapped around his waist. Gypsum had gone to the Dagr palace to bring Sparrow and Hawk to the Sumar palace.

Pearl's lips tightened as she appraised me. "Darling," she said in a voice so low even Slate would've strained to hear her.

I'd told her about our marriage and how I had no intention of hiding anymore. Her expression when we returned had gone from exalted glee, to concern, to despair. Now her emerald cat eyes looked empathetic. They'd all thought I'd lost my mind.

"I am of sound mind. I swear it on the lives of mine and Brass's children," I said, nocking up my chin. "Was there any issue enrolling me back into Valla University?" I asked in a casual tone.

Jett stopped his pacing. "You can't be serious. I saw Nirrin try to capture you and Indigo both. You won't be going anywhere; you can't be watched nonstop."

My brother's tan face had blotches on his tan cheeks as well, but Jett's were in anger and frustration. His turquoise almond eyes were hard on his chiseled face as he glared at me.

"We will continue to guard her," Shale answered, glaring right back at Jett as if he suggested she wouldn't be good enough.

Quick cleared his throat. "I intend to stick with Indigo. I will be with Scarlett while she is in classes. Shale can take up the night's watch and bring a cot up to the girls' room."

Jett shot daggers at Quick, who kept his eyes focused on Pearl as she leaned on the ivory chaise with a trembling teacup in her long-nailed hand. Brass placed a hand on my shoulder and I patted it with my right hand, appreciating his support.

"We re-enrolled you in classes. Since they did not expel you, there was no reason to bar you." Pearl said, pushing back her coppery waves as she sipped her tea to steady her emotions.

Indigo dropped her eyes to the hands she'd clasped in her lap.

"I am afraid his funereal is not up to me, but to Sparrow," Pearl said and, as if hearing her name, the exquisitely carved doors swung open.

Sparrow charged through with Amethyst and Cherry on her heels. "He's dead?" Sparrow said, holding a hand over her mouth.

Apprehension grew thick in the airy room as I rose to my feet. "Captured. Not dead," I said in a cool tone.

"The bond we held with him severed after they attacked him," Brass said, and described the scene which led to Slate's disappearance.

Sparrow crumpled. I'd never known another woman to suffer more grief than Sparrow. I didn't know how she did it, having lost so many people in her life. Tawny went to her side and held her. I left the room when they made funeral arrangements against my wishes.

. . .

Valla University was just as I left it. No one wanted me to go to classes the next day, but I had plans to set into motion and evil to undertake. Tawny, Cherry, and Jett hadn't come to classes. They believed Slate was dead. They were planning his funeral and I couldn't be anywhere near something so needlessly painful. In my heart, I had to believe Slate was alive. My mind would have it no other way.

I swept through the Valla University for Guardian Mastery vine carved portal doors and into the sprawling yellow stoned castle. Tapestries hung at either end of the long room, lit by pewter sconces between the doors. When I got to the room I shared with Tawny, Indigo, and Cherry, I found my four-post bed made with an apple green comforter much more modest than the blue and gold satins of the palace. The room had the same yellowed stone look as the rest of the enormous castle, tapestries hung on the walls, sconces or mirrors didn't occupy. There weren't any windows on the walls.

Braided pillars divided the rooms, three alcoves, another bed to the left, and one to the right. They had already settled my things into my trunk and I left the fourth floor second year girls' wing to head to our classes.

Halls of the second floor were filled with students. Girls in their floor length black caftan dresses trimmed in gold and wide red and yellow belts cinched at their waists. The young men in their black lightweight jerkins and black pants tucked into black boots. I wore a yellow belt being a second year.

My first class was Guardian History, taught by none other than Dahlia Natt, Ash's mother. They designed the room with stone stadium seating, cushions covering the seated portion. Wood desktops collapsed into slots in the front of each seat that pulled up into an 'L' shape. I took my usual cushioned seat next to Quick, and I flashed him a relieved smile. Things would be hard enough without my family here. Not having Quick would have made my day impossible, even with my resolve.

The pewter sconces lit the desk that Dahlia sat at with her projector and laptop sitting completely foreign in the Old-World style of the castle. Ash, Sage, and Hunter entered the room, and I kept my eyes straight ahead. It was going to be a long day.

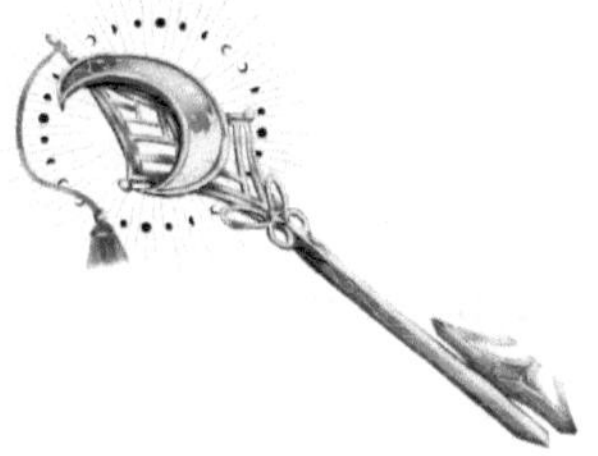

The days passed with agonizing slowness. My family hadn't returned to classes and wouldn't until Slate's mock funeral had taken place. Fury rose in me whenever I caught word of it, which they were careful to keep from my ears. His sham of a funeral was tomorrow.

I was eating lunch alone with Quick when he told me. I ignored the snickers and whispers against me as I walked through the halls, which were harder to ignore in a stationary position like the dining hall. Quick did his best to distract me and I did my best to pretend I didn't hear any of it? Soon I would make my moves and we'd see who had the last laugh then.

At night, I'd invited Shale into my bed. A cot was a ridiculous prospect since there was more than enough room for us both. If anyone understood my need to want to be close to others, yet not touched, it was Shale. I invited her on the first night and she'd not so much as grunted to accept. She'd slid in next to me and we fell asleep with the comfort of knowing we weren't alone, if only in the physical realm.

That I muttered to my unborn children about their stepfather didn't seem to bother her either. Neither did my tears when I tried desperately to reach out to Slate through our bond.

The funeral was open to all the greater families, which, if Slate was dead, he would have hated. He would have wanted something small and private, just the family. Maybe his ashes would mingle in falls behind the Sumar palace or into the lake by the Wemic. None of the pomp and frivolity planned.

Step one would begin that day.

CHAPTER 46

JETT

An empty pyre burned on the stairway they'd constructed in the center of the cloister at the Dagr palace. Lombard bands lined the grey stone monolithic columns that wrapped around the covered walkway that held hundreds of Guardians that paid their respects to Slate and the Dagr family.

Jett sat between his wives on the manicured lawn with the rest of the family. Despite her veil, Sparrow's tearful state was evident from the shake of her narrow shoulders. Hawk sat with a grim expression on her other side. His silver hair combed back in a pompadour; grey had streaked his thin, manicured beard. No doubt because of the added stress of the deaths in the family and Scarlett's penchant for getting caught up in trouble.

Speaking of Scarlett, she wasn't there. Neither was Indigo nor Shale. A group of thirty Shadow Breakers sat near the back of the cloister under the hot Thrimilci sun. Jett had spoken to Lera for the first time in years. Her olive face was tight, but she looked as sultry as ever. Jett didn't think the woman aged. Chafer and he had exchanged glares before they'd gone to sit with Brass and Quick.

Jett had asked Brass and Quick to sit up towards the front with the family, but they'd declined to sit nearer the Regn family and the Shadow Breakers. All the greater and lesser families were there except for Orion Vetr, which was strange. Not even Tawny seemed to know why he would decline to come.

To Jett's irritation, they granted the Hausts a position of honor in the second row of mourners. Peak Haust and Willow Natt sat speaking in hushed tones to one another while their children and spouses sat next to them. That meant that Ash was there. Slate would roll over in his grave to have seen Ash's cocky grin watching his body burn. Thankfully, there was only a useless pile of wood there.

Sorrow hung heavy in the cloister, and Pearl had finally lost her collected demeanor. His grandmother had raised him. Seeing her cry was a hot poker in his heart. Steel comforted his mother, since Tawny didn't need his solace. Events caught her between the facts and Scarlett's unwavering belief that Slate was alive. A whisper campaign had already begun at Valla U, that had gotten back to Jett. According to them, Scarlett was not in Chicago by choice as they sent there her because of her unsound mind.

A strong wind blew into the cloister from behind the seated Guardians, and Jett and the others blinked into the gust of wind. Jett's breath caught in his chest. Scarlett and Indigo dressed in white flowing gowns, heads held high, long hair streaming down to their waists. They looked like queens in their court. Both bore regal expressions of coolness. They weren't alone.

Orion Vetr walked a step behind them with four Guardians wearing the white auseklis sigil on red cloaks the color roses. Two other men flanked old man Vetr wearing the black cloaks of Guardians with the silver interlocking triangles that represented Valla. The dagaz rune marked their chests, the little double 'X' signified that they were interrogators like Quick. They could tell if you spoke truth or lies.

Indigo and Scarlett didn't break stride as they ascended the stairs with hundreds of eyes on them. Those people gasped as Indigo and Scarlett stepped directly into the flames that burned the pyre. Only then did Jett realize Scarlett was wearing her wedding dress from her ceremony. Scarlett reached the pyre first and instead of her dress catching in the indiscriminate flames of the inferno. They absorbed it into her. Her skin was lit from within in a red heat, Indigo a step behind her, doused the flames, making steam rise around them.

Jett stretched his neck to see what they were doing next. Vetr waited at the bottom of the steps with the Guardians. His hooded blue eyes watched the steam settle facing the pyre. People stirred out of their stupefied trances. Did Indigo and Scarlett just interrupt a funeral and ruin a pyre? Jett knew he wasn't the only one blinking bewildered at the stairway.

A clap that made Jett's ears pop blew the steam away in a punch from the platform to reveal Scarlett and Indigo, who had formed pillars of water and fire braided around one another. Jett's mouth fell open. He hadn't even known they could do that. Gasps resounded around the cloister. They had just let the world know they were elementals in the most dramatic way possible.

Indigo and Scarlett still had shape, but their calling extended past them. Their dresses existed inside the pillars they'd become. They ended their *calling* so you could see human forms. Indigo's form was like rushing water in a woman's form, her hair swayed around her face as if she was in fact under water. Piercing blue eyes like ice swept the crowd.

Scarlett was terrifying. Her fiery hair writhed around her molten face. Flames licked Indigo and steamed away in a hiss as she gazed out with hot coals for eyes and she lowered her hands to her sides, blasting the crowd with her oppressive heat.

"I am the true wife of Slate Dagr — his mate."

Scarlett's voice came out disembodied and sent chills down Jett's spine. The interrogators faced the crowd so they would all know if she spoke a lie.

"Do any contest my marriage and right by blood vow?" Scarlett challenged.

More gasps. Guardians didn't swear blood vows when they married. They said the oath's words but didn't exchange blood. What Scarlett and Slate had done would prevent either of them from being remarried should one of them die.

Scarlett's fire melted away into her skin so she glowed like a smithy's blade but flames no longer licked up her body and her hair settled against her back. "My mother was Wren Tio. My father, Alder Var. Both murdered. We are vengeance. The Mother's elementals. The first to be born in hundreds of years and we will find the men responsible for their deaths and Slate's capture."

She clasped Indigo's hand so steam brewed between them and Indigo and Scarlett winked out completely into two young women at the ripe age of twenty. They descended the stairs together, their imperious postures never wavering as they strode from the cloister.

Old man Vetr hung back and approached the patriarchs and matriarchs of the greater families. Straumr, Tio, Sumar, Var, Natt, Dagr, Geol, and Haust he handed scrolls that bore a sigil Jett had never seen before, but it was easy to guess Scarlett had created it. A turquoise seal of a canine's head before a blazing sun.

Jett clambered to his feet to chase after his sisters, only to find the way barred by more of Vetr's house Guardians in red. A smile played on old man Vetr's seamed face and Jett started. He was enjoying their display. Jett didn't think he'd ever seen the old man smile. It was especially bright when he handed the scroll to Cassiopeia, his estranged wife. Orion walked from the cloister the way the girls did and the Guardians moved aside for him and retreated once he was out of sight, leaving the stunned funeral guests to star at a half-burned pyre that smoke rose lazily into the air from.

"Let me see."

Jett couldn't help himself. His sisters had kept this a secret from everyone. As he looked around, it shocked him to see looks of astonishment on Brass and Quick's faces and Tawny and Pearl's. None of them had known. The attack had been nine days ago. Scarlett and Indigo had only had three days to plan. Jett's eyes met Lera's, where she held a scroll of her own and her red lips quirked. She'd known something was up. Damn the devious woman.

Jett snatched the letter from Pearl and apologized.

Greater Families,
An opportunity has arisen for your consideration.
Please join us at Vetr Castle in Elivagar

at week's end for dinner.
Sincerely,
The Mother's Wildfire

One guess who that was.

CHAPTER 47

INDIGO

Scarlett's palm was sweating as they hurried to the portal room of the Dagr palace. Vetr would be behind them shortly and they'd join him in Elivagar until the meeting on Friday. The plan had gone off without a hitch, despite Scarlett's nerves and the last-minute rush to the bathroom so she could void her empty stomach. Those twins seemed content to torment their mother with random bouts of nausea whenever it pleased them.

I squeezed her trembling hand as we waited in the portal room for Orion. The stone walls were lit by recessed lighting, making it look like a cathedral as it lit the sculptures of the Dagr matriarchs along the walls like saintly beauties. Would Slate get his own sculpture? He was the first patriarch ever for the Dagr line. Natt had been the ones being forced into a matriarchal line after Storm and Wind had died ages ago, so the two families could never marry.

"Hard part is over. It's out of your hands now. Do you feel better?" I asked, raising my brows at Scarlett.

Her face had paled as she trembled. "Sort of. I'm tired of lies and being pushed around. We are powerful, more powerful than most of the people in that room, and they treat us like rodents." She ran her free hand over her forehead. "Not that I want to bully anyone, but whoever killed our parents has to know we're coming for them. What I did with the Stygians before wasn't enough. Not if they had enough people to capture Slate and orchestrate that attack."

Shale had waited in the portal room, not wanting to see the other Shadow Breakers as she stepped up now. She'd been sticking to Scarlett's side since Ama's death. Scarlett gave her a reason to push through. Protect Slate's wife and her children. Help find Ama's murderers. It helped that Gypsum had been keeping Shale company during the day when she wasn't guarding Scarlett.

I was stuck at the Sumar palace when I wasn't in Elivagar arranging today's pronouncement and had seen Gypsum lacing his fingers through hers and pulling her into his bedroom when he should have been at the local school. I didn't think they were sleeping together. As far as I knew, Shale didn't swing that way. Stranger things had happened, though.

Orion strode through the doors with his Guardians in tow and the two interrogators flanking him. He smiled at us — his all but adopted as his granddaughters, and I saw Tawny on his heels with an unexpected guest. My own palms started sweating.

"Come along, ladies. The outcries will be swift. We must get you to Elivagar as soon as possible." He raised his white brows at Sterling, whose violet eyes fixed on me, making my heart leap into my throat. "Haust. You may come for now, but you may not stay." He told him boldly, and Sterling nodded.

We walked through the portal door.

The Vetr castle was surreal in white and black; I hadn't seen a single hint of color. Pristine white ceilings carefully carved in delicate lace-like patterns swept through every room, white pillars, wide-open windows, and marble floors were in every room. The only pop of color was the scarlet red of the Vetr sigil. It felt *too* clean and empty. There was an army of white and black clad staff in the castle that our mother had died outside of that did nothing to aid its warmth. The last time I spent an extended time here was for Tawny and Steel's wedding when Wren had plummeted to her death from an upstairs window.

I'd only visited briefly, for an hour or two, with Orion to relay messages from Scarlett about today. Sterling had fallen in beside me, and Scarlett released my hand as Tawny interrogated her. Sterling grabbed my arm around the elbow and Scarlett paused.

"Go on ahead." I told her, and her eyes narrowed at Sterling before she walked after Orion with Tawny.

I folded my arms under my breasts and lifted my eyes to Sterling. My pulse raced whenever I set eyes on him. Now was no different. His violet eyes glowed below his thick brows. With my heels on, I was eye level to his six feet.

"Indi, what in the name of the Mother was that?" he accused.

"What did it look like, Sterling? I'm an elemental, me and my twin. You don't know everything about me," I said with a sniff.

He ran his hand over his tousled espresso locks. They were always stylishly coifed to my irritation. Longer than Silver's but styled with purpose as his were.

"Does *he* know you are?" Sterling asked, trying not to sound hurt and failed.

"I spend a great deal more time with him than I do you. It hasn't been that long since I discovered this new... talent."

I was using Scarlett's empath abilities. I could *feel* his love for me and more. His pain and longing. If she *felt* that around Slate, I didn't know how she could have withstood it. Sterling's eyes dropped, and I suppressed a sigh as I took a step nearer.

"My father will not go to that meeting, but I can relay the message of being the heir," he murmured.

His tan cheekbones were wide and high, like his mother's. He didn't resemble his father in the slightest. Sterling even had her violet eyes and pink sensual lips. I couldn't stop myself from staring at those lips.

"He won't be included in that case. This concerns all the islands. If Mabon wants to be a part of progress, then he will come. If not, then he can fall behind and become obsolete with the rest of the islands who decide not to go along with our plan." I gave a shrug of my shoulders and he raised his eyes to mine.

"What do you two have planned, Indi? Why have you not told me of this?" He asked, knitting his dark brows.

"You've been with your fiancée. It's hard to speak to you at all since Sage and Ash told all the world about our affair." My stomach roiled with anxiety.

"Is there somewhere we can speak in private?" Sterling asked, looking over his shoulder at one of the red clad Guardians who guarded the portal.

I licked my lips and nodded. He followed me over the white marble floors with black skein, and up the grand staircase that led higher into the castle until we reached the room I'd be staying in until Friday so no one could cajole me into telling them of our plans. It might be too late for me if Sterling pressed hard enough.

My bedroom was simply decorated by greater family standards. The walls were white with black damask patterning the walls. The black bed had a red damask comforter with a trunk at the foot and a vanity against the opposite wall. A crown above the bed held black and white fabric that cascaded down to either side of the bed with a white chandelier that hung from the center of the room. There was no sitting room.

Sterling crossed to the bed after he closed the door behind him and made himself at home. He always did. I gripped my chiffon dress in my fingers as I moved to sit next to him. Sterling dressed impeccably well. He wore an indigo sleeveless jerkin in the Ostara style over snug grey pants that were tucked into black leather boots. His violet eyes followed me from beneath his lashes.

"I am sorry about Slate. Does Scarlett truly believe he lives?" he asked, leaning towards me.

"We believe it."

Sterling was nervous. We'd been in bedrooms so many times before I'd lost track in the years since we'd started our affair. At one point, it was just Sterling and me. Then Diamond became old enough to be interesting to Sterling physically. It had been a few years since their first time and since the reality of the life I'd been living became clear. Still, I'd stuck by him with his sweet promises and whispered, 'I love yous'. I knew he did. I loved him, too.

Had Silver seen Sterling come after me? By the Mother, I prayed not. I hadn't made Silver any promises, but they were unspoken. Though, Silver needed to hear me say it. He would have made me say it. I never asked if he'd been seeing someone else. I had no right to him. It didn't explain why I felt guilty.

Sterling's fingers touched mine on the coverlet, and a twinge shot through me that heated my skin. "Should I be worried about this meeting?"

"Not at all. It's an excellent opportunity. You know I would tell you if it was something bad, Sterling," I told him, leveling my eyes to his.

He brought his hand up to my cheek and I resisted kissing his wrist. "Even now."

"Always," I breathed.

We were no longer talking about meetings. Sterling leaned in to brush his lips against mine. I should have known what would happen by bringing him up here. There wasn't a bedroom we'd both been in that hadn't led to it.

I parted my lips to his, and he pulled me closer.

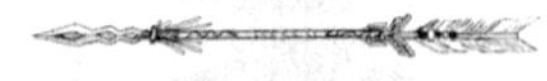

Sterling's body was as familiar to me as my own. We were good together. If the Norns had been kind, I would have known Alder was my true father years ago and as a Tio. We could have been bound by a betrothal. He held me tightly, our hot bare skin moving together. My breasts smashed against his chest as he kissed me. Sterling's mouth kept contact with mine as he made love to me.

It was the first time I felt guilty for having been with Sterling. Usually, I felt guilty about Silver, but something had changed. I couldn't quite put words to. I was still doing it, still enjoying the feel of Sterling sliding inside me. He knew my body so well. He'd been my first and I his. All of our firsts had been with one another.

Sterling had been upset when I bedded Rikke, but nothing like he'd been when he'd seen Silver and me together. Silver was incredibly good looking; I'd noticed him long before I bedded him. He also had a very nefarious reputation that I had counted on to keep him at a distance. Tio women had to be careful.

I heard the *snick* of the door opening and I gasped, pulling my mouth away from Sterling's. Hurt and outrage assailed me. I pushed Sterling off me, and that only made matters worse since I was completely nude.

I *called* the white robe that hung from the changing screen by the vanity and wrapped my arms through it as I faced Silver and his smooth expression.

"Silver," I rasped, pulling my lips between my teeth.

The look he gave me as I approached made me feel as if I had betrayed him. He'd been in my bed every night since we came back from the village.

"I am waiting, Dove," Silver said in a soft tone.

His pet name for me burned in my ears. Was I just cooing with Sterling? I licked my lips and tried to smooth my face, but my brows knit back together as if drawn by magnets. Sterling moved on the bed behind me, either dressing or pulling the blankets up around him. I couldn't be sure.

I swallowed hard. "Did you need something?" I asked in a squeak, hoping there wasn't a mirror in my line of sight so I wouldn't have to face myself afterwards.

Silver's deep chocolate eyes flitted between mine and my heart felt as if he squeezed it in his calloused hand. "No. I need nothing," he said in a disappointed tone.

I balled my fists to my sides as he shut the door and I turned back to the bed where Sterling was sitting up against the headboard. He hadn't pulled the surrounding blankets at all. He was as naked as the day as he was born and with his legs crossed out in front of him with a cool expression on his face.

"Better that is over before he hurts you. He is a known philanderer, Indi. Honestly, what could you hope to accomplish seeing a man like that? If you are going to be with another man, at least choose one who can give you a future. Hunter is a suitable match for a Tio," Sterling said.

I shut my eyes. He followed the Guardian rules. He'd marry and keep me if he could. Sterling would care that I slept with his friend but be glad I had made a good match.

"I'm not feeling amorous, Sterling. Silver is a good match for me. You choose to ignore the fact that he is one step below a greater family, your first cousin. His relatives have already bred into greater families. In truth, he would be perfect for me, and that's what you don't like." I crossed to the bed and sat down beside him, running my fingertips along my forehead where I felt a pressure build at the start of a headache.

Sterling guffawed. "He would not be faithful."

"As I would be?" I countered dryly, and Sterling leveled his eyes at me, cupping my face.

"No one will come between us. I love you, Indigo. You know that."

I felt myself being sucked back into his vortex of sweet words and familiarity. "Yes. I know. I love you too, Sterling."

FORTY-EIGHT

I eyed Quick warily as he sat down at the table in the Vetr castle. He claimed he would go get Indigo and came back red faced and sullen. Brass seemed to know what was on his mind and gave me a slow shake of his head to warn me not to ask.

Freya's burly boar! Indigo had better not have taken that Haust to her bed! Not that I was the one to judge, but she and Quick were doing so well.

The walls were white with lattice work around the plaster sculpted walls and ceiling. Black glass plates sat on a white marble table threaded with silver with white upholstered chairs. It made me afraid to touch anything or I might break it or stain it.

Wide windows displayed the snowcapped mountains surrounded the castle like a fairy tale hideaway. Any minute now, the snow queen would descend from a stairway made from pure ice. Puffs of smoke stretched to the sky from the faraway village. It looked like the north pole, or what I imagined the North Pole looked like with Santa's elves milling about making toys.

We ate the potato casserole with Salisbury steaks; it was hearty, and I was stuffed. I had wanted them fed before I started, so they would be relaxed and ready to hear my plan. Tawny, Cordillera, and Chafer sat opposite me, Brass, and Quick. Indigo breezed into the dining room with a cool expression and took a seat next to Quick, making him stare openly at her.

Well, that answered that.

Orion smiled and inclined his head towards her as a staffer brought her meal before her. The Vetrs were much more formal than the Sumars. I brought out the papers I had left with Indigo and passed them around the table. Shale detached from the shadows and took the seat next to Chafer. Cordillera and Chafer watched her like a rabid cougar, she hadn't been back to headquarters since Ama's death and had only spoken to me, Indigo, and Gypsum.

"How long have you been concocting this?" Quick asked leaning forward to look at my drawing again.

His black swirling tattoos peeked from under his collar and I caught Indigo's eyes running along them.

"Not long," I said plainly. I had no intention of elaborating.

"As long as it makes money, it may be of interest," Chafer said, leaning back in his chair.

I hated the patrons; it was personal and the idea of my friends getting married one day and their wives having to deal with their husbands being groped in a velvet room made me want to puke. Vegas. Where they said what happened there, stayed there.

"Well, that's it. Jett is going to inherit Ostara, Tawny is heir to Elivagar, and Pearl runs through Thrimilci. That leaves Mabon and Valla. If Sterling is on board, he's the heir to Mabon, and Indigo has a bit of sway over him. We might need to get the Straumrs included to do it in Valla, but luckily my brother is married to a Straumr and the only other Straumr female regards me as a sister. The Straumr men... well, Crag is my uncle's lover, and Fox and I got along. I don't think they will be a problem."

"Ash. He will never let this succeed," Brass said, gazing over my sketching of the arena for Valla.

I'd spent long nights with Shale before bed using the artistic skills I'd inherited from my mother to come up with Crash Courses for each of the islands.

"Good thing he's not up to be Prime yet," I asked nervously, looking at the people before me. "Forget for a moment how much it will cost to get it started. Do you think it's something Guardians would be into? You guys don't have any organized sports, so I think it would work and generate enough coin flow to make the patrons obsolete. Not to mention giving Lera's Breakers a cover and say a Guardian doesn't want to do menial tasks, has no family ties, and doesn't want to be a mercenary, this would be perfect."

Brass ran his palms against his pant legs. "If you kept the fees minimal and expanded the seating." He made a hopeful face. "I think it could work, provided you could get an arena on each island and provide safe passage."

I hadn't made love to Brass since the morning of my wedding. We hadn't touched or kissed. I'd been hiding out at Valla U, afraid to be close to him. My guilt for being pregnant with his children would crush him. I couldn't hide my love for him or Slate and how horrific I felt about having hurt Slate before he disappeared.

He had to be alive.

I smiled widely. "That's where Lera would get her bonus. We could use Breakers for escorts exclusively."

"Where do we come in?" Quick asked, with no small amount of skepticism.

"Teams would need managers and captains outside of the Breakers. I'm sure there are qualified Guardians."

"I can be very convincing." Quick's mood perked and he flashed me his patented panty dropping smile.

"Now what is this really about?" Brass said, pushing away the long white sheets.

I ran my teeth along my lower lip. "I think it would bond the islands back together and maybe we could even incorporate some tribes if they wanted. There needs to be a better line of communication between everyone. That's why nothing ever gets done. Everyone is trying to guard their secrets. This would be a foot in the door. Once everyone sees how easy it could be, slowly those lines of communication will come."

"A little ambassador of peace? I think it needs to happen and I even believe your plan may work, but people like their secrets." Cordillera finally spoke.

"They can keep some of them, but wouldn't it be nice to go to Elivagar or Ostara without worrying if another Guardian is going to welcome you? I bet some Guardians haven't even left their home islands because they're afraid. We could put an end to that. Reunite the Guardians to do our job and balance things once again and help the tribes help themselves," I explained.

"And get you into each of the islands to search for Slate," Brass added.

My cheeks heated, and I pressed my lips together. "It would help all Guardians search for lost loved ones. We lost my own great grandmother in Valla and didn't return for nearly fifteen years. That's why there are both male and female Tios."

"It's been over a week, Scar. If Slate was still alive, don't you think he would have come back to you by now?" Tawny said in a cautious tone.

Anger boiled my blood. "You either believe me or you don't. I know what it looked like and how he was acting, but shouldn't I feel like he's gone? Because I don't. I feel like he's lost and I have to find him. Doing nothing is driving me crazy. I want to be out searching for him, but unless I have a reason to go to these islands and search the lands, the greater families won't let me in. Especially in Ostara and Mabon. Indigo, what did Sterling have to say?" I asked, swinging my gaze at her.

Her cheeks reddened, but she held my eyes. "Peak won't come. He said he would, though. Perhaps if he's persuaded, he'll relay the ideas to his father."

"I bet you could manage that," Quick said with a too sweet smile.

Indigo stiffened and arched a delicate brow. "I'm sure I can."

They stared at one another until Jett barged into the room in a huff.

My giant of a brother took in the room, furrowing his brow, and took the seat at the foot of the table.

"Excuse my intrusion, Orion. I came to find out what *else* my sisters are plotting since they just revealed that they're elementals, that Scarlett is married to a dead man who has a dead wife. Pray tell, baby sis. Do you plan to pinch babies now that you have started down this diabolical path?" Jett's tan, chiseled features twisted into a sarcastic grin as he faced me.

"He's not dead," I ground out.

He waved a gigantic hand dismissively and saw the papers before him and gathered up those close to him. His turquoise eyes lifted to Lera and Chafer as if for the first time, and he cocked a brow at me.

"I saw Sterling leaving. Does that mean you've included him in this plot?" Jett asked, looking at Indigo.

Indigo started and blinked at Jett, breaking Quick's stare. "No. I was very vague about the details. He'll be there Friday."

Jett nodded as he looked over at the plans. "A public Crash Course for each island? No patrons? A night club in each arena? Scarlett, why didn't you tell me? Who would run it?"

He raised his brows in question, wondering if I meant to. I shook my head.

"I had hoped I could convince a lesser family. Preferably a pair of charming brothers without ties to any greater family in particular." I flashed Brass and Quick my best smile and Brass's amber eyes widened with amusement.

"To oversee all stadiums?" Brass asked, and I nodded.

"I'll have my hands full with two children soon and after that, I'd prefer to do something that would keep me close to home," I admitted.

"*We'll* have our hands full," Brass corrected

"Close to Slate, you mean?" Tawny snorted. She still didn't believe he was alive, and it irked me.

I ignored her comment. "We'd own it, but you'd run it. Orion had been gracious enough to offer funding, but I'm also going to enlist Pearl to take some of the burden."

Jett leaned back in the chair and ran his hand over his short, dark blonde hair. "I'm in. You should have told me sooner. This looks awesome, Scar. Pearl will be in too. Whatever she has to do to bind you to the family, she'll do it."

I let a smile curl my lips and looked to Cordillera. The petite brunette ran her index finger over her red lips, the same shade of a polish on her long nails. Her dark, high arched brows raised as her dark eyes scanned the sketches. She'd known the gist of it, but this was the first time she was seeing the sketches. I didn't want to force her out if she didn't go along with my plan, but I would.

"Exclusive escort rights? Plus, an arena to be run in Valla? Who would be in charge?" she asked thoughtfully, and I shook my head.

"I'm keeping it open. They'd have to respect Brass and Quick, but I may offer the position to be decided by the Straumrs to sweeten the deal. If not, then I was going to ask a Tio. Cyan Tio is low enough in the family that he doesn't have a lot of prospects for marriage or is in a prime position to be an ambassador. He also gets on well with Quick." I gestured to the youngest, Regn, and nodded with his thumb on his chin as he agreed with my assessment.

Jett nodded as well, and I looked at Orion. "We don't have anyone to run things in Elivagar, either. I'm open to input, of course," I said with a smile.

Orion inclined his head and gestured to Tawny. "She can decide. Steel works as ambassador, but perhaps running a home-based arena would keep him closer."

Tawny beamed at her grandfather. "Thank you. Steel would never give up his position. He was hoping Slate would take over for him with the Wemic so he could focus on the Merfolk, since they're so finicky."

"Slate *will*," I interjected. "So, we're all on board? I'll have something else drawn up, a bit more professional looking for the meeting on Friday. Pearl and I should speak before then," I told them and for once, things seemed to go my way.

I would show no weakness. Not even to Sparrow, who was like a mother to me. Pearl sensed my mood and kept silent as she watched me with feigned casualness.

"Slate is my husband. There is no reason for us not to be together any longer. When he returns, we will set things straight. That's what today was about. He's alive. I just need to find him. That's why I need these arenas. The Guardians have nothing to do in leisure, there aren't enough ambassadors, and the ties between the islands are thin at best, frayed at worst. The list goes on."

Pearl raised her hand from her tea and signaled that I need not go on. "Darling, any venture you should pursue, I would sponsor. I am only surprised that you sought Orion out instead of myself."

"I didn't know if you would believe me about Slate. I needed someone with the means to find me interrogators so they could let everyone know I was telling the truth. Orion had offered his help a few times and I've never accepted. Tawny trusts him, so I put my faith in him."

Sparrow's dark eyes fell to her cup. She didn't believe he was alive, and it galled.

"When do you plan to move in?" she asked instead of prying.

"I would like to decorate our own wing as soon as possible. I'd like to use your decorator, Pearl, if that's alright. Jett told me Slate destroyed the wing," I said, sipping my tea.

I couldn't see Shale, but I knew she was blending in with the shadows by the curtains. Pearl's gaze slid over her position occasionally and Indigo knew she was there, though she was doing a much better job of not looking at her. Tree and Bee sat in our laps. The stark white cats purred in contentment as we scratched their heads. I missed Tree. She'd been scampering around the Sumar palace while I was at Valla U, but tonight I would stay in Elivagar and return to classes tomorrow.

Pearl's emerald eyes glittered. "I will put her in touch with you so you may begin planning. Should I make an appointment with you so we may look for lands for the stadium?" She pondered, and I couldn't help the smile that bloomed on my face.

"That sounds fantastic."

I returned to classes the next day. Quick was back to his charming self. Cherry, Jett, and Tawny had returned to classes, and I was the topic of conversation since Indigo wasn't there.

The dining hall was longer than it was wide, with long tables and benches along its marbled floors. The walls were the same yellowed old stone, sculpted pillars lined the rooms and sculptured people lined the edges of the ceiling looking down at us. Chandeliers were on each side of the hall, two by two, all the way down. The most amazing part was the ceiling. Between chiseled rafters were circular stained-glass mosaics depicting the phases of the moon so realistically it looked like someone had pressed the moon into the ceiling.

"I thought he was gay," Tawny hissed as Garnet sat down across from Sage.

At the head of the hall was a fireplace, with long windows to either side. The head tables for the provosts were in front of them. Moon sat there, where he had been when Indigo had slapped Ash.

Ash and his cohorts had been eyeing me all day. I wanted to get the confrontation over with. Garnet had switched gears so quickly, I wondered if she'd only been a talented actress or if she'd ever cared about Quick. As it was, she was acting as if Sage hung on the moon.

"I've seen him with girls before," I said, and turned back to my chicken, artichoke, and feta salad, stabbing a sliced piece of chicken with my fork.

"Really? I suppose I have heard rumors..." Jett trailed off.

"Brass knew. He is funny that way. He knows everyone's secrets but does not tell them. What is the point of having all that gossip locked in your mind if you will not use it to your benefit?" Quick asked, incredulous.

"Brass only knew after the funeral." I corrected, "I'm not saying this because... oh, never mind."

Cherry giggled. "But how can someone go from sleeping with Quick to sleeping with Sage? Opposites, aren't they?"

I widened my eyes, nodding. "Exactly."

Tawny mulled it over, her hazel eyes taking in my half-brother with his combed back blonde hair from his fair skin and with a soft pout like his mother. His big, round, blue eyes flickered to our table, full of disdain. I didn't think he had another expression.

"His lips look soft. He's tall and good looking."

I made a face, then smiled wryly as Cherry giggled, patting Jett's back.

Ash slipped onto the bench next to me, on the other side of Quick. He placed his hand over mine while Jett distracted me, squeezing it in his grip. I gritted my teeth but didn't gasp.

"You can't possibly think that's a good idea after you saw what she can do." Tawny snapped.

Ash's light green eyes flared at me. "We will speak now."

"We can speak here," I countered, and Ash sneered.

"Very well," Ash *called,* and I felt his warmth flood through me from his hand.

"Don't do anything stupid, Ash," I gasped, and Jett's face went tight.

Quick's dagger was already out under the table should Ash try to harm the babies. Ash's cool expression never left my face.

"You never should have bedded the orphan. There is no one to see to your needs now, Scarlett. Who will protect you?" Ash whispered so low the others were leaning forward to hear him.

"I can protect myself." I hissed, and the corner of his mouth pulled up.

"You do not know how dangerous the game is that you are playing. You should have stayed with the myopics. Perhaps then the orphan would not be gone." I stiffened, and he loosened his hand over mine. "We would have been good together. When it all comes crashing down, I will still need a paramour whose *calling* can reduce the staunchest man to his knees." Ash rose with a fluid like grace that belied his deadly skill at fighting.

Quick let out a low whistle. "Fuck me. I think Ash believed he was in love with you. They all think you are having Slate's children."

I massaged my hand as he'd squeezed. "I know. He doesn't know what love is. He could love no one more than himself or his ambition. It's anger because not only did he miss out on a fertile Tio wife, but an elemental to boot. He sees me and he sees a missed opportunity."

Jett had gripped the fork so tightly it had molded to his fist. He dropped it on the polished wood table and it clattered against the plate.

"Stay away from him. I know a threat when I hear one. If something happens to your children, Scar..." Jett trailed off, but he hadn't needed to continue.

Jett would kill Ash, even if he wasn't directly responsible. That much was as clear as the Thrimilci sky.

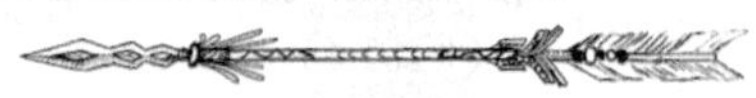

That night I brought Indigo to head quarters without a blindfold so she could train during the day with Brass while I was at Valla U. Word had gotten around I was married to Slate and pregnant with his children. Brass wasn't correcting anyone and I started to feel rejected. I had pushed him too far.

When I had asked Lera for my old position back as a delegate, she had laughed. "Girl, you have no use for us any longer. Why would you waste your time?"

Her blunt words had surprised me. "I like it here. The Shadow Breakers are like family. Maybe one day if you retire, I can run the Breakers myself. I'm not as shrewd, but I'll learn." I responded candidly, and she pursed her lips.

"That may be possible," she said.

Low hanging lamps from the ceiling of the rumpus room, and leather permeated the air even before we reached the room. The sound of pool balls cracked against one another. Spots of bright light existed between spots of darkness in the loft like room. There was a bar complete with bottles with tender, and stools. Two pool tables and four couches scattered around the random rugs of the dusky purple room.

They greeted me at the round tables where Breakers sat, the ones I'd recruited and were glad to have Brass back as their captain. Quick had taken over for Slate's team that was now splintered into so few now that Ama and Shale weren't training with them.

Indigo gaped at the underground room. "It's only three stories from the outside."

I walked over the walnut floors to get an ice water from the polished bar. Pinball machines rang out through the room and Shale glided in beside me. Her emotions were in turmoil being back. I planned on forcing her to go to the room she shared with Ama and start sorting things out, or at least grabbing a few of her own things and she could move into the Sumar palace.

"There are ten floors. This is the fifth. The lowest is the Crash Course and the prep room. They shared the one above that with the seats of the arena and the hot studio." Shale answered in her clipped tone.

Indigo nodded and was drawing more attention than I was strictly comfortable with. I'd dressed her in all black like the Shadow Breakers, though I wore a bright red shirt so I would purposefully stand out. I spotted Brass and Quick, who ate dinner with three women our age. Brass's eyes had slid over me and he smiled at something one girl said.

I would not get jealous.

"Come along. Let's get things settled." I told Indigo and Shale followed along.

I recognized the girls right away. I'd recruited all of them. They were Brass's team. They looked at him with more than an admiring appreciation, as if he was some trophy to be won. I clenched my fists and ignored the burn in my stomach.

It was what I wanted, wasn't it?

"Quick, once you're done eating, would you mind joining us in the prep room?" I asked in my delegate voice, letting him know he no longer had a choice; in case he was thinking of holding Indigo's indiscretions against her.

Quick wiped his lips with a napkin and stood from the table and brought his plate to the bar. He thanked the tender before heading back towards us. The girls had eyed me as girls usually did, weighing and measuring, but they knew I was not to be trifled with. The girl I'd beaten to a pulp sat two tables over with her brother. Mirage's eyes never left me as the other girls greeted me as a delegate.

We walked down the stone steps, my hand sliding along the wrought iron and polished wood balustrade to the lowest level of headquarters. I pushed open the metal double doors and into the modern prep room with black metal cubbies and gray marble tiles with white and black skein marble benches. I led them through until the end, where three massage tables and showers were off to the left. A screen that alerted the Breakers of their price and room number of patrons, rested blank against the wall, and I pushed through the second set of metal doors.

At the front of the Crash Course, were weapon racks and several combat rings. The left half had something we called the Guillotine with all its wicked looking blades. Tall trees stood in the center of the room looking like a small woods dividing it. A simulated earthquake, complete with falling boulders, was next, a lava pit with floating rocks on its surface after that, and wooden rafts that rested on crashing waves were its finale. It'd taken me three weeks to cross it the first time.

Indigo had never seen it from this angle. She'd been in the stone stands that wrapped around the arena and looked down on the course. The left half had two-way mirrors that hid Cordillera's suite, as well as the patrons' rooms.

"Indigo is going to be on Slate's team. Since you're acting team captain, you will train Indigo," I said, brooking no nonsense, and Indigo objected.

Quick looked at me coolly and I smirked as Indigo started making excuses. "No problem." Quick said, and Indigo shut up.

"Really?" she asked.

Shale snickered, and my smile deepened. There she was.

"Come on Shale, I'm getting rusty."

I led Shale to the prep room to head to the hot studio and leave Indigo and Quick to work out whatever was going on between them. Maybe they would work it out, or maybe they'd beat one another into the dust.

Either way, they'd get out some of their aggression.

CHAPTER 49
INDIGO

"Your sister did not even say hello to Brass," Silver said, removing his shirt and I licked my lips as he turned his muscled back to me.

I wanted to run my fingertips along his tattoos, so I balled my fists. Did I only want him when I couldn't have him?

"I think she's trying to give him distance. I have her empath abilities almost all the time. She's desperately in love with him. The problem is she loves Slate too, and when he was here, she could justify not being with him. With Slate gone and Amber dead... everything concerning Brass makes her feel horrible. As if her love for him orchestrated Slate's death. *Capture.*"

My mouth had suddenly gone dry, and I swallowed to replenish my diminished supply of saliva.

Silver walked back to me with a short seax like the one that Scarlett had strapped to her thigh and two daggers that he tucked into my boots as he knelt before me, his hands moving in a practiced way. Silver slid his hands up my leg to my thigh and buckled on the blade.

"You will need to get your own, so you are comfortable with it. I know you are an archer, but we work with blades here. Learn," Silver said, looking up at me from where he knelt. "Brass intends to lure her back by letting her see him with other women. I do not think it will work. He is not Slate. Your sister has always idolized him. If he acts out of character, I think it will make it worse."

By the Mother, what was that fluttering in my chest? Was I having a heart attack? Could twenty-year-old girls have heart attacks?

"I'm not afraid of the work, if that's what you're implying." I said bitingly to cover up the exhilaration I'd felt at his touch. "You're right about Brass."

Silver's lips twisted into an impish grin. "I know you are not afraid of hard, *long* work, Dove."

My cheeks flushed. "Silver..." I trailed off.

He arched a dark brow at me. "Yes, Indigo? Have something you wish to say?"

I'm sorry.

Why couldn't he be a mind reader like Brass? I shook my head, and he nodded as if I'd just confirmed something.

"We shall start simple. Pull your blade so you can get used to its hold," Silver said, and I did as I was told.

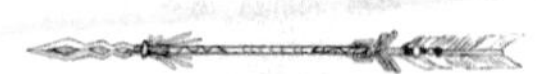

After an hour and a half of getting used to my dagger, Silver wanted me to draw blood. It was incredibly condescending, since he had no blade of his own and it exposed his top to my blade without even a thin shirt to buffer from the blade. It turned out he had needed none of it.

He disarmed me repeatedly, so I was grunting in fury as he smirked again and again. Scarlett made it look so easy when she did it. Finally, I charged him and he caught me by the elbow and belt buckle, flipping me effortlessly onto the floor of the combat circle and air whooshed from my lungs.

Instead of helping me up like he'd been doing every time he took me down, he braced himself above me on his hands and toes as I rubbed my head.

"Had enough, Dove?" he asked with glittering chocolate eyes.

Flecks of gold were spun into those dark eyes that were more prominent when we were inches apart, much closer than we were then. "Only if you're tired of me."

Silver's brow twitched, and I thought I saw his eyes drop to my lips. I licked them instinctually and tried to even my breaths. It satisfied that while I was glistening with sweat, a fine sheen covered the crease between his pecs and his forehead.

"It would take much for me to tire of you." Silver said huskily, and I felt something like excitement course through me.

"You seem tired now," I asked, probing, and Silver flashed me that heart-stopping smile of his that made me grimace.

"Only you frown at my smiles."

"Because they're inviting and you flash them —" I stopped myself.

By the Mother, what was I saying?

"Finish, Dove." Silver encouraged, and his arms bent as he came down to lower his body over mine.

He would call me out if I lied. "You flash them at *every* woman. Scarlett says Slate has a smile he only gives her."

I was doing it again. I pulled my lips between my teeth, hoping that would prevent anything else stupid from propelling out into the air.

"Slate is in love with Scarlett," Silver said, and I blinked at him.

"Of course he is," I snapped and shoved him off with a sharp gust of air before getting to my feet and dusting myself off.

Silver stood and gave me that unreadable look, making me glare. "Are we done for now? I'll be back every day. I can walk here with you after classes or meet you here once you've had dinner. Scarlett said Brass may train me in the mornings, so if you don't want to, he can."

"No. I shall train you. We are done for today," Silver said and gestured with a mocking bow to the prep room.

I tilted my chin and headed towards it. What I needed now was a hot shower and an ice-cold drink.

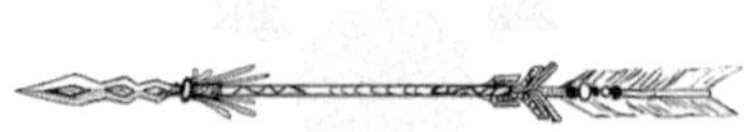

Outside the shower room were towels neatly rolled for everyone's use, which I grabbed two of as I walked into the black marble room while thanking the Gods it was vacant. Soaps dispensed within each shower stall, except there weren't really stalls. There were frosted glass partisans that retracted in an otherwise big, wet room. I pulled mine and hit the energy plate so the hot water flowed over my sore muscles. I'd be damned if I asked Silver Regn for healing. Scarlett would heal me once we met up.

I rested my forehead against the cool marble and chastised myself for being so passive aggressive with Silver. I couldn't give him an inch. He took five miles every time, and I never learned.

Case in point, I heard a shower start next to me and I wiped the stream from my face to look and see who it was. As if I didn't know.

Silver stood three feet away from me on the other side of the frosted partition under his own stream of water. "I suppose there are time constraints, so you had to shower right this second and directly next to me," I said, rubbing shampoo into my hair.

"How would you say it? *Oh*, that is right. Get over yourself," Silver said, and I spun around, gaping at him. "I have a date tonight. She would not appreciate me being late."

Oh, that didn't feel good at all.

I took a fortifying breath. He never told me about other girls. I just knew that they were a part of his life. I never wanted to know. My head ducked under the shower and let the suds slide over my body. I could always find Sterling. When we were together last, I hadn't been able to get into it. He'd finished and waited for an explanation that I didn't have. I couldn't tell him that the disappointed look in Silver's eyes haunted me.

I wished I didn't have so much stupid hair to condition when he slapped the energy plate and he stepped out of the shower, wrapping a towel around his waist. He didn't hide the way his eyes raked over my body as he sauntered past the open side of my partition and my skin grew tight all over my body. I rinsed the conditioner out and wrapped a towel around my head and one around my chest that fell down to my thighs.

Scarlett had told me where her cubby was that contained her spare clothes and I started when I saw Silver in the aisle with the damp towel on the marble bench. He didn't look up as I walked to the cubby and pulled out clothing only three cubbies down from him. I pulled deodorant and lotion from it and swiped under my arms.

While rubbing shimmering lotion over my skin, I felt rather than saw Silver's eyes watching me. I jerked my head up to find him in a snug pair of red boxer briefs that did little to cover him. I dropped my gaze again and let my towel fall before rubbing the lotion over my stomach.

Silver sucked in a breath loud enough for me to hear, and internally, I smiled. I pulled the towel from my hair and gasped as I felt his hands spin me around before I could lift my head from the awkward position.

He pinned me against the metal cubby with his body and pulled my arms above my head as he parted my lips with his. He caught both my wrists in his hand as his other hand slid over my damp skin.

"Sometimes I think I hate you, Dove," Silver breathed roughly, and I panted against his mouth.

"I know. I'm sorry, Silver."

He pulled back, astonished at my sweet, sincere tone.

"Truth," he whispered, and his eyes scanned mine before he slanted his mouth over mine again. "I want you. Gods cursed Tio women," he growled.

"Anyway you want me," I cooed and Silver moaned.

"Here now and then upstairs in my bed. Lots of kissing and me on top," Silver said in pants, and I grunted in agreement.

"Have I ever told you I have this theory that you could make a woman climax just through your kisses?" I whispered, as his mouth slid to my throat.

He moaned again and his hands slid under my thighs to lift me up. I locked my ankles around his back as he pushed into me, making me moan, and I tightened my hands on his shoulders. We were making a riot of noise with our breathing and the slamming against the partially open metal cubby door. I could tell Silver didn't give a fig.

"If you make me come in your *calling*. So help me," Silver said, pulling his mouth from mine to growl at me.

It made me laugh with a slightly hysterical edge that tightened the muscles inside me, and Silver groaned.

"Oh, Quick. You know that is against the rules."

My eyes flew open at the mocking feminine voice, and Silver's eyes locked on mine with a note of desperation. I broke his intense gaze and saw Mirage; the girl Scarlett had fought for antagonizing her after trying to seduce Slate. I knew Silver got around and it was no private place to be having sex, but the challenge in her eyes was there. I unlocked my ankles and Silver growled.

"Get out of here, Mirage." Silver had slipped from me but was still pinning me against the cubby, even though I was trying to push him back.

"Just waiting my turn, Quick. I will meet you in your bed again tonight. After last night, I am surprised you have the energy for this one." The tall blonde smirked as she walked away, her big blue eyes glittering like sapphires.

I made a strangled sound and elbowed Silver in the gut. He grunted, and I grabbed the underwear Scarlett had left me and stepped into them as I dressed. Silver pulled his briefs up and stood next to me, willing me to look at him.

"I know that is not your date. I used to find it reassuring you'd been with so many women because that meant you wouldn't force me into something with you. Now, I know you not only demand that I not see other men, but that you can spout off sweet words while still sleeping with several other women on the same day. You may be second, but your second of two. Two men, Silver. You've had more women than that in two days. I'm not passing judgement, but you should stop throwing stones in that glass house of yours." I slammed the metal cubby door and steeled myself for his gaze.

He was angry. Silver rarely got angry.

"Tell me, Indigo. I want to hear it."

"Save your childish games, Silver. Sometimes sex is just sex. Sometimes it isn't even very satisfying," I said caustically, and he flinched as if I'd struck him.

"Truth." He muttered as he turned to the cubby and I stormed past him.

CHAPTER 50
GYPSUM

Shale's angled chin dropped as she howled. Her insides pulsed around me, triggering my response. I gripped her trim hips as I moaned, and she fell down to my chest. Her poker straight hair stuck to the sweat over my chest and I felt her shift, pulling the strands away from her mouth.

I wrapped my arms around her back as she trembled with her tears. Most guys would freak to have a girl cry on them after sex, but Shale needed a release. Fighting wasn't cutting it and, for some reason, she felt like being with me reminded her of Ama.

I would be there in any way she wanted. Since Shale and I explored new avenues of our relationship with Ama, we'd become close. She was one of my closest friends. She was the only one whom I told aside from the Wemic, that the twins I'd been in the adobe with were missing. They'd come out to fight the Jorogumo and simply disappeared. I'd gone through the bodies and not found either of them.

Keen had told me they were Nirrin's little sisters. That they had probably left with him. My stomach twisted at that, but I didn't think the girls were traitors. They were probably afraid after Nirrin brought the Jorogumo into the canyons.

"Can we please get out of his room now?" I asked, and she laughed through her sobs.

Amber had a mirror installed on the ceiling above Slate's bed, and Shale had wanted to see what it was like to use it. I had been vehemently against it, but Shale could get me to do a lot of things I wouldn't normally do when she asked with uncharacteristic kindness.

I rolled us over so she faced the mirror and pulled her hair out of her face. "Scar would kill us if she caught us in here."

"Slate would kill us. Scarlett would understand," she said, wiping the tears from her cheeks. "Have I ever told you, you have one of the best asses I have ever seen? Man or female, show it off more."

I laughed, jerking us both onto the black tufted leather bed. "I'll work on that. Assless chaps maybe?"

Shale laughed, clenching around me, and folded her arms under her head. "You know we have been sleeping together for half a year already?"

Shale switched gears in her grief so fast, I could barely keep up. I rolled off her, but she locked her legs around my waist.

"I have been a third wheel for a year in less than two months." I reminded her.

Shale's dark eyes glittered as she swallowed hard. "Blonde women and dark-haired men. I do not know why Ama chose me. Perhaps she thought she could make me bright and shiny too. I think she failed that mission. The moment she saw you, I knew she wanted to take you home. You are the best third we ever had."

I gave her a lopsided grin. "Thanks, I think. Is it because of my great ass and girlish long hair?"

Shale chuckled. "And you never treated Ama like an object, or me, after you took my maidenhood."

"Shale, I think we've all agreed that what I did that night was not take your virginity. Merely allowed you to sleep with a man. There's a difference."

"Scarlett is pushing Brass away. It is not the right move. I cannot tell her because she is on the edge. Brass has waited so long for her, maybe he will wait forever, but perhaps he has had enough. I would hate for her to lose him and end up alone." A tear rolled over Shale's high cheekbone and I kissed it away.

She gave me a wry look, and I smiled again, though I didn't feel much like smiling.

"Like you?"

"No. I have you," Shale said with a small twitch of her lips.

She didn't say as much, but the feeling that she was trying to secure an heir for her family before she allowed herself to join Ama had slowly grown until it was too big to ignore. What was even more frightening was that I wasn't stopping it.

Once Shale fell asleep, I moved her next door into my bedroom and informed the staff the sheets in Slate's room needed to be changed.

Maybe he wouldn't come back, but maybe he would. He'd be pissed I bedded Shale in every God's known position so she could determine what her best angle was in the mirror in his monstrous bed.

Before too long, I'd have to check-in with Bee and Tree. Scarlett was deep in her machnations and Indigo was at her side. The skogkatts were fiercely independent so I wasn't worrying too much.

I was making my way from the bathroom I shared with Slate before he moved to the Dagr palace, when the knob to my room turned. One staffer must have been new and wasn't sure which room was Slate's, so I jogged over to the door so they wouldn't see me in my underwear to let them know they had the wrong room.

Diamond's thick mane of chestnut locks poked through the crack of my bedroom door and I froze in my orange boxer briefs mid step. She smiled, her full pink lips on her caramel face brightening the dark room.

"I didn't get a message," I said stupidly.

She crossed the room to wrap her arms around my neck, and I held my face away from hers. "I wanted it to be a surprise. I am so sorry about Slate."

"I'm sorry about Amber. I didn't like her, but she didn't deserve to die."

Diamond's smile turned down. Girls could have strange friendships. Diamond and Amber were more competitors than they were friends, but it was apparent Amber's death had hurt Diamond.

"You can help lift my spirits," Diamond said, leaning towards my lips again.

I took her arms down and she frowned prettily as she looked up at me with her lightest green eyes.

"Now isn't a good time. Any other night, I wouldn't mind you surprising me, but —"

"There is a girl in your bed?" she asked, knitting her delicate brows together.

"I wouldn't call her a girl. Not to her face, anyway. My friend lost her lover, and she's staying the night." I told her, feeling a tightness in my chest as Diamond's lower lip pouted.

"Do you love her?" she asked with a warbling voice.

"We're friends. I'm just keeping her company. The only woman I love is you." I told her firmly, and she crossed her arms under her chest.

"I want to see her."

I wiped my hand over my mouth and bit back a curse when I could detect Shale's sweet, musky scent on my hands and lips. "Fine, but if she wakes up, she'll know who you are. Give me a minute."

Before she could object, I darted into the bathroom and washed my face and hands before gargling mouthwash and spat it into the sink. Diamond stood in the doorway watching me with a dry expression on her face. I gave her my dimpled grin, and she sighed before moving away.

I wanted to kiss Diamond, but after what I'd done with Shale, I had to freshen up.

Diamond was already in the archway of my bedroom area when I stepped up behind her. Shale had curled into the fetal position under my brown sheets, but you could tell from the shadows that she was nude.

Diamond backed away and headed towards the door.

"I'm sorry, Diamond. You know I wouldn't have done this if I knew you were coming."

"We will go next door," she said, grabbing my wrist.

I stopped, jerking her to a standstill. "No. I can't leave her alone. She lost her lover."

"And I lost my best friend, Gypsum," she said, knitting her brows.

I'd never told her no. She was not used to hearing the word being a greater family daughter. I was glad our parents raised us in Tidings. It was easy to see why so many of the lesser families despised us.

She changed tactics. "Please. I want you to make love to me as only you can. Just once and you can return to your friend. She will not even wake up before we are done," she said, batting her lashes at me.

I held up my index fingers. "Once. In the linen closet and then I go back, Diamond. You wouldn't have to sneak around with me if you would leave him."

Once again, she made no comment about my proposal.

FIFTY-ONE

Indigo and Quick were worse.

Much worse.

She'd refused to talk about it but said she wouldn't train with 'Quick' Silver for all the silkworms in Ostara. I wasn't sure what that meant, but I let it go. Brass agreed to train her with his team during the day and she would be back in Elivagar at night caring for Tree and Bee.

The problem was there weren't classes the next day. I laid awake in the Elivagar castle, having given Shale the night off since the Vetr castle was one of the safest places with Tawny in it. I sensed a Shadow Breaker in every shadowed corner and realized that Orion and Cordillera were old acquaintances from our short time in meetings together.

Orion was the white-haired man I thought I recognized at my very first competition when they introduced me to her suite. He'd turned right away, but I was sure now it had been him. Shadow Breakers guarded over Tawny from the time he realized she was alive at my mother's Ragnarök a few weeks after we arrived in Tidings from Chicago.

I bit my lip hard enough to draw blood and slipped my ring finger into my mouth.

Were beds so big and cold before I met Slate?

I felt empty laying alone under the black jacquard coverlet. The bedroom door opened within minutes of me activating the bond.

"Were you waiting in the hall?" I joked, but my voice held no humor.

I heard weapons hit the floor and the sound of clothing being shed before Brass was on the side of the bed. I furrowed my brow, looking up at him.

"This bed is enormous." I swallowed hard.

"Need another body to fill it?" Brass asked, standing in nothing but his green boxer briefs before me.

"A non-lecherous one, preferably. Shale's with Gypsum tonight." I confided and turned down the coverlet and rubbed the spot next to me. "Do you hate me, Brass?"

Brass climbed over me, making my heart skip a beat until he laid beside me and I turned to face him. It filled his amber eyes with warmth and I felt my nose burn. How much simpler my life would have been if I'd fallen for Brass first.

"How are you holding up?"

I sucked in a shallow breath. "I hope I look stronger on the outside than I feel on the inside."

Brass laced his fingers through mine and pulled our joined hands up between us. The bond deactivated.

"You could have told me."

"I know. You're kinder than I am. I had to do something drastic. I hate all the secrets. Part of me feels released having it all out in the open." I swallowed. "What about you?"

Speaking of collateral damage.

His lips curled. "Your brother asked me at this year's induction cere-mony if I'd had my heart broken. I think I may have underestimated things."

I gasped and pulled our joined hands to my breast with tears pricking my eyes. "By the Mother, don't say that." I whispered roughly, "Hurting you is the last thing I would have wanted. To be honest, I'd rather hurt Slate over you. Mostly because he would have deserved it for some unknown evil I'm sure he's committed."

Brass chuckled and gazed into my eyes in the darkness. "I'll be okay, Scarlett. We must all have our hearts broken once. How else do we appreciate when it is full again?"

"Does it hurt you to be here now?" I ran my teeth along my lower lip. "If it does, you don't have to stay. You don't owe me a thing. I owe you."

"May I kiss you, Scarlett?" Brass asked and my heart played a new tune with all the beats it missed.

"Just a kiss. Don't seduce me, Brass Regn. We both know I've never been good at turning you away, even though I should have."

He left me breathless.

No such thing as just a kiss with a mind reader. He had to break us apart, and he turned my body, tucking me to him with us both breathing raggedly and I squeezed my eyes shut. Slate had to be alive. I couldn't have given this up for nothing.

Brass was gone before I awoke that morning.

I went to headquarters, and he came back with me after dinner that night, as well as the next. Indigo was smart enough not to utter a word about it.

Since Quick was keeping his distance from Indigo, he didn't know his brother was spending the nights I wasn't at Valla U with me. We didn't kiss again. That one was more than enough to let me know he would wait for me if I chose a different path.

I wondered if we were ever just friends, and all Slate's jealousy and suspicion had been with merit. I thought it was. Looking back, Slate knew if I let Brass into my heart just a little, he'd kick open the door with his mild temper and honesty, to which I had no defense. The exact opposite of Slate and yet, somehow similar.

There were only three months left until the Ragnarök challenge. Classes had been trying before, but now they were grueling. It was only somewhat eased with the provosts giving me extra lessons after classes. My red-headed uncles and aunts had each given me an extra book to bring back to my rooms and study. Tawny and Cherry alternated staying until bedtime, helping me catch up on seven months of missed classes.

In the meantime, Indigo found us an architect in Valla after training with Brass during the week. He'd gone over my sketches and drafted new, more professional ones on an actual computer. We paid extra for the rush, but by the night of the meetings, they were ready.

Brass opened my bedroom door and strode over to where I sat at the vanity trying to give myself a pep talk. He rested his dark honey hands on velvet clad shoulders. The traditional dress in Elivagar differed from in Thrimilci. Wool and velvets replaced chiffon and satin. Layers of petticoats and corsets went under thick boned bodices and high collars that still showed an impressive amount of bosom.

I wore a deep red long sleeve dress that was cinched at my waist with a gold belt and gold embroidery along the sleeves. The plunging neckline went to my bodice. It weighed a ton, but all the Elivagar dresses kept the wearer warm in the land of perpetual winter.

Hair was worn differently here as well, to better display the fashionable collars and designs embroidered along the shoulders of the dresses. They pinned mine up in a low chignon at my nape. Brass's thumbs slid over my nape and I turned to smile up at him.

"Elivagar suits you," he said in his smooth, deep tone.

"Save all that charm for our dinner guests. They didn't come, did they?" I queried, and Brass gave me a rueful smile that made me sigh. "I knew they wouldn't."

"Your grandmother is here, though."

I gave him a wry smile. "Of course she is, she's fronting me —"

"Not that one," Brass said with a genuine smirk.

"Oh!" I exclaimed.

Ruby Geol had come. Only three Geol women lived. Ruby, Amethyst, and Gigi. From my reports, she owned land in Ostara. She could've been there to bring word back to my father's father or she could offer her own lands for the arena. I had expected none of them to show. Ruby had never expressed an interest in the past.

"What about the others?" I asked.

"Peak and Cassiopeia are not present, but you knew they wouldn't," Brass said, trailing his thumb down my throat and I blushed.

His amber eyes glittered in the mirror when I didn't say a word about it. I missed him. All the guilt that sat on my chest every second of the day couldn't make me stop caring.

"That leaves Orion, Pearl, Sparrow... Moon, Reed, Sterling, Jett... am I missing anyone?" I asked, rising to my feet.

"Their spouses, Cordillera, Chafer, Tawny, Steel, Gypsum, Silver, Indigo, your uncle Jackal and Crag. Scarlett, Ash came with Quartz," Brass said with sympathy.

I groaned. "Do they not understand this was invite only? What's the point of sending invites for specific people if they all come, anyway?"

Brass didn't hesitate to pull me into his arms and rest his jaw on top of my head. "Orion planned. He is good at the Guardians' games. They moved everyone into the great hall and more food was prepared. There are nearly thirty people down there waiting for your idea."

"Diamond's here as well?" I asked, and he made a noise of ascension in his throat.

I looped my arms around his hips loosely and breathed him in, calming my nerves, drawing his calm into me.

"Tell me I can do this. That they won't leave laughing in my face because I'm barely more than a girl."

"You don't need me to tell you this. You'll do it because you need to traverse the islands and find Slate. Which you cannot do it alone," Brass said and withdrew, taking my chin in his fingers so he could level his eyes at me. "The woman who prodded my honor after I disarmed her in a darkened alley could do anything she put her mind to. Even blind a fool into bringing her into an assassin's guild when she was a naive girl. You are no longer that naïve."

I searched his eyes. "I knew you would be prickly about your honor, that you didn't want to hurt me. Those people down there are not all on my side."

"So sway them to you."

The rap of knuckles sounded on the door, and I started pulling away from Brass. I'd been staring too intently on his lips and we'd stopped talking. Quick peeked his head in and saw me smoothing down my skirts and smirked.

"Getting lonely, Scarlett?" he chided, and I shot him daggers.

"Do not start," Brass warned.

"Everyone who is coming is seated," Quick said, shutting the door behind him and looking around my room.

My cheeks heated when he saw Brass's beads in a bowl on my vanity and his black Shadow Breaker clothes thrown over the trunk at the foot of the bed. Quick's eyes swung back to us, twinkling.

"It's not like that," Brass said in a soft tone I recognized as the danger zone.

Quick scoffed. "Sharing her bed, but not her body. I think I know exactly what it is like, brother."

I clenched my jaw and moved to skirt Quick and leave the room. He'd been confrontational ever since I pushed Brass away. No one understood how hard it was for me to keep my distance.

"Just because you and Indigo are fighting, don't take it out on us," I said, slamming the door behind me.

I strolled to Indigo's door and found it open and Indigo looking breathtaking in her namesake's color in a thick velvet dress with a mock collar whose neckline cut across the swell of her breasts with a sheer white pleat that poked up from it and from the hem. Her they pinned corn silk hair high in a fashionable knot that exposed her fresh tan face.

She pinned her earring to her ear and crossed to me and shut the door behind us just as Quick and Brass exited my room. "Ignore him. He's grumpy today," I warned.

She looked at Quick coolly. "That shouldn't be a problem."

Quick narrowed his eyes at her and she spun on her heel away as we walked down the white marble hall.

I HELD two scrolls that came by messenger shortly after the guests had left. A pile of signed blood contracts sat on my left.

Notice Of Engagement

Sage Var and Garnet Lodda have signed their marriage contract.
A betrothal ball will be held at month's end with invitations to follow
All Hail The Happy Couple!

I IGNITED it like a flash paper. That wasn't what I expected, but it wasn't what troubled me. Brass read the second one, leaning over my shoulder.

Mrs. Slate Dagr
I have been hasty in my dismissal. Sterling has informed me of your plan
of an arena with the potential to bring revenue into Mabon.
If you would do me the honor of being my guest this coming week's end, I would like
to hear your business plan in private before I make my decision.
Peak Haust

"I can't see anything wrong with it on the outside, but it feels wrong." I told him, holding it up to him for him to take.

Brass scanned it over. "I am curious whether he wrote it before or after Sterling returned. Perhaps this was his plan all along, but then, to what end? Will you go?"

I sighed, and Brass pulled the pins from my hair, letting it fall to my waist. It was nice to have a mind reader around.

"I don't see what other choice I have. Moon and Crag sided against Ash for me to get the arena built in Valla, Ruby and Jett's signatures offer her land in Ostara... It'd all be for naught if I didn't get Mabon. I don't want to wait until Peak retires and for Sterling to agree to have the arena built there."

Quick grunted. "Indigo could coerce his father since she handles the son so well."

"Quick!" I admonished in shock.

Indigo regarded Quick with piercing ice-blue eyes. She didn't realize her anger shone through her elemental eyes.

"I could. I've been told I'm a skilled lover. Granted, I haven't slept with half of Tidings."

Brass's hand on my shoulder kept me from interrupting what would inevitably be a verbal knock down drag out fight. Quick's powerful jaw jutted arrogantly as he looked down his nose at her.

"Being told by one inexperienced person you have a certain skill set does not make it so. There are such things as fact and fiction."

I winced visibly under Brass's firm hand. Indigo's lips curled, though, and my eyes widened as the room grew cooler.

"Being told by hundreds of brainless twits that you *do* is *fiction,* when one inexperienced person has known those supposed skills and found them lacking is *fact.*"

Quick shot to his feet, knocking his chair askew, and pointed his finger at Indigo. "You said a great deal of pretty things to me, Indigo. Do not pretend you did not."

She flashed him a mocking smile and didn't so much as blink when she spoke icily, "Pretty words to a pretty *boy*. Words mean nothing."

Quick's jaw clenched as I saw hurt pass through his dark eyes. Everyone knew words meant the world to Quick. That's how he judged the world. Their words he separated into fact and fiction through his talent.

"Truth. All of it," Quick said harshly, "Why did you waste your time?"

Indigo gave a small lift of her slender shoulders. "I didn't think you had feelings to be hurt."

Had they forgotten we were there? Was Brass holding his breath as I was?

"Truth," Quick said raggedly, as if she wore him down with her words alone. "Did none of it matter?"

Indigo sniffed. "Your feelings for me are absurd. If you want more pretty meaningless words, my pretty boy, you may warm my bed whenever it isn't occupied."

The veins in Quick's neck bulged and pulsed as he glared at Indigo, who still sat with her hands under the table. They had forgotten about us — an empath and a mind reader. They were hurting one another on purpose. Indigo had carefully crafted her words, so she didn't lie, but they *were* lies. I could *feel* it, and Brass would know as well.

"You belong in this castle of ice with your frozen heart and biting words. I thought Scarlett was heartless the way she breaks men's hearts, but she is honest, if indecisive. She does not say things, she does not mean. When she tells my brother she loves him, I hear the truth. Same as when she tells Slate. It is not like that for you, though, is it, Indigo? Go on. Keep fucking Sterling and carry his bastard. I will watch it all play out from the sidelines and when you are discarded, do not come to me. There are plenty of women who welcome me with *warm,* open arms."

"And legs." She added with a wicked smile and Quick blinked. "You can go Silver; I won't be stopping you."

Quick stared for a moment longer and I thought I couldn't take it another second longer. Was he waiting for her to apologize? To take it all back? Would he take her back if she did? I thought I knew the answer, and I shut my eyes, unable to bear it.

Quick nodded for no reason I could see and left the great hall, slamming the double doors behind him. Indigo sucked in a swell of breath and started yanking at her bodice.

"I can't breathe with this thing on." She cried as her nails dug at the fabric.

Brass released my shoulder, and I flew up from my seat and she leaned forward so I could unclasp the dress and I untied the strings of her corset. She sat there half-dressed and sucked in deep, steadying breaths. She leaned her forehead against the white marble table as her back shook. I rubbed her back soothingly as Brass took my seat.

"Why?" I asked, and she gave me a bitter smile.

"Better to push him away than give him what he wants and have my heart torn out." She scoffed. "Things were getting too serious."

"Did you have to cut him down so much?" I asked her.

"Yes. Silver is persistent." She smiled prettily. "I don't feel any better. For some reason, I thought once I was free of him, I would. He's been sleeping with Mirage. She walked in on us after we trained and let him know once he was done with me, she'd wait for him." She straightened and gestured for me to retie her corset.

I helped her dress and felt a pang of empathy for Indigo. "Want me to kick her fanny pack for you again? I don't mind at all."

Indigo let out a soft chuckle. "I'm not supposed to care enough to let his exploits bother me. I have Sterling."

I bit my lip. "Do you though, Indi? I wonder if you pushed Quick away because Sterling didn't like how close the two of you were getting. Quick is more than a suitable match for you. Sterling knows that. With these arenas, Brass and Quick will be elevated to a standing with the greater families. That they are more loved than the Vars in Ostara certainly counts in their favor."

She gave me a dry smile as I clasped her dress closed. "Quick doesn't want to marry me. He wants me to himself or for him to do whatever he pleases. Spare me his feelings. I know he thinks he loves me, Scarlett. It's only because no one turns down the illustrious 'Quick' Silver Regn. Except you, but then that's because you're in love with his brother." Indigo's ice blue swung to Brass's amber, and he lifted a brow at her.

"You lie to yourself. If there is a Tio curse, that is it." Brass got to his feet and looked at me. "Are you coming to bed?"

My cheeks heated, and Indigo scoffed. "Who lies to themselves, Regn?"

I did. He did. The better question was, who didn't?

Without him, all I had was anger and pain. That's what I told myself as I traced his dark honey muscles, running my fingertips through his dusting of dark hair over his chest with my cheek pressed against his shoulder.

"Are you going to come with me when I check out the sites?" I asked him.

His fingers trailed up my spine, my long satin night dress catching on it as he ran it back down the curve of my body. "If you wish," he said drowsily, and I laid my palm flat over his heart.

"You think he's out there, don't you, Brass?" I asked in a voice so low it was almost inaudible.

"Do you, Scarlett? Sometimes I think you hold tight to the idea because giving up on him is not something you are capable of. Then I think I would not be in your bed, even as your friend, if you thought he was."

"I don't like when you make so much sense." I mumbled as he slid his fingers through my hair. "You're right. About all of it. Part of me believes the Faunelle were right, while the other part knows I felt the bond break," I squeaked.

"Your heart and your mind. It is a futile struggle." Brass reassured me. "Sleep now, Scarlett. Stop thinking about bedding me or my resolve to wait until you are ready again will waste away."

The insides of my ears burned with my blush and I turned my back to him so he could fuck me into him. I felt him *call* to check on our children. The children he was so careful not to bring up because my fragile mind couldn't take one more thing.

I broke away from Brass's stolen kiss. My skin had prickled and my thoughts were rampant. No more kisses. That was it.

If I didn't have an appointment with Peak, I would've brought Brass back up to my room in the Vetr castle. I hadn't crossed that line yet. Brass stroked my cheek and my chin lifted traitorously to receive another one of his warm, seductive kisses.

He smiled against my lips, and I bit my lip, ducking my head. "Gods, stop that," I whispered.

"I'm waiting patiently, Scarlett. There is no rush. They are only kisses."

"There is no such thing as only kisses with a mind reader. I've known that since the very first one and that feeling has only increased with each one ever after."

My chest felt tight with emotion and I pulled away from him as I smoothed down the emerald velvet dress I wore for my meeting with Peak Haust. Another week had gone by and still no sign of Slate. It'd be three weeks in two days. Shale detached from the shadows and I held up my hand.

"Watch Indi for me, Shale," I told her and she nodded, crossing the room.

She'd become a wraith in the darkness that followed me wherever I went. A part of me wondered if she didn't sometimes hide in my bedroom on the weekends when Brass spent the night in Elivagar. Indigo leaned against the wall across from us with Shale, her and Brass were going to headquarters until I sent word that I returned.

Brass gave me one last squeeze and released me as I turned and swept through the portal door to the Haust castle.

CHAPTER

FIFTY-TWO

High rib vaulted ceilings spanned the long room, dimly lit by incandescent light from wrought iron multitiered chandeliers. A brown clad servant waited for me with her hands loosely clasped in front of her and turned once I got my bearings. Fringed rugs covered the grey stone floors and tapestries hung along the walls. Once again, I felt awful for their cleaning staff.

The medieval castle was something right out of a movie and I was glad I was wearing the Elivagar clothing instead of the loose flowing Thrimilci which would have been out of place here in the rich dark textures and fabrics of the land of perpetual fall.

I had only gone to the Dagr palace once in the last three weeks. Amber and Slate's wing needed repainting and was refurnished. Then I chose a first-floor wing close to the cloister, so we could have picnics outside if we chose. I met with the decorator then and picked out everything within hours. It had been simple. I wanted to replicate the rooms

391

Slate had created in the Sumar palace for us, the only exception being a larger nursery for the twins, plus any children Slate and I would have.

Hawk and Sparrow were in much better spirits, and Sparrow had apologized profusely for having revealed Slate's need for an heir pushing me to abandon him. The only person I was mad at was myself. Never had it crossed my mind to be upset with Sparrow. Hugging Hawk and Sparrow made me feel like I was back in my Chicago, and with Hawk withdrew from me, I almost expected my mother to embrace me next.

I didn't stay after that. Since the wing was being remodeled, I would have to choose another room to sleep in, so I went back to the Elivagar castle. My dirty little secret was that I had actually gone back because the enormous castle was almost always empty and Brass could spend his weekends with me. He didn't ask me if I'd lost hope. He waited, holding me in his arms three nights a week, keeping me company. Shale was still sleeping in my bed at Valla U, though most nights I didn't think she slept so much as rested her eyes.

Gypsum had hinted that they'd been doing more than keeping one another company on the weekends, which baffled me. He said he thought she did it weirdly to be closer to someone who had been with Ama in how she had. He wasn't upset about it, but he had also hinted that one night Shale had come early and had found a certain girl there and there had been another night where Diamond had walked in on him and Shale.

Diamond and Gypsum were still seeing one another.

If I doubted it, I didn't anymore. It explained the uncomfortable tension between them when they'd come to my meeting the week before. Sterling and Quick had been shooting one another volatile glance the entire time and... well, Ash.

The woman opened a set of double doors after leading me up several sets of stairs. Grey pillars with composite capitals lined the enormous bedroom. The doors shut behind me and a felt a surge of panic.

"*Ah*. There you are. Come change. That dress is not suitable for travel."

Peak came from behind a bronze changing screen, fastening blades to his biceps. I'd never seen the Haust Patriarch in anything other than his brown and gold ambassador robes. Silver threaded his onyx hair at the temples and with a bit more curl than Slate's, but he was just as big as his nephew, with the same bronze skin. I hadn't realized how fit he was under his robes. He was older than my father, but Guardians aged differently. We slowed at the ripe age of twenty so we could live well past a hundred.

His eyes were so bright they almost looked lime colored from between his long, thick black lashes. He was a strikingly handsome older man with a full mouth. This too was like Slate's. Gods, I must have been blind. His only fault, if you could call it that, was the tip of his nose was broad and rounded. I liked a little character to men's faces though, too perfect could get boring. Maybe I only told myself that because of my too full lips.

Peak was no handsome young man there to court me. He had a disingenuous sweetness to him that put my guard up. No respectable man would meet his nephew's wife in his bedroom. He raised his thick brows at me from his chiseled face.

"There are clothes on the table for you, as well as a pack with a roll. I have sent a messenger letting them know we have this last-minute excursion," Peak said.

I would not splutter. I held my chin high as I crossed the room to the screen and found the clothes he'd mentioned. With great effort and a feeling of uneasiness that crept over me, I disrobed.

"Will your wife and children be joining us?" I asked, finally having calmed my nerves.

"Willow is visiting her mother in Elivagar at the Natt castle. My children's spouses are all Straumrs and once a week they have dinner together at their palace. Any other personal questions you wish to know, child?" Peak asked dryly.

I pulled the thick cream sweater over my head as I blushed. The outfit fit, as did the sturdy brown boots I tucked my forest green pants into. I ran my hands over my hair after I removed the pins and emerged from behind the screen. His lime green eyes scanned me and he nodded.

"I didn't bring any weapons," I confessed, as I counted the blades around his body.

"Surely an elemental can take care of herself, Mrs. Tio," Peak said dryly, and my cheek twitched.

I picked the pack off the floor and found a roll, a change of clothes, and two meals securely packed in the bundle. I slung it over my head so it rested against my back and carefully folded my velvet dress over a chair so it wouldn't wrinkle.

"Will your wife wonder why a woman's garment is in your bedroom?" I asked, and he laughed deeply, making me flush again.

"Dear child, you do not threaten my wife," Peak said, giving me a smug smile, and I dropped my eyes.

The bedroom threw me off, but I couldn't very well change in the hallway or the office. I'd keep my guard up, as I'd intended to do.

Peak held a cloak in his hand as he crossed the room to tower over me and swung the deep brown cloak over my shoulders before lifting my hair from my neck with his *calling* and pinning it at my throat with a gold jumis button. His manicured hands slid over my shoulders, looking down approvingly before he spun back to the door and walked without looking back.

I had no choice but to follow him out.

My heart hurt.

Mabon reminded me of Slate, from its crisp fallen leaves scent to the memories of us having been together after months of separation and making love.

Frigga's sweet grass. How I missed that man.

I'd been having terrible nightmares, the same nightmare I'd had since as long as I could remember, and seeing Slate lying dead in my dreams tormented me. Shale and Brass had gotten very good at comforting me when I woke up in tears. Fiddlestick, it was embarrassing.

At some point, as I walked along Peak through the dark lush grass that covered the undulating knolls and stone bridges that covered the creeks and streams that ran through Mabon, he stopped talking to me as one would a disobedient child. I felt emboldened as I listened to him speak about his childhood and Slate's father, Lark. He captivated me. I smiled and laughed as he regaled me with stories of Hawk and Lark when they were adolescents.

"I never knew Hawk was such a hellion."

Peak's lime green eyes gazed down at me with a knowing mirth and I smiled up at him. He pointed ahead through the forest and we came to a large clearing at the top of a hill.

"We shall camp here tonight," Peak said, laying down the pieces of wood he'd collected as we walked.

I frowned. "This is far from the town portal gate, isn't it? Not really conducive to travelers."

Peak gave me that belittling glance he'd given me in his bedroom and bit my lip. Peak was Slate's uncle. I now probably knew more about his father than he did. Slate had a chance to learn a great deal from Peak, and I realized I had wanted to impress him. It wasn't too late; I had more time on the way back to dazzle him with my wit.

Peak started a small campfire in the clearing, and I set out my roll. "Orion does not confide in you, despite appearances."

I sat down on my roll and pulled my carefully packed dinner from my pack and ate the apple that Peak's staff supplied.

"What makes you say that?" I asked in a casual tone.

We'd walked for three hours. We could have done this tomorrow, unless it was like he said and he'd only thought of it tonight. "Orion has been trying to create more portals. Who do you think helped repair the Dagr gate?"

"I hadn't thought about it. He offered to procure me a gate when I had moved outside of Tidings." I noted. "Has he come up with a way to create them or only repair them?"

Peak snapped out his roll next to mine and I distracted myself by taking another bite of the sweet and tart green apple.

He was an attractive older man, but he was married and Slate's uncle. I had more than enough trouble on my hands. Besides, I was a callow girl. Willow was a cultured woman of renown beauty. The idea he would be interested in his nephew's wife was utterly ridiculous. Still, I was on edge.

There was his scent. Yes, that must have been it. It was detrimentally close to Slate's with its smell of fallen leaves and vetiver, subtle but undeniably masculine. He sat down next to me and ran his hand through his obsidian curls that bounced back once his hand had left them. He raised a dark brow over his lime green eyes that seemed to glow against his bronze skin as his lips curled and I slowly looked out towards the fire, not wanting to give him the impression that he'd caught me ogling.

I wasn't; I was making comparisons.

"Wine?" He offered a wineskin up to me, and I bit my lip.

"I'm pregnant, Peak," I said, and he chuckled.

"Willow had a glass of red every time we supped while she carried the children. Live a little, Mrs. Tio."

Peak pushed the wineskin into my hand, and I gave him a reluctant smile as I balanced the apple on my lap to drink from it. Peak clapped his hands and drank deeply when I passed it back to him. I went back to eating my meal and carefully folded the wax paper back into my pack before pulling my cloak tightly around me.

"Cold?" Peak asked, as he finished his own dinner of cheeses and dried meats.

"No. I don't get cold anymore," I said, and he leaned back so he rested on his elbow with his legs crossed in front of him towards the fire.

"Ah. The fire elemental. I imagine you would not. Tell me, Mrs. Scarlett, what did you say to the other greater families to win them over? I hear there is not an island who has not bowed down to your wishes." Peak's eyes glinted in the firelight, making my breath catch. "Being from outside of Tidings, you cannot fully appreciate the accomplishment."

Maybe my uneasiness came from him being a condescending tool bag.

I drank from my finger *calling* water and laid back to look at the stars that reminded me of Brass. "I told them the truth. That we have broken the bonds between the islands for two decades and they needed something that would unite them. I may own the arenas, but men from Ostara will oversee it. Each arena will have an individual from a different island to see to the day to day. People will flock to each arena every other week. Each team having their own competitors. If it all goes well, we could introduce tribesmen. Personally, I find they are more civilized than some Guardians." I flushed when I remembered who I was speaking to. "I'm sorry —"

Peak leaned on his side, and I could feel those eyes on the side of my face. "Ash was not kind to you, was he? I suppose your half-brother has never hid his disdain."

"Until we broke off our engagement, Ash was very kind. We weren't a good fit. Sage... he's his mother's son," I said, heaving a sigh.

Peak chuckled. "An apt statement."

I turned my face towards him with a smile and started. With his eyes closed when he smiled, he looked like Slate. I turned my head back towards the sky. It hurt to look at him.

"Do you believe he is truly out there?" Peak asked, not needing to refer to whom.

"He has to be," I whispered.

"He resembles my brother and myself." Peak said, resting his head on his balled-up pack facing me.

"He does," I admitted.

"You are not sleeping alone tonight, Scarlett. I imagine you have not needed to since he has been gone. A beautiful girl such as yourself must have suitors already waiting in line." Peak murmured.

I bunched my pack under my head. "I have good friends who take care of me. When Slate returns, he'll be grateful so many came to his wife's aid and note the ones who turned on him."

"Good night, Scarlett," Peak said, and I chewed the inside of my cheek.

"Good night, Peak."

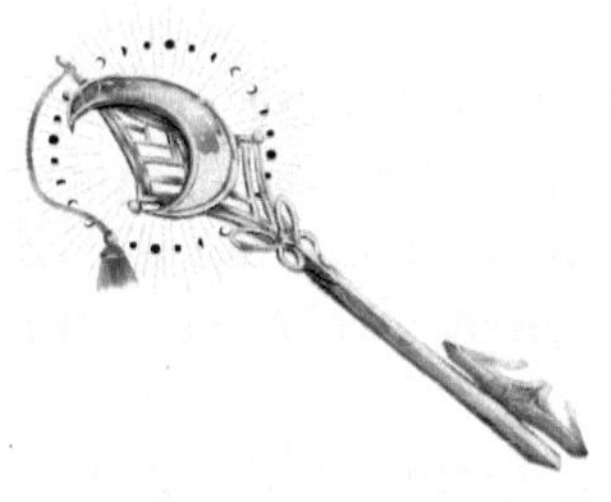

I'm walking through the carnage. I feel her; I hear her. She's standing in a white dress, arms held out. She is my mother. She tells me I can fix this. I try not to look at the bodies, the battleground alongside Valla University. Not everyone is dead. Frozen angry faces stare up at angry faces in the castle. I can't even tell if the faces are human. They all look like monsters to me. The wind is whipping at me. I look up at the sky, even the sky is angry. Black clouds, lightening without rain. She's all around me. "You are night."

I stand in the middle of a circle, people around the edges. Slate lies on the ground in a pool of blood. Light and gushing wind blasts from my body, my hair, my hands, shoot up. My mouth opens in a silent scream.

I didn't normally jackknife awake after the dream, but when I opened my eyes, feeling disoriented. Dawn was peeking over the trees and the scent of fall filled my lungs, making me choke.

"Oh, Slate," I whispered, covering my face, remembering where I was.

A heavy hand rested on my shoulder, making me jump. Messy grey hair framed Peak's face as he regarded me with lime green eyes full of speculation.

"A nightmare?" he asked, and I nodded, not willing to try my voice and have it come out weak and strangled.

I must be strong. This man is not my friend, no matter how kind he was being on the trip.

"What are your thoughts?" Peak asked, not removing his hand from my shoulder, and nodded to the clearing.

I rose to my feet, letting his hand slide from me, and looked around. I walked to the edge and looked down, wrapping my cloak around me. What I thought were shrubs last night was actually a tree line that fell from the plateau. The arena would have a gorgeous view of lower Mabon.

"It's beautiful," I breathed, watching the sun's lazy climb into the sky.

Peak moved up just behind me, so his chest brushed the back of my head. "I have lived nowhere else. You may put your arena here, Scarlett."

Excitement shot through me, and I turned too quickly and lost my balance. I wasn't completely awake yet, and he gripped my shoulders, looking down at me.

"You won't regret it," I said, searching his eyes.

His full lips curled. "I imagine I will not. Come. Night falls early in the land of autumn. We will sign your contracts over an early dinner."

WITH MY MOOD SKY HIGH, the walk back to the Haust castle went quickly as I took in the trees that grew in the warm colors of autumn. Slate's home island was beautiful and rich with its scents. Peak came to wild rose bushes and plucked a crimson rose from the shrubbery and slid it behind my ear with a smile. I thanked him, blushing, and we started forward again.

We didn't speak as much on our way back. I was too busy mentally scanning the construction companies Indigo had interviewed for me in the last week. Gods, we had been so busy. Once the sites started going up, we would have our excuse to be seen traveling around all the islands and I could finally find Slate.

We crossed over a mossy stone bridge and Haust castle came into view on its hilltop like a portal through time with its grey stone ramparts and barbican. The deep brown clad Guardians that stood at the moat didn't make eye contact as Peak led us into the castle and his servants rushed to meet him, taking our packs from us.

"Baths have been prepared," a staff member said, and Peak nodded as he climbed the impressive stone stairs.

I sniffed myself and frowned. I didn't stink.

"Show her the way," Peak said dismissively, and I grimaced as they led me up another staircase.

FIFTY-THREE

After I argued with the servants who would not leave the bathroom that housed the tub that could have fit five people in it, I growled as I stripped and got into the bubble bath they prepared. I drew the line when they tried to scrub me with handled brushes. Honestly, I was glad Pearl was so independent from her staff that they were more like friends than servants.

I pursed my lips as they dressed me in Mabon fashion. A heavy teal silk dress with a low squared neckline. There were fewer skirts than the Elivagar style, but with a small bustle. The fabrics were lighter also, taffetas and thick silks. Ivory silk spilled at my three-quarter sleeves and around the back of my collar.

Servants opened the double doors that led to the dining hall, where Peak stood next to a roaring stone fireplace. Contrary to the halls in the castle, the floors in the dining hall were a gleaming gold and brown marble. The walls were painted in grand fight scenes that supported the groin vaulted ceiling from which hung three wrought-iron chandeliers.

Peak turned and smiled at me. He oiled away his hair from his face, which made him look younger than he had yesterday. Peak wore a long sleeve brown satin jerkin with gold leaf buckles that trimmed the edges in a metallic gold. He held up a golden chalice before drinking deeply from it.

"You look lovely, Scarlett," he said, and I unwittingly ran my palms over the tight teal bodice.

"My thanks." I wasn't sure if I should compliment him on the return, so instead I gestured to the long-polished wood table and he nodded.

I almost sighed in relief as I crossed the room to the place sitting that sat on the right of Peak's seat. Peak beat me to the square wooden chair with a gold jacquard upholstery and pulled out my seat for me. His fingers brushed the side of my neck as he backed away, and I swallowed. Purely by accident, I was sure.

He sat down and servants brought out our first course. Women dressed in brown bustled dresses served us broths with golden spoons. My life had taken a turn. A gild freaking spoon.

A salad with turnips and nuts came next with vinegar and oil dressing.

"Wine?" Peak asked, as I sopped up soup with a buttered slice of freshly baked bread.

"Just a glass, then I must stick to water."

"Of course," Peak said and pulled the top off a small crystal decanter and poured a burgundy liquid into my gold chalice.

I drank deeply; the wine heating my stomach, and I made an embarrassing noise of contentment. I blushed and Peak smiled at me over his chalice with glittering lime eyes.

"Excuse me. I rarely enjoy such delicious repasts now that I'm back at Valla University."

"Too few women eat with such zeal. I find it charming," Peak said, as the firelight danced in his eyes.

I ran my teeth over my lower lip and drank the rest of my wine. A flaky blackened white fish was next to a creamy sauce, followed by roasted mutton. I could hardly take a bite with my corset pressing against my ribs. I caught myself fanning my face and froze.

"I'm not used to the heavy dresses. Thrimilci has such loose fabrics," I said gustily, and Peak filled my goblet with water.

As I took the glass from his hand, he slid his fingertips over mine and my skin prickled. The swell of my breasts tightened visibly to my eyes in my low-cut dress. I drank from my goblet, hoping my fever would extinguish. I wasn't sweating, just feeling hot and achy.

My heart thumped in my chest as servants brought out a chocolate mousse. It hurt my stomach to even look at. Peak's spoon dipped into the mousse and he lifted it to his full lips. A soft pink tongue licked across the golden spoon as he took it into his mouth and my lips parted in a low moan. My eyes widened and looked down at my desert.

"Could you possibly heal me? I am feeling... out of sorts. It's warm in here, yes?" I asked, resisting the urge to unbutton my dress.

Peak's lips curled, and I caught his scent. That fire inside me, the rousen, never let die. My over developed pleasure center that caused me to scent pheromones flared into awareness. I sucked in a sharp breath as he shifted in his seat and reached over to place his hand over my wrist with a featherlight touch. I felt his warmth slide into me like a caress and my insides coiled with pleasure.

"You carry my nephew's sons," Peak asked, looking at me through hooded eyes.

Gods, I knew that look. Slate had given it to me enough times that I was intimately familiar with it. Carnal desire barely leashed. I thought about cutting my hand so my blood would activate my bond with Brass. Judging from the way my body was responding to Peak though, I doubted by the time he reached me I'd go with willingly, if Brass could even reach me.

"No," I breathed in a gravelly tone.

Peak pushed from his seat and the doors at the end of the hall sealed, and a bar fell across them. Peak took his hand and pushed me away from the table. And slid his hand into my hair at my nape, making me look up at him. I did through slitted eyelids and kissed the inside of his wrist. His full lips parted into a deeper, more sinister smile. Not like Slate at all.

Peak unbuckled his jerkin as I sat in numb adoration. "Did you know a barghest can only mate with one human? We mate for life. We are very particular about who we choose. She must have all our desired attributes. Some die without knowing what it is like to lie with a human woman in our barghest form."

We?

Barghest?

Frigga's sweet grass!

"*But* did you know we can mate with tribeswomen in our barghest form without it forming a bond?"

"No," I breathed, unaware of where the thought came from.

"I thought not. Lark never had time to teach his son how to be barghest. All the secrets there are to be told." Peak laid his jerking over his chair and removed his sleeveless white linen shirt and unbuckled his snug brown pants. "If he had wanted or needed to, he could have forced you to mate with him after the first time. It bonded you to him after that. You could never deny him if he pressed. Pressed, not forced, mind you. You are as bonded to him as he is to you. Your rousen training has given you a unique advantage, making you more resilient. Unfortunately, my nephew will not be back to claim you."

Peak grabbed me up under the arms and lifted me to my feet and I struggled with my urges, fighting against them with everything I had. My mind floundered and failed to make my body react in any way that would deprive me of the pleasure Peak promised.

Peak hands swept the polished wood table, sending the golden utensils and plates to shatter on the marble floor. He picked me up by my hips and sat me on the wet table where the goblets had spilled before crashing to the floor. My chest heaved and Peak's eyes glowed in truth. No normal human had lime green eyes.

Peak kicked off his boots and revealed his bronze naked body that did not belong to a man over twenty years my senior, when his bones stretched. His skin darkened and hair forced from his follicles. Two sets of horns grew from his scalp and tusks pushed from his elongating jaw. He was a barghest shifter. A moan pulled from my throat as he took a step towards me.

He wasn't the dark charcoal grey with sleek fur like Slate. He was a heather grey that made his eyes gleam above his snout full of long, sharp teeth. Peak smiled at me with those teeth as long as my hand.

"I knew he had shown you his true self. I have waited decades to claim a mate, Scarlett. You understand the privilege I bestow upon you? Not even my wife has had me in my true form," Peak rasped, still managing to speak in a civilized manner Slate had not managed yet.

"Why?" I croaked.

I knew it would be the last word I uttered before I slipped under deep in the whirling tide that drowned me even as I placidly sat there. His wolfish grin deepened.

"I heard your resistance was high. I promise. It will only be this once. I will not have to resort to such underhanded tactics in the future. You will be *mine*, Scarlett. My mate. I take care of *mine*. You may keep my nephew's bairn, but then you will carry my son. Barghests never lose their fertility, as Guardians do." Peak took another step towards me, so he stood between my legs, looking down at me.

That wasn't what I was asking, and he seemed to see it in my eyes. "Whether you like it, you are a khoraz now. With my help, you will attain power and command respect as a powerful, well-bred barghest khoraz. It is puerile to mention that you are one of the most beautiful women in Tidings, young, supple, and fertile. Who knew Alder and Wren's daughter would have a beauty to surpass us all? You are familiar with a claiming, I take it?"

I was.

Before Slate had laid claim to me, he had given me a tongue bath so his scent was all over me. He'd done it again in a more... intimate way on the lake shore of the Wemic lands. When he'd finally claimed my body bonding us together as a barghest and his mate, I'd been deep in a rousen stupor. I remembered being incredibly sore the next morning. The beast had come out in him and Peak had been just as violent.

The teal dress laid in shredded tatters on the dining hall floor when he carried me in a tapestry he'd yanked off the wall upstairs to the bedroom he shared with his wife. It wasn't for my modesty. I had none at that point. I only wanted Peak to give me pleasure and to give it a return. It was because I was his mate and, like Slate; he was possessive, like some primitive animal. The servants that usually lined the halls to await his needs had disappeared. Nowhere in my mind would I have cared if they'd seen us naked in the halls.

After a while in his marital bed, he'd changed back into a man. He had the stamina of a much younger man and years seemed to shed from him as he took me over and over. I was helpless to it; I encouraged it — basked in it. At some point I passed out whatever had built up in Peak over the years. He's shed onto me, wearing me out.

He kissed my swollen lips, waking me from my slumber and climbed over me to pad across the room to where a long robe laid across a chaise lounge. He slipped it over his shoulders, tying it loosely around his waist, and walked over to the door.

I rose to my feet quickly, wincing at the soreness while he was distracted. Slate was never so rough with me. I took the sheet with me, wrapping it around my body as I walked over to the changing screen.

"Bring me the contracts." Peak called into the hall.

He turned around, and a smile played on his lips as I hurried with downcast eyes to where my dress draped over the chair I'd left it two days ago.

Two days.

Light shone in through the stained-glass windows that lined the medieval bedroom. I heard the servant lay the papers on the desk against the wall across from the changing screen, and Peak appeared at the side of the screen where I stood in only my corset and petticoat. His bronze muscles peeked from the long robe, not hard like Slate's, but that of a man who still took care of his body. I did whimper pathetically then when I realized I felt a certain attraction to him now that he claimed me.

"Did you not find last night pleasurable, sweet Scarlett?" Peak said, pressing closer.

"You drugged me with rousen." I accused, and his lime green eyes flared.

Not Slate. Not even close. This man had none of the compassion

Slate had towards me and my big mouth. I always knew I lived at the barghest's leisure, now I had one who had forced himself on me and would probably be indifferent to my death. He'd tear my throat out like one might swat through a spider's web.

"An unfortunate necessity. I hope I will not have to repeat," he said sternly, and I tried to look away to hide the tears that threatened.

Peak gripped my face like a vise.

"You are *mine*."

Something had snapped at the words Slate had said affectionately, coming from a man who planned to use it as a weapon. My heat blazed to life, and I squared my shoulders.

"You *forced* me. Make no mistake about my willingness last night. You drugged me. I may be a barghest khoraz, but I have a choice. I'm married to your nephew. You are married. You chose me because I'm beautiful and powerful? Did you think I would so willingly submit once you'd taken me because I've always been so compliant with my lovers? I fight — always. I'm good at it. Consider last night a onetime gift." I narrowed my eyes at Peak who had steadily grown.

"Your life is a small flicker of a flame that I can extinguish as easily as I breathe. With just as much effort. I am giving you your arena; I can take it away," Peak threatened.

"I paid my price in flesh. It's mine by right," I countered.

"Take the contracts, Scarlett. Go home and lick your wounds. I will forget this transgression. You would not be a Tio woman if you did not reject acceptable offers in favor of disreputable ones," Peak said, turning his back to me.

"Acceptable?" I laughed. "Call it whatever you want, but it doesn't change the fact that you took what I did not offer. It will not happen again."

I grabbed my dress hastily in my hand and skirted him as I went to the desk to find all the contracts signed with the deed to the land for the arena. I rolled them up in my free hand and started towards the door when Peak grabbed me around the wrist and yanked me back.

"You think because you are an elemental, you are protected, sweet Scarlett? Did you know your husband murdered Jonquil Kaldr? Snapped her neck. She could not run fast enough." His lips curled at my appalled expression. "I did not think he told you. He is an animal. I am an animal. You want a rightful claim to being forced, my sweet? I can oblige."

He switched his grip, and I winced as his big hand wrapped around my frail throat. Pain exploded in my face as he backhanded me, and darkness crept into the corners of my vision. The room spun as he dug his fingers into my belly and I flared to life. I didn't care about the consequences of burning Peak to ashes. I wanted him dead.

He clicked his tongue. He wasn't burning.

"I must teach a lesson today so I do not have to repeat myself."

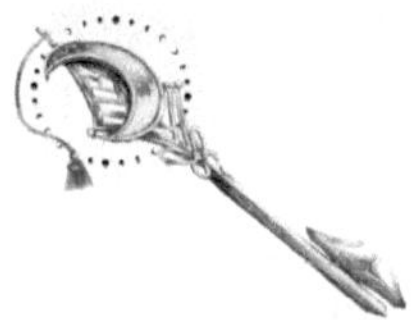

With trembling fingers, I pulled my emerald velvet dress on and fastened the clasps. I licked my swollen, bleeding lower lip and tried to smooth my hair down. My heeled boots crunched over the mirror we'd broken in our fight, and I stepped over the writing desk that Peak had shoved at me when I'd reached the door. I broke its legs after I'd taken one off to swing at him like a club. I'd been screaming, and no one had come. A patch of hair was missing at my nape, where he'd gripped it. I knew my mouth would push someone too far one day.

Peak had turned into the barghest, and I fought tooth and nail against him as an elemental. My heat barely fazed him. When I'd tried to use the table leg as a club, he'd plucked it from my hands like a parent would snatch away a dangerous object from a toddler and kicked me in the stomach, sending me sprawling. I'd given up then, unwilling to risk the lives of Brass's children.

He'd made me pay for my insolent words, but it wasn't the abuse I expected. He fought me to prove that I could throw everything I had at him and he would still win. Resistance was futile and my life hung in the balance.

Peak slipped his robe back over his shoulders in his human form and walked over to me with the rolled-up contracts. I'd clawed his flesh with my nails until they'd broken and blood trailed down his bronze chest and his cheeks. He held out the contracts, and I took them limply from him.

"My babies," I whispered and flinched when he brought his hand to my stomach.

Warmth spread through me. "Two boys. Healthy. I swear it." Peak looked down his nose at me. "Scarlett, it was not my wish to hurt you, but you need to be humble. You cannot hope to win against me. The sooner you accept it, the happier you shall be. This need not be an untoward arrangement. You are my mate; I wish to care for you and you me." He cupped my face, and I lowered my gaze. "I would have you know you are quite a talented lover. Be proud, sweet Scarlett."

Peak kissed my broken lips and withdrew, leaving a wet spot on my cheek where his blood brushed my skin.

"You may leave. I shall call on you when I need you again."

I started to the door and opened it to find the hall empty.

"*Oh*, and Scarlett." Peak called after me, and I stopped to look back at him. "Your mouth is definitely the most talented I have experienced. I would heal the rest of you, but a little humility would go a long way."

I shut the door behind me as I hobbled down the hall. Not even the Merfolk had done this for me. It was different. It wasn't about my body; that was about Peak's power over me. Wanting to break my spirit and cow me. By the Mother, how I hurt.

Servants didn't spare me a second glance, and I wondered if Peak had done it before. I doubted it. A man in his position, with his looks, wouldn't have a problem getting women to lie with him, but maybe he didn't like the willing kind. My mind turned over the events of the last two days and I hobbled to the portal room, trying to decide where I could go to receive healing, where no one would judge me. I could only think of one place.

The Mother granted my prayer, and I stepped out into the Shadow Breaker's secret portal door. I shut the studded wood carved door was against the dark grey wall and opened the door on the opposite end that led to the hall at the top level of headquarters. Navy walls lit by golden sconces appeared extra bright as they gleamed off the polished wood floor.

The next door was Cordillera's, and I knocked softly on it, hoping she was in and not in a compromising position. I had no idea what time it was, but assumed it was after breakfast. My stomach churned, but I had no desire to eat. The door opened to reveal a surprised, undressed, Chafer. His dark hair was messy, and his thick, slanted brows were high on his angular face.

"How —" He started and then took a step back, seeing that I was bloodied and bruised.

I could feel my nose swelling and my left eye had shut on me. My right arm felt broken. It was pulsing with lightning pain that shot to my elbow and shoulder. The rest of me would be mottled with bruises. Gods, I hurt.

"I didn't want my family to see me like this. I'm sorry I used the secret portal."

Anger, frustration, and hate were my bedmates. Cordillera pulled the door open and her red lips pinched together as she took me in.

"Put some pants on, Chafer." She scolded, and his wide mouth grinned wickedly at her as he walked away.

She tied her red robe tight and brought me into the room. Red velour bedding with a matching canopy on a cherry wood pillared bed, tapestries over walls with red as the prominent color, dark wood floors so polished they reflect the light from the gold sconces along her bedroom walls. The adjoining closet was as big as some people's bedrooms. Chafer made himself at home sprawling across a maroon couch in her sitting area a dozen feet from her floorboard, shirtless, to expose his torso that had zero percent fat on it.

She led me to the couch opposite Chafer and had just sat down when we heard pounding coming from the hallway. Chafer hopped to his feet, chuckling.

"He must have run. Just a moment," Chafer said, closing the door behind him.

My eyes went wide, and I shot to my feet, forgetting how bad my legs felt, and toppled to the floor with a cry. Cordillera's arms hooked under mine and was lifting me when Brass, Quick, and Indigo burst into the room.

So much for not letting my family find out. My hair had fallen in front of my face and I peered out pathetically at them.

CHAPTER 54
INDIGO

I'd been training with Brass late both nights, with Silver not making any pretense of watching, as if Brass or I would do anything together. It was such an absurd notion that we hadn't bothered to correct. Training with Brass had also made me absorb his talent, and it attuned me to Scarlett's mind.

When she suddenly appeared nearby, feeling vulnerable and in pain, Brass had run. Silver had said if Brass ever ran, run with him. I knew he was going to Scarlett and Silver hadn't asked a single question as we charged up the stairs and beat down the door.

Brass knocked Chafer up against the wall, who had known exactly what door she would be behind. I strangled a wail when we came through the door to find Scarlett on her knees, being lifted by Cordillera back onto the couch.

Hair matted to her head in snarled tangles. Her left eye was turning black and was so swollen I couldn't see the eye beneath it. As were her lips — swollen and cracked, so dried blood caked the seams. Her cheekbone bore a purple bruise, and one look at her nails told me she had put up a fight. They were jagged with blood beneath them.

She lowered her eyes, and I saw a tear fall from her good eye. "Don't look at me," she croaked. "The babies are okay."

Brass hadn't broken stride and now he was on his knees in front of her and Cordillera slid away to where Chafer stood. I stepped to her other side and Silver put his hand on my shoulder. Brass's hands hovered around her face until he settled for brushing her hair from her eyes. She looked up at him piteously and tried to lubricate her lips with her tongue.

"Please don't pry into my mind, Brass. I'm begging you." Her chin wobbled.

"I can't do that," he ground out.

Brass held up his hand to heal her, and she flinched away. She raised a turquoise eye to me.

"Indi," she rasped and swallowed visibly.

... Don't tell them what you find...

Brass swung his head to me and back to Scarlett. Brass would not allow that. He grabbed Scarlett's knee, and she whimpered. I couldn't help myself as I touched her other knee and recoiled. My head turned, and Silver wrapped his arm over my back. I had no right to cry in front of her.

How had she gotten there?

Her facial injuries were just the ones we could see. Undressed bruises would have covered her. The attacker broke her arm, and it was a miracle the babies survived the attack. Whoever it was must have healed her.

It made little sense and then I saw what she gripped in her hand. I reached for them and her hand tensed reflexively until she opened her healed eyes and released them.

"The deed to the land in Mabon for the arena. We'll have all five islands," she said, sounding clearer.

Her throat had been raw from screaming. No one had helped her.

"Who?" was all I could utter, pulling away from Silver's comfort.

Scarlett licked her now healed lips and looked at Brass. She was doing a good job of not revealing who it was, which meant it was someone we knew. Brass's mind was running rampant as well as Silver's, but only Brass was thinking about taking Scarlett into his room here so he could replace the other man's abuse with his own gentle caresses.

I was at a loss. I wasn't the only one. Brass turned to Cordillera.

"Lera, we need to use your bathroom," he said in a soft, dangerous tone.

Cordillera strode across the room to a door next to the headboard and the sound of running water followed her out. Cordillera and Chafer both walked into a closet, and Brass helped Scarlett to her feet. All of our hard work trying to show people we were to be respected. That the men responsible for our parents' deaths should be afraid. Now they abused Scarlett in the most fundamental way they could abuse a woman. Why save the babies?

She looked behind to me and I got to my feet to follow them in. Silver walked with me, and I shot him a look.

"I have seen your sister naked as many times as I have seen you naked." Silver shrugged and I kept walking, determined not to argue.

Scarlett leaned against the black granite counter as Brass kneeled, unzipping her boots, and then unclasped her dress. Her eyes were far away as Brass pulled her dress over her head to reveal a bloodied corset and petticoat in tatters. Long strips hung from it. It looked like claw marks and I was suddenly wishing we'd done that before we'd healed her to see the extent of the marks, but as long as she was healed, it was all that mattered.

"Get out, Silver." Brass's voice was little more than a growl.

Silver didn't argue. There wouldn't be much he could do to help, and Scarlett wasn't herself. She wouldn't be yelling at him to leave in her condition.

"Scarlett, may I bathe you?" Brass asked, and she blinked blankly at him.

"Do you want me to?" I offered giving her an option.

Scarlett turned her matted head towards me.

... Brass...

She thought, and I nodded before I stepped out of the bathroom. Silver's head was in his hands where he sat on the couch and Cordillera and Chafer sat across from him, dressed and speaking in low tones.

"Slate would kill us all if he found out we let this happen to her. The Mother protects us if he is dead. He will haunt us until we join him in the afterlife," Silver muttered into his hands.

I sat down next to him, unable to form a full sentence in my mind. "The babies are okay. That's what matters. Scarlett's strong. She'll survive it with our help."

I ran my palms over my black pants and Silver slid his arm around my shoulders and pulled me to him. He kissed the top of my head and I leaned into him.

"Sure she will, after we find the bastard and kill him," Chafer said like he was talking about going out for dinner.

"What I do not get is that she must not have shifted into her elemental form," Silver said, and I sighed.

"You didn't feel her injuries, Silver. Whoever did this was very strong. You can't shift if you're unconscious, or in Scarlett's case, if they threaten to kill her babies. She'd do anything to keep them, even let a man do *that* to her."

Silver ran his hand along my biceps in a soothing gesture, and a high moan came from the bathroom. Chafer ran his hand over his mouth.

"That is one way to make her feel better."

I pressed my lips together and glared at Chafer. They weren't sleeping together. I picked that much up from their minds. Not yet, anyway.

"Do you think someone in Mabon... Obviously it happened in Mabon. Someone we know from the way she's hiding it." I licked my lips. "Peak wouldn't, right?"

Cordillera leaned back and clasped her hands in her lap. "Anything is possible."

FIFTY-FIVE

Brass slid into the bathtub behind me and washed my body with feather light caresses. I rested my head back on his shoulder and shut my eyes, intent on pretending we were back in Chicago and Slate was safe. The weekend never happened.

Brass washed my hair and untangled it with gentle fingers and massaged my scalp. He kissed my throat as he rinsed my hair, and then he trailed those kisses over every inch of my skin. Cleaned and healed. I still had a phantom soreness. Brass lifted me up to the lip of the tub and kissed along my legs until he reached the apex of my thighs.

My fingers twined in his thick hair as he kissed and sucked until I moaned aloud, trying to bite my lip to keep the others from hearing. Brass pulled me back into the tub and into his arms so I straddled his lap. I buried my face in the crook of his neck and he kissed my cheek. The stubble of his jaw grazing my skin as I wrapped my arms around his neck.

My body shook with tears that wouldn't come, and he held tight. "Tell me who did this to you."

"It's over. He'll get his," I whispered, and Brass pulled back to look at me.

"Scarlett, I know you know this, but I have never said the words." He tilted my chin up and pressed my lips with his. "I cannot let this go. I can be smart about it, serve my revenge cold. Scarlett..." He lifted my chin with his thumb as he held my nape. "I am in love with you. I love that you will be the mother of my children and want to spend the rest of my days with you."

His amber eyes were inches away from mine and kissed me deeply, forcing my mouth wide and I gave myself over to Brass.

"I don't want to feel his hands on me," I whispered harshly, and Brass carried me out of the tub.

He laid me on the white plush foam rug that laid over the black marble and Brass looked down at me. "I want to make love to you, but only if you're sure."

I nodded. I wanted him to scour the feel of Peak from my body.

"Make love to me, Brass. Slowly, please."

When I ran my hand up the bed, it ran into a warm body. Panic welled up in me and I tried to jump away.

"Relax, Scarlett. It's me," Brass said, banding an arm around my naked body.

We were in his room at Shadow Breaker headquarters. "How did I get here?" I asked.

"I carried you in Lera's robe." Brass nodded to the red robe over the back of his brown microfiber couch.

I sighed and rubbed my palms to my eyes. "The others?"

"Are keeping it quiet. Indigo is staying with Silver. Chafer and

Cordillera sent the deed and contracts to your room at Orion's. It was Peak Haust. I know, Scarlett. You touched me enough that it shown through. He's a barghest, Slate did not know." Brass's tone was measured, and I felt his eyes on me.

"I shouldn't be here," I said, but made no move to get up. "He claimed me, Brass. He gave me a hefty dose of rousen and —" I choked off and Brass pulled me close.

"I know. Are you hungry?" he asked.

He was very naked. "I am, but... I really shouldn't be here."

I scooted up in his bed and ran my hands over my hair, touching the tiny bald patch at my nape. I pulled his sheets to my chest and Brass pushed up next to me with the sheets in his lap.

"You still need to eat, don't you?" he asked, sliding his hand into mine.

"I am hungry," I admitted. "What time is it?"

"Around ten. I will go grab you dinner and then you can stay the night. Clothes, no clothes... your choice," he said, leaning forward and hovered just before my lips, and I tilted my chin to meet his. He smiled. "I will take care of you, Scarlett. I swear it."

CHAPTER 56
INDIGO

"Stay, Indigo. We will just sleep. I swear it."

Likely story.

I tugged at my arm that Silver held at the wrist. "You're so full of it, Silver."

Silver drew his brows down. "Fine. Then come back to my bed and let go. I care about you, dove." He let go of my wrist and wiped a hand over the dark close-cropped hair at the back of his head.

I stopped struggling and stood facing him. "Silver. We are not compatible. I lied about the sex not being good, but everything else was the truth. If Peak did this to Scarlett, then Sterling needs to know."

Silver took a step forward. "It always boils down to him, does it not? The son of a brutal rapist."

"The son is not responsible for the father's sins," I said coolly.

"Is Scarlett still here?" he asked.

"She's staying the night." I couldn't help the blush that rose to my cheeks. Scarlett was vocal about her appetites.

Silver's lips curled. "Good. They are happy together."

I arched my brow. "Like you care..."

"I do. My family and your family are the same." Silver took a step closer.

"Does that make me your sister? Forget it, Silver. I'm not staying with you. Not now, never again."

I shut the door behind me and slid down it. Freya's burly boar! He never gave up. What did I have to do to make him not want me anymore? It was only a little flattering. I turned my head as a woman walked down the hall and got to my feet.

"Come. I need help," Shale said, carrying boxes down the hall.

I got to my feet. She finally wanted to pack up Ama's things. She shouldn't be alone while she did it.

"She had a crush on you."

I gave a lopsided grin. "I didn't know that."

We'd finished packing up Ama's clothes and sat leaning against the bed eating bowls of ice cream. Shale dipped her spoon into the mint chocolate chip as I ate chocolate.

"Ama had hoped you would invite us to join you and Quick some day," Shale said with a smokey laugh.

My cheeks flushed. "Gypsum said you two were..."

"Fucking? Yes. I have not asked him yet, but I am trying to give my mother what she wants. He is more observant than he seems, so he likely knows I have not been drinking my tea." I barely absorbed her bomb drop when she went on. "I did not sleep with Quick though, if that is what you are getting at. It had been some time since we had invited Quick to bed with us."

"He is free to sleep with whomever he wants, as I am," I told her with a shrug.

Shale laughed. "Life is too short to pretend like you do not feel. Hold tight to those you love. Dance with abandon. Laugh often. *And* howl when you come."

She tossed back her head and howled that broke into laughter when I turned a dangerous shade of red. Her laughing tapered off, and she sobered.

"Amalgam died fighting like a warrior. Her big heart had wanted to defend the Wemic pups. She would not have had it any other way. I should not be here without her," she whispered roughly, and I filled my mouth with chocolate, not knowing what to say.

FIFTY-SEVEN

"You can say those things out loud. I hear them regardless," Brass said as he kissed up my stomach.

His hair was loose and unbraided, so it tickled my ribs as he moved along me. "I'm sorry. I can't stop thinking about him. It's going back on my word and sleeping with you and..."

"And going through what you went through and having him not save you..." Brass continued.

I swallowed hard and nodded. "If Slate was alive, he would have come." I swiped at a tear I had not given permission to fall. "If I had known how long..."

"You would have activated the bond with me. I know, Scarlett. I appreciate you wanting to spare my feelings, but not when you risk your own." He folded his hands under his chin above my belly button and peered up at me.

"I didn't want to torture you again. I should have kept my mouth shut. It may not be too late to report him to the Guardians or something. Not many must know he is barghest. Brass, what if the Faunelle's prophecy isn't about Slate? What if I'm destined to carry Peak's son, and he's Grar Dyr?"

Brass's eyes darkened. "I will never let you come near that man again. If it was up to me, I'd take my team in tonight and rid this world of him."

"We need a better plan than that." I chewed my lip. "I need to ask you something about Slate, and I don't want to be lied to."

From his resigned look, he already knew what I was going to ask. "Yes. Slate has killed many people before. Jonquil included after Ash slapped you that night at the cottages. You do not hurt Slate without him retaliating. Your family, Silver, and I are the only ones I know of that he did not lash out at after being challenged. Nevertheless, he shifted on Jett before. Jett had hit him in the face with a barbell to get him off."

Things were finally coming to light now and stories they'd told, warnings they'd given were making much more sense. My husband was a murderer. I wished I was more than surprised.

"Brass, delve, please," I asked, searching his eyes.

The corners of his mouth quirked as he set his hand to my stomach. I watched as his eyes widened and his smile broadened.

"Boys," he breathed, and I nodded, biting down on my lip.

"Your sons," I whispered.

Brass sucked in a shuddering breath. "I have been waiting for you to come around. I cannot help how happy I am that you are having my sons, Scarlett."

I kissed his stubbled jaw and nuzzled his face. "Me too, Brass. Everyone thinks they're Slate's. Why haven't you corrected them?" I asked, trying to not let the hurt seep into my tone.

"The only reason Peak did not let our sons die is because he thought one would be the Dagr heir. We know they are mine, as does your family. Until we take care of Peak, we can keep up the ruse. I fully intend on claiming my children if that's what was upsetting you."

I pulled my lips between my teeth and nodded, feeling relief wash through me. I should've known Brass wouldn't shirk his fatherly duties. I felt nothing but love from him.

"One more time. I don't want to go to classes today." I ran my hand along his stubbled jaw and Brass kissed the inside of my wrist.

"You must go. You have missed too much already. I'm not going anywhere. We can clean out your room in Elivagar tonight and you can stay here with me until you're ready to move into the Dagr palace." I made a face and Brass sat up, leveling his eyes at me. "You want to raise your children there? You know you do. We will only be apart for a short time and then I can move in as your paramour until you are ready." *For more.*

"Paramour? I think you've been my hand-fasted spouse for some time now." I squeezed my thighs at his ribs and he smiled.

"That I have. Have any intention of making an honest man out of me and revealing that information?" Brass teased and I reached for his face and brought him back down to mine.

"Never. You're already much too good for me and I need to keep you in your place." I licked along his lower lip.

"And where is my proper place?" Brass asked huskily.

"Right here." I breathed, wrapping my arms and legs around him until he gave into another go around before classes.

Indigo knew which meant Quick knew. She and Quick had fought yet again. I had all but lost hope Slate was alive. Guilt weighed me down after I left Brass in the morning. I shouldn't have been smiling and making love all hours of the night. Maybe that was why I couldn't accept it. I couldn't fall down into that pit I might never claw my way back out of.

Peak Haust.

My intestines writhed and I did not know what to do about it. I wanted him dead. I was afraid to go to the Guardians and tell them what happened and lose the little of standing I'd gained in their eyes with my declaration at Slate's funeral and from the meeting we'd had about the arenas. Peak in his hybrid form was just as big as Slate's and more controlled, thus, more dangerous and less prone to make irrational mistakes. He'd proven that when I'd tried to outwit him during our fight. If he took Brass from me... I didn't know what I'd do.

The physical pain had only lasted a few hours. The emotional... well, we'd see about that. Brass had tried to erase all memory of Peak from my skin, but he was still there. His claim on me under my skin, not as deep as Slate's, thank the Gods. I couldn't help but feel like if I'd shut my big trap, I could've walked away from it minimally scathed. Because I couldn't and I'd not wanted to keep more secrets and tell lies, I'd told him exactly how I felt and didn't hold back. He'd beat me down for it. It was about power. He did not force himself on me after the beating, which seemed an extremely small concession.

He'd flexed his will over me and now I lived in dread that I'd receive a messenger summoning me to his castle. I'd go. I knew I'd go. If he caught me as he promised he would hurt my sons... I'd subject myself to it over and over if it would guarantee that he'd leave them unharmed. Hopefully, next time, I'd remember to keep my mouth closed and just endure. Nothing lasted forever, and as soon as we found a way, we'd put an end to Peak Haust.

Part of me expected to be wearing a sign that read **BARGHEST KHORAZ** in bold dripping red letters as if written in the blood of my dignity, but the other tyros at Valla University didn't seem to stare at all. There was the whisper campaign, but rumors about our family were a dime a dozen.

What I was waiting for was a side glance, a smirk... from Sage or Ash, one at their table that would tell me they knew what had happened, the way they always seemed to be so well informed. The looks didn't come. We confined Peak's actions to me, the five who had been at headquarters, and the deaf mutes for servants at the Haust castle who hadn't answered my screams.

I received a messenger from Sparrow while I dined in the hall at Valla U. "They finished the wing," I said numbly, and lifted my eyes to Jett and Cherry, who sat across from Quick, Tawny, and I.

Only Quick knew at this table about my previous weekend and he was doing a dreadful job of treating me with the same sarcastic charm he usually reserved for women. To him, I was like one of those fragile glass menagerie pieces, the kind that caught the light to shine rainbows around the room, a giraffe or maybe a jackass. Jett's observant eyes had been following the way Quick seemed determined to do everything for me and to be attached to my hip.

Since there was no way anything physical would have developed between us, Jett knew if Quick was taking extra care of me, it meant something else serious.

I speared another bite of Italian chicken with rotini pasta, black olives, and mozzarella and Jett spoke, stopping my bite to hover in front of my lips.

"Are you with Brass again?" Jett asked thoughtfully, then added, "No one is judging. It's been over three weeks. If Slate could have come back by now, he would have." Jett clenched his arrogant jaw as he ground out the last words, thick with emotion.

"I'm leaving Elivagar. I have all the contracts; Indigo found an architect with enough crews to begin construction on three island sites at once. We'll do them within the next two months, I am assured. Orion and Pearl are financing and Cordillera has recruiters out for teams. Everything is going to plan. Tomorrow I'm joining Pearl to find a location for the arena. You all may join us. I have the deed to the land in Mabon already and this weekend Tawny is taking us to Elivagar where Orion thinks will be prime for the arena."

"That doesn't answer my question at all." Jett smirked at me.

"I can't completely give up on Slate. If I do..." I didn't finish, and Jett nodded. "But... Brass has been —"

"You do not owe anyone an explanation," Quick interjected, catching us all off guard. "Slate is not here. I promise if he knew Brass was taking care of you, he would approve."

Cherry giggled, "Quick, has she finally won you over?"

"She won me over a long time ago. I am just an ass. Scarlett is like a sister to me. I would kill whoever hurt her," Quick said fiercely, without looking at me.

Tawny leaned forward to give him a look. "What has gotten into you today? You are being so... serious and stuck to Scar's fanny pack."

"Newfound respect."

The dining hall hummed with conversations punctuated by the occasional laugh. If you didn't know we were all bred from the first chosen Guardians for our strength and beauty, you'd never know we were all teeming with the 'M' word: magic.

I felt his presence the way I used to feel Slate's electricity crackle in the air and that tug to him that led straight from my heart to his. This was different. There was that attraction, this need to breed as if I was coming down from rousen. Vetiver and fall leaves. I let out a whimper and Quick's head whirled around. My hand tightened over his where he'd drawn his dagger.

Peak was almost to us from where he'd been speaking to Sterling and the others at the other table. They looked as surprised as I was to see the Haust patriarch at Valla U and striding towards us. His lime green eyes glittered like a cat who'd caught a mouse it had no intention of killing and wanted to play with. Bile splashed in my mouth, and I swallowed convulsively against the bitter spew.

His hand landed lightly on my shoulder and I felt his *calling* warm me. "How are my nephews this evening, sweet Scarlett?"

His familiarity with me made Tawny's lips part and hazel eyes widen like someone who'd just been confronted by a Wemic wearing a three-piece suit and Italian dress shoes. Jett watched with two observant eyes and if my hot-headed brother found out what Peak had done, he'd try to kill him here and now.

I met those eyes with great effort. "Very well, thank you."

The problem with healing was that sometimes you should feel pain to remind you of your stupidity or to warn you.

Peak's eyes glittered at me.

"I have arena business to discuss with you tonight. If you would be so kind." Peak dared me to outright deny him with a curl of his lips.

"The wing I've been remodeling for your nephew is complete. Sparrow asked if I'd come see it tonight." I held up the scroll for him and he plucked it from my fingers, his hand sliding up my shoulder so his thumb ran up and down the nape of my neck, hidden behind my hair.

"Regretful." Peak sighed in that false kindly way he'd always spoken in before. "Tomorrow suits me just as well, sweet Scarlett. No need to sup here, I will have dinner arranged in my great hall. I relish in your zeal for eating." Peak moved away in a swirl of his sleeveless ambassador's robes with the gold jumis emblazoned on the back of the deep chocolate fabric.

I shut my eyes and quickly opened them and forced pasta into my mouth so Jett wouldn't suspect. Quick wasn't as nonchalant.

"Say the word, Scarlett," he growled.

"Scar, your admirers have already flocked to you now that you are a fertile Tio again and your husband…" Cherry's big cobalt eyes glanced away. "Now that someone can court again you."

"He's married," I said flatly.

Cherry giggled. "Maybe Patriarch Haust wants you to be his paramour. He is handsome, and he's your type. Tall, dark… it would be weird that he's Slate's uncle," she conceded.

They all knew people thought Brass's sons were Slate's. If they thought it was strange, they kept it to themselves. Only Quick and Indigo knew the real reason for our deceit.

"Get out of here, Straumr," Jett warned in a low tone.

My head snapped around to find Ash's usual table staring at me and Ash right behind me. "You are more ambitious than I gave you credit for. A friendly warning though, Natt's do not take kindly to paramours. If you take Patriarch Haust to bed, you may get more than you bargained for."

"Thanks for the warning, Ash." My lack of sarcasm made his brows knit. "I promise you my only ambition is to be left alone, to find my parents' murderers, and get Slate back."

"Truth." Quick ground out red faced from the force it took for him to not go after Peak, who was speaking with the provosts at the front of the hall.

"You never play by the rules, Scarlett," Ash said.

Was that…? *No.* Did he feel sorry for me?

"I don't like the game. I have no interest in being anyone's paramour, Ash. If Peak is interested in me, I do not return the sentiment." Ash searched my eyes and then glanced to Quick.

"Truth."

Ash looked like he wanted to say more. Like he wanted to take me aside and confide in me and thought better of it as he looked back to Peak, who was watching Ash. Ash's face pinched.

"Patriarch Haust wants you, Scarlett. Make no mistake. I could have protected you from the advances of men like him."

"She has us," Jett said icily, and Ash sniffed before walking away.

Tawny shifted her body to face me. "Mabon is the only island who has given you the deed already?" she asked, and I nodded. "Scar, if you tell me right now you did not sleep with that man, I'll believe you."

"Did you have sex with Ambassador Haust to expedite the build?" Cherry asked, leaning forward in an excited whisper.

I denied it, to get indignant. How would anyone think I could do something like that? Then I thought better of it. Peak had been too familiar, and his coming there was too bold. It wouldn't take that long until someone started asking anyway, and I wouldn't lie to my family.

I kept an impassive face and slid my hand to Quick's knee and gave it a squeeze. "When I went to visit the prospective site, he made me an offer I couldn't refuse. I stayed the night with him and now he wants more."

"Scarlett!" Tawny hissed.

"No —" Quick started, and I pinched his leg.

"He reminded me of Slate." I shrugged. "I miss him."

All true. Not one lie. I was getting good at it. I'd rather my family think my flesh was weak than a victim.

Brass met me in Elivagar and packed the few things I had there to bring to his room in Valla. He did not take Peak's appearance at the university well.

"By the Mother, Scarlett, we cannot let him do this to you."

Brass laid on his side in the black jacquard bed as I touched the bald patch on my scalp. Peak had ripped the jade canine fetish I'd taken from Slate from my hair. I wanted it back, but there would only be one way to get it. I pushed him onto his back and slid my body against his.

"I don't want to. What choice do I have? You know how many it took to capture Slate. I'm one woman, you're one man. Even if we had your team, Quick, my brother, and Indigo against him... he'd catch me eventually and what would he do to our sons? I can't risk it and I won't run again."

Amber eyes were molten against his dark honey flesh. "You pay for our children's safety with your honor."

"I'd pay anything I *have* for their safety. Honor and pride be damned, I'd give him both my arms and a leg if he let me have our children."

"This plan is full of holes. What happens once they're born? They will be too small to defend themselves from him. He will try to get you with his child, Scarlett."

I dropped my eyes and looked at him through my lashes. "You wouldn't let that happen."

Brass's plump lips parted as he sucked in a ragged breath and spun us over, so I lay on my back and his tongue found mine. I couldn't keep my hands off him. I could still feel Peak on me and willed Brass to dull the memories with ones of him.

"Scarlett..." he trailed off, and I nipped at his lower lip.

"I don't regret Chris, but I never should have left Tidings. I should have gone with you to Ostara."

"You never should have left Slate, you mean," Brass stroked my cheek.

I kissed his jaw. "You're right, but I don't regret what I have with you, either."

"I should hope not since you have asked me to be your paramour and we are having children together. What an oddly flattering proposition," Brass teased, and I smiled ruefully at him.

"Do you think Slate forgives me?" I whispered as if words could grow wings and they could find him wherever he was.

"The better question is, could he stay angry with you? I say no. He never could, just as you could deny him nothing. We will find a way to thwart Peak."

Sparrow, Hawk, Tawny, and Gypsum joined me on the open gallery that framed the cloister. Sparrow had staff bring out a pitcher of iced tea and we let the warm breeze kiss our skin under the clear starry night. The constriction of my chest could not be mistaken for anything other than heartache.

"I can't believe how well it turned out," I said again.

"They did a splendid job. It was worth all the ruckus," Hawk said with a playful smile. "How are my nephews?"

"Content," I sighed, "losing hope."

Silence greeted my unprompted honesty.

"We didn't have to give him funereal. That was a mistake. I see that now," Sparrow said, finding my hand that hung over the wrought-iron chair. "What's more, I shouldn't have pushed him to settle down. You both needed time. You didn't see him while you were gone. He gave up."

As much as I wanted to tell her it was alright, it wasn't. I dropped Sparrow's hand and sipped my tea, rubbing my chiffon clad stomach with the other hand.

"You know people think the boys are Slate's, but they're not. I wouldn't want to give you false hope for an heir. They're Brass's, beyond a doubt," I said to them.

"We've begun talks with Steel and Tawny about a possible son inheriting. We should've gone that route to start because Slate never had interest in governing. Sparrow wanted to give Sea and Lark something. Anything." Hawk rubbed his trimmed beard as the silence stretched. "Is Brass Regn amenable to moving in?"

I shook my head ruefully. Of course, they knew where it was going. There was a lazy vibe to the late night gathering. If my mother was alive, it would be the group that had come over from Chicago so long ago.

"Brass loves Slate. I want to give it more time." *Before I gave up.*

"At year's end, if Slate has not returned, Brass may come to live with you here. Brass is a middle son; he has no properties to care for and all the experience to help you here with your sons." Sparrow's lips parted in a smile. "Your mother thought you and Slate would marry. Lark would approve."

Hawk chuckled. "He would. They are watching over you now."

"When are you going to take over for Pearl?" I asked Hawk.

He raised a brow at me. "I don't want it. I never have. When she wants to retire, Gypsum will be old enough to become the patriarch."

It was obviously the first Gypsum was hearing about it. "I can't. I don't know the first thing about running an island," he spluttered.

"It's high time you look into finding a suitable wife. Dating one girl would be a pleasant start," Sparrow said, leveling her dark, knowing eyes at her son.

Gypsum's dimples sprung to his olive cheeks as he gave her a killer smile that disarmed her. "Next year I'll be at Valla U and the dating pool will be easier to wade through."

"Shale is from a lesser family," Tawny teased.

Gypsum laughed; his copper beads that threaded his dozen braids clicked. "Shale never plans on marrying."

"A smart, faithful wife from a respectable family," I agreed. "They'll flock to you next year. You're the last unmarried patriarch. We won't be there to keep the parasites away."

Gypsum sighed, "Trust me. I know."

Tawny raised her brows at him but said nothing.

The others had gone to bed, and I sat outside alone with Sparrow, not ready to go to Brass's bed yet.

"I still love Slate," I said suddenly, "Brass too. A lech like my brother. It's like the involuntary muscles that work my lungs or eyelids. As easy as blinking."

Her eyes tilted towards the stars. "I loved Ridge Vetr — Hawk too. I would never have stopped loving Hawk. When Ridge had come with Orion to ask for my hand, it came as a shock." Sparrow let her long, dark tresses slide through her knuckles with a small smile. "Ridge was laid back and funny. Many of the girls tried to court him because he was the heir to the Vetrs. Wren and I didn't hang out with the Guardians from

Elivagar or Ostara, so we'd never expressed interest. I think that's what he liked best. Mabon and Thrimilci back then were one in the same. Flint and Pearl held dinner parties with the Hausts and my parents while us younger kids would play. The older kids, like Peak and my sister Sea, weren't interested in our games, so they stayed behind. When Sea finally came to a dinner, Peak was there, and he was smitten with her. They dated casually until Lark stole her away. I don't think Peak ever forgave him." She sighed. "Sea was beautiful. You remind me of her. You have that same fierce spirit and righteousness. Not quick to anger, like Tawny and me. More like Wren, I think that's why Lark married them both."

It was time I told Sparrow about the wight.

CHAPTER 58
INDIGO

"He said tomorrow. I don't know how to stop her; she doesn't want to go. She's at the Dagr palace now. Scarlett won't go there without telling one of us."

I crossed my arms over the black Shadow Breaker shirt as I spoke with Shale, Brass, and Silver.

"She will go. I have tried to speak to her about it. She will not listen. If there is a small chance it will put the babies at risk..." Brass shook his head.

Shale pursed her lips. "Ama would say it is only her body. Patriarch Haust will not influence her mind. As long as he does not beat her again."

"How very *practical* of you, Shale," Silver said dryly, and she smirked at him.

"She is doing what she needs to survive. I would do the same in her position," Shale said with stunning sincerity. "Time will dictate the appropriate action to exact revenge for her."

Brass's soft amber eyes burned at the prospect of letting Scarlett lie with Sterling's father. Short of killing him and facing a lifetime in Karkinos, we didn't have a lot of options. We would still kill him, of course, but we had to be smart about it. If Slate were there, he'd have done it no matter what any of us said. Of course, he was also prone to fits of destructive rage being the seven-foot-tall primitive beast that he was.

"I am off to bed. If Scarlett is staying with you tonight, then I am off duty." Shale gave me a questioning look with a sly smile.

Gods, did the woman have to be so obvious? Brass and Silver looked at me with gaping expressions, and Shale chuckled as she sauntered away. Silver's sensual mouth pinched as he looked down his nose at me.

"You slept with Shale last night."

I rolled my eyes but didn't stave off the blush. "*You've* slept with Shale before."

"Yes, but you are you and I am me," Silver said, flushing.

My chuckle wasn't mocking. "Yes, Silver. I think that's how being two separate people works."

He took a step closer while Brass looked everywhere but at us as we stood in the prep room of headquarters. "I asked you to stay with me last night and you chose Shale?" Silver asked in a hushed tone.

"I didn't choose her over you. I helped her pack Ama's things. We ate ice cream, then she brought up some wine. She was lonely and I don't belong to anyone," I said, as if it was obvious.

I hadn't planned that night, it just sort of happened. I liked to think I believed in love and that it didn't stop at one gender or the other. It was a feeling, not a box to check. Box one for female, box two for male.

"A pity fuck?" Silver said bitingly, and my face darkened.

"Do not go there, Silver. Her tongue is as sharp as your seax," Brass inserted before walking towards the stairs that led to the rumpus room.

"Sorry," Silver grudgingly muttered, and I let my anger roll from me.

He was giving me that inexplicable look again and leveled my eyes at him with a look that said, *got something to say?*

"Do you want to get a nightcap?" he asked.

"Would you being trying to get me drunk so I'll go to your room?" I rebuked, and he flashed that dazzling smile of his.

"Mayhap I am a glutton for punishment and would like your searing words to char my ears for trying to court you."

I chortled. "Court me? Is that what you call it?"

He ran the side of his thumb along his lips, drawing my attention there in a purely male gesture of impish speculation. "Mayhap, when you let go, all your bitter words melt from my mind. Mayhap, your *kind* company is worth the caustic."

I narrowed my eyes at him. "What's your game here, Regn?"

He pulled his tongue between his teeth, teasing me. "Say it, Dove."

"You might be insane."

"Please?"

"Not a chance. Besides, I have to go speak to a son about a father. He should know what his father is doing to my sister."

It was warm for October, so I left my cloak in the cubby and buckled on my borrowed short seax to my thigh. Silver hadn't moved, and I knew he was getting ready to argue with me. Last time we were in this prep room alone was the first time he trained me and I'd ended up walking out on him in the middle of our coitus.

I rose to my feet, readying for his strident tone. Silver looked at me with hooded chocolate eyes flecked with gold, and for a moment, I was dumbfounded. By the Mother, I hated that look he gave me. He stepped towards me, pivoting his body, and I backed up on reflex to get out of his reach and knocked my head into the cubby door. I winced and rubbed the spot I'd hit it.

"Ouch."

Silver's lips curled.

"Don't."

"I have done *nothing.*"

"Yet."

"Truth." He placed his hands on either side of me and his scent that stuck to my skin for days inflated my lungs.

Patchouli and sandalwood. The black lines of his tattoo peeked from his collar and I balled my fist to keep my index finger from tracing the air in its pattern.

"If you're going to kiss me, do it so I can leave. I told you; you can warm my bed. You just can't keep me from having anyone else in it."

I didn't want to be any crueler tonight, so I'd put my coldest words in a truthful sentence. Silver faltered but kept coming. He'd never give up.

His hands rested lightly on my hips as he pressed his against me, making me crane my neck to look up at him. "Such ugly words from such a lovely mouth," he whispered.

I licked my lips as if he willed it, and the corner of his mouth quirked.

"Do you want me to kiss you, Dove?" he purred.

"Now or ever?" I asked, trying to diffuse the moment so I could clear my mind.

"Now."

My eyes flickered to his lips. I hated he knew if I was lying.

"Yes. Now hurry. I don't want to stay at Sterling's too late."

Silver sighed. "Go on then." He moved aside and gestured for me to leave.

My brow twitched in confusion. Gods, I didn't know what the hell I wanted anymore. I waited another moment, and we stared stupidly at one another before I got my feet to move.

Sterling's violet eyes glowed in the low light of the candle I'd lit at my bedside. I sent my message, so he knew to meet me in my old room at Valla U. Nothing had changed. We were alone in a bedroom and couldn't stop ourselves. I hadn't even told him the horrible news.

"Where to begin?" I said, pushing my blonde locks from my mouth.

"The beginning is usually a good place to start, Indi," he teased with a sated expression.

My expression matched his. The tips of my fingers combed through his hair.

"I know you and your father don't get along. Did he ever... strike you?" I fidgeted with a lock of my hair and averted my eyes.

"No. Why?" Sterling asked, stroking my arm that rested above the comforter.

"I know you're a barghest, Sterling. Slate is, and we know your father is." I blurted and Sterling's boyish good looks turned into a man's as it hardened.

"Keep that to yourself, Indi. If my father found out you knew, he would make sure you never told another soul. You do not know how manipulative he is."

"I might have some idea. You trust me, don't you?" I asked hopefully, and Sterling smiled wryly.

"Indi, I love you and I know you love me. I trust you more than anyone else in my life."

My insides swelled with love and pride. "Your father revealed himself as a barghest to Scarlett when she went there for a meeting about the arenas."

"No. He would never," Sterling denied without a second thought.

"He claimed her," I whispered, and Sterling shot up.

"No, Indi. That is not possible. My father would never —"

"He forced her, Sterling," I said as much as I could without trying to hurt him with the monster his father was.

Sterling sat up in my bed with his head in his hands, elbows resting on his knees. "He told us to stay another night at the Straumr's. When we got back, the tapestry from the great hall was missing. I knew something must have happened. By the Mother, Indi I am so sorry. Is she okay?"

He believed me. It was a miracle.

"As good as expected. Scarlett bottles things until she explodes. Slate and now this... I don't know when, but it's going to be bad. I think the twins are the only things keeping her from shutting down."

"I thought it was strange he came to the dining hall today. I will do what I can to keep him preoccupied so he cannot force her to meet him. Gods, Indi, if my mother finds out..." He shook his head, lifting it to me. "She will have her killed. I am not exaggerating. You cannot tell anyone."

"I don't think you have to worry about that. We're not exactly advertising it, and Scar would rather meet him than admit to her abuse."

Sterling rolled over me and stroked my hair away from my face. "Please believe that I did not know he was capable of that. I know he has had affairs before. A fling here or there. Once he started taking a servant to bed and mother... I did not see the woman again. Never has he forced himself. I will say an oath about it."

"I believe you. I think it was more about her rejecting him afterwards than anything. You should have seen what he did to her, Sterling. I've seen nothing like it. He really *hurt* her."

"Do you hate me, Indi?" he asked, looking at me with his glowing violet eyes.

"No, love. I have to ask, though. Your wedding is coming close. I won't be able to see you as often. I'll always love you, but I may start seeing someone more regularly so I can have a husband of my own."

Sterling looked genuinely surprised. "You want to see me less?"

"No, but Diamond will want to see you more, and that is what would eventually happen. I'll still be here. Whomever I find will have to deal with it, as Diamond does."

I was a terrible person.

"Not Quick, Indi. I mean it."

I smiled softly at him. "My love." I kissed his lips. "That is up to me. I did not pick Diamond."

"Indigo! Get up! I need your help!" I shot up at Scarlett's belligerent shouting and blinked at the bright light.

She had dressed hastily and wore a hot pink tank top with a pair of jeans tucked into black boots. Scarlett was buckling her daggers around her hips and tucking blades everywhere. She even had her wrist blades on with her Yggdrasil necklace and silver torque. She looked completely out of place, as if she didn't know where she was.

Sterling was sitting up wide eyed, and she hadn't even noticed him yet. Scarlett yanked the blankets off us, and Sterling fisted the blankets in his hand to keep himself covered.

"Gods are you listening?" she shouted.

I swung my bare feet over the bed, and a bra and shirt hit my face. "I would be if you were making sense," I muttered.

She looked crazed. Her face flushed and eyes glassy. "Slate." She hissed and pressed her hand to her heart. "He's alive. I can feel him. We have to get him before the bond fades. I don't know why it took so long, but —"

Silver charged into the room, and I yanked the blanket over my bare bottom. He took in Sterling and me, then Scarlett gripped his shoulders. She was hysterical and temporarily distracted him from us. Sterling pulled his clothes back on as I grabbed for underwear and pants.

"Quick, my bond." She pointed to her lower lip as he steadied her. "He activated it. I don't know why it took so long, but he's alive. We have to go right now."

She shook violently and Silver pulled her tight as she fought against him. "Truth, as you believe it."

She shoved him hard. "There's no time for that. Fiddlesticking fine if you think I'm crazy. I'm going to get my husband with or without your help." She charged out of the room, and Silver hooked his arm around her waist and tossed her back into the room.

"Stay here. Let me get Brass and Shale at least. It will only take five minutes." Silver's eyes slid to Sterling, who was buttoning his pants shirtless.

"What are you doing here, Silver?" I asked in my hardest tone.

"Fucking down the hall, Indigo. You?" Silver said coolly.

I nocked my chin up and let my eyes slide to Sterling. "Using my lovely mouth for lovely things, Silver. Thanks."

Sterling gave me a disapproving look that I ignored. Scarlett seemed to see him for the first time.

"Tell your father I'll have to miss our appointment tomorrow. I don't know when I'll be back," she said in a rush, and Sterling's lips pressed into a grim line.

"I will hold him off as long as I can, Scarlett," Sterling said like a knight swearing his allegiance to the crown.

She inclined her head at his offer, and Silver snorted derisively. Scarlett turned on him. "You're still here? Go, Quick! So help me, I will leave. I'm going to portal jump until I figure out what island he's on."

Before we could stop her, she knocked Silver out of the way and ran down the hall, leaving Sterling and Quick with me. Silver crossed his arms as Sterling buckled his jerkin.

"You must be happy. Indi tells me she is thinking about marrying you," Sterling said, violet eyes flashing.

As far as I knew, it was the first time they'd addressed one another. My heart had lodged in my throat.

Silver's eyes bugged comically from his face, and I didn't know whether to laugh or be angry that the prospect of marrying me made him look like someone was strangling him.

"I didn't say that."

"Did you not, love? I thought you said you wanted a husband. I asked you not to see Quick, and you told me it was not up to me. Did I hear it wrong?" Sterling asked smoothly, and I narrowed my eyes.

He was chasing Silver away. I wanted to slow clap at the manipulation. Silver certainly looked like he wanted to bolt.

"I said something along those lines. Don't put words in my mouth, Sterling." I chastised.

Sterling's lips quirked. "But I love putting things in your mouth."

"I haven't been with Silver in weeks, and if you're going to act like this, I don't want to see you either. Do not belittle me because you can't stand that I find pleasure with another man." I could feel Silver preening by the door. "GO!" I shouted at him.

He chuckled and *called,* yanking me to him, and covered my mouth with his. I was gasping when his tongue plunged into my mouth. He pushed back, and I swung to Sterling, who watched with pursed lips.

"Wondering what that taste is, I can elucidate for you."

Silver laughed richly. "I do not care. Be right back." He took off the way Scarlett went.

I licked my lips and faced Sterling. "Why?" I asked.

Sterling skirted the bed to stand in front of me and pulled me close. "What he has with you is an illusion. He only has it because I allow it. If they did not betroth me to Diamond, he never would have had you, Indi."

"That doesn't make me feel very good at all."

"Tis life, love."

FIFTY-NINE

I couldn't wait. I'd fallen asleep in the chair while sitting with Sparrow under the stars, and Hawk or Gypsum must have moved me into the big white bed replica of our former bed. Pain blossomed in my mind where the knot of emotions that were Slate's usually resided and woke me. After I realized what it was, I'd grabbed whatever clothes I could find in an old box and ran through the portal. It happened to be a box from Chicago so I wore an eclectic blend of modern clothes and Old-World weapons.

In my haste, I'd forgotten to tell the others who slept in the palace. Goodness, Indigo had looked at me like I'd lost my mind. Maybe I had. I looked like I had with this ridiculous hot pink tank top on and jeans. No one wore jeans in Tidings, but all I had was a slinky chiffon dress. I'd found the clothes in a box they'd moved there from my Chicago items.

I'd needed my weapons, so I went to Valla U. I did not know Indigo would be there. I wasn't thinking clearly. Good thing I'd run into her or I would've gone off alone. Quick had been there too. That was good. I didn't know how I felt about Brass being there, but he'd do what was right.

Gods, the adrenaline was rushing through my body so I couldn't sit still.

I went to the portal room and went through from island to island until I determined he was in Mabon.

My bond with Brass activated and didn't look back as I ran over the rolling hills. I tried to send Slate reassurance through the bond. I was coming and would save him. He was in so much pain! I hadn't been paying attention to where I ran in the pouring rain. I fell more often than not and mud caked my jeans from where I slid down a hill.

My hair hung in limp ropes around my face and when I reached the edge of the island I started screaming.

It couldn't be. It didn't make sense. I'd gone to every island; that one was where my bond with him was strongest, yet he was further out. I didn't blink. If I did, the bond might disappear. I couldn't leave the cliff side. I was afraid to let it grow faint again.

Sitting there waiting for the others made me restless. It was pitch black out with the storm brewing. Clouds hid the moon and stars. I got up and paced when a flash of thunder lit on something near the water. Alarm washed over me and I half climbed, half slid down the cliff side, skinning my arms and cheeks in the process until I saw what it really was.

A twenty-foot-long blue dory was tied off by the rocks with two sets of oars. I thanked the Gods and trudged to the boat.

"SCARLETT!"

I heard Indigo's shout over the rain and, when lightning flashed again, saw the outlines of four people. I waved moronically and felt Brass's bond flare up with irritation.

I'd tossed the tie line into the boat and climbed in by the time Brass, Indigo, Shale, and Quick reached me. Brass threw a cloak at me and I buckled it around my throat as I readied the oars.

Brass grabbed me under my arms, and I cursed. "Stop! I can feel him!"

Brass cupped my face and looked into my eyes, keeping me still. His healing flooded me, and he slowly shook his head.

"We believe you. Get your head on straight. Wherever he is, it's against his will. Can you imagine what might be able to keep Slate away from you for almost a month? Because I cannot. Other than you yourself, that is." I smiled at his attempt to lighten the situation.

"Sugarfoot, Brass," I sobbed and flung myself at him.

I fisted his cloak as I buried my face in his chest. I'd given up on Slate, no matter what I said out loud. In my mind, I was already playing out my life with Brass.

"Did you tell anyone else?" He asked stroking my head.

"No, I freaked. I wouldn't have even thought to get you if I hadn't needed my blades. That was only because Indigo was at Valla U and Quick heard us talking. It was Quick's idea to get you." Brass tilted my chin up with a finger and we gazed into one another's eyes.

I kissed him passionately and pushed all my feeling into it. I fed him what I'd imagined for us, not to hurt him, but to let him know what we had was real. He was the father of my children, but Slate was my husband. We'd lost a child together and could have more. I pulled away and Brass held his forehead to mine.

"I know, me too. Let's go get him back." Brass cleared his throat and took the spot I'd been in taking up the oars.

Quick took the other set and Indigo started wiping at my face with a piece of fabric that was coming away full of mud.

"You look like a lunatic," she said, raising her powder blue eyes to mine.

"I feel like a lunatic." I told them which way to head and suffered Indigo's fretting.

"Did you say goodbye to Brass?" she asked in a hushed tone.

"He's not going anywhere," I said.

She nodded, and Shale's dark eyes met mine. "You will not get any judgement from me."

The bond grew stronger until we floated in the ocean within sight of Mabon and another island I couldn't identify. I was swiveling my head around, making my neck hurt.

"He's right here," I said in an unnaturally high pitch.

I looked at the others, and Brass and Quick were having some silent communication. They stood and started taking off their cloaks and boots. I watched for a moment before it dawned on me. I shrieked.

"Karkinos," Shale cursed.

I started pulling off my boots and Brass put his hand on my shoulder. "No, love. You're not in the right frame of mind." His eyes were soft and jaw set with determination.

I stood unclasping the cloak and began unbuttoning my jeans. "I would like to meet the person who would stop me," I said, feeling my eyes burn in my skull.

Brass sighed. "Indigo, we need someone to stay with the boat."

Indigo looked indignantly at Quick as if this was his doing and he dazzled her with a smile. Maybe it was his doing. Shale was in her long black sleeve shirt and a pair of black boy shorts with blades strapped all over her taut body.

"Good thing I do not date men," she muttered.

I stood buckling my seax to my thigh and tying the blades I had in my boots to my biceps. My hot pink tank top and white boy shorts looked ridiculous in such a serious situation. Indigo sat sullenly fully dressed and watched Quick take off his shirt to reveal all his black Celtic tattoos. Her index finger moved on her thigh as he strapped blades across his chest. Brass was doing the same to my left.

"What is the plan?" Shale asked.

"Blast our way into the highest tower and keep away from the claws," Brass said, tying back his hair in a knot at his nape making his biceps bulge.

"Sounds good," Quick said enthusiastically, "Still there?"

"Still there," I said, leaning over the side of the boat to peer into the watery depths.

I couldn't see anything in the ocean that was dark green in the storm. We all looked like drowned rats in the downpour and I flared to life. My elemental fire a beacon.

A torch in his darkness.

"A kiss for luck," Shale said, and I turned my head of writhing hair.

Indigo blushed and got to her feet. I looked at Brass, who gave me a lopsided smile as Shale laid a very serious kiss on Indigo, making me look away. Indigo took a swaying step back and Quick grabbed her elbow and spun her to face him.

"My turn, Dove."

He didn't give her a chance to object. Shale chuckled as she jumped overboard and Quick wrapped his fist in Indigo's long hair as he kissed her so deeply I thought I could see the toe of her boots curl. She stopped fighting him and slapped her hands to the sides of his face and slid them up into his short, styled hair. Quick pulled back, and she smiled puckishly at him as he pushed his hair back with an equally amused expression.

I turned to Brass in my elemental form. "For luck," I told him.

He had no chance to object either when I stood on the seat and yanked his head back to kiss him so thoroughly he'd forgive me for everything to come. I drew back, and he laced his hand through mine, deactivating our bond. At that moment, I was so glad I'd learned to keep from burning everything I touched. Brass looked spellbound.

"I will miss this," he whispered, and I had to look away before I started blubbering.

He turned to face the churning water where Quick and Shale bobbed and held my hand as we jumped off the dory.

I *called* an air bubble and dove beneath the surface and started down, using air to propel me faster. Brass held my hand and Quick held my ankle with Shale holding Brass's so we wouldn't get separated in the murky depths. I swam towards a darkened spot and I would have gasped if we weren't in the water.

Claws the size of houses back in Chicago rested on the ocean floor. It looked black in the dark, but it was burnt umber with a khaki underside that squatted in the sand. The colossal crab, Karkinos and the shadowy pillars that stretched in several stories above it which housed all of Tidings's criminals. One level touched each of the towers that protruded from the shell of Karkinos.

I winked out and zeroed in on the tallest tower. Karkinos was sleeping. We approached at a decelerated rate and as we approached; I realized the flaw in our plan. Someone would have to stay behind to keep the water from rushing into the prison.

The towers may have been black once, but now they were homes to the ocean life that grew alongside its bleak surfaces. There were no windows, and it looked like parts of it had worn down to nothing. They sealed two of the towers' top floors after having collapsed. I wondered who cared for it.

I took us right up to the tower and placed my hand on its surface and almost gagged at its slimy feel. I flared to life and used my heat to scour into the room. The circle I'd made blew in with a rush, pulling us all in after it. I lost my grip on Brass and slammed into a wall. Someone's barefoot connected with my head and suddenly the water pressure let up and I coughed and hacked as I got to my feet.

Shale was kneeling in front of the hole I cut with her teeth grit and hands outstretched. "Go get my captain," she ground out.

We didn't debate it. The top cell was empty. Flat metal bars that ran top to bottom and side to side barely opened enough to stick a hand through. I winked out, and Brass stepped up to cut a hole through it. Quick caught it so it wouldn't clatter to the floor. The stone floor was a drab grey and the walls. If there had been a drearier place in existence, I didn't know of it.

Everything was wet, and a dankness hung in the air. We stepped through and into a short hall that led to stairs.

"I know nothing about this place. Are there guards or something? Where is the portal door? Maybe we can send him through and we'll go the long way?" I asked in a whisper that seemed to echo in every corner of the tower.

"There is a center tower where the guards reside. That is where the portal door is that leads to Moon's office at Valla U," Quick said from behind me.

Brass let me believe I was leading, but really he was. His dark honey muscles tightly bunched as we walked down the stone steps. The only sound we made was our breathing.

"Is he in this tower?" Brass asked, and I shook my head.

"Somewhere lower. I can't be sure until we're closer."

I sounded as distressed as I felt. If his bond broke while we were this close, they would have to keep me in a straitjacket until the babies were born and then put me out of my misery.

If I never had to be inside Karkinos again, I'd die a happy woman. It sucked the life out of you. My very soul felt oppressed within its walls. My happiness must have fed the colossal crab, because it seemed to seep out of me the longer we stayed.

"Check on the babies," I said, suddenly feeling ill.

Brass ran his palm over my stomach and offered me a smile. "This place is supposed to steal your will to live. The babies are okay, Scarlett. It's in your mind."

I nodded hesitantly, and we continued.

Seven more flights of stairs with more halls of metal cells. All kinds of tribes within them calling out to us as we hurried lower. For once, I was grateful I was so miserable at languages. If I had to guess what they were saying, I'd say it was somewhere between 'Help me' and 'I will kill you.' None of which I wanted to hear.

We were out of stairs and had reached a long hall that opened up in two directions. I turned around and started down it, staying close to the walls and calling a shadow to mask our approach. We heard the slide of a door and voices reached us down the hall. There wasn't anywhere to run. Brass grabbed my arm and called open the first door and pulled me in after with Quick on my heels.

Quick shut the door, and we waited in a pitch-dark room to hide us or if they had a talent like Brass or mine, that would sense us at a distance.

"We are clear," Brass said from behind me.

Quick slid the metal door open a sliver and looked out. He gestured for us to follow. We continued down the hall and reached another fork of halls. I went left. The drab halls were lit by circular globes that seemed to be charged and hung in a conical basket above our heads. It offered little light, and its fluorescent color was depressing.

"This way," I whispered as we reached another stairwell. "He's above us now."

Brass pushed me in my chest and Quick didn't hesitate to grab me and turn me around, so his body protected me. Shouts erupted and Quick held an arm around me as *calling* lit the halls.

"Time to run." Quick shouted at me as he tossed me over a shoulder effortlessly and ran up the stairs with Brass falling back to guard our backs.

"Put me down! I'm fast!" I protested and Quick laughed.

"They do not call me Quick for nothing," he shouted as he took stairs two at a time.

"*HERE!*" The adrenaline was back and my heartbeat in my ears.

Quick charged down the hall of the third floor and skidded to a stop to put me down. My legs were pumping before I hit the ground and I took off with Quick and Brass defending my back as I reached a cell with a busted light inside it so I couldn't peer in.

I wrapped my fingers around the metal and leaned in close. "Slate?" My voice came out high and frail.

I held my breath for what seemed like minutes as the fight continued down the hall. The halo of let out by the globe of light breached the cell and a dark paw came into view.

"Scarlett!" Quick called frantic as —

Oh Gods, Karkinos was swarming with Crathode!

The Red Kings were free. They came at Brass and Quick with clawed hands snapping and stabbing. The crustacean hybrids' beady eyes were wild as they attacked a grossly outnumbered Brass and Quick. They were as tall or taller than the brothers. I didn't think I *called*.

A circular hole about five feet across blew towards me, and I stepped to the side so it could tumble to the floor. I moved to step inside when the front paws of a beast came into the light. At first I thought it was the enormous wolf creature the Stygians kept at their pit to eat the defeated competitors, the one they called Fenrir.

A double row of off-white horns curved along its spine on a ten-foot-long frame. The three pairs of horns on his head were of the same color. Tusks jutted from its jaw, another set curved back from behind his ears, while the third poked up from behind its pointed ears. His muzzle was like a wolf's, but his teeth were much longer. His body was bulkily muscled, thick across his chest and arms, but he moved with unnatural grace. In all that was a human eye, silvery grey that looked out at me.

It swished a long, thick tail with a barbed tip just before I saw its muscles tense. I went full rabbit. It was not a barghest hybrid, that was a barghest. The biggest and scariest thing I'd ever seen and nothing like the mist monsters we faced at our Wild Hunt challenge. I couldn't help the shriek that I loosed when it pounced and I threw up my hands to protect my face, not even thinking to *call*.

"What the fuck!" Quick shouted.

My pink tank top caught on its tusk as it sniffed me where I laid pinned under its massive chest. Its fetid breath stunk of clotted blood and death. I whimpered pathetically and *called* out to Slate through the bond. The beast's wrinkled snout pulled back and a wide, coarse tongue slid out and licked me from my chest to my hairline.

I gagged.

"It's… it's Slate. I'm alright," I shouted, hoping Quick would hear me and wouldn't blast him.

One of Slate's silver eyes peered down at me from the barghest's face in expectation. I tried for a smile and it lifted its head and tore my shirt with its razor-sharp tusk. I didn't bother trying to free my shirt from its tusk and instead slid up on my palms to sit in front of it, *er*, him.

Distracted by how terrifying he was, I didn't realize he was injured. Patches of his sleek charcoal fur were missing and where his left eye should have been an infected open wound. I placed my palm on his face and he closed his good eye as if happy for my affection.

I *called*.

I shut my eyes and took into myself a deep power that made the lights flicker and the room grew silent as I stole the sound from them. When I opened my eyes, Slate had two eyes, but scars riddled his sleek, furred body. I took my hand away and got up. Slate snarled.

"You have to shift back to a man. We have to get you out of here," I said, aware Brass and Quick had retreated closer and we were at a dead end.

None of us might make it out alive. The beast looked at me but made no move to change. In my mind, he was very base and had only three things on his mind. Fighting, feeding, and fiddlesticking in no particular order. Knowing him, he'd want seconds.

"I'm activating my Shadow Breaker bond so Shale knows to collapse the room and escape. There's no way we're going to make it out that way," I said, getting to my feet and Slate's head pushed into my hand.

Quick turned around and his brows rose. "That is a big puppy."

It bared teeth as long as my forearm at him, and Quick started. I stepped up beside Quick, leaving Slate back, and shifted into an elemental.

"I'll clear a space. Slate will follow me. Come in behind him."

I didn't check to see if they agreed. I knew they wouldn't. Not with me in front. I did it anyway. My fire scoured the hall and, as I suspected, Slate was hot on my heels. Brass and Quick killed the Crathode that survived my inferno.

"Conserve your energy!" Brass shouted at me.

I slowed and winked out as we retraced our path back to the highest tower. Slate didn't even trot as we jogged through the hall. He breathed open mouthed, and I gagged again.

"By the Mother, Slate. Close your damn mouth, you are going to make Scarlett faint," Quick said, making a face.

A group of Crathode turned a corner in front of us, and we skidded to a halt. Two men led the group and my stomach flip-flopped. The bearded Mint twins, Spear and Pepper. Their eyes snagged on me and I was sure the one named Spear chuckled darkly, holding his stomach.

"I cannot tell if you are stupid or if you think you are clever. In any case, you are a very foolish girl to come into the lion's den. To rescue your beast? See what he is now? Do you like what we have done? Do not worry. After we kill these two, I will take good care of you." Spear's smile held no warmth.

"Kill the men," Pepper said, and the Crathode started forth.

We didn't have time to react when Slate sent us sprawling and charged into the dozens of snapping and dicing claws. I screamed, and he picked up seven-foot-tall hybrids and shook them in his massive jaws. It was a bloodbath. Brass and Quick took up his flanks and started *calling* to disperse the Crathode so we could get by.

With the melee, no one noticed the shadow that floated towards me until I saw Spear detach from it and lunge for me. I bit my teeth together to keep from screaming and fell onto the chilly stone floor. He didn't have any weapons on him and he wrapped his fingers around my throat, squeezing so tight I couldn't see straight. I grew frantic and clawed at his finger with stubby broken nails. All my training flew out the window. He wanted to strangle me with his bare hands and that thought shook all rational from my mind. He *hated* me.

It lasted mere heartbeats. Then fresh blood poured over my face where Spear's head was. It spurted into my mouth as I choked for air. Slate's jaw crunched as he chewed on Spear's head and swallowed it. I turned my head and started puking.

"Freya's burly boar! Did he just eat that guy's head?" Quick shouted.

Pepper wailed.

Brass grabbed my arm and Slate snarled. I held up my hands and tried to wipe warm blood from my eyes with the tatters of my shirt. Quick was holding them back and straining with the effort. Slate nudged my hand, and I frowned.

"You have horns back there." I protested and it, *um*, he knelt down.

Brass grabbed me around my waist and lifted me onto Slate's back. The space between the horns was just big enough for me to fit. "I hope he doesn't come to a quick stop," I muttered.

I gripped his flanks with my thighs and tried to make myself a smaller target as Slate raced forward. I flared to life, so I absorbed their fireballs and deflected their weapons. Brass and Quick ran in our wake as I tried to direct Slate which way to go. Not just Crathode, but Minotaurs and Anguillan chased us. The hybrid eel Anguillan moved in a way that sent shivers up my spine. They infested Karkinos.

There was no way we were making it to Shale. I *called a* shadow into the inguz rune at my hip. Every Shadow Breaker would know we had activated it and Shale would know exactly where I was and to leave the floor.

"I'm going to blast through this wall!" I shouted.

"Do it! This place is a lost cause. It will cause Karkinos to surface!" Quick shouted behind me.

I bit down on my lip and faced the stone wall. I created a shield of air around us and sent a rocket of air into the wall. The air shield forced the water to our sides as I looked behind us and saw the rushing water narrowly miss Brass. Slate's sides brushed the walls as he forced his way through and then we were in the ocean.

I tried to rein Slate in so I could *call* my shield around Quick and Brass. I saw them hit the water, and they *called,* propelling them further from the hole.

I formed air bubbles around Slate's muzzle and my mouth, then led him up to the highest tower. I could see the light of dawn through the water's surface as we climbed higher and saw Shale dive into the waters above me. She slowed, and I watched her wade in place.

That's when I felt the water move around me. Karkinos were rising and the force of his movement was pulling us under. I held tight to Slate and turned around to see Brass and Quick grabbing onto one another. I knit my brows, wanting to call out to them when I saw Shale zoom past. She started *calling* to steady the waters around them and they forced their way out from Karkinos's pull.

Slate climbed higher, his paws paddled as I rode him back towards the sky. I checked over my shoulder and saw Quick release Brass. Quick swam to Shale, who was floundering after using so much *calling*. Brass started towards me and I screamed as Karkinos's claw rose. I lost my bubble of air and Slate's as I *called* to knock away the massive claw.

Shale lifted her head, seeing my spear of air shoot into the claw and she shoved Quick away. It wasn't far enough. My spears barely penetrated its hard shell and my fire was useless against it. Karkinos's claw clamped down. Brass saw my expression and turned around to see Quick's torso get caught in the pinch and the red fluid burst around him. Shale disappeared into the claw.

The bond snapped and in my mind's eye I saw Shale's dark up tilted eyes gazing blankly at the ocean's surface. Quick curled round himself when Karkinos released him. Shale's broken body drifted down and Quick caught it.

Brass reached them as Karkinos was opening its claw again. I searched frantically for a soft spot and found its black, beady eyes. I *called* just as it lowered to the brothers. The claw snapped up as its eye popped. The waters churned, and I saw another torpedo of water hit the surface and shoot towards Brass and Quick. It was Indigo.

She zoomed in as her elemental form and took Quick from Brass and didn't falter as she arched back to the surface. Brass floated, mending Shale, and then shot like an arrow straight up. I squeezed Slate with my thighs and realized he wasn't moving. I hadn't *called* his air back. My *calling* got us to the surface.

I puked up water when I reached the top. The rain had stopped, and the air was cool. I kept *calling,* trying to find the boat.

Indigo was pulling Quick into the dory, and blood streaked the side of it. I *called* into Slate's barghest body, forcing the water from his lungs, and I heard his hacking cough. I laughed hysterically, drinking in more water and *called* us closer to the boat.

Brass was pushing Shale into the boat as I climbed over. Slate paddled in the water, too big to climb aboard. Indigo was sobbing over Shale, whose glassy-eyed stare faced the dawn sky that looked lit by fire. Blood poured over Quick's lips, and a chunk was missing from his right side. I could see his ribs through the wound.

I shoved Brass aside, who looked lost as he clutched Quick's hand, and Indigo moved from Shale to hold Quick's head, peppering his face with kisses.

"Silver! Don't die on me! By the Mother! Frigga's sweet grass! You can kiss me whenever you want, I'll let you be on top." Quick's eyes focused on her and he gave her a grisly smile, laughing as he coughed up more blood.

She laughed with a hysterical edge. Everything was happening too quickly. We lost Shale, we couldn't lose Quick too and their healing was taking too long!

I closed my hands over Quick's wound.

"I love you, Silver. Do you hear me? I love you! Call me Dove. Tell me it's the truth." Indigo cried, and she lowered her mouth to his, kissing him over and over.

I shut my eyes. No more death. I wouldn't lose Indigo's one chance at happiness while trying to save my husband. I refused.

A soundless thunderclap struck the air as I sucked in the elements. I *called* everything I could get my hands on and I heard Brass and Indigo choke because I stole the very air from the earth's surface. The light of dawn darkened in a nimbus around us as I stole it. I would've stolen the very ocean we floated on is I could. The skin knit beneath my fingers and his flesh warmed beneath my hands.

I fell back and gasped. Brass and Indigo were taking wheezing breaths as I scrambled on my hands and knees to the side of the boat. Tears poured down my cheeks. I pulled myself up to look into the water where Slate was still paddling.

"Slate. I need you to shift. You can't come in the boat as you are. The shore —"

I broke off and looked around and squeezed my eyes shut as I loosed a ragged sob.

"Karkinos moved. I had to follow you in the boat." Indigo was saying, and my eyes fluttered shut.

I turned to Slate, whose giant charcoal head was bobbing in the water. "Please. I'm not strong enough to save you." I cried.

Slate's silver eyes watched me, and he hit the boat with a paw. The boat rocked, and I yelped as the boat rocked back and I fell over the side. I floated for a moment as the streaks of orange fire gave way to sky blue.

My eyes fluttered again, and Brass's face appeared above mine. He didn't grab me and then darkness descended.

CHAPTER 60
INDIGO

Silver couldn't stop laughing. I couldn't stop kissing him.

"If you tell me you're no longer interested in me, I will throw you back into the ocean as crab food." I told him as I straddled his lap and kissed more of his face.

"By the Mother, I just woke up. Give me a moment. Where are we?" Silver laughed richly and made no move to stop me.

I smiled at him and slid off his lap. We were inside a floating room made of wood that hung from a towering tree. A short wood rail ran along the edge of the floor, which only held a chamber pot and a stuffed mattress covered with blankets. I moved the heavy curtains away that enclosed each hanging "nest" and showed Silver where we were.

He gasped and leaned back. "The Aves."

I pulled my lower lip into my mouth and nodded enthusiastically. "The bird hybrids saw us struggling off the coast and swooped down, saving us! We are on their floating island in the sky!"

Silver didn't look over the side again. Hundreds of the "nests" hung from the tall branches of the tree that reached ten stories into the Ostara sky. Its roots were in a floating land mass that traveled above Ostara all year round. No one got onto the Aves island without them bringing them. My mother was their ambassador before she died, the first one to contact them in almost twenty years.

At the trunk of the massive tree were more tiny houses built against it where their sachem lived, their meeting halls, and school, all connected by rope bridges. Aves flew between the hanging platform nests, some even walked down the stairs that connected branch to branch. A peacock hybrid male had flown me into this nest and I helped them bring in Silver with a bright red cardinal woman. Her human torso and legs ended in bird's claws, while a long red crest flowed down her back like hair. She had black eyes with a human face, but a bird's beak. Her feathers tapered from where her brow would have been. She had feathered hands which had made me start when she'd helped roll Silver onto the mattress.

Rope ladders hung from the branches so we could climb up or down to reach the staircases and the tree trunk. That high, the usually warm air of Ostara had a sweet cool breeze. I let the panel fall back and shifted back to Silver. They had given me two pieces of fabric to replace my clothing. I'd wrapped the longer piece brighter than the sun around my hips like a sarong and the second piece like a tube top of a purple jewel tone.

Everything in Ostara was bright and cheery. I'd almost forgotten how much I loved the sweet aroma of flowers that would flow through my bedroom window in the Var castle. I watched as Silver slept and the Aves wrapped Shale's body in a white gauzy fabric. A toucan man then carried Brass to the nest next to the one we sat in now. I promised we'd activate Silver's bond with him as soon as we were ready to talk.

Scarlett was unconscious, and they'd had a hell of a time getting Slate to let them take her. Luckily, they'd seen him and had brought tranquilizer darts. A pigeon man had shot Slate full of the stuff and it took four Aves to lift him. Brass had dragged Scarlett into the boat and a blue jay woman had carried her off. Brass was last to be taken by a bright yellow canary hybrid.

I scuttled back to where Quick was now sitting up against the woven wall with the blankets pooled in his lap. I straddled his powerful thighs and tucked my hair behind my ears.

"Kiss me, Silver," I purred, running my fingers over the flawless skin Scarlett had grown back with her own two hands. "You shouldn't be alive right now. She grew back so much of you."

I rubbed my nose along his, forcing his mouth up to mine. He kissed me once, twice, then slid his hands around my hips, pulling me closer.

"Did you mean what you said?" he asked, and I felt my cheeks flush, but didn't stop kissing him.

"On the boat?" I asked, feigning ignorance. "You're the interrogator, Silver. You tell me."

My hands slid up his impeccable chest to his face and held him away from me so I could peer into his deep brown eyes. "You love me." He purred, and I rolled my eyes.

"Get over yourself," I said, fighting a smile.

"I believe you said I could kiss you whenever I wanted and I could be on top." Silver rolled us, overexposing his taut backside that tattoos also covered on his left side. "You said I could call you Dove." He kissed my jaw. "And that you love me."

"Stop gloating. It's smug and arrogant and entirely to Quick*ish*."

He kissed along my throat. "Do you want to hear the words?"

"It'd be nice to hear that you like me," I said breathlessly.

I felt Silver's teeth as he smiled against my skin. "You make me want to be a one-woman man, Dove."

I laughed throatily, and he pressed his hips into me. "Really? Is that the best you can do? I think I feel a case of amnesia coming on. I don't recall saying anything pleasant to you as you laid dying."

Silver's teeth caught my earlobe, and he purred. "*Oh, Dove.*"

CHAPTER
SIXTY-ONE

My skin stuck to itself as I took a deep breath. The air was clean, with a hint of jasmine. As I stretched, my hand bumped into something meaty and I open my eyes, expecting to see Brass. I took air in so rapidly it made me cough, but Slate didn't stir.

I knew that the white underwear I was in was all I wore since before we went into Karkinos and someone neatly piled my blades next to the blankets we slept on. I knelt at Slate's side and ran my fingertips down the scar that stretched from his hairline to just below his cheekbone in a jagged silvery white, as if he'd had it for years. Prying his eye open, his pupil didn't react, but it was winter storm grey.

I slid my fingers under his head and felt where the Shadow Breaker tracker should have been and found another scar, one deeper and puckered. They'd skinned him sloppily, but you'd never see it since they'd not cut his midnight mane of waves, which brushed halfway down his hard muscled chest. He was gloriously nude, with a stock of scars that marred his flawless bronze skin. His silver Celtic etched beads threaded through his hair and the fetishes he always wore.

Slate. My Slate. Alive!

I ran my fingers over his body to make sure he was whole before I unbraided his hair and found a small wooden bowl, which I collected them in.

We were in a hall of sorts, except instead of chairs, they had a long bench that was more of a cylinder than a flat surface. An odd bench lined three of the wooden walls, which brightly dyed fabrics swathed.

I did not know where we were or if everyone else was okay.

Shale was dead.

I felt the bite of anguish and sat back on my heels to gaze down at my husband. She'd died rescuing Slate and saved Quick from being cut in two as she had been. Brass had bound her pieces together in the ocean. I didn't even know where that was.

I continued to unbraid Slate's hair as I peered around the room. It was long and slightly curved like a crescent. What I thought initially was wood paneling, was actually tree bark peeking out from between the bright fabrics.

Where were we?

Pulling Slate's head into my lap, I *called* water and wash him with my hands in a slow, methodical way. If someone wanted to hurt us wherever we were, we'd be dead already. They wouldn't have left the pile of fabric. I hoped was clothing, either.

I touched every inch of his body unabashedly in a way I hadn't done in almost a year, then attempted to sort myself out after I laid a thin red dyed fabric over his hips. I took out my fetishes, pearl, and beads to scrub at my scalp and then braided the items back in before rinsing my body off and picking up a jungle green sarong and a royal blue piece of fabric that I tied at the top and bottom like a tube top and pulled the opening at my back for modesty's sake.

My memory was kicking in as well as lessons from my Tribal Relations class with Butterfly Rot. We had to be with the Aves. The warm weather and brightly dyed clothes alone suggested the fine feathered tribe.

My mother was their ambassador. She'd contacted them and hadn't wanted to tell me what they'd discussed because it was too dangerous. Could I find her contact or would they seek me out?

I sat staring at Slate in disbelief that he was really there. I delved and found him healthy. They have healed me because I didn't feel the slightest soreness. I got to my feet and stared at Slate again. I loathed to leave him, but I had to make sure the others were safe.

Barefoot, I padded over to the woven double doors and pulled them in. The sight took my breath away. I stood at the base of a giant tree trunk whose limbs stretched high overhead to disappear into the clouds. From so high, I could see the ocean stretch for miles and below us, the lush green jungles and gardens of the land of perpetual spring. It smelled like spring with its floral bouquet in the very air. Spring and Brass.

I had to find him.

Birds as tall as I was flew to and fro, oblivious of me as they went about their day. Smaller trees lined like orchards covered nearly every free inch below the giant tree in the land mass that bore the tree's thick roots. Bright fabrics hung everywhere from the branches and bridges to the stairways and off of the platform that hung from the branches like nests. There were lit torches that connected along the stairs to light your way as you traveled since dusk had fallen.

I looked back at Slate. He was alive. I put my hands on my stomach as if I could hug my babies through my skin and let them know we were on the path to happiness.

"I promise not to screw it up this time," I whispered.

"I wonder where that leaves me."

I turned to the shadows I should have known concealed a man and smiled fondly at Brass, who detached from the side of the hall. I crossed to him and took him into my arms.

"I'm so glad you're okay," I said, pressing my cheek into his warm flesh. "I'm sorry about Shale," I whispered.

His arms hung loosely around me, and his stubbled jaw grazed my forehead as he kissed it. "She reunited with Ama. Perhaps she would have recovered in time, but Shale was not happy without her. She died as she lived. I imagine she's smirking down at us right now."

I smiled and inhaled his cinnamon spring rain scent mingled with a hint of sweat. "Quick?"

"Under your sister's care, who has a new appreciation for him." I could hear the smile in his voice.

"I saw. He'll never let her live it down."

"No, thanks to you. He will torture her for many more years to come."

I withdrew, leaving our arms clasped around one another. "It's my fault to begin with. She didn't need to be here. If I hadn't antagonized the Stygians, Ama wouldn't have died either."

Brass pressed his index finger to my lips, and I couldn't resist kissing it. He was wearing loose red drawstring pants that folded at the ankle, obviously made for trading with Guardians or stored for visiting ones. His feet were bare, and he didn't wear a shirt. The light fabric of his pants molded to his skin where the warm floral breeze hugged us.

"You are not responsible for the actions of others, even if something you did led to the circumstances that led to the situation. You did not contract the Stygians to capture Slate. That contract has been out for almost two years. Silver is whole. You have my eternal thanks."

"No, I should thank you. If he hadn't talked some sense, very little sense that seeped through, I would've gone alone and likely died for my rash efforts."

The firelight caught in Brass's amber eyes, making them look like they'd caught fire. "It's over. We need to move Slate into a nest so they can have a feast. He would not fit in his barghest form. He's…?"

"Sleeping. He's scarred, but I'm hoping that's just skin deep. The pain I felt through the bond…" I shook my head, dropping my eyes. "If he endured that all month, Brass. I don't know what kind of mental state he'll be in."

There. I said it out loud. I'd stick by him no matter what, but Slate was dangerously powerful. If he'd come unhinged… I saw him *eat* a man's head.

"Cross that bridge when we get there, love," Brass said tenderly and led me back into the hall.

When Brass and I floated Slate securely into one of the larger plat-forms, or nests as they called them, Indigo was leading Quick down one stairwell to us. Quick's face was an unhealthy pallor, and Indigo seemed to drag him by the hand. She waved and Quick's hand snapped to the railing.

Brass chuckled. "Not a fan of heights."

"I see that."

Night had fallen and with Slate secured and still sleeping, the Aves had brought in platters of food into the hall. Quick wore a pair of royal blue pants that matched my top in the same style as Brass. He gave me a rakish smile as he approached, and Brass had only just stepped aside when he lifted me into the air like a child and swung me around.

I tolerated heights when both my feet were on the ground. Now my face paled, and I gripped his wrists until my knuckles whitened. Quick laughed boisterously and set me on my feet before he squeezed me tight to his chest.

"Every time I luxuriate in life, I will think of you, Scarlett," Quick said, kissing me on both my cheeks.

My cheeks heated, and Brass placed a hand at the small of my back to steady me.

"Certainly not every time," Indigo said with a sly smile.

Quick's head swiveled to her and her playful tone and his dazzling smile deepened to positively sinful. I had to avert my eyes for fear of getting caught up in its undertow and catch myself standing naked in front of him. He should need a license for that smile.

Indigo took a step forward and hugged me. "You look good, tired, but good. He's okay?"

I nodded, feeling a sudden surge of relief that brought tears to my eyes. "Hormones." I gave an awkward chuckle as I swiped my cheeks. "We should get bonded with Jett like Quick and Brass have."

Indigo delicate brows raised with a smile that made the beauty mark on her cheek lift. "That's a great idea. Jett would love to know where we were. Oh Gods! No one knows where we are!" She slapped a hand to her mouth.

Quick sucked on his teeth. "That is a problem. With Shale's bond being broken, they may think the worst."

"I deactivated my tracker," I told them. "Should I maybe reactivate it?"

"No. Best to wait until Slate wakes and we can speak to him. We don't know who all was involved with his capture and we should not lead people to the Aves," Brass said.

The surrounding atmosphere seemed to change, and I stepped back from Indi to look around. As their wings beat, the wind picked up around us and three Aves lowered themselves to the planked walkway that bordered the hall. Two birds of prey, by far the broadest and tallest of the other Aves I'd spotted, landed before the third.

A golden eagle with a man's torso and legs with great golden-brown wings cocked his head to look at our group with round walnut eyes. A bald eagle man landed next to him. They both had crests of feathers instead of hair that began at their human brows. The bald eagle's intelligent eyes watched us as a predator might, assessing our threat level to the third that came to rest between the others. They each had beaks in the style of the birds that they replicated as well as human mouths.

The third carried a staff with brightly colored rings and plumes that dangled from it. Its chest was grey, but head and wings were black. A crow who landed gracefully with clawed human legs on the planks. Its human mouth smiled below its crow's beak as the three stepped forward as one. More Aves were flying directly into the open double doors behind us in a constant stream.

The old crow didn't speak as it approached Brass and held out a strip of violet silk. Brass held out both his hands and accepted it with a slight bow. The old crow placed its hands on Brass's head. Being shorter than Brass, he bowed again to the crow, and it sniffed him. Brass straightened, and the crow smiled.

"Where do you hale?" It asked in a croak of English.

"Ostara, sachem," Brass replied.

"How is your father?"

"With my ancestors."

Brass asked how the crow's father was and it gave the same reply. Then, Brass stepped back to tie the swath of silk to the railing that ran along the planked walkway. Other sun faded, well-worn strips flapped in the breeze. Brass's violet strip was the first strip to be placed there in quite a while.

Quick was next, and he received a lemon-yellow strip of silk with a bow of his head and tied it alongside Brass's as the crow moved to Indigo. She grinned as she told him she was from Ostara as well. Her face was bright with excitement that I wished I shared, but I had no suitable answer to his question. I fidgeted with my sarong, but kept my stance proud and respectful.

The crow's black eyes landed on mine and I saw all the sharp intelligence and wisdom that lurked there. He held out a plum-colored strip of silk and I accepted with both hands and an inclination of my head. He took it in its feathered hands and sniffed my hair with a sigh.

"Where do you hale?" It asked with a kindly smile much warmer than formalities would dictate, as if he expected a numskull reply.

I didn't disappoint. "Chicago?" I replied, my voice going higher, insinuating I wasn't all that sure myself.

The crow's eyes glittered, and I started when it cackled with a laugh. Its eagle guards started chuckling, and I heard Brass and the others join in. My face turned as red as the pants Brass wore as I wished there were rocks for me to hide under in the enormous tree.

"Sisters?" The crow asked, "Brothers?"

I licked my lips. "We're sisters and they're brothers, but they're not our brothers."

The crow's human mouth below its beak quirked, and I realized he already knew that. I blushed again.

"You are Wren Tio's hatchlings?"

My heart flip-flopped and I couldn't find my voice. I nodded and hoped it wasn't disrespectful.

"Come. We will join the banquet and I shall tell you about our time with your mother." The crow said and held out the hand that didn't hold the staff to me.

"Thank you, sachem," I murmured and tied my cloth to the railing before following in the crow.

The hall was a flurry of movement as Aves flew along its high ceiling and clutched the cylindrical bench with their clawed feet and squatted as platters were spread out along the long tabletops.

"This is the first banquet. When they have filled their bellies, the next shift will eat. All are welcome to stay once they have had their fill. I am called Corvus, sachem of the Aves."

The crow said as he led us to the table at the far end of the hall that faced the doors. The wood floors were bare except for the Aves that swarmed.

"These are Aeetus and Aquila, my sons." Corvus gestured to first the bald eagle, then the golden. They inclined their heads to us, giving me twin smiles that belied the amusement they held from my ever so clever replies.

A stunning yellow canary that was unmistakably female sat in a place of honor at the long table we approached and she smiled amiably at us, her blue eyes hitching on Brass. I had no claim on him anymore. I had to squelch the unanticipated flicker of jealousy that heated my blood.

Tweets and whistles trilled through the room, and we took our seats. The eagle twins pointed to with Indigo on the sachem's left, and me on his right. Aquila took the seat next to Indigo and then Quick while I sat next to the yellow canary with Brass on her other side and Aeetus to his right.

The canary introduced herself to Brass. "Serinus. Corvus's daughter. And you are?"

Her speaking skills were much clearer than the others I'd heard chattering and rivaled Corvus's. Her voice was high with a singsong quality that reminded of tinkling bells. They had a way of cocking their heads as you spoke that set my teeth on edge with its rapid, inhuman movement.

They made no special proclamation as the sachem filled his plate and passed me a platter. I libelously piled a fruit salad onto my plate filled with pineapple, strawberries, peaches, and baby spinach. They had forks placed for us, though they used beaks to shovel the pieces into their human mouths with well-practiced moves.

Aquila had taken as keen an interest in Indigo as Serinus had in Brass. Quick's irritation was palpable, but the chatting duo was clueless. Perhaps I was getting as irrationally irritated as Quick because I found myself wanting to leave the banquet.

"I don't mean to be rude, Corvus. Do you think I could have some broth so I may tend after my injured man?" I asked, leaning into where I hoped the old crow's ear was.

"Already taken care of, my dear. When you placed him in the nest, Lidae volunteered to watch over him. She will feed him about this time."

My sharp new jealousy was warranted. Another woman, bird hybrid or not, didn't sit well with me. Corvus cackled a laugh in his rough, quavering tone.

"Thank you," I said and tried for a smile that came out tight.

"I cannot discern which one is your mate. Is it the injured one or the one Serinus fancies?" he said in a mirthful tone.

I should have blushed, but I only sighed. "It's a long story."

Corvus rested his inky feathered hands on the tabletop and cocked his head to peer at me with one eye and then the other. "I enjoy a good story."

My mood was ideal for a vent, so I told him how I'd married Slate, not knowing who he was and thought I was barren. I explained how I left him so he could find a mate who he could sire children with. That I'd eventually come to have feelings for Brass, which led to a relationship and found out I was not, in fact, barren, but pregnant with twins. I told Corvus how we thought Slate had died after he was captured and that Brass and I had picked things back up recently and had made plans for the future.

I left out that I had made love to Brass only yesterday morning, and until about three o'clock that morning, had planned on having him move in with me at the Dagr palace at Yuletide. That I'd allowed myself to love him without the all-consuming guilt for about five minutes and it had been marvelous.

Corvus startled me when he placed his hand over mine. His soft, sleek feathers were smooth over my skin. He looked at me with oddly kind eyes for a crow.

"You love them both. Who will you choose?"

"Slate is my husband, and he's all alone. What's more, Brass doesn't need me. He loves me, but he can fall in love again. I don't think Slate can. Brass's heart is open, while Slate's is closed. I wish I had two lives-"

I cut off, aware of more than one set of eyes on me. So deep in my mind, I hadn't noticed the table had quieted and Indigo was looking past Corvus to me with gleaming eyes. I chanced a glance to my other side to find Serinus and Brass watching me. I dropped my eyes to my half-eaten plate and swallowed hard.

"I'm sorry. I shouldn't have-"

Corvus patted my hand. "Thank you for sharing, daughter of Wren. Your honesty is refreshing. I believe I owe you a true story in return, though I'm afraid it is not nearly so romantic and tragic."

Serinus had turned to Brass again, but it enraptured Indigo. "Your mother was the first Guardian we allowed into our nest in a score of years. Frankly, it was because of her name that we continued to treat with her as she traveled along Ostara, following our nest, hoping we would let her up." Corvus smiled. "I could not deny a woman by the name of Wren to our nest."

A tear fell from Indigo's powder blue eyes to streak her cheek.

"We suspected wrongdoings going on in Ostara, so we sequestered ourselves away. Sensing a change in the times, we allowed her in on the promise that she not reveal she had treated with us. For it would jeopardize her. I fear by her absence that our warnings did not save her."

I shook my head and Corvus turned to Indi and gave her a sorrowful smile. "May I?" he asked, turning back to me.

I slapped a hand over my stone pendant necklace tucked into my tube top. "I'd prefer to keep it on my person," I said in an apologetic tone, and Corvus's smile deepened.

"Clever girl. I'd expect no less from Wren's hatchlings."

I pulled the pieces from my top to rest across my breasts and Corvus's eyes flitted from them to my eyes. "You have begun to collect them. That is good. You should carry the Grar Dyr's son, daughter of summer and spring."

My eyes must have widened at the retelling of the prophecy the Faunelle mentioned. Corvus reached behind him where his colorful staff rested and unwound the brightly colored threads.

"Beware your spring family, hatchlings. The Anguillan had a piece of the great work and someone in the family extorted it from them. I know not who. That was when we removed ourselves from the Guardian world as best we could. Now, the Mother is ailing and we must fight to protect her. Your injured man, he is Grar Dyr?"

Indigo met my eyes, and she gave a nod. "He is," I whispered, hardly audible over the tweets and whistles of the Aves' native language.

He nodded in a bobbing of his head, his black crest rising above his human-like face. "The barghest — it felt safe to assume you were the one we were waiting for, from the way your sister seemed attached to the marked man."

Indigo turned away, and I saw the tips of her ears redden. "Yes. She is." I admitted.

"From your reaction, you are aware of the prophecy?" Corvus asked, and I nodded. "Ah, here we are. For your collection, my dear."

Corvus held out a smooth square stone about the size of my stone pendant Pearl had given me. I gasped as he slid the piece from an orange thread and into my palm.

"I do not know where the work is, or where the other pieces are. I know that there are nine pieces. One of which is in the custody of the Vars. I have sent my people out in search of the works and it is not visible from our skies. I wish we had more information to offer you," Corvus said as I slid the piece onto my chain that now held three of the nine pieces.

"No. My goodness. I did not know what I was going to do to find these pieces. Not being visible from the sky is a tremendous help. You've searched all the islands?"

"We have," Corvus confided.

A stunning red cardinal woman with a long red crest entered the hall and strode over to the long table. She would have been radiant in any race; her looks were comparable to a statuesque woman's. Her skin was black around her eyes like a mask and a pale red over her face and down her torso and legs. A light tapering of shimmering red feathers covered her human breasts and hips.

She smiled at me and Corvus as she reached our table. "Your injured male took the broth; he is still unconscious. Citta is with him for now."

"Thank you," I said, inclining my head and her honey eyes swung to Serinus and Brass.

I suppressed a sigh and sipped from a carved cup of water while everyone was indulging in a fermented milk drink that was alcoholic. Kumis, I'd heard them call it.

"Please enjoy the festivities in your honor," Corvus said, perhaps sensing my desire to leave again.

Aves brought out drums, and some whistled an upbeat tune. Male Aves gathered in the cleared space and began a sort of jumping competition that sent the dining crowd to cheering and laughing.

"Whatever happened to your mother?" Corvus finally asked, and since I was expecting the question, I told him about the wight in Mabon that now possessed Wren and Alder's souls.

Quick had hauled Indigo away from Aquila and the golden eagle man had taken up a dance of jumping and spinning with a fellow Aves. Serinus and Lidae, who both seemed determined to win him from the other, accompanied Brass to the dance floor.

Corvus politely listened to my story and gave his condolences before excusing himself and leaving the hall. I was readying to leave when a stunningly plumed peacock with broad shoulders and a mohawk crest of brilliant blues and greens swaggered to where I sat. His teal eyes were black lined, and he had a smile to rival Quick's as he approached and spread his plumage for my admiration. His iridescent feathers made me jump as they snapped out with his courtly bow.

"My goodness," I breathed, and his already bright smile broadened.

He was absolutely beautiful. When we first arrived in Tidings I had hoped to find peacock Aves, but my imagination of what that would look like did not do him justice.

"May I be so bold to ask you for a dance?" He asked in a quavering baritone.

I couldn't say no. He was the most breathtaking being I may have seen in my entire life. My eyes didn't rest on any part of him for long before flitting to another vivid part of him.

"Yes... my name is Scarlett," I said, as he followed me to the end of the table.

He had the strut of a confident man. "Pavo. Pleased to make your acquaintance."

Pavo spoke in the whistling tweets of his native language, and I gave him a rueful smile. "I'm sorry. I am terrible at tribal languages. Your

English is very good," I said, hoping he'd revert to a tongue I understood.

He took my arm and with his plumage; he stood well over a foot taller than I was. Indigo floated into view, spinning with Quick and was laughing as she looked at us.

"He asked if your 'plumage' under your clothes is as golden as the 'plumage' on your head." Quick laughed heartily as they spun away.

Never had I been more embarrassed. "That isn't an appropriate question for a woman you just met," I said stiffly, and Pavo turned me to face him, cocking his head.

"You see all of me. It is all the same soft texture. Touch me." He took my hand and ran it down his chest and lower.

I snatched it away, spluttering. "Stop that. I have to wear clothing because I don't have feathers to cover me."

He was incredibly soft and his feathers had shimmered under my fingers tips. His smile returned when he saw my eyes flicker to his chest.

"Having my feathers stroked by one such as you gives me great pleasure, Scarlett. Do it again," Pavo said boldly, and I wondered if Quick and Indigo had sent him to me just to watch me fluster. They came around again, laughing at my reddened face.

Unwittingly, I searched for Brass and found he'd left. The canary and cardinal were no longer dancing in the hall as well. My confused heart fluttered painfully, and I took Pavo's hand.

"I will not stroke you, but I will dance with you," I said, dragging him out onto the cleared square.

Pavo was a bit of a ladies' man and I got my fair share of dirty looks from the female Aves who had hoped to catch Pavo's teal eye. The hall grew warm, and I tied up the end of my skirt to jump and hop with Pavo's spinning dance more easily. I was having fun. Aquila and Aeetus cut in to dance with me, since Quick was not letting Indigo get away from him.

Pavo waited patiently, not taking any other dance partners as the eagle twins led me around the square. My skin glistened with sweat and Aeetus offered me a feather to twist my hair up. I took it gratefully and Pavo appeared at my side and took the feather from my hand.

"Nice try, Aeetus," Pavo said with a wry grin that held no scorn.

Aeetus laughed. "Go on then."

Pavo plucked one of his iridescent green feathers and slid it into the bun I held my hair in with a hand and I felt it secure and dropped it.

"My thanks," I said with a smile and took Aeetus's feather from his other hand. "It's rude to turn down a gift. Thank you, Aeetus."

Aeetus's feather was nowhere near as beautiful as Pavo's, but I could sense this had something to do with courting my affection and I would not play that game. I threaded Aeetus's plain white feather into the knot of my jungle green skirt and smiled warmly at them both.

"Now. Who is going to make me dance until my feet fall off?" I asked, placing my fists on my hips.

Pavo's eyes glittered and didn't hesitate to take my hands and immediately swung me around, much to my delight.

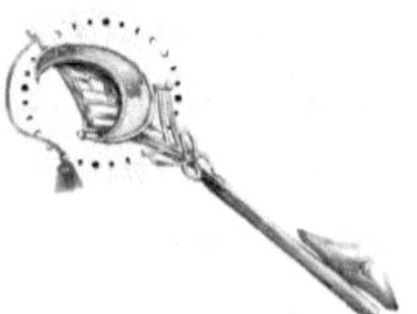

When the music finally stopped, I found I'd lost all my human companions but had gained a stalwart group of male Aves admirers. I tried to let them down gently when I told them I had to return to my ailing husband and they tried to get me to stay and tell them stories about outside of Tidings. I'd told them a few already.

"I really must tend to him. What kind of wife would I be if I left him to Citta?"

"Citta is a very honorable Aves. She will care for him while you are here," Pavo insisted, and I smiled at him.

"I could use a lift to the nest to get me there sooner. I seem to have tired out of my feet," I said jovially, and my admirers laughed.

Pavo put a feathered hand to my back as I said my goodbyes and he led me to the others. We exited the hall, and the air was refreshingly cooler.

"I should have come out here for a breather ages ago," I said, fanning myself.

"I could have escorted you," Pavo said, cocking his head in that peculiar bird like way.

"I suppose so," I said with a coy smile. "I wasn't making it up. My husband really is ailing. This was a pleasant reprieve from my reality, though. My thanks, Pavo."

"Thank *you*. Will you keep my feather? Wear it in your hair as you do these beads?" he asked, running his feathered hand along one of my narrow braids.

My brow quirked. "You'd want me to?"

"To remember me. They strictly prohibited us from interacting with Guardians for fear of imprisonment. It is not exactly legal that we refrain from your governing. I have not spoken to a woman of your kind."

"I didn't know that. I love your feather. All of them. You are a very handsome Aves."

Pavo grew emboldened. "A kiss for thanks?" he said with a stunning smile.

I laughed and placed my hand on his chest. "I see your game now."

I stepped forward with my hands on Pavo's chest, and he sheltered us with his wings. My eyes widened in awe as I looked around our little cocoon.

"My goodness," I breathed.

"You have said that already," Pavo jested.

"Not very modest, are you?" I said with a smile as I reached up on my tiptoes and planted a chaste kiss to his human mouth.

Pavo sucked in a breath and let out a loud cawing noise three times in succession, making me jump as his eyed plumes spread out behind him. Laughter sounded from within the hall and, inexplicably, I blushed.

Pavo seemed as surprised by the reaction as I was as he cocked his head, dropping his wings, and looked into the hall. "I will take you now."

I pointed to the platform Slate was on and Pavo stepped close so his body was flush with mine. "Hook your arms around my neck. Hold tight. I cannot carry you with my hands as I fly."

I bit my lip. "If I can hold on tight enough... and I'm not too heavy for you, maybe we can take a detour?" I asked shyly, and Pavo started cawing again with my arms around his neck.

His human mouth pressed into a line to stop himself. He gave me a rueful smile.

"You seem to pull it from my throat involuntarily, I apologize." Pavo said, and he lifted from the planked platform.

My hands locked over my wrists as I bore my weight, and he rose above the floating tree. "Would it be strange if I locked my ankles?" I asked sheepishly.

I was terrified, with my feet dangling free as we climbed higher, but I didn't want to stop. The air was cool, and the sky was clear. I felt like one with the stars and I didn't want to give it up yet.

Pavo's face turned down to me with narrowed eyes. "You would have me sound my mating call again to embarrass me?"

My eyes widened. "*That's* what that call means?"

Pavo's face smoothed, and he laughed. "Yes. That is why I apologized. Hold tight, however you wish. If you fall, I will catch you." He promised, but I pulled my legs up anyway, pushing my sarong to my thighs and locked my ankles around his back.

Pavo's feathered brow lifted as he looked down at me as he leveled off. "You are sure I cannot steal you from your husband?"

I actually laughed as I turned to look at Ostara below. "Many have tried. One... may have succeeded, but I'm afraid I am his and he is mine. We are bound by more than love."

"Pity." Pavo muttered, and I chuckled again.

Pavo flew elegantly through the sky with a grace I would never accomplish in my lifetime and twisted and turned so I could get the best views of Ostara below. He took me past the Var castle with its white glass like shine and the mirrored globes that glowed green along the sleek bridges.

My mind had been preoccupied since rescuing Slate. I'd been so happy to have him back, I'd forgotten about Karkinos and that now we'd have to tell the council about how it was overrun with rogue tribes. We'd have to confess to breaking into it and face the consequences if the prisoners had all drowned when we escaped. I hoped not. Imagining those people locked in their metal cages as they were helpless against their own deaths made me sick to my stomach. Then again, that place had probably made them welcome death.

Shale would have to be brought to her mother; Asp Sandr was provost of Calling at Valla U. Shale was her spitting image. Ama had no family to speak of. The Shadow Breakers were her family. They'd be celebrating Shale's memory tonight without us having felt her bond break.

"You may stroke me, Scarlett. I find it brings comfort," Pavo said, sensing my dark mood.

My fingers loosened on my wrist and I let them glide over his sleek feathers. "You're not going to caw in my ear again, are you?" I asked teasingly, and I felt him smile.

"It is a possibility. You are very attractive and would find myself honored to mate with you."

I scoffed. "Be wary of pretty girls with husbands, Pavo. We are nothing but trouble."

"I like trouble," Pavo said rakishly — of that I had no doubt.

Pavo beat his wings as he landed on the little plank outside our nest. I unlocked my legs and set them down slowly on the platform since they were stiff from how tight I'd held Pavo. I slid my hands from his neck and he clasped my wrists in his feathered hands.

"A boon?"

"Another kiss, you mean?" I said with a knowing smile.

Pavo's stunning smile lit his blue-skinned face. Loud trill cawing made us both look to the nest that hung a little further down the branch. Its thick drapes prevented us from seeing in, but from Pavo's guffaw, I needed no other context.

"Your man friend is giving Lidae and Serinus bragging rights for the rest of their lives. The Aves have not bedded Guardians for decades," Pavo said, and my insides heated.

"I must go," I said curtly, and pecked Pavo's cheek before pushing back the thick apple green drapes to find a beautiful bluebird woman crouching with her eyes closed near Slate's feet.

A candlelight cast shadows over the small nest and I stepped in on cats' paws, not wanting to wake them.

"He sleeps deep," the bluebird, who must have been Citta, said.

Her sky-blue crest rose as she did to stand just shorter than I was on her clawed feet. Her human skin was stark white with smooth, light blue feathers that covered the rest of her.

"Thank you for watching over him. I'm afraid the banquet is over," I whispered as she cocked her head. Eyes that matched her wings assessed me.

"It has been for some time. Was that Pavo's mating call and who dropped you off?" she said plainly, and I pursed my lips.

"Yes. Your tribe seems to miss interaction with the Guardians. I will have to do something about that once I get back. There's no reason for us to be segregated."

She raised her feathered brow. "You have that sway?"

I held myself prouder. "My husband is the patriarch of a greater family and I come from lines on both my mother's and father's sides. My mother was the most recent ambassador to the Aves. You may have met her, Wren Tio."

Citta's face softened. "Yes. She spoke of you often. I assume from your fierce comportment that you are Scarlett."

I felt the corner of my mouth quirk. "I am."

"But this is not Ash," she said, pointing to Slate.

"My goodness, no. This is Slate."

Citta's eyes brightened, and she started laughing. It grew until she held her stomach. I looked at her as if she'd lost her mind.

"Forgive me. Wren was my contact. When she visited, I was the one who she spent most of her time with. She told me about Slate." Judging from her smug expression, my mother said some unflattering things about me.

Still, I was excited to hear whatever my mom told her. "What had she said? Please tell everything. No matter how insignificant." I gestured for her to return to her seat, and she nodded in understanding.

I moved to check on Slate myself and saw he was unchanged; his face had a healthy glow, so I put my worries to rest as I trailed my fingers down the scar that marred his eye. It didn't matter. Disappointment washed over me as I kissed his lips and felt the bond fade.

I sat to face Citta and crossed my legs in front of me as I poured us both water from a pitcher that rested next to the mattress. She inclined her head.

"Wren said you were smitten with an adopted young man you call Slate. The son of a man she called Lark, who was not your father. I remember his name because I too had a first love, that was a lark. We are mated. She said it was her fault you had agreed to the marriage with Ash, but that she hoped you would break it off before it was too late. That Ash was not a good fit for you. She said that when you and Slate were in a room together, that the sparks flew around you two."

I sighed.

CHAPTER 62
INDIGO

Despite Silver's best efforts, my mood was not improving as the Aves brought us to the edge of Ostara and lowered Slate on a makeshift stretcher so we could be carried home. Scarlett had transformed overnight. No more flirtatious smiles for Brass or warm hugs and kisses. If I were her and seen the way Lidae and Serinus preened at Brass all morning, I would've barely been able to stomach down my breakfast.

Scarlett had done an impressive job of letting her eyes coolly slide over him and forcing down her entire bowlful of porridge down before she prepared Slate for departure. She asked for my help; I suspected, so Brass wouldn't offer. Not that he could have with the ketchup and mustard colored bird brains so close to him you couldn't see where their feathered hands were groping.

Silver had been right to keep me close.

Scarlett had a flock of admirers, including the sachem's two eagle sons, who anticipated her every want with impressive accuracy. Then, when the blue jay woman and the eagle twins were lowering Slate down to Ostara, the absolutely gorgeous peacock man swooped down and threw his wings up, so she disappeared within them. Judging from her reddened cheeks when he flew off again, he'd kissed her for what I suspected wasn't the first time.

The peacock flew back, and she lifted her arms. His head slipped within the loop she made and her legs pulled up to wrap at his waist as he angled towards the ground. That was not the first time she'd done that, either.

I smiled at Silver, who grimaced. "You will be doing none of that."

I laughed and let myself be carried by the clawed feet of Aeetus while Silver was carried by Aquila who entertained himself by pretending he'd injured his wing and Silver had shouted as they soared towards the land. Brass's pretties had carried him down and planted kisses on his lips, one after the other, before flying away.

Corvus had joined them for breakfast and saw them off, letting them know they welcomed us back whenever we wished. I didn't think Scarlett understood how monumental that gesture was. I decided right then and there if I could become the ambassador to the Aves, I would.

Scarlett had busied herself with making sure Slate's unconscious body was covered while Brass made out with the birdbrains. The tension in her body was visible. She wore her jeans again and the sarong she wore last night wrapped around her torso so it almost looked like a halter top. All her blades were on, and a fresh addition to her fetishes shimmered in her golden hair. One of Pavo's feathers, as well as a white one that had likely belonged to Aeetus.

She ran her fingertips over the silver scar that sliced down his bronze skin, forming a gash in his blue-black brow. She said she'd checked his eye, and it was sound. It bore no marks from the cut. Again, she asked if I would steer the makeshift stretcher as she *called* to lift it from the ground so we could make better time.

Brass and Silver did the same for Shale's gauze covered body on a stretcher of her own with Silver steering the petite body behind us.

Scarlett walked with one hand on the stretcher as we cut from the Ostara jungle that lined this part of the island where no tribe had reigned and into the town's heart. Her other handheld the stone pieces of the great work we needed to find and had no clue where to look.

We walked over crunching white glittering stones that made up the roads through Ostara's heart that was lined with gardens of flowers of all colors, sending their sweet cacophony of fragrances into the morning air. Women in bright caftan dresses entered and exited pastel houses and shops with white trim like lacework. Men in dapper waistcoats and lightweight jerkins inclined their heads to us as they caught sight of our comrades.

Ostara's town gate was the only one not in the actual town. We walked up the road until the castle came into sight. Its white, glittering turrets and towers reflected the bright morning light. The Aves had left us only an hour's walk from the town and we'd made excellent time.

The portal gate waited ahead, Ostara's residents coming in and out of it in a loosely formed line. The rounded arch was a white marble its creator had chiseled to form two tree pillars on either end and a lace-work of branches and leaves painted a metallic gold that fanned over the top.

Valkyries in cream-colored robes cinched by brown silk ropes approached us with seamed sorrowful expressions. Since the disbanding of the Brotherhood of Paragons, they were the only religious type sect of women had their hoods down, exposing their shaved heads to the warm day. They must have heard a word about us traveling through town. It was their duty to help with the deaths of Guardians and the raising of orphans.

The women nodded to us and took up positions on either side of Shale, seeing that Slate was alive, if in a coma.

We stopped a dozen yards away from the gate, and Scarlett signaled for me to let go as she set Slate on the ground to turn and face them. Her normally bright tan face with her big turquoise almond eyes was closed off and uncharacteristically cold.

She looked directly into my eyes when she spoke. "I'm taking him to the Dagr palace alone. Could you please bring my things from *his* room to the palace?"

"Of course," I said without hesitation. "You want to go alone?"

"Yes. I think I should." She swung her gaze to focus on Quick. "I cannot possibly find the words to express how sorry I am about Shale and Ama, but I thank you sincerely for all your help. You can bring her body to her mother?"

Quick arched an eyebrow at her and nodded. "Truth."

"Once I get settled in our wing, I'll have messengers sent to the greater families for a council to be convened. I would appreciate if you could all come to support my telling of events."

"Scarlett —" Brass said.

"My thanks." She cut him off and spun on her heel and lifted her palm.

Her *calling* was stronger than any of theirs. Slate's body floated next to her as the bright white light of the portal engulfed her.

Silver blew out a gusty breath. "There is a new Slate in town and his name is Brass Regn. I have only seen her be that frosty to Slate after he slept with whomever the flavor of the night was. Could you not wait until we were back before you found someone new? That is not like you."

"It's for both of us. She will thank me later. It will be easier for her to focus on him without worrying if it will hurt me," Brass said softly, and I snorted.

"Let's hope he wakes up from his coma because if he doesn't and you've pushed her away, she'll run. I think you could've waited a few days for the mother of your children, Brass. You're the Gods' cursed mind reader." I sneered. "Whenever you're ready." I gestured to the portal gate.

Brass looked away. "Aves were ideal because they expect nothing from me. A woman would. This way, no one gets hurt."

"Lie," I said in a biting tone. "Except for the fact that Scarlett will expect nothing from you. You can be sure of that. I'll collect her things. You don't need to be there for that."

Silver shouted after me. "Do not take this out on me, Dove."

I turned around to face him. Gods, he was devilishly handsome. After last night I was having a hard time saying anything cutting to him. He loved me.

The poor fool.

BIBLIOGRAPHY

"For Whom the Bell Tolls" by John Donne
"A Crazed Girl" by William Butler Yeats
"A Woman's Shortcomings" by Elizabeth Barrett Browning
"Stopping by Woods on a Snowy Evening" by Robert Frost
"I Thought I was not Alone" by Walt Whitman